DUCHESS BY NIGHT

Duchess Harriet of Berrow has been a wallflower for far too long. Now London's most beautiful widow has decided to seek a little pleasure of her own, beginning with one of the most disreputable men in the country, Lord Strange. Given the high-staked games of lust and chance that rule Strange's household, Harriet decides to swap her hoops and corsets for a pair of breeches and transforms herself into the Duke of Villiers. Will Harriet decide to stay in her disguise or will she reveal herself to be a real duchess by night?

DUCHESS BY NIGHT

DUCHESS BY
NIGHT

by

Eloisa James

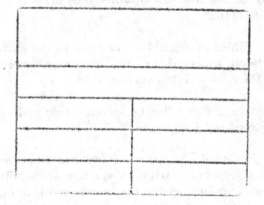

Magna Large Print Books
Long Preston, North Yorkshire,
BD23 4ND, England.

British Library Cataloguing in Publication Data.

James, Eloisa
    Duchess by night.

    A catalogue record of this book is
    available from the British Library

    ISBN   978-0-7505-3274-7

First published in Great Britain in 2009
by Hodder & Stoughton Ltd.

Published in Large Print 2010 by arrangement with
Hodder & Stoughton Ltd.

Magna Large Print is an imprint of Library Magna Books Ltd.

Printed and bound in Great Britain by
T.J. (International) Ltd., Cornwall, PL28 8RW

This book is dedicated to Georgette Heyer. Though a few writers before her did dress women in male clothing (Shakespeare comes to mind), Ms Heyer's brilliantly funny cross-dressed heroines set the standard for all modern romance novelists.

I couldn't get my character into clothing at all without the help of three fabulous people: my editor, Carrie Feron; my assistant, Kim Castillo; and my research assistant, Franzeca Drouin. I am enormously grateful to each of you.

Finally, the readers on my bulletin board (www.eloisajames.com) are a constant delight, provocation, and source for ideas. Please stop by and join us!

PROLOGUE
Justice by Duchess

December 15, 1783
Shire Court
The Duchy of Berrow
Honourable Reginald Truder, presiding

'I didn't mean to marry both of them!'

'The problem,' said the duchess, leaning forward, 'is not marrying twice, but marrying a second husband while the first is still alive.'

'Well, I didn't want Avery to *die*,' Loveday Billing explained. 'I just wanted to marry John, that's all. I couldn't stop myself. I was that tired, and lonely, and he ... he sat with me of an evening.'

The judge snorted and Loveday thought he might have woken up, but then he started snoring again.

The Duchess of Berrow had very kind eyes, but she shook her head at Loveday. 'You were already married to Avery, that is, Mr Mosley, when you married John.'

Loveday hung her head. 'Avery left me three years ago,' she said. 'I didn't know as how he wanted me any more, because he

11

said I was stupider than a sow in spring-time.'

The duchess had a quiet sort of prettiness about her, like a preacher's wife. Her gown was black, but it had a shine to it. Her hair was lovely too, looped and frilled and ruffed over her head, the way fine ladies did those things. And her eyes were so forgiving that Loveday suddenly felt like telling the truth. It was as if she were a youngster back in her mother's kitchen, having stolen a cake.

'I ain't really married to Avery Mosley,' she said. Out of the corner of her eye she saw Avery swing up his head. 'I was already married before I married Avery. And I didn't really marry him because it were an Irish minister named Usher and he told me privately that it weren't a real marriage.'

Avery probably fell off his chair at that news, but Loveday was focused on the duchess. 'My da married me off the first time, when I was twelve.'

'Twelve!'

The duchess looked a bit stricken, so she tried to explain. 'It wasn't so bad. I had developed, you see, and I was worth something, and it wasn't so bad.'

'What is his name?'

'That was Mr Buckley. But he died, so after Mr Buckley passed on, I married Harold Eccles.'

'I don't suppose that Mr Eccles is dead?'

The duchess sounded hopeful.

'He's about as alive as anyone could be in debtors' prison. I always visits him when I'm in London. Two hatbands and a coat, they got him for. He's been there almost eleven years now.'

'So I married–' she paused for a moment, just to get it right '–Monsieur Giovanni Battista. He was an Italian man, and he said he'd take me away. But he gave me a pair of gloves, and then he went away instead.'

'And then Mr Mosley came along?' the duchess asked.

Loveday nodded. 'I shouldn't have done it, I know,' she said. 'I knows as I shouldn't have. But I didn't know what to do, and he asked me. But he left.'

'You were in a difficult position,' the duchess said. 'If I have this right, your first husband died, the second is in prison, the third went to Italy, the fourth was not a real marriage, and the fifth–'

'I had no one to care for myself and the babes because my da doesn't speak to me after the Italian man.'

'Children?' The duchess looked through the long pieces of paper that were floating around the table. 'There's no mention of children in these pleadings.'

The fancy London man standing next to John answered. 'It was not considered relevant to the matter at hand, Your Grace.

13

My client married her in good faith as the certificates indicate. And may I point out that these court proceedings are highly irregular? Surely the Honourable Judge Truder should be roused?'

The duchess ignored him. Loveday could have told the London man that in Berrow, this was the way of it. Truder was a drunk, but it didn't really matter as he and the duchess did the business together, just as it was in the old days, and that was good enough for the town of Berrow.

'Whose children are they?' the duchess said, turning back to Loveday.

'All of them, really,' Loveday said hopelessly. 'I gave them each one. Except for John, of course, because we only married a bit ago.'

'You've four children?' the duchess asked.

'Five. Harold, him as is in prison, has two.'

There was silence in the courtroom. Loveday could hear John moving his feet. If only ... but it was too late.

'You are really Mrs Eccles,' the duchess observed.

Loveday nodded. 'I know as how you're right, Mrs Duchess.'

'Your Grace,' a man next to her hissed.

'Your Grace,' she said obediently. 'But Harold is in debtors' prison.'

The duchess looked over at the box, so Loveday looked too. There was John, with his blue eyes. And Avery with his angry small mouth, just like always.

'Why did you pursue this indictment, Mr Mosley?' the duchess asked.

Avery burst into words, but the gist of it was that he wanted her back, even after the things he had said about her.

The duchess looked at him steadily. Then she turned back to Loveday. 'Have you any money?' she asked.

'Oh, no,' Loveday said. 'I've no money but what my husbands give me.'

There was quiet for a moment, and then the duchess said, even more gently, 'Is your father still alive, Mrs Eccles?'

'Yes, but he–' and she stopped.

The duchess folded her hands and looked so sweet. 'He's ill, isn't he?'

'I heard so,' Loveday whispered.

'And your father has some money that he might leave you?'

Loveday looked back at John's blue eyes, and she felt like a fool. 'That's why Avery wants me back. Because of the mill. And John... I suppose that's why John courted me. For the mill.'

John got up and left, so that sort of spoke for itself.

Avery left too, so Loveday cried for a little bit, and then the duchess said, 'You were very wrong to marry so many men, Loveday.'

15

'I know,' Loveday said, sniffling.

'I'm going to advise the judge to acquit you. But you mustn't marry again. I want you to bail out Mr Eccles. And then live with him.'

'I will,' Loveday promised.

The duchess reached over and poked the judge. He snorted once or twice and woke up. She said something to him and he snorted again and said, 'Case dismissed!' Then he slumped back down in his chair.

Loveday stood there for a moment before she realized she was free to go. Except the duchess wanted to see her. So she went to the front, and the duchess took her hand. She told her a fairy tale, about how Mr Eccles – that would be Harold, in prison – should treat her like a princess, because she was to be a mill owner.

Loveday just smiled and smiled. That duchess was the most lovely, best-smelling woman in the world. She had a funny way of talking, and daft ideas, but you couldn't help liking her. Especially when she sat right there, holding Loveday's hand – Loveday, who everyone said was as stupid as a sow though she wasn't.

And finally the duchess gave her five pounds, which she could use to get Harold out of prison right away. Harold didn't owe more than a pound or two, even counting charges for board, so Loveday tried to give some back, but the duchess wouldn't take it.

Then the judge woke up again and he seemed to have a terrible problem with wind, so the duchess smiled at Loveday just as if she were a normal person, and they both left the room.

Loveday Billing had never been so happy in her life.

A duchess liked her, and had quitted her, whatever that meant, and told her what to do.

And she did just that.

1

In Which Cinderella Dresses for the Ball and Her Fairy Godmother Brings a Goose Instead of a Pumpkin

January 6 (Twelfth Night), 1784
Costume Ball
The Country Seat of the Duke of Beaumont

Nursery tales are full of fascinating widows, although they aren't always the nicest characters. Cinderella's stepmother likely put on a dazzling gown for the prince's ball, even if her daughters did inherit her big feet and sharp tongue.

Harriet, Duchess of Berrow, realized soon after her husband died that there are glamorous widows, and then there are widows who live in shoes with too many children, like poor Loveday Billing. There are widows who dance all night with younger men, and then there are dowdy widows who are offered only pinched smiles.

Harriet had no illusions about what kind of widow she was. She was the kind who lived in a shoe, and never mind the fact that she had no children and her estate was much larger than a shoe.

Her husband had been dead for two years and no younger – or older – men were lining up to ask her to dance. Most of her acquaintances still got a tragic sheen in their eyes and promptly moved away after greeting her, as if sadness were catching.

Apparently, if one's husband committed suicide, one automatically became the unappealing type of widow.

Partly it was her fault. Here she was at the Duchess of Beaumont's impromptu costume ball – but was she dressing as a glamorous character? Or even an evil one?

'Who are you?' her friend Jemma (the aforesaid Duchess of Beaumont) asked.

'A nursery rhyme character. Can you guess which one?' Harriet was wearing a motherly nightgown of plain cotton that her maid had recruited from the housekeeper. Underneath she had three petticoats, as well as four woollen stockings in her bodice. Just to show off a bit, she arched her back.

'A nursery rhyme character with big breasts,' Jemma said. 'Very big breasts. Very very—'

'*Motherly* breasts,' Harriet prompted.

'Actually you don't look motherly as much as wildly curvaceous. The problem will be if one of our houseguests lures you into a corner and attempts a cheerful grope. Wasn't there some nursery rhyme about lighting the way to bed?'

'I'm not on my way to bed,' Harriet said, somewhat deflated. 'And no one ever tries to grope me. What character are you?'

Jemma's gown was made of a clear pale pink that looked wonderful with the dark gold colour of her unpowdered hair. There were small silk poppies sewn all over her skirts, and poppies tucked in her hair. She managed to look elegant and yet untamed, all at once.

'Titania, Queen of the Fairies.'

'I'm Mother Goose. Which fairly sums up the difference between us.'

'What are you talking about!' Jemma scolded, wrapping an arm around Harriet. 'Look at you, darling. You are far too young and fresh to be Mother Goose!'

'No one will know who I am,' Harriet said, pulling away from Jemma and sitting on the bed. 'They'll think I'm a fat white ghost.'

Jemma started laughing. 'The ghost of a murdered cook. No, all you need is a clue to your Mother Goose status, and people will admire the cleverness of your costume. Wait until you see Lord Pladget as Henry VIII: he has a hearth rug tied around his middle and he looks as big as a barn.'

'I already look as big as a barn, at least on top.'

'A goose!' Jemma said. 'Of course, you need a goose and I know just the one!'

'Oh, but–'

Two minutes later, Jemma was back. With a goose.

'Is that real?' Harriet asked warily.

'In a manner of speaking. I'm afraid it's a little stiff. It usually flies along the wall in the south parlour. My mother-in-law had a morbid attitude toward decorating that involved arranging all kinds of dead animals on the walls. You can use the poor goose tonight, darling, and then we'll set him free to fly to a better place, if you understand me.'

Harriet took the goose in her hands rather dubiously. It was stuffed so that its neck stayed stiff, as if it were in flight.

'Just tuck it under your arm,' Jemma said. Harriet stood up and tried it. 'Not like that. Here, turn his head upright so he looks like a friend whispering in your ear.'

Harriet stared down at the bird's glossy

eyes. 'This is not a friendly goose.' It looked ready to lunge from her hands and peck someone.

'There is no such thing as a friendly goose,' Jemma said. 'I must go to see how Isidore is coming with her costume. I checked on her earlier and her maids were frantically tearing apart two dresses. She says she's going to be a queen, but I'm afraid she's going to enter the ballroom wrapped in a handkerchief.'

'Why doesn't Isidore go by her title of Duchess of Cosway?' Harriet asked. 'Last night she was announced as Lady Isidore Del'Fino.'

'I don't think she's ever met the duke. Her husband, I mean,' Jemma said. 'Or if she did, it was for five minutes years ago. So she uses her own title, although for tonight she's the Queen of Palmyra.'

'If you had told me that you were planning a Twelfth Night costume party,' Harriet said, putting the goose down, 'I could have been a queen as well.'

'Apparently queens don't wear much clothing, so you'll definitely be more comfortable this way And I'm sorry about not warning you, darling, but it's so much fun doing it last minute. You should see people rushing about the house looking for costumes. The butler is going mad! It's wonderful.'

And with that, Jemma sailed out of the

21

room leaving Harriet with the goose.

It was absurd to feel so sorry for herself. Every time she walked into Judge Truder's court she heard of people whose lives were far more desperate. Why just last month there was a girl who stole half a jar of mustard and six oranges. Truder had actually woken up and had wanted to give the poor child hard labour, fool that he was.

But she, Harriet, had no need to steal oranges. She was a duchess; she was still relatively young; she was healthy...

She was lonely.

A tear splashed on the goose and she absently smoothed his feathers.

She didn't really want to be a queen, either of fairies or Palmyra, wherever that was. She just wanted a husband.

Someone to sit with her of an evening, just like Loveday had said.

2

Another chapter in Which Breasts Play a Not-insignificant Role

Zenobia, Queen of Palmyra, threw back her head and laughed. Her bodice gaped, precariously clinging to the slope of her breasts. The dapper man before her twirled on his toes, one hand up in the air, like a gypsy dancer at Bartholomew Fair. Zenobia laughed again, and flung both hands in the air in imitation of him.

The Queen of Palmyra's corset, if one existed, was thoroughly inadequate.

It crossed Harriet's mind that a true friend would alert Zenobia – more commonly known as Isidore – that her breasts were about to make an appearance on the ballroom floor.

But Harriet was tucked in a chair at the side of the ballroom, and Isidore had her eyes fixed on the man she was seducing, though seducing wasn't quite the appropriate word. Harriet had the idea that Isidore was chaste. Just bored. And Harriet couldn't possibly catch her attention. She felt invisible; she certainly seemed to be invisible to most of the men in the room.

Widows dressed as Mother Goose were not as much in demand as half-naked queens, no matter how much stuffing their bodices contained. What little cloth existed in Isidore's bodice was thickly embroidered with peacock feathers, the eyes picked out in jewels.

In short, peacock eyes were more popular than goose eyes. Lord Beesby, for example, didn't seem to be able to take his eyes off Isidore's bodice, whereas Harriet's goose put men off. It was lying beside her, head drooping from the chair so that its beady eyes stared at the floor.

Isidore twirled again, hands in the air. A lock of hair fell from her elaborate arrangement. The dancers nearby paused in their own steps, entranced by the sway of her hips. There was something so un-English about Isidore's curves, her scarlet lips, the way she was smiling at Beesby as if he were the king himself. It had to be her Italian ancestry. Most Englishwomen looked – and felt – like Harriet herself: dumpy. Maternal.

Though she, Harriet, had no reason to feel maternal, given her lack of children. At this point, the only man likely to approach her would be called Georgie Porgie.

Harriet bit her lip. She'd welcome Georgie Porgie. Who knew it would be just as humiliating to sit out dances when one is widowed, as when one first entered the marriage market? Yet another one of life's charming surprises.

Lord Beesby was dancing as he had never danced before. One hand still in the air like a gypsy king, he capered and pranced before his partner, his knees rising higher and higher. He reminded Harriet of nothing so much as her beloved spaniel, Mrs Custard. If Beesby had a tail, he'd be wagging it with pure bliss. He was rapt, enchanted, in love. According to the pattern of the dance, he should have long ago moved to another partner, but he and Isidore had – scandalously – eschewed exchanging partners, and the dance had continued without them.

Suddenly, out of the corner of her eye, Harriet caught a glimpse of an irate-looking Lady Beesby making her way toward the couple. Isidore's bodice was at the very point of disaster. Harriet jumped to her feet, caught Isidore's eye, and inclined her head in the direction of Lady Beesby.

Isidore flashed one look at the matron heading toward her, drew back, and shouted, 'Lord Beesby, you do me wrong!'

Caught in a dream, Lord Beesby didn't hear and circled blissfully, one more time.

Isidore bellowed something else; Lord Beesby started blinking and stopped short in the midst of a turn. Isidore's hand flashed out and she slapped him.

The entire ballroom went stone silent. 'You led me to believe that you found me attractive!' Isidore shrieked, with all the bravado of an Italian opera singer. 'How dare you spurn me after presenting me with such temptation!'

Jemma appeared from nowhere and wrapped an arm around Isidore's waist. 'Alas, Lord Beesby is a man of high moral fibre,' she said, with magnificent emphasis.

'Oh, how shall I recover!' Isidore cried, casting a drooping hand to her brow.

Jemma swept her off the dance floor. Harriet barely stopped herself from applauding.

Lord Beesby was still standing there, mouth agape, when his wife reached his side. Harriet thought she looked at him with a measure of new respect. It was one thing to have one's husband making a fool of himself on the dance floor with a gorgeous young woman. It was another to have that same husband spurn the wench in a public arena.

Lady Beesby even smiled at her husband, which had to be the first such affectionate gesture in days. Perhaps years. Then she spun on her heel and marched off the dance floor, her smaller, bemused husband trailing after her. It reminded Harriet of when her fat sow Rebecca would suddenly march off in indignation. Rebecca generally trailed at least one piglet behind her. Or – Harriet stopped.

Her thoughts were made up of spaniels and piglets. She was so tedious that she bored herself. She was countrified, tedious, and melancholic.

She could feel her eyes getting dangerously hot. But she was tired of tears. Benjamin had died over two years ago. She'd wept when he died, and after. Wept more than she thought it was possible for a human body to cry. Wept, she realized now, from a mixture of grief and rage and mortification.

But her husband was gone, and she was still here.

Dressing in Mother Goose costumes wouldn't bring him back. Sitting like a mouse at the side of the ballroom wouldn't bring him back. Nothing would bring him back.

Yet what could she do? Widows were supposed to be dignified. Not only that, but she was a duchess. Given that Benjamin's nephew, the current Duke of Berrow, was only eleven years old and still at Eton, she wasn't even a dowager duchess. She was a duchess and a widow and a twenty-seven-year-old woman: and which of those three terms was the most depressing she couldn't even decide.

She swallowed hard. Could she bear to spend the rest of her life growing paler, as her hair faded and her shoulders stooped? Would she merely watch other women seduce and entice, while she mused about fat piglets and loyal spaniels? A dog, no matter how loyal, is only a dog.

She couldn't spend the rest of her life clinging to the sides of ballrooms, dressed as the mother she wasn't and never would be.

She had to do something. Change her life! Start thinking about...

About...

Pleasure.

The word popped into her mind unexpectedly and stayed there, with all the gracious coolness of a drop of cool rain on a blistering day Isidore was obviously enjoying herself, flirting with Beesby. He had loved their dance.

Pleasure.

She could think about pleasure.

Her pleasure.

3

In Which the Geography of Pleasure is Dissected

Harriet found the Duchess of Beaumont and the Duchess of Cosway – Jemma and Isidore – in a small parlour after a dismaying search of other rooms. Every alcove held a pair of heads, male and female. Every settee featured people paired off like robins in spring. Or, since it was a costume party, like a sailor and the Queen of Sheba.

She pasted a cheery Mother Goose type of smile on her face and kept saying mindless things like, 'Oh, very sorry! Right then, I'll just – just move along, shall I?' The sailor didn't even look up when she walked into the yellow salon. His head bent over the Queen of Sheba's with such tenderness and possession that Harriet felt as if her heart would break in two.

She and Benjamin never ... of course not. They had been a married couple, hadn't they? Married couples didn't kiss at balls.

But had Benjamin *ever* kissed her like that? He used to kiss her in a brisk, affectionate manner. The way she kissed her spaniel.

'You saved me!' Isidore cried when Harriet finally located Jemma and Isidore in the small sitting room. 'Lady Beesby would have eaten me for breakfast.'

'Darling, come and sit beside me; I'm feeling blue,' Jemma said, peering around the side of her chair. They were seated by the fire.

Harriet rounded the little circle and halted. Her least favourite acquaintance in the world, the Duke of Villiers, lay on a settee just to the left of the hearth. He was recovering from an infection caused by a duelling wound, and his face was angular and pale. Even so, one look at him made her feel every inch an unattractive, dumpy widow. His dressing gown was made of Italian silk, dark lavender embroidered with a delicate border of black tulips. It was exquisite, unexpected, and utterly beautiful.

'I apologize, Your Grace,' she said. 'I didn't realize you had left your chambers.'

'I was threatening to rise to my feet and dance the saraband,' he said, in his slightly drawling accent, 'so my dragonish valet finally allowed me to be near the festivities, if not part of them.'

Harriet sat down stiffly, promising herself that she could leave within five minutes. She could plead a headache, she could say the fire was too hot for her, she could say that she had promised to meet someone in the ballroom... Anything to get away from Villiers.

'As you entered, Harriet,' Isidore announced, 'I was just saying that I have decided to create a scandal.'

'Poor Lady Beesby,' Harriet said.

Isidore laughed. 'Not with Beesby. That was just entertainment. No, I mean to create a true scandal. The kind of scandal that will force my husband to return to England.' Harriet suddenly noticed that Isidore had a very firm jaw.

'I hate to use my misbegotten history as an example,' Jemma said, 'but my husband never found my scandals an adequate reason to travel from England to France. And your husband is somewhere in the Far East, isn't he?'

Harriet silently agreed. Propping up a drunken judge had caused her to see any number of cases involving scandals caused by women. Often their husbands didn't bother to travel to the next county to rescue them. But then, dukes and duchesses never showed up in the shire court of the Berrow duchy, and presumably the duke cared for his reputation.

'I pity Cosway,' Villiers said languidly. 'Jemma, have you a chess set in this parlour?'

She shook her head. 'No. And you know that the doctor told you to stay away from chess. You need to recover from those fevers, not exacerbate your tired brain by thinking up intricate plays.'

'Life without chess is paltry,' Villiers growled. 'Not worth living.'

'Benjamin would have agreed with you,' Harriet said, before she thought. Her husband had killed himself after losing a game of chess.

To Villiers.

There was a drop of silence in the room, a moment in which no one breathed. Then Jemma said, 'We all wish Benjamin were here to play chess with us.'

Villiers turned his face to the fire and said nothing, but Harriet felt a rush of acute shame, along with the memory of his stammering apology. Villiers had been dying, literally burning up with a fever, and he'd come all the way to Jemma's house just to apologize to her for winning the game that led to Benjamin's suicide.

'I wasn't referring to his – his death,' Harriet scrambled into words. 'Merely that, if a doctor had told Benjamin that he couldn't play chess–'

'For a whole *month*,' Villiers put in.

'Poor Benjamin would have been enraged. Crazed.'

'I would be rather crazed myself, I think,' Jemma said.

'That tyrannical Scottish surgeon of yours could at least allow us to continue our match,' Villiers growled. 'One move a day ... how difficult could that be for my festering brain to handle?'

'You truly can't play chess for a month?' Harriet asked.

'It's not so terrible,' Jemma said. 'You can read books. Though not books about chess, of course.'

'A *month*,' Villiers said.

There was a world of leaden boredom and misery in his voice, so much so that Harriet couldn't help smiling. 'You'll have to find other interests.'

'Women, wine, and song,' Isidore suggested. 'Classic male occupations.'

'I can't sing.'

'Beautiful women, preferably mermaids, are supposed to sing while you quaff wine,' Harriet pointed out, rather liking the image of the Duke of Villiers surrounded by sirens. If she were a siren, she would try to sink his vessel.

'If you know of any mermaids, do send them in my direction,' Villiers said, closing his eyes. 'Right now I am far too tired to pursue a woman, fish tail or no.'

He did look white. Given that Harriet loathed him, she was feeling provokingly sympathetic.

'I know! I can use you in my scheme,' Isidore exclaimed.

'No,' Villiers stated, not opening his eyes.

'I never join schemes.'

'A pity,' Isidore said. 'I am quite sure that the news that his duchess was frolicking with the infamous Duke of Villiers would summon my ne'er-do-well husband. Cosway's solicitor last indicated that he was somewhere in Ethiopia. Apparently he's discovered the source of the Blue Nile. And aren't we all happy for him?'

'But if the duke returns to defend your reputation, poor Villiers would have to fight another duel,' Jemma said. 'Your husband probably fights off cannibal tribes over his breakfast Isidore.'

'I'm in no shape to emulate the cannibal hordes,' Villiers said, ladling his voice with such a layer of dramatic gloom that they all started laughing.

'Then I need someone with your reputation,' Isidore said.

'You can't be serious!' Harriet exclaimed. 'Are you really hoping that a scandal will make your husband return?'

Isidore looked at her, one eyebrow raised, her lips curved in a hard little smile. 'Can you think of one single reason why I shouldn't try? I am married to a man whom I have no memory of meeting. He shows no concern for my whereabouts, and has never answered a single communication I sent to him, though I know he receives my letters.'

'Surely post goes astray between here and

the Blue Nile.'

'Occasionally I receive a note from his solicitors in London responding to something in a private letter I wrote to him. I am tired of this situation. I am married to the Duke of Cosway and I want to be a real duchess.'

'Why does Cosway stay away from England?' Villiers asked, opening his eyes. 'Are you so very terrifying?' He peered at her in an interested kind of way

'Why don't you go to him?' Harriet asked, at the same moment.

'He is an *explorer*,' Isidore said with withering scorn. 'Can you see me on a camel, trotting around looking for the Blue Nile?'

Harriet couldn't help grinning. She herself was a sturdy type who probably could – if she had to – clamber up onto a camel. Isidore, on the other hand, looked as exotic and delicate as an orchid.

'Can't his mother summon him?' Jemma asked.

'She pleads failure,' Isidore said. 'And says that nothing will bring him back home, that he is the most stubborn of her children.'

'I met Lady Cosway several times,' Jemma remarked. 'If she put her foot down, the King of England would bow to her will. I'd back her over her son.'

'That's just what I think. I'm trusting her to gauge the scandal and force him to return.'

'How long has it been since he was in England?' Harriet asked.

'Eighteen years. Eighteen! I could divorce him on some sort of grounds, I suppose.'

'Non-consummation would be a possibility,' Villiers noted.

'But I'm not stupid. It is a great deal better to be a duchess than not to be a duchess. I've lived on the Continent. I visited Jemma in Paris, and spent a great deal of time in my favourite of all cities, Venice. But now I want my life as an adult woman to begin. And I can't do it while caught in this half-life!'

Harriet blinked at her. It sounded as if Isidore were voicing the same things she had just been thinking to herself.

'To be brutally honest,' Isidore continued, 'I'm tired of sleeping alone. If Cosway turns out to be a horrible sort of man with whom I don't want to spend time, well, then I might leave him and return to Italy. But at least I won't have this talismanic virginity any longer. And I might have a child.'

Harriet choked, and even Villiers opened his eyes. 'Did I hear the word virgin?'

'Isidore, you are being deliberately provoking,' Jemma said, handing her a small ruby glass of cordial. 'You are trying to shock us. I assure you that I am horrifically shocked, so you can relent now.'

'Virginity is a woman's most valuable possession,' Villiers said, looking not in the least shocked.

'Nonsense,' Jemma said briskly. 'Since we're all being so remarkably intimate, I don't mind pointing out that a virgin without a brain is a useless creature.'

'Ah, but a virgin *with* a brain is beyond the price of rubies.'

'I have beauty too, I might point out,' Isidore said.

'Vanity, thy name is woman,' Villiers said. But he was smiling. 'I gather you intend to impress upon your husband the possibility that you might birth a cuckoo to inherit his dukedom.'

'More to the point,' Jemma put in, 'impress it upon his mother. Because if Cosway were interested in his estate, he would have come home years ago.'

'You truly mean to lose your virginity?' Harriet asked. It was so fascinating to see another woman face loneliness – and do it with all the courage that she, Harriet, lacked. Isidore wouldn't sit around on the side of a ballroom weeping onto a stuffed goose.

'I haven't made up my mind yet,' Isidore said airily. 'I shall make that decision based on how long it takes my husband to return. I just need a potent kind of man.'

'In order to father your child?' Villiers asked. 'May I say that this is a fascinating conversation? I can't say I've ever seen adultery planned with such ruthless lack of emotion.'

'I'd prefer he were potent in terms of scandal,' Isidore said. 'Someone like you, Villiers. If I were flirting with you, the news would travel to Africa by the end of the month. Harriet, you must know who's the most scandalous man in England besides Villiers.'

'Oh, Villiers isn't truly scandalous,' Harriet said.

Villiers opened his eyes. 'You surprise me, Your Grace. Truly, you do.'

'I don't know why. You never really step beyond the bounds of the commonplace.'

'I have children out of wedlock,' Villiers said, looking slightly wounded.

'What nobleman doesn't?' Harriet retorted.

'I am lowered by a sudden sense of my own inadequacies,' Villiers said. 'Not truly scandalous. Commonplace. My pride is dashed to the ground.'

Harriet ignored him. 'There are no interesting men in the *ton*.'

'Worse and worse,' Villiers mumbled.

'Then who is the most scandalous man in England, to your mind?' Isidore asked.

'Lord Strange, of course,' Harriet said.

'*Lord* Strange?' Isidore asked, knitting her brow. 'Surely a lord is part of the *ton*.'

'Not Strange,' Villiers said, sipping a glass

of water. 'Strange is the richest man in England, give or take a shilling or two. At some point the king gave him a title. After all, he keeps rescuing the English economy. Strange could certainly afford to pay for a dukedom if he wished, but he told me that the only reason he accepted the title was because he liked the sound of Lord Strange.'

'He's odd, very intelligent, and truly scandalous,' Harriet said. 'Not like the men who claim to be rakes in London but really just trot around after opera singers–'

Villiers groaned.

'He's mad for architecture, by all accounts, and has built his own replica of the leaning tower of Pisa,' she continued.

'I've seen the original,' Isidore said. 'Surely Strange didn't gain his interesting reputation by copying defective Italian architecture?'

'His reputation stems from the motley collection of loose people with whom he lives,' Harriet said.

'Actors and actresses,' Villiers put in. 'Those who work the streets, and those who work the court. Inventors. Scientists. Strange boasts that every interesting person in the country passes through his estate at some point.'

'It's true,' Harriet said. 'I no sooner read about someone powerful in government, or at one of the universities, but the gossip columns note that he's visiting Strange.'

'How did he come by all his money?'
Isidore asked. 'Is he a merchant of some
kind?'

'Oh, no, his father was a perfectly respect-
able baronet,' Villiers answered, 'with a beaky
head, like an old eagle. There was some sort
of problem with the family years ago. Could
be his mother flew the coop. Or a sister.
Perhaps an aunt? At any rate, Strange is a
gentleman born and bred, but you'll never
see him in the normal haunts. He goes where
he wishes, while hosting an endless house
party.'

'I would *love* to pay him a visit,' Jemma
said. 'I bought a gorgeous little chess queen
that he had sold to a curiosity shop. He
promised me the whole set if I gained the
courage, as he put it, to pay him a visit.'

'Brilliant!' Isidore said. 'I shall travel there
at once!'

'Oh, but–' Jemma said.

'But what?' Isidore interrupted. 'I wish to
make a scandal, and this man appears
ideally suited to create one for me. I shall
brush shoulders with all those light-skirts
and theatre people and have an excellent
time doing so. And meanwhile I shall flirt
madly with my host, thereby creating a
scandal that will burn its way straight to my
husband's ears.'

'You're planning to flirt with Strange himself?' Harriet said. 'Your reputation could be

40

ruined throughout England, merely by walking through the doors at Fonthill, let alone by flirting with Strange. No one flirts with Strange.'

'Why on earth not?' Isidore asked. 'Is he hideous? I flirt with everyone! Unless–' she wrinkled her nose '–is he shorter than Lord Beesby? There are certain physiques in which I cannot feign interest.'

'Oh no, he's actually quite good-looking,' Harriet said.

'Then *I* shall be the first to flirt with him. In a very public way, naturally.'

'He doesn't flirt,' Harriet explained. 'From what I understand, he beds women but doesn't toy with them.'

'He shall flirt with me,' Isidore announced. 'I've yet to meet the man who couldn't be taught to flirt. All one has to do is lead him to think that bedding is a possibility and *voilà!*'

Harriet laughed. 'I'd love to see your lessons!'

'Then you must come with me,' Isidore said, grinning at her.

'*I?* I could never do such a thing. You couldn't really mean to visit Fonthill. It's just not done. Not done by – by us, I mean.'

'Us?' Isidore said scornfully. '*Us* is short foolish men like Beesby, and tall, uncaring men like my husband. What do I care for us?'

'It is useful to have a good reputation,'

Jemma said.

'How would you know?' Isidore demanded. 'You left your husband years ago, Jemma. Left him in England and went to Paris – and don't tell me that you were tending to your reputation all those years! Not when you had parties that even Marie Antoinette hesitated to visit–'

'Though she always did,' Jemma put in.

'But you have skirted the edges of propriety for years – yes, and well beyond propriety,' Isidore stated. 'And now you say there is a place in England that you dare not visit? Why? What could happen to you there? Will you be struck by a great desire for an actor and have an *affaire* with a man from a different class?'

'Well–'

But Isidore was just gaining her stride. 'Because that is what you are really talking about!' she said, her Italian accent increasing. 'You, all of you, are saying that Strange is scandalous and not one of us because he is a mere baronet's son. Because he, unlike all of us, is not a duke or a duchess!'

Harriet looked around. Until that moment she had not realized that they were all duchesses, except for Villiers, who was a duke.

'Apparently, we live in such a rarefied atmosphere that we cannot flirt with men who do not have a ducal crest on their carriage door,' Isidore said scathingly. '*You,*

42

Jemma, you who set Paris on its ears with your parties of half-dressed satyrs, you cavil at the idea of Strange because he is not a duke!'

'The problem is more complicated than you present it, Isidore,' Jemma replied. 'If a man flirts with a duchess, he flirts with her rank. When they feign affection and you don't see the foot-licking behind it, you are a fool. No man ever forgets your rank at the moment he kisses you – if your rank is the highest in the land.'

'I don't believe that!'

'You will never truly be able to forget your rank either,' Jemma said remorselessly, 'unless you are in a room like this one, in which we share the title. The scandal caused by your flirtation will undoubtedly be greater due to Lord Strange's low birth, but it will temper your pleasure. At any rate, I cannot accompany you. I am done with scandal-broths.'

'And why is that?' Isidore demanded.

'My husband requested it of me. Beaumont has many responsibilities in the House of Lords, and it is not helpful to his career when his wife makes herself a byword on the street. And believe me, Isidore, anyone who visits Fonthill will be a byword.'

'Fine!' Isidore said. 'A byword is precisely what I wish to be. I shall write to my mother-in-law immediately and tell her of my plans, and then I'll write to Cosway's solicitor, and tell him to send me funds at Strange's house.'

'In my experience, when a woman has decided to lose her virginity, one can't stop the impulse,' Villiers said, grinning. 'It would be like trying to dam–'

'Don't finish that sentence,' Jemma said.

'I've been invited to Strange's and was planning to travel there after this party,' Villiers said, 'but I can't take you with me. That is, not unless I put together a party. Or you find a chaperone.'

'I gave up my chaperone two years ago,' Isidore snapped. 'When I turned twenty-one and there was no husband in sight, I let my aunt return to Wales. I shall travel alone.'

Villiers looked at Jemma. 'Please tell your fiery friend that she cannot arrive at Strange's house unaccompanied and – I might add – uninvited.'

'I am a duchess, even if I don't use the title,' Isidore said instantly. 'Show me the house that will deny entrance to the Duchess of Cosway!'

'Strange doesn't like titles,' Villiers said. 'You're more likely to be admitted as Lady Del'Fino.'

Jemma shook her head. 'I cannot accompany you, Isidore. I really can't.'

'I'll take her,' Harriet said.

She heard the words in her own ears with that queer double sense one gets when one hasn't thought out a comment. It just sprang from her lips.

There was a moment of dead silence. All three turned to look at her.

'*You?*' Isidore said.

And: 'You mustn't take Isidore's starts so seriously,' Jemma said. 'She'll forget about this scheme of hers by tomorrow morning.'

'No, I won't,' Isidore stated.

'Why shouldn't I go?' Harriet said. 'If the Duke of Villiers accompanies the two of us we won't be turned away.'

Villiers gave a short laugh. 'You must be as feverish as I.'

'You can't go, darling, because you are not a wastrel like myself,' Jemma said, 'nor yet a wastrel-in-training like Isidore.'

'I may not be a wastrel,' Harriet said, 'but I'm not really anything else, either. No one recognizes me, because I've lived in the country for so long. Like Isidore, I am a duchess without a duke. But unlike you, no one's career would be diminished by the tarnishing of my reputation.'

'Everyone knows you!' Jemma said, horrified. 'You are our own, darling Harriet.'

'I am a dumpy widow who lived in the country during my marriage and thereafter,' Harriet said flatly. 'My husband committed suicide, and those of the *ton* who don't blame me for his death are morbidly sorry for me. No one will pay the faintest attention to whether I go to Strange's house or not.'

'They don't blame you for Benjamin's suicide,' Villiers said. 'They blame me. And God knows, they're right to do it.'

She gave him a little half-smile. 'It was his life – and his decision. There's no one to blame.'

To her shock, he reached out his hand. And she took it. There was no need to say anything else. His hand was surprisingly comforting for someone as sharp-tongued and uncomfortable as she considered Villiers to be.

'How long ago did your husband take his life?' Isidore asked. 'And please forgive me for not knowing the answer; I have only been in this country for a few months.'

'Two and a half years ago,' Harriet said. 'I am well out of mourning and can attend whatever party I wish.'

'Then I would welcome your company,' Isidore said.

'I just can't imagine either of you at Fonthill,' Jemma exclaimed. 'From what I've heard, Lord Strange's household is one long bacchanalian orgy.'

'Splendid!' Isidore said immediately. To Harriet's mind, she looked ready to throw herself straight into the fray.

Jemma shook her head. 'Harriet isn't–'

'She certainly isn't dressed for an orgy,' Villiers interjected.

Harriet looked down at herself. She'd forgotten she was dressed as Mother Goose. But why shouldn't she be part of an orgy? 'I want to go. I am dressed in a nightgown; I'm halfway to the bedchamber already.'

There was a wry smile in Villiers's eyes.

'We can both wear our costumes. I'll announce myself as an actress.' Isidore had a wicked grin.

Villiers was shaking his head. 'Everyone dresses like that at Lord Strange's house and they don't bother with explanations. He owns the Hyde Park theatre, so his house is haunted by actors. I do think it's a good idea to go in costume,' he said to Harriet. 'And under a false name.'

'Something like Isidore's dress? I couldn't.' She couldn't wear a scrap of fabric that barely covered her breasts.

'No,' Villiers said. 'More of a disguise than that. As I said, Strange is not fond of titles and he wouldn't welcome a duchess – or two – on his doorstep.'

Harriet felt a stab of humiliation. Naturally Villiers didn't want to see her in a scanty costume like Isidore's. 'What are you suggesting? I go as a man?'

It was a joke. The word flew from her lips but–

'You couldn't be so brave,' Isidore said laughing.

'Her Grace need offer no proof of her

courage,' Villiers said. 'Please recall that she just carried a goose into the ballroom while wearing a nightgown. One doubts Saint George exhibited such steel while setting out to fight the dragon. Yet I am not certain...' His eyes rested thoughtfully on her chest.

Raising her chin, Harriet reached inside her voluminous sleeves and pulled out a rolled woollen stocking. And another. A third and fourth.

Then she flattened the fabric against her chest. 'I think,' she said coolly, 'that I shall look very well as a man.'

'Indeed,' Villiers said. 'The idea has possibilities.'

4

In Which Sin & Silver Boxes are Itemized and Explained

January 7, 1784
Fonthill
Lord Strange's Country Estate

'I don't like his blue hair powder,' Eugenia Strange observed. 'Papa, are you listening to me? Today his hair is all covered with red powder, and yesterday it was blue. I think he looks better in red. Do you agree, Papa?'

'Absolutely.' Justinian Strange, known to his closest friends as Jem, let his eight-year-old daughter's words flow by him as he frowned down at the architectural drawing on his desk.

'Do you know what Augusta did to him, Papa? She locked him in the wardrobe. She said that she was tormented by being surrounded by foolish men and she only allowed him out of the wardrobe when he promised to have her coach relined in yellow silk. It's going to cost two hundred pounds. But she says that her diamond earrings cost three hundred pounds, and those were given to her by Mr Cornelys. I asked if she locked him in the wardrobe as well, but she didn't.'

'I expect not,' Jem said, looking up from the drawing he had spent the afternoon creating. 'Eugenia, what do you think of the idea of putting this false floor in the ballroom? It's quite ingenious, you see.'

His daughter came around the table and stood at his shoulder. 'This mechanism would cause the platform to rise, Papa?' she said, putting her finger in precisely the place.

'Exactly.'

'Why?'

'Why? Because it would be striking,' he said, rather lamely. 'The table would rise suddenly in the air when it was time for supper.'

But his daughter shook her head. 'Striking is not a good reason, Papa. Striking is why Mr Hodes is wearing blue hair powder, and I assure you that is not a good decision.'

He drew her little figure against him. 'You're my Sensibility,' he said into her curls. 'Did you spend time with your governess today?'

Eugenia didn't answer, but said, 'Papa, did you know that Mrs Mahon brought fourteen silver filigreed boxes with her? She carries them everywhere.'

'She's the new lead from *The Beggar's Opera*, isn't she? I haven't met her yet. Whatever does Mrs Mahon keep inside her fourteen boxes?'

'Love notes. I believe that she has had fourteen protectors, which is a great many. Miss Linnet told me that when *she* was playing at the Hyde Park Theatre a prince gave her ten pairs of diamond earrings, one a night for ten nights. I should very much prefer diamonds to silver boxes.'

'A prudent observation,' Jem said, pushing back in his chair. 'A box is worth a few pounds, Eugenia, but a diamond might be very expensive. Though I trust you shall never have a protector. I'll give you any earrings you wish.'

Eugenia had her mother's turned-up little nose and sweet brown eyes, but other than that she looked just like him, which meant that she had an awkward face for a child. He glanced at himself in the mirror. He looked the same as always: pale, too gaunt. Clever, he supposed. The kind of hawkish cheekbones he had looked acceptable on a man in his thirties, but rather odd on a young girl. One had to hope that she would grow into them. Or out of them.

In fact, she looked rather odd today in other respects as well. 'What are you wearing?' he said, peering at her.

'My riding costume. But I put a silk petticoat underneath it, because I like the way the dark serge looks against this pink. Look, Papa.' She twirled, and sure enough, there was a light flutter at the bottom of her sombre habit. 'It makes me feel more festive to be in pink. And I pinned these roses here and the scarf breaks the colour, you see?'

'What did your governess think of that?'

'We haven't seen each other today. She's in love, you know.'

'I didn't know. Who is she in love with?'

'Well, for a long period of time she was in love with you, Papa.'

Jem blinked. 'With me?'

'I think she has seen too many plays. She was convinced that you would discover her and I would stop being a motherless child. She's always saying that I'm a motherless child, and no matter how many times I point out that not having known a mother, I

51

feel no lack of one, she doesn't understand.'

Jem could sympathize with the governess. Eugenia's practical nature had deflated many a dream, including that of a spectacular false floor.

'But she finally realized that you weren't going to notice her.'

'I do notice her,' Jem protested. 'Don't I?'

'Well, you didn't notice when she left for ten days, Papa. What colour is her hair?'

'Miss Warren's hair?' He paused.

'I don't think you've ever really *seen* her, Papa.'

'Of course I have, Eugenia!' She was making him feel guilty now. 'I employed her, didn't I? And we've had several conversations about your progress in French and mathematics.'

'She hates mathematics. She has to learn it with me, you know. And she's not very good at it.'

'Why didn't you tell me that she left for ten days?'

'I thought I could use a rest from schooling,' Eugenia said serenely 'I would have told you eventually, Papa, but she came back again. And now she is in love with a footman.'

'A much more suitable choice than myself,' Jem said. 'Which footman?'

'The one with beetling black brows,' Eugenia said, leaning against his shoulder.

Jem pulled her onto his lap and she sat

there, long legs dangling almost to the floor, but still as light as a feather. When she was a baby, she seemed so frail that he had been afraid her bones were like a bird's, with air in the middle.

'Will you ever fall in love, Papa?' Eugenia asked, resting her head back against his shoulder so she could look up at him.

'I'm in love with you, poppet,' he said. 'That's enough for one man.'

'The house is full of beautiful women,' she observed.

'I suppose so.'

'Many of them would like it if you fell in love with them.'

'Unfortunately, these kinds of things can't be arranged on demand.'

'Mama would have liked it if you fell in love.'

He snorted. 'How could you possibly know, given that your mother died before you knew her?'

'She and I are very similar,' Eugenia said without hesitation. 'She would like precisely what I like. And I think you would be happier if you had someone of your own, Papa.'

'Falling in love is merely a way of getting something you desire,' Jem told her. 'Like a silver box. If I want an ornament, I'll buy it.'

'Mrs Mahon probably can't afford to buy silver boxes,' Eugenia observed. 'She has a beautiful muff, but her shoes are quite shabby.'

'A perfect case in point. She falls in love in order to get herself silver boxes. Luckily, I can afford all the silver boxes I want.'

'There's more to love than that,' Eugenia said, wiggling happily. There was nothing that Eugenia Strange loved more than a lively discussion in which she bent her wits and argumentative skills against those of her papa. 'You are focusing on finances, which is a weakness of yours.'

'What should I focus on?' Jem asked cautiously. While he had early on established his child-rearing practices as promoting a clear-headed sensibility in his daughter, he wasn't sure that he wanted her clarity to include bedroom matters. Not at this age. And certainly not if he had to explain them.

'Love is a matter of the heart,' Eugenia said. 'Shakespeare says that nothing should stand between true lovers.'

'We agreed that you wouldn't quote Shakespeare to me for at least a month,' Jem pointed out.

'I didn't quote. I merely condensed.'

'I'm not certain that Mrs Mahon is talking about that kind of love,' he said, more cautiously still.

'Well, of course, Mrs Mahon is a concubine. Or perhaps it is more accurate to say that she occasionally plays the concubine,'

Eugenia said promptly.

'Waa–'

'I see her as a character in a play. There's an old play called *Cupid's Revenge* in the library, and a very naughty woman named Bacha says in Act One that she means to "embrace sin as it were a friend, and run to meet it."'

Jem started thinking about some suggestions he might give Eugenia's governess as regards reading materials the next time he saw her.

But Eugenia didn't even pause for breath. 'Mrs Mahon is embracing sin as a friend. Because really, what else can she do? She must eat.'

'And get more silver boxes,' Jem said, unable to resist.

'Love is not about sin, precisely,' Eugenia told him. 'And it's definitely not about silver boxes. To think about love, we need to consider my governess, in love with the beetle-browed footman. Because love is blind, Papa.'

'That's a quote! We said no quotes.'

'It's an aphorism,' she corrected him. 'It happens to have been repeated in many plays, but its provenance is unknown.'

The good news was that the governess was obviously earning her salary, since his daughter was nimbly using words like *provenance*. The bad news... 'The only time I ever fell in love was with your mother, poppet. And that only occurred because my parents forced the marriage. So you'll have to discard the idea of dancing at my wedding.'

'You simply haven't met the right woman,' his daughter told him.

'As you said, the house is full of beautiful women. Loads of them.'

'Beauty is not everything, Papa.'

Jem looked down at his daughter's oddly angular little face. 'But I don't want to fall in love. It is my observation that only people who wish to fall in love do so. A case in point: your governess developed an affection for me, but transferred it promptly to a hairy footman when the opportunity presented itself.'

'That makes a great deal of sense,' his daughter said, after a moment.

It was a sad reflection on his life, Jem thought, that he was most thrilled by praise from an eight-year-old.

'However,' Eugenia said, rallying, 'perhaps you simply don't know what you want. That's a common state of mankind. While the playwright George Chapman—'

'Don't,' Jem said.

'I wasn't going to quote him,' she complained. 'I was merely summarizing his argument.'

Jem shuddered. Who would have thought that his household would be invaded by a child whose prodigious memory had nothing better to do than memorize large swaths of drama? Obviously it was his fault for inviting actors to rehearse their plays at Fonthill. Parenthood was full of these traps, it seemed to him. An obvious decision – have the actors out to Fonthill so he needn't travel to London for their performances – became fraught with complications once it intersected with Eugenia.

Meanwhile she hopped off his knee. 'I shall devote myself to finding you a mate,' she said.

'What?'

'A mate!' She paused at the door and looked back at him, a beloved, enchanting, awkward little combination of himself and Sally. 'Unless you would like to reconsider the question of my governess?'

'No,' he said firmly 'I don't want a wife at all, Eugenia.'

But she was gone.

5

In Which Masculinity is Described and Detailed

January 7, 1784
The Country Seat of the Duke of Beaumont
Overheard at Tea

'The key to being male,' the Duke of Villiers said, 'is to think like a male. It's really quite simple.'

'That's exactly how I would have described it,' Isidore said, laughing. 'Simple.'

Villiers cast her a look. 'Ribaldry aside, if a person looks male, everyone assumes he *is* male. If a bystander appears doubtful, say you're going to take a piss. Men never expect women to know that word. Or say something about your pole.'

'My what?' Harriet asked, and then felt herself turn pink. 'Oh, of course. I can do that.'

'You'd better stuff your breeches in front,' Villiers said.

'Thereby aligning yourself with the larger part of English males,' Jemma put in.

'This is all so vulgar,' Harriet complained.

'Men are vulgar,' Villiers said. 'If you are

naturally rarefied and delicate in your thinking, then do not put on a pair of breeches.'

'I can be vulgar,' Harriet said instantly.

'If you can manage vulgarity, you're halfway to being male. Men are direct while discussing bedroom matters. We never say that a couple *dances in the sheets,* or any of those euphemisms women employ. Good old Anglo-Saxon words prevail.'

'Talk about yourself most of the time,' Jemma suggested. 'For a man there is no nobler topic than himself.'

'But,' Harriet said confusedly, 'there won't really be a myself, if you see what I mean.'

Villiers eyed her. 'Lived your life in the country. You'd better be my second nephew Cope. He's an odd duck who is never seen in town. He has a doting mother: that explains the effeminacy.'

'I'm not–' Harriet began and realized the absurdity of what she was saying. 'I suppose I will be a trifle effeminate.'

'You'll have to figure out how to walk like a man. I can get you fitted up with clothes,' Villiers said, 'but walking is important. Can you smoke?'

'Absolutely not. But I shall enjoy the clothing. I loathe wearing panniers. I'm always bumping into doorways, not to mention people.'

'What about your hair?' Isidore asked. 'If you cut your hair now, you'll never be able to wear it high again.'

Harriet smiled. 'I don't wear it high now.' She gestured toward her modest arrangement of curls and puffs. 'Most of this was added by my maid this morning. My own hair barely reaches my shoulders.'

'Very clever,' Jemma said. 'I keep meaning to try a hair piece.'

'I doubt you could do it successfully,' Harriet said. 'Your hair is such a beautiful gold colour. But mine is dull brown, and it's easy to match.'

'Your hair is not dull!'

Harriet shrugged. 'Who would know, what with the hot iron and crimping and powdering? I shall positively relish being male if it means I could stop trying to straighten my hair.'

'Men do not straighten nor curl their hair,' Villiers stated.

'Some do,' Isidore put in. 'I am quite certain that Saint Albans curls his hair. And he wears lip colour as well.'

'I shan't,' Harriet said.

'I wouldn't let you,' Villiers said. 'If you're going to do this, you're going to do it properly. And that means you'll be my creation.'

Jemma laughed. 'Created in Villiers's image: you're going to be a huge success, Harriet!'

Harriet bit her lip. The idea of being Villiers's creation, after the time when she had tried to seduce him and he had rejected her, was mortifying.

She wasn't the only one remembering that night. In the depths of his black eyes there was a mocking spark that said: you can't do it. After all, when she had kissed him in the carriage, he had done something so shocking that she had actually slapped him. He knew her to be a conservative, tiresome country woman.

'There's no need to go to these extremes,' he said now. 'We could simply dress you as Isidore's elderly aunt from the country. You'd make a fine chaperone and no one would question you.'

The anger in Harriet's chest felt like fire. She had played the fool when she had tried to seduce Villiers, and he had been right to scorn her. Benjamin had been his closest friend, and she had kissed him in a misguided impulse to make Benjamin notice her.

But she was no elderly aunt from the country.

'I shouldn't think I'll have the slightest problem playing a man,' she said. 'I shall merely remember to rearrange my breeches in front at least once an hour, thereby drawing attention to the padding I carefully placed there in the morning, and I'll blend in perfectly.' She let her eyes slide below his waist.

'A low blow,' Villiers said.

'Low indeed!' Isidore crowed.

'Lucky I brought my tailor with me,' Villiers said. 'You need everything from boots to periwigs.'

'You can be measured for boots and I'll send to London for them,' Jemma said.

'I must return to Berrow for quarter sessions before I can travel to Fonthill,' Harriet said with a frown.

Villiers raised an eyebrow.

'A sot rules the shire court in my village,' Harriet told him. 'So we abide by the old customs. He sleeps off the brandy of the night before and I make the rulings. Otherwise he simply gives everyone hard labour, no matter the offense or the truth of it.'

'Who's the current duke?'

'He's eleven years old, and at Eton,' Harriet said.

'You must know of his mother, Lady Brewyn,' Jemma put in. 'She is currently living in Paris with a man twenty years her junior. A cheerful woman, by all accounts.'

'I'm taking care of the estate for my nephew,' Harriet said, 'and that includes the shire court, at least until he is of age or the current judge is replaced.'

'I shall wait for you to return from the quarter sessions,' Isidore said. 'Meanwhile, I'll send a letter to my husband declaring my visit to Strange. I'm sure it takes a while to return from Africa.'

'I am immensely amused by this scheme,' Villiers said.

'There's nothing better than an occasional act of folly,' Jemma said. 'You would be the better for it yourself, Villiers.'

'The fact that His Grace lies there recovering from a duel suggests that acts of folly are second nature,' Harriet said gently.

Then she smiled at the narrowed eyes of Villiers – and the amused eyes of Jemma.

She felt like a new Harriet.

Not a widow.

Not tedious.

A wild Harriet, a Harriet who engaged in folly, a Harriet who saw life as a challenge, not a failure.

6

Justice By Duchess, Part Two

February 1, 1784
Shire Court
The Duchy of Berrow
Honourable Reginald Truder, presiding

'If I understand you correctly, Mr Burch, the defendant pretended to be a barber.'

'And then he stole my fish!' Mr Burch said, keeping his eyes imploringly on the duchess. He'd heard as how she was the only one who saw to it that justice was done.

'Your fish,' the duchess said.

'What fish? What fish?' barked the judge. He had deeply flushed cheeks and a beak of a nose. He looked more like a convict with a headache than a judge.

'It was the fish that he pretended the haberdasher sent to my wife,' Mr Burch said. He skewed his eyes toward the duchess again. Anyone could tell that she was the only one really listening; the judge was swilling out of a flask again.

'It wasn't just the fish,' Mr Burch continued. 'First he pretended to be a barber and gained entrance to my house. Then he stole a silver cup that my wife had sent over from the silversmith, by pretending that he'd come to deliver the fish.'

'So it wasn't your fish?'

'Well, it was – I suppose it was his fish. He came back and took the fish anyway, telling my wife that–'

'Hard labour,' the judge stated, glaring around the court.

The duchess put a hand on his arm. She spoke quietly, but Tom Burch still heard her. 'I'm just getting to the bottom of it, Reginald.'

'I don't like fish,' he said.

She patted him again and said, 'So we can discount the theft of the fish, Mr Burch, because the defendant sent you the fish, and then took it back again. But that was a stratagem to allow him to gain access to your house and steal your silver cup.'

'He was caught with it!' Mr Burch said triumphantly. 'Caught red-handed! In the deed! With the cup!'

'The defendant claims that you asked him to carry the cup back to the silversmith and have it engraved.'

'If that's the case – and it isn't – why was it under his bed?'

'Hard labour,' the judge said after another swallow. 'I insist this time, Yer Grace. The man's a fish-stealer.'

The duchess sighed and turned to the dock. 'Oscar Sibble, this is your third appearance before this court, all three of which were for rather creative escapades involving stolen objects.'

Burch noticed that Sibble didn't even hang his head, the way any proper man would. He grinned instead. 'No one was hurt,' he said. 'The cup's back home with Burch.'

The judge's eyes narrowed. 'Transport him!' he suddenly bellowed.

The duchess patted his arm again. 'We can't do that, Reginald. The colonies are at war, remember? We don't transport people there any more.'

'Then drop him in the sea offshore,' the judge said. 'He can swim over to them tarnishing Americans, most of 'em transported from this county anyway.'

'Two weeks hard labour,' the duchess said. 'And Mr Sibble, the only reason you're not facing imprisonment this time is because the cup was recovered. You appear to have had a merry time of it, delivering the fish, stealing the fish again, pretending to be a barber, ending up with a silver cup. But life is not a game, Mr Sibble.'

There was a moment of silence in the court.

'If you appear again in this shire court, you will face imprisonment.'

'For life,' the judge added thirstily.

The constable hauled Sibble away, and the duchess turned to Mr Burch. 'It sounds as if you've had a distressing time of it, Mr Burch. I want to commend you on your restraint in the face of these indignities.'

Tom Burch stood up taller. Everyone had been hooting, saying he was a fool because of losing his silver cup due to a fish. But the Duchess of Berrow thought he'd showed restraint.

He put on his hat and marched out of the court. She wasn't a real judge, of course. But she was what they'd got in Berrow, and it was better than nothing.

Everyone nodded to him on the way out.

7

In Which Strange Guests Arrive at Lord Strange's House

February 5, 1784
Fonthill
Lord Strange's Country Estate

Lord Strange never quite managed to ignore his butler, although he frequently tried. Povy felt the need to make announcements three or four times a day, and although Jem had frequently pointed out that he had no interest in household matters, the butler persisted in informing him.

So Jem didn't look up when he heard Povy's tread in the hallway, and merely reminded himself to install a latch on the inside of the door as the butler came to a halt before his desk.

'Visitors have arrived, my lord. Perhaps you might wish to greet them.'

'I'll greet them this evening, as usual.' He'd woken up in the middle of the night with two ideas simultaneously: one for a bridge suspension system, and the other for a madrigal. He had the bridge drawn in charcoal, and the madrigal in four parts and on the whole, the madrigal was the success. The bridge looked very pretty, but he rather thought the weight-bearing beams might be overburdened. Perhaps if he lowered the arch itself...

'The Duke of Villiers has arrived,' Povy announced.

'He likes the velvet suite, doesn't he? Relishes all that frivolous splendour. Tell him I'll see him at supper.'

'He is accompanied by the Duchess of Cosway.'

Jem looked up. 'Who the hell is that?'

'To the best of my knowledge, the Duchess of Cosway is some sixty years of age and lives a retired life in Colchester.'

'Oh dear,' Jem said, grinning. 'I gather that Villiers's companion is not an antique countrywoman?'

Povy coughed. 'It is remotely possible that the young woman in question is the wife of the current Duke of Cosway, son of the aforementioned duchess. I understand that he contracted marriage at a very early age, but since he left the country thereafter, Collin's Peerage does not credit the marriage as having reached full sovereignty.'

'Not consummated, in other words,' Jem said, tracing the line under the bridge again.

'Precisely.'

'Do you or don't you think this young

woman is the bride-to-be?'

'It is possible.'

'But equally possible that Villiers has brought a fancy piece with him, gusseted up like a Christmas lamb. I will greet the supposed duchess at supper as well, Povy. Put Villiers and the young woman in adjoining rooms.'

'Yes, your lordship. They are accompanied by a young man whom the duke introduced as a relative, Mr Cope.'

'Never heard of him either.'

'He is quite young,' Povy said. It was evident in his tone that Povy considered the young man too young for the exuberant nature of a Strange house party.

'That's not our problem, Povy. Has my new secretary, Miss DesJardins, settled in yet?'

'The young Frenchwoman seems quite comfortable, my lord. She is planning an entertainment for tomorrow, Something called a Tahitian Feast of Venus.'

Jem started smiling. 'I knew she would liven up our entertainments. They've been deadly dull lately. Tahitian as in the country of Tahiti?'

'My sense would be that there is little connection, except perhaps that the land of Tahiti is a very warm country, which encourages lack of clothing,' Povy said repressively. 'Miss DesJardins has requested that the fires in the South Ballroom be lit to their highest capacity and kept there.' He cleared his throat. 'You might want to encourage the Duke of Villiers to confine his relative to his quarters tomorrow. Miss DesJardins is talking of twelve virgins.'

'*Twelve?*' Jem said, barking with laughter again. 'She must be trafficking in miracles. There isn't one in the house!'

'Mr Cope...' Povy began.

Jem narrowed his eyes.

'The lad has a remarkably innocent face.'

'Innocence is a time of life, not an irrevocable blot.'

But Povy had known his master for many years, and he gave him a stern look. 'Mr Cope is not prepared for the Feast of Venus.'

Jem got up with a sigh. 'I suppose I'll come down. I might as well assess this child for myself. What a fool Villiers is, to bring an innocent to my house. Povy, you do remember Wilkinson, don't you? He had an innocent face, but my word!'

'A very different kind of look in Wilkinson's face,' Povy said.

Jem hated to leave his work, but he paid Povy a prince's ransom just to know this sort of thing. His house sometimes shook from sins collected under its roof, but the one thing he could not and would not tolerate was the defilement of innocence. No young woman played a Tahitian virgin in his house unless she did it for pleasure. And no Mr Cope was going to lose his wide-eyed purity unless he wished to.

Though honestly, he couldn't remember the last young man whom he thought needed shielding. Villiers's young relative was probably straining at the leash.

'Wasn't there a time of life when you would have lusted to see a feast of Tahitian virgins, Povy?' he asked, leaving the room.

'No,' Povy said.

That seemed to answer that, so Jem continued down the stairs.

Fifteen minutes later he entered the small Rose Salon without being announced, paused for a moment to survey his visitors, and then swore under his breath. Povy was an intelligent, canny miracle and he should never have doubted him.

There was only one word for Mr Cope: adorable. He had curly brown hair, pulled into a simple pigtail at his neck, with just a dusting of powder. He wore a beautiful coat; he could hardly be Villiers's relative without exhibiting a fine sense of style. But his eyes gave him away. They were exquisite, and not just because of their colour and a fringe of lash that could have graced a princess. They were – fresh.

Jem shot Villiers a look through narrowed eyes. There was something peculiar about this. For one thing, Villiers wasn't sleeping with the woman he'd dragged along with him, the supposed Duchess of Cosway, the duchess who didn't exist. She was a pretty piece, all right, as glittering and sultry as a peacock, but Villiers was talking to her without the faintest desire in his eye.

On the other hand, Jem wasn't sure that Villiers could feel desire for anyone, not if he were as ill as he looked. The man had to have lost three stone.

Mr Cope was standing close to Villiers, with his eyes as round as saucers, staring at a statue Jem had shipped from Crete on an impulse. That kiss between Mars and Venus *was* on the risqué side. Of course, they were married (mythologically speaking). But the whole question of marital virtue was somewhat offset by the fact that Mars was wearing a helmet – but nothing else.

'Villiers,' Jem said, walking forward.

The duke turned around and swept him a bow. Even gaunt as Villiers was, he looked every inch a duke.

'We'd better get you in bed,' Jem said by way of greeting. He'd heard Villiers was ill, but hadn't realized how close he came to death. It gave him a queer feeling, so Jem said roughly, 'You look like hell.'

'I'm better than I was. But I'm not supposed to play chess, so I'm relying on you and your dubious charms to entertain me, Strange.'

'You'll have to entertain yourself,' Jem said, turning to the so-called duchess and bowing. 'Good morning, Your Grace.'

Instantly he saw that she *was* a duchess. A rather gaudy one, in an Italian style, but he knew instantly that he was looking at the Duchess of Cosway. Or perhaps the future Duchess of Cosway was the proper terminology

It was a miracle that she managed to curtsy, given that her travelling dress appeared to have been sewed onto her body.

'You do me too much honour,' Jem said with patent insincerity. This was not the sort of guest he enjoyed. He disliked the way that titles, especially the higher-up ones, seemed to give their holders the right to behave like despicable fools. She would be fussy, and shocked, and likely stamp out in high dudgeon in a day or so.

But then she smiled at him, a lush armful of warm Italian skin and sweet ruby mouth, and he changed his mind. There was something wicked about that mouth, a hint of a kiss or a kiss-to-be-taken hanging in the corner.

She may be a virgin, but she didn't look shockable.

Mr Cope, on the other hand, was so new-fledged that he bobbed his bow like a schoolboy.

Jem was rarely shocked by life, but he was

conscious of a little surprise now. In the course of throwing his house open to anyone he (and Povy) deemed interesting, he had seen all sorts of desire. Very little of it interested him – and none of it surprised him.

But he was surprised now. Surprised by a little surge of interest in himself – shamefully – for Mr Cope. For a stripling with big eyes and not even a sign of a beard. For a male. For God's sake, Jem thought with disgust. If this is getting old, I want nothing to do with it.

And he made a mental note to stay far away from Cope.

'Just how old is that youth you've brought along?' he managed to ask Villiers *sotto voce*, a few moments later.

'Twenty-two,' Villiers said. 'I know he looks like a cherub, but don't be fooled, Strange.'

'What do you mean?'

'He's a hardened reprobate. Plays the innocent because it pulls the ladies. Wait till you see him with them. They fall over him screaming. Fall backwards, really. He's a nice lad, though, and doesn't take advantage.'

'Try another one,' Jem said, his voice hardening. 'This house may be a byword, Villiers, but I'll thank you to pack him up and send him home to his mother.'

Villiers's eyes narrowed dangerously, but Jem had never backed down to any duke's desires, and he wouldn't now. Especially to one of the few men in England whom he thought of as being of his own weight intellectually.

'I dislike the idea that my house is being treated as some sort of proving ground for innocents.'

There was a thread of anger – and an odd strain of amusement – in Villiers's voice. 'All right, he's not a rake-hell. Far from it. But he *is* twenty-two. And he's got as much right as anyone else to a full life. Surely you'd be the first to say that?'

'What do you mean? What's his life been up till now?'

'His mother is eccentric,' Villiers said. 'She lives in the country and has kept him close by her side.'

Jem glanced over at Cope. He was standing with the duchess as they examined the intertwined bodies of Venus and Mars. The marble cleverly blended into one piece during the crucial encounter. The corner of his mouth quirked as he saw Mr Cope point to the relevant spot.

Villiers followed his gaze. 'He's a willing learner.'

'Did you rescue him?'

'Something of the sort. I promised him a look at life that wouldn't hurt him. He's twenty-two, and – I hardly need to say it – a virgin. I could have taken him to a brothel in

London, but I didn't want that dewy look of his dashed when he had to hand over coins to the lass of his choice.'

Jem didn't like the reasoning. Yet he couldn't deny but that it made sense. If he had a son, he wouldn't want him in a brothel either.

'The same diseases are to be found here as elsewhere,' he said, a warning in his voice.

'Then I'll trust you to steer him in the right direction, Strange.' Villiers made a sour face. 'The trip took more out of me than I expected. My Scottish devil of a doctor told me not to travel, but I overruled him. And now I think he was likely right.'

Villiers's face was a pallid white, with deep bruises under his eyes. Jem jerked his head at Povy. 'You'll stay in bed,' he said, 'and I'll watch over your fledgling. And what of that duchess? Or should I say, half-duchess? Am I to watch over her as well?'

Villiers gave him a faint smile. 'You might want to warn your guests she's in the house.'

'A wild one?'

'Jemma had a Twelfth Night party – do you know the Duchess of Beaumont?'

'I met her once. Dared her to come to visit, but she didn't have the backbone.'

'Or perhaps the desire,' Villiers said mildly. 'Not everyone thinks that an invitation to your house is a ticket to Paradise, you know.'

'I'm glad you succumbed.' And he meant it.

'The duchess had all the married men at Jemma's party running in little circles around her. It was like a trained dog act.'

Jem snorted. 'You weren't one of them?'

'Not in the cards at the moment,' Villiers said. 'I didn't even make it to the ballroom, just languished in a side room waiting for visitors.'

There was a note of self-mockery in his voice. He didn't want sympathy. 'You deserved every moment, playing the fool with a rapier. We're too old for that.'

'I'm not allowed to play chess,' Villiers said, sounding as if he were announcing a ritual castration.

'Says who?'

'Dr Treglown, the Scottish devil who saved my life. I was in and out of a fever for months, and apparently I did a lot of raving about chess. He says I have to take a break and rest my brain.'

'Ah, so a visit to the house of tarnished angels is a perfect convalescence. Though I still don't quite understand why you dragged along those two, I'll take care of them for you.'

'Put them in adjoining chambers,' Villiers said.

'*What?*'

Villiers looked at him. 'I thought it was impossible to shock you,' he observed. 'I'm off to bed, if you please.'

Povy ushered him away and Jem stood for a moment, staring at the odd couple still looking at the statue. They were no longer examining the salacious point at which female marble blended into male. Instead, Mr Cope was running his finger down the arch of Venus's neck.

It was one of Jem's favourite aspects of the statue. Venus had her head thrown back, her face a mixture of desire, joy, and despair. The genius who sculpted it had captured, to Jem's mind, the joy – and the grief – of marriage. Venus's head fell back, her body ravished by a pleasure she couldn't control and somewhat resented.

Jem wrenched his eyes away from Mr Cope's slender finger. Really, it was time he took a mistress again.

He really meant it: if this oddness was part of growing old, he wanted nothing to do with it.

8

The Definition of Marital Success

The same day
Before dinner

Harriet couldn't stop giggling, once she was alone in her bedchamber. She'd done it! She'd really done it! She had bowed to Lord Strange, and murmured something in as gruff a voice as she could manage, and he had believed her to be male. She didn't see even a flicker of disbelief in his eyes.

The first moment she saw him, she thought the jig was up. She always considered Villiers rather terrifyingly intelligent, with his heavy-lidded eyes and sardonic comments.

But Villiers was nothing compared to Strange. Strange had a lean face that had seen use, but the sardonic lines by his mouth only emphasized the beauty of his bones, the banked sensuality of his eyes, the long body that reminded her of the coiled energy of a greyhound. Put together with the fierce intelligence in his eyes, and the charm ... God, he had charm.

But it was his intelligence that made him frightening. No wonder Villiers had called him a genius. He looked like one. And yet – he hadn't seen through her disguise!

She dropped to the bed, and froze for a moment before she realized that the odd feeling in her legs was due to her breeches.

She lay back and swung her legs into the air. It was utterly bizarre to see her legs in the open like this. She never looked at herself in a glass unless she was wearing a corset, camisole, panniers, petticoats, and a gown on top. Somewhere under there were her legs, one had to suppose.

But now, wearing this ridiculous male attire, they were exposed. Thanks to Villiers, who had ordered her an array of clothing fit for a young prince, her breeches were closely shaped to her leg, ending at the knee. They buttoned on the outside, and had a closure in the front that made her laugh. Even her knees were entirely visible, clad in pale, violet-coloured stockings.

Actually, her legs looked shapely and strong. The truth was that while Harriet always felt smothered in women's clothing, she was starting to think that she looked just right in breeches. Her body was a kind built for endurance, with muscles in her legs that came from the way she walked for miles after breakfast.

Benjamin never liked that habit. He

preferred to see her reclining on a couch, waiting to hear about his latest chess match. Not strolling over to see how the sow was faring with her new piglets. 'That's not duchess's work,' he would tell her. But then he would laugh. Benjamin had been a great laugher. He never truly hated her penchant for walking. Nor her legs.

Though come to think of it, her husband had likely never seen her legs this clearly.

The adjoining door opened and Harriet sat up so fast that her head spun.

'It's just me,' Isidore said. 'I'm sorry; I should have knocked.'

'Do come in,' Harriet said, lying back again. 'I'm admiring my breeches.'

'They are lovely,' Isidore said, wandering into the room. 'But if I were playing the man I would want oval-shaped knee buckles. Oh – and perhaps knee ribbands.'

Harriet wrinkled her nose. 'Too feminine. I have to look as masculine as possible.'

The odd thing is, Harriet, that you do look masculine. I mean that you look perfectly feminine and delectable in a gown, but there's something, oh, out-doors-ish about you at the moment. I really wouldn't guess that you were a woman in a man's costume. I wonder if I could get away with it.'

'No. Your features are far too delicate.'

'So are yours,' Isidore persisted. 'You have a little pointed chin, and those big eyes.

How on earth did you get your brows to look so dark?'

'Villiers's valet drew them on,' Harriet said. 'His name is Finchley, and he's going to help me dress when necessary.'

'It adds a masculine touch,' Isidore said. She peered closer. 'Did he do something to your chin as well?'

'He put some dots here and there that are supposed to make me look as if I have a beard coming.'

'Less successful,' Isidore announced. 'Though it looks as if you might have spots, which would make sense if you're a very young man.'

Harriet decided to forego the nearly-beard spots in the future.

'What are you going to wear tonight?' Isidore enquired. 'I was so disappointed that there weren't any Paphians languishing around the entranceway, weren't you? I mean, there was that statue, but given that the bottom half was all one blob of marble, you couldn't really see the relevant bits.'

Harriet thought the relevant bit was the look on Venus's face, but she didn't say so. Isidore, after all, was a virgin. Which brought her to something she wanted to say. She propped herself up on her elbow.

'You aren't really thinking of bedding someone, are you, Isidore?'

'I might,' Isidore said, pinching her cheek

to make it a bit pinker. 'If there is someone truly delectable. Let's face it: since I'm here, ruining my reputation, I might as well have fun.'

'Don't,' Harriet said, catching Isidore's eye. 'I've been married before, and I know what I'm talking about. Please don't do that.'

'Why not?' Isidore turned around, hands on her hips, and there was a flash of genuine rage in her eyes. 'You can't tell me that my husband has been parading around foreign parts like some sort of eunuch.'

'Eunuch?' Harriet said, before she realized what Isidore was talking about.

Isidore gave her a wry smile. 'The truth is that you are far more innocent that I am, Harriet.'

'Perhaps about some things, but I know marriage. I understand it. Unfair though it may be, your husband will be sorely disappointed if he finds you are not a virgin.'

'*If* he interrupts his travels long enough to return and discover the state of my body,' Isidore pointed out. 'At this rate I'll be a withered virgin of eighty.'

Harriet shook her head. 'I think your instinct is right, and the dowager duchess will force her son to return. But in the longer sense, what you really want is a good marriage. Chastity is a very good way to start it on the right foot.'

'No one is chaste in their marriages these days,' Isidore said. 'Look at Jemma.'

'Jemma was entirely faithful to Beaumont until she interrupted him making love to his mistress. And I believe she was chaste for years when she first moved to Paris, and was waiting for him to fetch her.'

'But he didn't fetch her, did he? She was his virgin bride, and he didn't give a damn. Which just shows that your rosy idea of marriage is far from the reality of things.'

Harriet didn't think anyone who had survived her own particular marriage could have a rosy view. 'Jemma gave it her best possible try. If you come to the marriage with experience, you risk not having a chance at success. And then you might wish that you had.'

'It depends on how you classify success,' Isidore said. 'I define a successful marriage as one in which people live together without too much acrimony, long enough to have children. I would like that. A successful marriage is not necessarily one in which there is no scandal. I would judge Beaumont and Jemma to have a very successful marriage, for instance, although she disappoints me.'

'How so?'

Isidore's lip curled. 'I didn't want to tell her, but it's paltry the way she has bowed to her husband's demands. If she wants to play chess with Strange, she should have accompanied us. I am not one to accede to foolish commands.'

Harriet looked up at the ceiling. It was impossible to explain the dance of will and compromise that had been her experience of marriage.

'Was your marriage a success?' Isidore asked, uncannily echoing Harriet's own thoughts.

Isidore's maid, Lucille, pushed open the door. 'I need to get you into pantaloons for this evening, Your Grace,' she said, looking faintly harassed. 'Mr Finchley, the duke's valet, has given me a list of what you should wear. He'll be stopping by later to arrange your cravat.'

'I can't wait to see you!' Isidore said, nipping back into her own chamber. Leaving Harriet with her question. *Was your marriage a success?*

She and Benjamin had had no children. Her mother-in-law saw it as an utter failure on those grounds alone.

Then her husband had committed suicide. That fact would make most of London unhesitatingly condemn her marriage as a failure. Surely a good wife, a beloved wife, would be enough to keep a man from shooting himself.

But...

Life was so much more complex than

markers of that type. *Was your marriage a success?*

'Yes,' she whispered to the empty air.

I loved Benjamin. And he loved me.

He didn't love me enough to live. But he loved me. Surely that was the definition of marital success?

9

Of Mathematical Angles and Men in Flesh-coloured Silk

Jem was unable to focus on his structural drawings when he returned to his study, and so spent a gruelling three hours with one of his secretaries, the one in charge of foreign investments. He agreed to sell a grove of Italian olive trees, confirmed the purchase of two Flemish brigantines (to be used to haul cotton from the East Indies to his cotton mills), signed a sharp letter addressed to the House of Lords complaining of increasing privateer action, and approved expenditures of twelve hundred pounds in the next year towards armour-plating his trading vessels.

He finally retreated to his chamber with a headache. After a quick bath, he pulled on some clothing and went to the nursery.

The west wing of the house was, as always, locked away from the greater house. At two o'clock every afternoon, all doors leading to that wing were locked and guarded, forestalling the possibility that a drunken guest might wander toward the nursery in a state of disarray or worse.

As he approached, the footman standing at the door bowed and unlocked the door. He nodded at him, and then remembered Eugenia's comment. Did he really not observe people? The footman had a rather shaggy peruke, a bovine look, sweet eyes.

'Is your name Roberts?' he asked, knowing it wasn't.

'James, my lord.'

'James,' he said, committing it to memory. James: the bovine footman with the bedraggled peruke.

Eugenia was sitting in front of the fire, skirts spread out on all sides. 'May I come downstairs?' she asked, jumping to her feet. 'Look, Papa!'

'No,' he said automatically, coming over to look. 'What are you drawing?'

'I'm ciphering,' Eugenia said. 'It's so much fun, Papa. I learned it in this book. If you take an angle *here*, and add that outside one together, and divide it by this, it ends up at 360. And it does that over and over. Isn't that fascinating? I'm trying to figure out what else comes to 360.'

Jem squatted down. She was working on the same angles he'd been playing with as bridge supports. 'It's very interesting,' he told her. 'Here's another amusing thing. You take a five-sided shape.' He quickly drew it on her foolscap. 'Now extend all the angles. What do you think the sum of all five of these outside angles will be?'

'360?'

'Good guess. Try it out and see.'

She bent her head over the paper, clumsily moving the brass protractor into place.

Jem made a mental note to have a protractor made to her measure. 'Where's your governess, sweetheart?'

'I told her she could go to have her supper downstairs,' Eugenia said absently. 'She doesn't like angles. She'll be back upstairs in a while. She's reading me Chapman's Homer.'

'The *Iliad?*'

'We finished that. It's the *Odyssey*, and I like it much better.'

'You are frightening sometimes, Eugenia. Do you know that?'

'Well, you say so, Papa,' Eugenia replied, with complete unconcern in her voice.

He walked out wondering, once again, whether he ought to have provided – or ought to now provide – a playmate for his daughter. She never showed any signs of loneliness, but surely children were supposed to play, not sit around splicing angles for fun. But then, she seemed happy.

And, in truth, providing a playmate, an appropriate playmate, would mean sending Eugenia away, to school or to a relative. Parents of a properly brought up little gentlewoman would never allow their daughter to visit Fonthill.

The idea of sending her away was impossible, and he shook it off. Still ... it was a nagging thought. Eugenia was the dearest person in the world to him. Why was he raising her here? A better man would turn himself into a model of ethical standards, dismiss all his guests and half of the servants, and replace them with puritanical types with pinched noses and pure souls.

The problem was that he didn't value moral qualities as he should. In fact, he thought they were damned boring.

It was a conundrum and made him wish that Sally hadn't died. If he had a good woman around Fonthill, it would all be easier. Women were so good at lecturing. Sally could lecture him into obedience, and he would complain to the fellows behind her back, and that would be that.

The picture of English marriage.

The real problem was that he was free to please himself. Pleasure was vulgar – and generally wicked – but so interesting.

As he entered his study, Povy came forward

to give him his nightly report. Jem threw himself into an armchair and gratefully took the glass of wine handed him by a footman.

It was his indulgence and (if he admitted it) one of his passions. He drank sparingly. But he began most evenings with a small glass of the very best wine. He raised an eyebrow at Povy.

'A French claret from Bertin du Rocheret. I will serve it with the beef. The menu tonight: turtle Madeira soup, followed by the *relevé de poisson*, which is salmon in champagne. To be followed by roast beef, lamb chops, capons with a béchamel sauce, and a plate of roast goslings with puréed apples.'

Jem nodded.

Povy turned to another piece of foolscap, though he had it memorized. 'Some comments on a few guests. Mrs Sandhurst left this morning, sending you her most fervent gratitude. She wished to speak to you herself, but I indicated that it wasn't possible.'

Jem raised an eyebrow. 'And *is* she?'

'Indeed, I believe that she returns to London to seek consultation with an *accoucheur;* the child is hardly imminent, but naturally she will need to inform Mr Sandhurst of the event.'

'Or not,' Jem said. 'Did she leave Troubridge behind?'

'Indeed,' Povy said. 'Troubridge declared

himself *desolé,* but he spent the day hunting with one of the Graces.'

'So far this sounds terribly tedious.'

Povy turned the page. 'Miss Moll Davis and Mr Cooling are practising their performance of *The Five Hours' Adventure.* Monsieur Batelier, Sir Carteret, and Mr Pedley stay on.' He looked up. 'I believe that Sir Carteret may be drawing Mr Pedley into an unlikely and improvident endeavour, something to do with the Committee of Tangier.'

'He's of age,' Jem said. 'Are the Oxford scholars still here?'

'Yes, there was a most lively discussion of glass-making at breakfast, and then they all repaired to the dairy, which has been temporarily transformed into a glass-blowing studio. They are trying the effect of adding lead oxide in combination with a touch of copper. The Spanish ambassador was much taken by the idea, and has spent the day with them in the dairy, though he will be at the Game tonight, of course.'

'Excellent,' Jem said, feeling a spark of interest. 'I shall stop by the creamery tomorrow.'

'As you know, the commissioner of the navy brought in three wagonloads of prize goods last week; the Duke of Wintersall wrote with the request that he bring the commissioner to the Game in the near future. I took the liberty of replying in the affirmative.'

'Good,' Jem said. These days the Game – the heart of his house party – tended to populate itself.

'Tonight is a simple dinner, with a mere thirty-three to sit,' Povy said, turning the page. 'Your valet has laid out your flowered tabby vest and the coat with gold lace at the wrists.'

'That seems rather grand,' Jem said, watching the wine swirl in his glass.

'We have a duke and a duchess in the house,' Povy said with mild reproach. 'Although His Grace the Duke of Villiers is feeling poorly and won't join us. He doesn't have a fever, but is much pulled. I asked the cook to make him an *eau de poulet rafraîchissant.*'

'Chicken tea?'

'For the unwell, there is nothing better,' Povy said. 'Beetroot leaves, yellow lettuce and chicken, skimmed of course.'

'You are a miracle of knowledge, Povy.'

Povy put aside his book and Jem finished his wine. At the end of their evening talks, Povy generally added a few valuable particulars about his guests, tips that he had not committed to paper. But tonight he hesitated.

'Don't tell me that you are undecided about something,' Jem said.

'I am not entirely comfortable with Mr Cope's presence at Fonthill. Your lordship has always ensured that no innocence is besmirched under your roof.'

'I share your concern,' Jem said, swallowing the last few drops, 'but I promised Villiers I would look out for him, and I will.'

'I believe that he might find himself an object of interest to many,' Povy said.

Jem raised his eyes. 'Oh?'

'That particular kind of near-feminine beauty will find many admirers.'

'I shall watch my little chicken carefully then,' Jem murmured. 'Damn Villiers for bringing him here anyway.' He hesitated. 'Villiers seems to want his ward introduced to the pleasures of female company, but...'

Povy didn't blink an eye. 'It may be that Mr Cole has another inclination.'

'Well, I'll ensure that he makes his own choices,' Jem said, hating the fact that even the slightest hint of desire had crossed his mind when he saw this Cole. It was enough to make him dislike the man, but that was unfair.

'The Duchess of Cosway's reasons for visiting Fonthill were initially unclear to me,' Povy said, with just a hint of frustration in his voice.

'You surprise me, Povy, you do. I thought nothing in the human heart was unclear to you.'

Povy allowed himself a small smile. 'However, I now surmise that she intends to create a scandal, thus drawing her husband back to this country.'

'Ah.' Jem nodded. 'It will probably work.'

'She sent out some twenty letters this afternoon, asking me to frank all of them for you. Since she could easily have had her travelling companion, the Duke of Villiers, frank those letters, I gather she wanted your stamp on the letters, thus establishing her residence at Fonthill.'

'Well, the scandal-broth brewing in this house ought to be good for something,' Jem said. 'Is that it, Povy?'

'A final thought about your new secretary, Miss Caroline DesJardins. I am slightly worried that her ideas may be too outré.'

'Is it possible?'

'For the entertainment tomorrow night, she is employing several footmen – those with the better physiques – as "primitive men".'

'And what does that entail?'

'Flesh-coloured silk with a small apron of fig leaves embroidered on the front.'

Jem barked with laughter.

'The silk is sewn to fit the body with the utmost exactitude,' Povy said a bit gloomily. 'The effect is indelicate, to say the least.'

'I shall look forward to it,' Jem said, chuckling. 'No, I think that Miss DesJardins is a welcome addition to the household, Povy. I, loved her stories of the fêtes she designed in Paris for the Duchess of Beaumont.'

Povy bowed and retired. Jem made his way upstairs to put on the suit with gold lace at the wrists (for he never disobeyed Povy), thinking all the time of wild French designers and errant duchesses.

10

In Which Plans are Made for Lord Strange's Enticement

Harriet looked at herself in the glass and felt as if she'd drunk too much champagne. Staring back at her was a beautiful young man. Really. *Beautiful.* He was wearing a velvet jacket of a dark lilac, over which spilled the finest cream-coloured lace. Little epaulets at the shoulders gave him form, and the jacket laced in the front in a manner which (incidentally) concealed the so-called man's breasts.

But what Harriet kept staring at was her face. She never felt beautiful as a woman. She always felt overpowered by the huge hairstyles demanded by fashion, by her panniers and multiple petticoats, by the way her corset pushed up her breasts and made them seem plumper than they were in truth.

But in a simple pair of pantaloons and a velvet jacket, with her hair pulled back in a ribbon, you could see her face.

Harriet just kept looking at it. Without all those powdered curls towering over her forehead, her face looked both delicate and strong. Her mouth was actually quite a nice shape, though she shouldn't be the one to say so. The way the valet had coloured her eyebrows showed that their arch was a graceful wing that emphasized her eyes. She'd always liked her eye colour, but thought they looked faded to the same tired brown as the rest of her. But now they picked up the colour of her coat, and her eyes seemed almost purple. Exotic. Utterly unlike her in every way.

The only problem was ... her rear. Harriet turned around and peered back there again.

She could hardly believe that she was even contemplating walking through the door like this. Her breeches fitted her body like a glove. That was one thing from the front, but when she craned her neck to see her behind, she felt palpitations coming on. Her bottom ... her bottom was exposed. Very exposed.

It was round. She had a very round bottom, as it turned out. Who would have thought? With all the petticoats, and panniers, she'd never given her bottom a second glance. But there it was.

She tried to think about men's bottoms but couldn't remember that she'd ever seen any that were quite as – as curvy as hers appeared to be.

Would everyone know the moment she walked into the dining room? If they discovered her secret, she'd have to go back to wearing a huge wig and panniers. The very idea struck ice to her backbone. She couldn't do that yet. Not when she felt beautiful and powerful and free – for the first time in her life.

Harriet pulled back her shoulders. If anyone suggested she was a woman, she would deny it with her last breath. She hesitated for one moment, wondering whether to add a bit more padding down there, in front.

She couldn't bring an image of the front of a man's breeches to mind either. Had she ever really looked at a man's body?

Apparently not. Likely it was better to be discreet about the size of her pizzle, then, at least until she had a chance to investigate male breeches.

She marched out of her room, hesitating when she reached the top of the stairs and realized that Lord Strange was lounging at the bottom, almost as if he were waiting for her.

Of course he wasn't waiting for her. He

probably greeted all his guests there. He had remarkably broad shoulders for a man who was so lean through the hips. What she'd really like to see was his bottom, but he was leaning against the railing, staring intently at a sheet of foolscap.

She walked down the stairs as solidly as she could, squaring her shoulders. At the bottom, she swept an acceptable bow, flourishing a hand before her forward knee, just as Villiers had taught her.

'Good evening, my lord,' she said, deepening her voice.

Lord Strange looked up. 'Mr Cope.' He folded the sheet.

'If you'll point the direction to your drawing room, I'll join your other guests.' She could hear a clatter of laughter and voices coming from the other end of the corridor.

'I'll escort you,' he said, looking irritated for some reason. But he didn't look as if he suspected her of being a woman, so Harriet felt a surge of triumph. She automatically reached out to take his arm, and then quickly dropped her hand. Thankfully, he didn't see her error as he was tucking the paper away in his waistcoat pocket.

'What are you studying?' she asked, moving to the side so that their shoulders wouldn't touch.

'An auction catalogue I just received from

London. A man named Bullock is selling off his collection of hummingbirds.'

'What a lovely name, hummingbirds,' Harriet said, before realizing that men didn't use the word *lovely*. 'I mean, the name is enjoyable ... the hum and so on.' She sounded like a fool.

'Hummingbirds are small birds from the Americas,' Lord Strange replied, ignoring her stupid comment about hums. 'I am curious about them.'

'How many are there?'

'Two hundred and thirty-two.'

'That many birds! Dead?'

He glanced at her. 'Quite dead. Stuffed.'

She managed not to shudder. Men liked to kill things and stuff them. Even Benjamin had given up the chess board now and then to tramp around the woods with a gun over his shoulder. 'Excellent!' she said as heartily as she could. 'I love to shoot partridge myself.'

The sardonic lines by his mouth deepened. He was probably laughing at her, but he didn't say anything. They reached the door of the salon, and a footman whisked it open. Lord Strange stopped her for a moment.

'Mr Cole.'

'My lord?'

'Villiers asked me to look after you. I shall endeavour to note your whereabouts, but I must ask you to seek me out if anything happens that seems uncomfortably novel.'

Harriet was practically dancing on her toes, she was so anxious to see something novel, uncomfortable or not. 'Thank you, Lord Strange,' she said. 'Please–' and she gestured toward the door.

After a lifetime of sailing through doors ahead of men, she wanted him to go first. So that she could examine his bottom.

He shot her a look, and there was something curious there, something she didn't recognize. 'Don't play the fool too exuberantly.'

'I shall endeavour to do otherwise,' she said, giving it a chilly emphasis.

'Excellent.' He turned away and walked through the doors, only to disappoint.

His coat fell lower than his bottom. True, it was a glorious coat. The sleeves were pricked out in a faint tracing of metallic embroidery. His sleeves ended in lace, lace of a dull gold colour. The combination gave him the dark brilliance of a pirate king, Harriet thought with a thrill.

He was everything she would have thought a man of his reputation to be: dangerous, sullen-looking, probably tired from all the degenerate orgies in which he'd participated. He looked like someone who never found himself surprised. Even the sensual line of his mouth signalled he had experienced all the pleasures life had to offer.

It was really a shame that his coat fell so low. His breeches were quite as tight as hers, but of an even finer fabric, and his legs were far more muscular. In fact, her muscles were feeble compared to those defined in his legs. It was fascinating. How could she not have noticed men's legs before?

He turned around, eyes indifferent. 'Come on, then. Villiers says that you need to turn into a man, and my house is certainly the place to do it.'

Her mouth fell open. 'He said–'

Lord Strange shrugged. 'Nothing embarrassing about that. We were all urchins at some point.' He eyed her from head to toe. 'I know all about your mother and how close she kept you. The fact you've had no male companionship shows in the way you walk. And talk.'

'He told you?'

'We're old friends.'

Harriet gulped.

'I'll help you,' he said, turning away. 'Tomorrow. Tonight, try not to get yourself over your head. Do you have a French letter?'

Harriet blinked at him. 'What?'

'A French letter,' he said impatiently. 'Tell me you know what that is?'

She shook her head and he made a sound, half a groan, half a sigh. 'I'll tell you tomorrow. Tonight, try and keep yourself out of anyone's bed, do you understand?'

'Yes,' she managed.

'Damned if you don't stand like a woman,' he said, sounding disgusted.

She pulled her shoulders back. 'Better,' he said grudgingly. 'Do you know how to fence?'

She shook her head.

'I'll teach you how to fence tomorrow. You need to move like a man, not like a molly. Maybe having a weapon in your hand will help.' He looked rather unconvinced. 'And for God's sake, remember that men don't smile at each other the way you're doing now.'

'Why not?' Harriet said, the smile dropping from her face. It was a false one anyway, since she was getting more than a tad annoyed by Strange's arrogance.

'You look like a lounger,' he growled at her.

She blinked.

'Look, you're at a disadvantage.'

She put her hands on her hips and then dropped them when he gave her a disgusted look.

'Trust me, you just are.'

'You could at least clarify your criticism.'

His jaw set. 'Let's just put it this way: nature gave you a raw deal. It's not your fault.'

'What sort of deal? What are you saying?'

'Your lashes are too long,' he said, leaning toward her. 'And your – your–' He waved at her figure. 'You just don't have the physique of a man.'

Harriet was conscious of a bubble of laughter inside her chest, but she put on a look of furious dignity. 'I assure you that nature has given me everything I need to play a man's role.'

'I didn't mean *that*,' he said, sounding horrified.

'Good,' Harriet said. And then, to prove her point, she deliberately adjusted the button-placket on her breeches, as she'd seen men do hundreds of times.

'We'll discuss it tomorrow,' he said, stepping back. 'Villiers asked me to help and I will. But it's going to be a hell of a task. I suppose we might as well start by introducing you to a woman.'

'I can manage on my own.'

She snorted, and then turned away, eyes searching the crowd. They didn't look like the cluster of degenerates Jemma had described. In fact, they didn't look very different from the people who attended Jemma's Twelfth Night ball. Of course, they weren't wearing costumes, though there was a young lady off to the side who appeared to be dressed as a shepherdess. No shepherdess on Harriet's lands wore her gown open to the waist.

Strange followed her glance. 'Good choice,' he said. 'You've picked out a lady who would likely be quite happy to usher you into the throes of manhood. And I believe she might even do it without giving you a disease. Just don't look so eager, for God's sake. No woman wants to bed a man who pants at her hem.'

Harriet swallowed. This was going a bit faster than she had anticipated.

'Come on.' He strode off, and she followed, to find herself bowing before the young shepherdess a moment later. She had strawberry red hair and breasts that burst from her costume. In fact, she was just the kind of woman who normally made Harriet feel miserably inconspicuous.

'May I introduce Miss Nell Gale?' Strange said. 'Miss Gale, Mr Cope.'

Normally a woman like Miss Gale would get terribly nervous talking to a duchess. Yet if she actually happened to *look* at Harriet, she would instantly label her a woman who was neither a challenge nor a confidant. Then Miss Gale would curtsy, rather clumsily, and flutter away to laugh with more interesting women, the kind who knew scandal.

But Mr Cope, it seemed, was not as intimidating as a duchess, and certainly more interesting. Harriet guessed this because Miss

Gale – or Nell, as she quickly asked to be called – immediately did a complicated little manoeuvre with her hip that made her chest jiggle in a startling manner.

Strange drifted away a few minutes later, and Harriet found herself chattering to Nell about her shepherdess costume, which was for a play she was rehearsing.

It was surprisingly enjoyable. Nell had a wonderful gift: Harriet found herself convulsed with laughter by the way she imitated a stuffy matron's distress when her dog peed on the Lord Chancellor's robes. They both accepted glasses of wine, and before long were seated cozily on a settee at the side of the room.

Harriet was so absorbed that she almost forgot she was dressed as a man, except when she crossed her legs. That was so diverting she kept crossing and uncrossing until Nell asked her if she had a strained ankle.

'No,' Harriet said, remembering again to deepen her voice.

'I expect you're nervous, it being your first night here,' Nell said encouragingly. 'Don't worry. It's not nearly as bad as I thought before I came. I thought there would be an orgy before my very eyes.'

'Hum,' Harriet said. 'So did I, of course.'

'Well, being a man, you're probably looking forward to that,' Nell said, dimpling in the most delightful manner.

'Not really,' Harriet ventured.

'I believe we must be the same age,' Nell said. 'Or perhaps I'm a bit older. I shall be your tutor, for I can see that you aren't quite ready for this life.'

'Are you?' Harriet asked.

'If you're asking whether I'm a courtesan, I'm not,' Nell said readily. 'I'm an actress. Lord Strange owns the Hyde Park Theatre, and he likes to have final rehearsals at Fonthill. And just so you know, Lord Strange doesn't allow true ladybirds in his house. People do get up to all sorts of naughtiness–' she lowered her voice '–but there's no exchange of money, if you see the difference.'

Harriet did. 'What does your family think of your visit here?'

'I don't have much of a family,' Nell said, dimpling. 'You don't think that I'm a *good girl*, do you, Harry?' For she had promptly discarded 'Mr Cope'.

Harriet couldn't help smiling. She'd never met anyone like Nell before, anyone so cheerfully sinful.

'I've no need to be a courtesan,' Nell said. 'I'm a very good actress. I'd never want a man to support me; they're an erratic bunch. I don't mind telling you, since I can see that you've yet to come to London, that I mean to be a lead actress some day. But even now I earn a pretty penny.'

'I can imagine,' Harriet said.

'There's only one man here whom I truly have a fancy for,' she said, leaning confidentially close.

Harriet breathed a little sigh of relief. She wasn't sure that she was ready to fend off Nell. She had the distinct impression that if Nell decided to join someone in bed, that man would have little choice in the matter.

'It's Strange. But he's impossible to approach. I'm sure I could make him love me. You saw how he looked at me, and how he brought you over to me directly. I think he has a secret affection for me, but he doesn't know how to express it.'

'You think he can't express himself?' Harriet asked dubiously. Strange struck her as the kind of man who would know exactly how to express any emotion he wished. In fact, the very idea of Strange expressing desire made her feel a little weak behind the knees. He would look at a woman and she would – she would–

'I think he desires me, if that doesn't shock you too much, young Harry,' Nell was chattering. 'But I'm young and beautiful, and he's *old*, you know.'

'How old is he?'

'Thirty-two,' Nell said. 'I looked him up in this book full of birthdays and he's thirty-two. Really old. He has a daughter, you know, though I've never seen her. I've heard she's absolutely brilliant and speaks in mathematical equations.'

Strange was five years older than Harriet. Which did not feel *old*. Quite the contrary.

'The problem is that he doesn't have much to do with women,' Nell was saying. 'I've been watching him for the last week, ever since we came here.'

'He never has anything to do with women?' Harriet said. 'I thought he was notorious for his *liaisons*.'

'He is, but I can't understand why. Well, you only have to look at him to know that he's had lovers,' Nell said. She had an utterly blunt way of talking that Harriet found enchanting. No woman in the *ton* ever spoke like this.

'Perhaps he does have a lover,' Harriet suggested. 'Look at him now.' Strange was dancing with an older woman. She was beautiful in a terrifying sort of way.

'Mrs Cummingworth,' Nell said, with a curled lip. 'She's ancient. She'd fall into a dead faint if he'd even give her an interested look, but he won't. Look at his face. He's listening, but he doesn't give a damn. He looks like that quite a lot of the time.'

It was true. 'How peculiar,' Harriet said. 'How long has his wife been dead?'

'Eight years. She died in childbirth. He can hardly be mourning her. Besides, everyone knows that he had an *affaire* with Corisande de Grammont.'

'Now Lady Feddrington?'

'Yes. She never comes here any more, but apparently before she got married she was so desperately in love with Strange that she threatened to throw herself off a bridge if he didn't sleep with her.'

'And?'

'He slept with her. But he said afterwards that if anyone forced him to spend a second night with her, he would be the one to jump off a bridge.' Nell gave a little shiver. 'It's a challenge. I know – I just *know* that if I could have him in my bed for one night, I could make him love me.'

Harriet thought Nell was an adorable, funny actress. And she thought that if Strange ever found himself in Nell's bed, he would be bored.

How she knew that, she couldn't quite say.

'I wonder who *that* is,' Nell said sharply.

Harriet looked up, to find that Isidore was in Strange's arms. Compared to Nell, Isidore was like a vivid flame. Nell was pretty; Isidore was beautiful. And more: Isidore had a wild intelligence about her that made watchers think she was about to throw off her clothing, do something daring, kiss the man before her.

Harriet felt a pang of envy. She herself wouldn't have a chance interesting a man

109

like Strange, and yet how could he resist Isidore? He couldn't. He wouldn't.

'Just look at the way she's smiling at him!' Nell said. 'She'll discover soon enough that Strange isn't taken in by such obvious manoeuvres. He's not–'

She stopped.

Isidore's hair was piled in towering curls above her head, and if Harriet's face looked overpowered by that kind of hair, Isidore's just looked more beautiful. It was as if a queen had entered the room and chosen her consort.

Everyone was watching them. All eyes saw how Strange smiled back, the way she had him laughing a moment later.

Harriet sighed inside. Of course, Isidore had said that she meant to flirt with Strange. And Isidore had yet to meet the man whom she couldn't entice.

It seemed Strange was just as much a man as the rest of them.

She glanced sideways at Nell. Poor Nell … her mouth had turned into a hard, glum little line.

'She's going to take him before I even get a chance,' Nell said. 'It's not fair. I know I could make him laugh. I was planning on sending him a letter. But I couldn't figure out how to get the letter to him. You only have to look at Mr Povy to know that he doesn't deliver a lady's letters. But mine would be different! I could truly make him fall in love with me, not like those others, who just want him because he's so rich.'

She sniffed. 'I don't even care that he's rich.'

Harriet patted her arm.

'It's the way he moves,' Nell said. 'I don't know why but I just can't stop watching him. And the way he looks amused, mocking, as if the world were happening only for his entertainment. He's inaccessible, you know? I want to make him come to fire, wake up, look at me. I want–'

'He's teaching me how to fence tomorrow,' Harriet said.

'Lucky you,' Nell said longingly. 'I'd love to see him with a sword in his hand.'

Harriet thought that might be a *double entendre*, but she wasn't sure.

On the dance floor, Strange was bowing before Isidore. She turned away from him as if he didn't exist, straight into the arms of another man. That was pure Isidore. She never, ever let the man in her sights know that she was interested in him.

Strange actually stood still for a moment. His face was unreadable.

'Look at that,' Nell said, her fingers gripping Harriet's arm painfully. 'She left. Maybe she's not interested after all.'

'Perhaps,' Harriet said.

'She's dancing with Lord Winnamore

now,' Nell said. 'He's a roué, if you know what that means. Why, I heard that he took three of the Graces to bed at the same time.'

'The Graces?'

'A musical troupe,' Nell said, wrinkling her nose. 'There are eight of them. I have to admit that they sing very well. But they spend most of their time on their backs. You're fencing with Strange tomorrow?'

'Yes,' Harriet said.

'Then you could give him a letter from me.'

'I–'

The fingers on her arm tightened. 'You will, won't you? I'll stay up all night and write it, and put it under your door tomorrow morning. Won't you? Please? As a friend?'

Were they friends?

'I'll do something for you in return,' Nell said. She dropped Harriet's arm and pulled back. 'Are you interested in women?'

Harriet was so startled that her mouth fell open.

'You're such an innocent,' Nell said, shaking her head. 'It's a fair question, Harry. You have a look about you that is very attractive to certain men.'

Harriet gulped. 'I do?'

'I suppose that means you do like women?'

'Oh, definitely!' Harriet babbled. 'Definitely. Of course. All the time.'

Nell laughed, but it was a nice laugh. 'I'll do something for you too, Harry. You get my letter to Strange – and make sure he reads it – and I'll introduce you to one of the Graces. A friendly Grace, if you take my meaning.'

'You don't have to do that,' Harriet said hastily. 'I'd be happy to bring the letter. What sort of thing do you plan to write?'

'I'll tell him to visit my room,' Nell said, brightening up. 'Men like women to be very straightforward about these things.'

Harriet shot a look at Strange. He was dancing with a young woman who was smiling at him lavishly. She was exquisitely dressed in a cream gown embroidered with flowers, worn with an overskirt of puckered gauze in a ruby colour. The flowers shimmered under the gauze. Harriet felt a stab of pure feminine longing.

'I can see what you're thinking,' Nell said, giggling. 'You can't possibly afford her. That's Sophia Grafton. She's monstrously extravagant. I heard that she sometimes visits the mercer and pays thirty or forty guineas for a coat of winter silk, and then purchases two or three more. And she doesn't even wear the extras, just gives them to her maids. She has *four* maids, just for herself. Can you imagine?'

'But you said there weren't ladybirds at

113

Fonthill?' Harriet asked dubiously.

'Well, if you want to be strict about the label,' Nell said. 'But you'd never win Sophia Grafton with a simple offer of money, if that's what you're thinking. At the moment she is accompanied by Lord Childe. See, he's over there on the side of the room, talking to one of the Graces.'

The Grace in question had a blowsy, huge hairstyle with six or seven jewelled combs stuck in at various angles.

'I expect Sophia Grafton would drop Harrington like a scorched potato if Strange showed any interest.'

'Well, that's my point,' Harriet said. 'I'm not sure that a simple letter inviting him to your bed will be sufficient. Surely Miss Grafton has also issued such an invitation, in writing or otherwise.'

Nell looked offended. 'I hardly compare myself to Sophia Grafton! Why, she has to be twenty-six if she's a day. I'm sure she has wrinkles around her eyes. Just look at her. She's the sort who lies around on a chaise longue all day long and sighs. *Not* very much fun in the bedchamber, if you'll excuse the familiarity, Harry.'

Harriet saw exactly what she meant. 'But I still think that Lord Strange has received many an invitation. You need to intrigue him somehow. Make yourself stand out.'

Nell was silent for a moment. 'I know! I

could paint myself all over with gold and stick pearls on my body. Lord Strange's new secretary is a Frenchwoman, and she was telling me that Frenchwomen sometimes do that.'

'But...' Harriet said dubiously.

'I could have myself brought to his room in the guise of a statue,' Nell said. 'And then the statue could come to life! And do such things as he would never forget!' She was grinning. 'It would be positively Shakespearean. He wrote that play where a statue comes to life, you know.'

Harriet was starting to feel very affectionate toward Nell. She'd never met anyone like her. 'Just what sort of things do you have in mind?' she asked curiously.

But she'd forgotten that she was dressed as a man, and Nell burst out laughing. 'You'll have to discover those from some other woman, Harry my dear.'

'I think gold paint sounds sticky and uncomfortable,' Harriet said. 'And while you may be thinking that I have little experience, Nell, that is not the case.'

Nell hooted. 'You're a regular rakehell, Harry! I can tell it just by looking at you.'

'My point is that it doesn't sound very comfortable to be made love to if you have pearls glued to your body. Nor yet to kiss gold paint.'

'No kisses?' Nell said, horrified.

'I suppose your lips won't be painted,' Harriet said, 'but I doubt that Strange would kiss you anywhere else.'

Nell pouted. 'I may be planning to make it a night Strange won't forget, but I certainly didn't plan on skipping my own pleasure.'

'Write a letter that will intrigue him,' Harriet suggested. 'Keep him guessing about who you are. Perhaps with a riddle, or something of that nature.'

'A riddle?' Nell asked. 'The only riddle I know has to do with a chicken and an egg.'

'Then perhaps not a riddle, but how about a poem, some sort of verse that he can't understand immediately?'

'I'm not very good at poetry,' Nell said dubiously. 'I can read and write, you know. But poetry might be a little...' She looked at Harriet. 'You could write a poem.'

'This is *your* seduction, Nell.'

'He would never know. And I think you're right. Look at him now.'

Strange was still dancing with Sophia Grafton.

'He looks bored,' Nell said. 'Even if Sophia pasted herself all over with pearls, he'd still be bored.'

Harriet had to agree. Strange looked like a man who had bedded many a woman and lost interest in it, pearls or no. She had thought she had no interest in bed too, ever since Benjamin died. But now she couldn't

116

help looking at Strange's muscles and wondering…

'I hope you're looking at Sophia with that look in your eyes,' Nell said. 'Because otherwise you are truly unlucky. I never heard a peep about Strange being a molly, if you don't mind my bluntness.'

'So you really don't think I can afford her?' Harriet asked, making herself sound wistful.

'Never,' Nell said. 'Not unless your father owns forty flour mills, or something of that nature.'

Harriet shook her head.

'Then don't even look at her again,' Nell advised. 'Think about her wrinkles. Meanwhile you can plan the letter we're writing to Strange.'

'*We?*' Harriet asked.

'We, or rather *you*,' Nell said. 'The more I think about it, the better your suggestion is, Harry. Of course you should write the letter, because you can make it intriguing and intelligent and mysterious. Whereas I would just ask him to pay me a visit. Which,' she added, 'works for most men, I assure you.'

'I'm sure it does,' Harriet said. 'But I can't write your letter, Nell.'

'Yes, you can. If you do, I'll introduce you to my favourite Grace. Her name is Kitty and she's lovely. If she were an actress I would be hideously jealous of her.'

'So the Graces are not actresses?'

'I don't enquire too much about what they do in their performances.' Nell grinned. 'They pose for gentlemen's paintings mainly. If you have enough money, you can have all of them pose for you at once.'

'Naked?' Harriet squeaked.

Nell giggled. 'How else?'

How else indeed? It was fascinating to see how more open relations between men and women seemed to be in Lord Strange's world.

'I believe they employ some gauze scarves here and there. But I am going to get you–' Nell paused impressively '–a private showing with Kitty. She generally plays Erato ... do you know what she inspires?'

Harriet shook her head.

'Erotic poetry,' Nell said cheerfully. 'Apparently she knows reams of it and can recite in three different languages.'

'That's it!' Harriet said.

'What?'

'Erotic poetry. You need to send him snippets of verse. He'll be intrigued by it.'

'Not if he thinks I'm Kitty, he won't. Kitty would be lovely for you, but she's a bit of a giggler. I don't think Strange–'

'We can make that clear,' Harriet said. 'But don't you see how well this will work? You can send him a verse or two each day for a time, and then arrange a place to meet.

Then you can do all those things you won't tell me about, and you won't need letters any more.'

'You are wonderful, Harry!' Nell said. 'Wonderful! And it's so useful that you know about that kind of poetry. I suppose it's because you're a man. No one ever writes me poetry.' She looked rather wistful.

'I've never read any,' Harriet said bluntly.

'Oh. Never mind,' Nell said, patting Harriet's hand. 'I'll ask Kitty to share some of her books with you. I think she travels with them all the time. You can pick something out.'

'Shouldn't you pick the poem?' Harriet asked.

'Too busy,' Nell said quickly. 'We have to rehearse first thing in the morning, you know. In fact, I'd better go to bed. I'll ask Kitty to bring you a book of verse this very evening. In your *bedchamber*. So think about that, Harry. And you will deliver my letter in the morning, won't you?'

And with that she pressed a kiss on Harriet's cheek and left.

11

'Yet Still She Lies, and to Him Cries, "Once More!"'

Kitty turned out to be a lovely little person with pale gold hair with a faintly brassy tone that suggested it didn't come from nature. She had the air of someone with no ambitions to be a lady, but a good many ambitions to enjoy herself.

She appeared at the door of Harriet's room, thankfully before Harriet had disrobed. 'Nell told me as how you did her a *favour*,' Kitty said with an enchanting giggle. 'Do you mind if I sit down? I'm that tired from all the dancing.'

She sat down – on Harriet's bed.

Harriet backed up so that she was against the door. 'It is very kind of you to lend me a book.'

'It's one of my favourites. Gentlemen do like me to read it out loud. You do know that I'm the muse of erotic poetry, don't you?'

Harriet blinked. Did Kitty really think she was a muse?

Kitty was busy riffling through the book. 'Would you like me to read you a poem?' She looked up with a mischievous smile. 'It would be absolutely free, of course. I can't tell you how many times I've had to read for a gentleman for whom I personally could not feel a bit of attraction.'

Her smile broadened, and Harriet realized with a little burst of panic that apparently Kitty had no problem feeling attraction for Mr Cope.

'This is a funny one,' Kitty crowed. 'It's all about a man's yard. Listen to this line: *It is a pen with a hole in the top, to write between her two-leaved book.*" Isn't that clever?' She laughed merrily. 'Two-leaved book!'

Harriet smiled stiffly..

'"*It is a dwarf in height and length, and yet a giant in his strength*",' Kitty read. 'You know, I've really come to know something of men. I know if a man is a dwarf.' She got up and drifted toward Harriet. 'Mr Cope, you don't mind if I call you Harry, do you?' She stopped just in front of Harriet and ran a hand along her cheek. 'Your skin is so smooth; it's as if you never had a beard at all.'

'Umph,' Harriet said, moving quickly away. 'That's a very humorous piece of verse, Miss Kitty.'

She followed. 'What I was saying, Harry, is that I can tell when a man is a dwarf, and you're more along the lines of a giant, wouldn't you agree?'

Less padding in the front was definitely

called for.

Harriet turned around and cleared her throat to say something, but there was a brisk knock on the door. She swung around to find Lord Strange in the doorway.

He looked from Kitty to Harriet, and then raised an eyebrow. 'You surprise me, Mr Cope. You truly do.'

Kitty dimpled at him. 'I was just lending Harry a book to read, Lord Strange. From my special library.'

A flash of something crossed Strange's eyes, but Harriet was too embarrassed by the fact that her face was growing hot to interpret it. Did men blush? She couldn't remember seeing a man blush, but Harry Cope was definitely turning red.

A second later Strange had Kitty by the arm and was escorting her from the room, telling her that she needed her beauty sleep.

Then he put his head back in the chamber. 'Don't invite women to your room until you can control your blushes – though that's not as bad as losing control of your timing, if you understand me. I'll see you in the morning. We are going riding.'

Harriet would have been angry at his high-handedness, except that she was so grateful to have Kitty removed. She had the distinct impression that Kitty was about to make a grab at her supposed pen and try to get her to write. One had to think that her visitor would be surprised to find herself holding a rolled-up woollen stocking.

Lucille helped Harriet take off her tight jacket and the roll of cotton bands that kept her breasts trapped. Finally Harriet climbed into a steaming tub of water with a grateful sigh. 'Lucille, would you give me that book of verse on my bed?' she called.

Lucille was darting around the room, grumbling to herself. She wasn't used to 'doing' for two young women, let alone one who was dressing as a man, but they could hardly have brought along a separate lady's maid for Mr Cope.

'Don't worry,' Harriet said. 'You take care of Isidore. I'll ring for someone to take away the water.'

Lucille whipped around, hand on her hip. 'And how will you do that, Your Grace? One look at you in that nightgown of yours, and the footmen will know what's up.'

'It's quite plain,' Harriet protested. 'It could easily be a man's gown.'

'It's not the design, it's what you can see of your legs when you stand in it,' Lucille said, exasperated.

'Oh,' Harriet said. 'I am sorry to be so much work.'

'I'll just run over to the other chamber and take out her night clothes,' Lucille decided. 'Here, you read your book and then I'll wash your hair later. That's the one blessing about all this foolishness. Your hair is so short that it doesn't take me more than a minute to wash.'

She handed over the book.

Harriet skipped over the poem marked 'A Man's Yard'. She couldn't see Strange being intrigued by a bawdy poem about a man's pole, no matter how cleverly it rhymed.

The following page was a ballad called 'Walking in a Meadow Green'. It seemed there were lots of primroses in that meadow, but also a lass and a lad lying together.

Fine, except...

The lad performed once ... the lass wanted more. Harriet could hardly believe what she was reading. *'Yet still she lies, and to him cries, "Once More!"'*

It was like reading about a different world than the one she had inhabited during her marriage. In fact, the contrast made her smile. What on earth would Benjamin have done if she lay under him and cried, *'Once more!'* She couldn't even imagine it.

And ... why would she say that? The way she'd always understood it, it was men who wanted to make love over and over.

It wasn't that marital intimacies were unpleasant. She had always enjoyed it. She loved being with Benjamin, and every time she could pry him away from the chess board felt like a personal victory.

She shook away that thought and turned

the page again, to find another poem about a penis, and then a third. She was starting to think that men mostly wanted to hear verse about their own accoutrements, when she finally found a ballad for a woman's voice. *'His lips like the ruby, his cheeks like the rose, He tempts all fair maids wherever he goes.'*

Strange certainly didn't have cheeks like a rose, but he did seem to be tempting all the maidens. Not that Nell was a maiden, of course. And neither was Harriet. It was just ... for some reason, she couldn't stop looking at him if he was in the room.

Earlier, when he had suddenly appeared in the door of her bedchamber, her heart had started beating so quickly that she thought it might be visible. Even his voice seemed deeper, huskier, than other men's were. That wicked voice, combined with the stark intelligence in his eyes...

As far as Harriet went, put the voice and eyes together and it was far more tempting than a man with cheeks like a rose.

She kept reading. What the lass said she wanted to do to – and with – her lover made Harriet's heart start beating fast again.

No wonder Villiers thought she was a tiresome old woman when he touched her – and she slapped him. According to these verses, women kissed men everywhere and they returned the favour. All he'd done was touch her.

The ballad was unlikely to tempt Strange. All this bawdy, funny talk about women's and men's privates was fun, but she thought of the look on his face when he had danced with Sophia Grafton and shook her head.

It would have to be a great deal more sophisticated than this. More enticing. More erotic.

If she were writing the letter for herself...

The very thought made her whole body prickle.

If she were writing a letter to entice Strange, she would pitch it toward his intelligence. Make it intriguing, rather than erotic. She could picture him opening her letter, puzzling over it.

She would make him wait. He was a man who'd had too many things – women – given to him too easily. She would lead him on a dance of temptation and desire. She would–

Harriet snapped out of her daydream. What on earth was she thinking? She was at Strange's party *dressed as a man!* Not to mention the fact that she was a staid duchess, even though she didn't feel like it at the moment. She had no business falling into scandalous fantasies about her host, no matter how much she...

She went to sleep with rhyming words in her head: delight and night. Even, salaciously: little and prickle.

She went to sleep smiling.

12

In Which Manhood is Achieved...
Albeit With Some Discomfort

February 6, 1784

Harriet dreamed that she was dancing. She was wearing her male clothing, which meant that she could move far more gracefully than in skirts and hoops. She was dancing with Benjamin, so she said to him: 'Why didn't you ever ask me to ride on your prickle?'

He laughed at that, and said, 'What? What's that?'

She was trying to explain when he slipped away with a friendly wave, walked through the doors to the balcony outside the ballroom.

'Wait,' she said, 'I'm coming too. I want to talk. I want–'

A hand gave her shoulder a brisk shake. She opened her eyes, looked up, and uttered a little scream.

'Time to get up, youngster,' Strange said.

'Yip,' Harriet managed, and pulled the quilt to her neck.

'I exercise in the morning, so if I'm going to teach you fencing, I'd rather do it now. But I thought we could go for a ride first.' He turned around and walked to the windows, throwing open the curtains. 'Where's your valet? Do you always sleep away the morning?'

'What time is it?' Harriet stammered.

'Almost six on a gorgeous cold morning. It's a woman's trick to sleep away the morning, Cope.'

'Ah – right,' Harriet said, remembering to lower her voice.

'Your valet?'

'The Duke of Villiers has been kind enough to share his man with me.'

'For God's sake, Villiers couldn't pick up an extra manservant for you? I'm sure I could find–'

'There's no need,' Harriet said hastily. 'Really. I have a valet at home but he broke his arm and couldn't attend me so this is just for a short period of time and it's not an inconvenience to the duke.'

Strange shrugged and walked to the door. 'I'll see you downstairs in ten minutes. We're missing the light.'

Light? Light? What on earth was he talking about? Harriet pushed back the covers and shivered. It was February, after all, and a quick look out of the window showed bundles of snow and a lowering, grey dawn.

She fled through the door into Isidore's room.

'Isidore! Wake up! Strange is taking me riding.'

Isidore sat up for a moment, stared at her, fell back down and rolled over, pillow on her head. Harriet pulled Isidore's bell cord to summon Lucille.

Lucille bundled her into a pair of buckram breeches that buttoned tightly at the knees, and then a riding coat. 'Why are the jacket flaps buttoned back like that?' Harriet asked, craning to see her rear in the glass. At least her bottom would not be in evidence. Last night she kept edging around the corners of the room so that no one saw her from behind.

'So you can flip them up when you sit on the saddle,' Lucille said. She was wrestling with a pair of boot garters. Suddenly she looked up. 'Oh, Your Grace, you're going to have to sit astride!'

'That's all right,' Harriet said. 'I did it as a girl once.'

'It looks perilously dangerous to me. What's to stop you from sliding right off the end of the horse? All right, I'm ready for you to put these boots on.'

Harriet stamped into the boots. They were heavy, with a turned-over top. 'Now these garters,' Lucille muttered to herself, 'they fix to the boot and then pass around the leg over the breeches, like this. I think.'

Harriet looked in the mirror. 'Why?'

'I don't know,' Lucille said. 'But that's what Finchley, Villiers's valet, said to do. He's a terribly knowledgeable man, you know.'

'Well, I might as well go downstairs,' Harriet said. She had her hair tied back, but no powder.

'Your hat!' Lucille said. She opened the wardrobe and then hesitated. 'I'm sure he said the bicorne for horseback. Or perhaps a round hat.'

The round hat had a brim that stuck out all around, and a little cockade on the side. Harriet thought it looked stupid, but she grabbed it and jammed it down on her head. 'I have to go or Strange will come up and find you here.'

'I can't believe he walked straight into your bedchamber,' Lucille muttered. 'You're that fortunate he didn't know it on the instant.'

'People see what they expect to see,' Harriet said, reassuring herself as much as Lucille.

'It's perishing cold outside. Just look at the frost flowers on the windows. Here, I'll put another cravat over that black one. No one will know the difference, and at least it will keep your neck warm.'

Harriet had to make a conscious effort to pick up her feet since her boots thumped so loudly on the wooden stairs that she felt as if she were waking the whole house. Given that she had stolen off to her room around eleven in the evening, when most of the party appeared to be just starting to enjoy themselves, she would feel truly guilty to wake them.

Strange was at the bottom of the stairs. In the morning light his hair gleamed the colour of dark mahogany. She was overcome by a giddy sense of exactly how much fun she was having.

He glanced up and said, 'I might as well have been waiting for a woman to dress, Cope.'

'Good morning to you too, my lord,' she said. The butler was waiting with their coats. When she had struggled into her greatcoat (Villiers's tailor had padded her shoulders so that she looked more manly), Strange eyed her from head to foot.

'You don't look warm enough,' he said brusquely. 'And you're as pale as Villiers. We'll work up a sweat soon enough.'

Harriet smiled rather weakly and strode through the door. Outdoors the air was as cold as ice, catching the back of her throat and emerging from her mouth in great puffs of steam.

Groomsmen were holding the reins of stamping horses. Strange's mount threw up his head in greeting. Strange said over his shoulder, 'Don't get your nose out of joint, youngster. I gave you a filly, rather than a gelding, but that's not meant as a comment on your horsemanship. She's got a beautiful stride.'

A lad with a shock of white-blond hair and freckles on his nose was holding Harriet's horse. Harriet walked over and held out her hand so the filly could blow warm air into her palm. Then she pulled on her gloves.

'Let's go,' Strange snapped.

He must be irritable by nature, Harriet decided. She checked the belly strap of the horse as she watched Strange swing into the saddle. She'd seen countless men mount horses, but she never expected to ride astride herself.

Finally Harriet put her left boot into the stirrup and flung herself into the air.

Plop! She landed on the saddle and gathered the reins as if she expected to find herself there.

Strange started down the driveway without looking back, so Harriet signalled to the boy to let her horse go. He stepped aside but then said in a low voice, 'If you'll excuse the presumption, sir, grip with your knees.'

Harriet nodded in a dignified sort of way, and let her horse start picking her way down the icy path. The sun was up, and Strange was right about the light. At this hour it had a peculiar, dancing clarity that edged every blade of glass with silver. Ice crackled under her mount's feet, and hung in great dripping rows from the fence beside the road.

'We can let them gallop at the end of this road,' Strange shouted over his shoulder.

Gallop? When she was growing up, her mother considered horse-riding unladylike. Horses were regarded as little more than moving sofas. Riding excursions tended to be ambling trips through the woods to a picnic spot, with a groomsman leading each horse to ensure that it didn't startle. Certainly, there had been no wild gallops down icy roads.

She slowed her horse even further, but the end of the road arrived anyway. She found her host prancing about on a caracoling horse. 'For God's sake, Cope,' he said, 'you're riding like a maiden aunt.'

She scowled at him and he cocked an eyebrow. 'Tetchy about getting up so early? Worse and worse. I'm not sure I *can* teach you to be a man.'

'You sound as if you belong to some sort of exclusive club,' she retorted. 'As far as I can see, the definition of a man has nothing to do with whether he thinks it's masculine to be out breathing ice and clopping around on a dangerously slippery road.'

'Fear is not manly,' he told her, with an insufferably condescending look on his face.

'The list grows more and more interesting,' she said, intent on distracting him so that she could avoid galloping off down the lane. 'Men get up at dawn, feel no fear, and – what was that you told me last night? – stay away from women's hemlines.'

'Look, you're at a disadvantage,' Strange said.

'As you already indicated.' Harriet put her nose in the air. 'I find your rudeness insufferable.'

'Look at you!' he erupted. 'You look exactly like a – well – you probably don't know the word, so I won't use it. But you'll never find a woman at this rate.'

'Kitty seemed to have no questions about my manliness,' Harriet pointed out. 'She said I was very handsome.'

'You are handsome,' he said, and then made a funny strangled sound in his throat. 'It's just that you – look at your hair!'

Harriet frowned at him. 'I'm wearing a hat.'

'It has golden streaks in it,' he said. 'Like a woman's hair.'

'Well, yours has streaks too,' she retorted. 'It looks just like mahogany.'

For some reason his face froze with horror. He spun his horse around and said, 'Bloody hell!' And the next moment he was pounding away down the road.

Harriet let out a little snort of laughter. Strange was cracked. But her horse was straining at the reins, so she gripped with her knees just as the stableboy had told her. It felt odd, but perhaps it would keep her in the saddle.

'All right,' she said to her mount. 'Go, then.' She loosed the reins.

She would have screamed, but the icy air blowing in her face stole her breath. She would have stopped, but pulling on the reins did nothing. Her horse was intent on catching up with Strange and clearly considered its rider an afterthought. She would have fallen off except she couldn't loosen her knees from pure terror. So she held onto the reins and screamed silently. Her hat flew off. Her ears froze.

The horse seemed to eat up the ground with its long legs – and every time it lurched forward, she flew into the air and then came down with a crash. Ow! Ow! Ow!

Through narrowed eyes streaming with tears from the cold, she saw that somehow she was catching up with that devil, Strange. A moment later, her horse actually started to pass him, except that Strange bent over and shouted at his horse until it drew ahead again.

At the end of the road she drooped over the horse's neck, panting. She didn't even look at Strange. If he dared to say something about her being a poor rider, she'd – she'd – kill him.

But when she finally looked over, he didn't

have that sarcastic sneer any longer. 'You're not a bad rider,' he said. 'That's something. I had no idea that Bess had it in her.'

She glared at him.

He was looking pleased with himself. 'We'll go back now – but we shouldn't gallop again, I'm afraid. It's too cold out here for the horses to be sweating this much.'

Thank God, Harriet thought.

He talked all the way back to the house about manly things like fencing moves and boxing matches. She ignored him and thought about whether she had suffered irrevocable damage to her most tender parts, her female parts. She was very fond of that part of her body and didn't want it battered to pieces. She couldn't feel anything between her legs at the moment. It was all numb.

By the time they arrived home, she was regaining sensation – and those sensations were not pleasant.

Strange jumped off his horse and threw the reins to the groomsman. 'I'll see you in the portrait gallery in ten minutes, Cope,' he bellowed.

'No, you won't,' she said.

He frowned at her. His plan seemed to involve keeping her in motion for the next twelve hours.

'I want breakfast.'

His face cleared. 'Right. Beef and beer,

that'll do the trick.' He went into the house without waiting for an answer.

He must be insane.

The freckled stableboy was standing at her side. He had a nice face, so she gave up her attempts at dignity. 'I'm not sure I can get off this animal,' she told him.

He looked around, but the other grooms-man had led Strange's horse away and there was no one to be seen but a footman huddled just inside the front door, waiting for her.

'Swing your right leg over, miss,' he said quietly.

'*What?*'

He grinned at her. 'I won't tell anyone.'

She swung her right leg over and squealed. 'Ouch!' And: 'How did you know?'

'Lord Strange must not have looked closely at your riding,' he said. 'You ride just the way my sisters do. The trick is to grip your knees and keep yourself a little above the saddle. Brace your boots in the stirrups.'

He reached up and pulled her off the horse. Harriet looked around hastily, but the footman at the door had retreated in-doors and there was no one to see.

'Thank you!' she said breathlessly. 'I'd give you a tip, but I couldn't figure out where to put my money since I can't carry a knotting bag.'

He laughed. 'Gentlemen have pockets

sewn into their garments. You'll find them. I'm just happy you didn't sail into the air and land on your rump.' He looked a bit uneasy. 'If you'll forgive the familiarity, miss.'

'Believe me,' she said, smiling at him, 'I'll forgive a great deal from the man who just told me how to avoid such a bone-jarring ride. What's your name?'

'Nick. I'll make sure that I come tomorrow morning as well.'

'Thank you!' she whispered fervently, and started to limp toward the house.

Though tomorrow was a moot point. She'd be lucky to walk again.

And if she ever *did* ride again – no more padding in front! She surreptitiously adjusted her breeches.

Ouch!

13

A Chapter in Which the Delights of Swordplay and Manhood are Confused

Jem waited in the entrance hall until Cope finally walked back into the house. Probably Villiers's protégé was out there caressing his mount's nose or some such frippery. Cope finally entered and handed over his greatcoat to Povy. He seemed to be a little stiff.

Good. He needed muscle. If Cope had more muscle, he would lose that effeminate look.

'Beef,' he said, striding off to the breakfast room. 'Come on, Cope.'

The butler stopped him. 'Lord Strange, if you cared to eat in your private dining room, Miss Eugenia would be very pleased to join you.'

Jem allowed very few of his male guests to meet Eugenia – but Cope was far from a rakehell. He was practically the girlish playmate Strange had thought of finding for his daughter.

'All right,' he said, reversing direction and heading up the stairs. He stopped halfway when Cope hadn't followed him. 'What are you waiting for?'

Cope glanced up at him. 'Did you say something, my lord?'

'We're having breakfast in my private dining room.'

The man had the impudence to grin at him. 'That must have been my invitation. So sorry I didn't hear it before.'

Jem ground his teeth. Cope practically *coo'ed* his little retort.

He should go upstairs right now and tell Villiers that there was no way he could turn a mooncalf into a bull. But Cope was walking up the stairs. And the odd thing was that

Jem actually liked him.

He liked the way that Cope made it through that ride, even though he was obviously one of the least experienced riders ever put on the surface of the earth. He didn't complain, though. And he didn't look *too* sissy in a riding jacket. He looked delicate in some lights, but he had a good strong chin. The real problem was his eyes. What man had eyes of burned velvet brown?

Swallowing an oath, he turned around and went back up the stairs.

Just when had he ever wasted time thinking about a man's eyes? He was truly losing his mind.

'I'll wash my face and hands in my chamber,' Cope said. 'Where shall I join you?'

Jem rolled his eyes. Washing. 'End of the corridor to your right,' he barked.

In the end he went to his own chamber and washed his face too, though he was plagued by the idea that his guest's over fastidious habits would be contagious in more than one sense. He strode into his private dining room to find Eugenia there.

She ran over to give him a hug. It was pure Sally, that hug. His wife used to think that if people would just be kinder and nicer to each other, all problems could be solved.

'Remember when you used to carry me around on your shoulders, Papa?' Eugenia asked, scooting into her chair.

'Yes. We're going to be joined by a gentleman named Mr Cope.'

'I hardly ever get to meet a gentleman,' Eugenia said, her eyes shining. 'There was that Oxford professor, the one who was an expert in water rats. Is Mr Cope a scientist?'

'Not that I know of,' Jem said. A footman offered a huge slab of red meat, so rare it practically quivered. He gestured toward the empty spot. 'Our guest is starving. Give him a large piece.' He himself took just a sliver. He didn't need red blood, the way Cope did, and he preferred eggs.

'So what does he do?' Eugenia asked.

'Nothing,' Jem said. 'Most men don't do anything.'

Her brows furrowed. 'I'm glad I'm not a man, then.'

'Most women do less than nothing.'

'It's impossible to do less than nothing,' she observed, accurate as always.

'I mean that they create busywork for themselves.'

'You are very cynical, Papa. From what I have observed, many women work hard, all day long. For example, my chambermaid's name is Hannah. She works from the very moment of dawn until after dark. Did you know that there are nine separate stages to washing lace, Papa? Imagine how long that takes. A great many of my dresses are edged in lace. And your shirts too.'

'I didn't mean the chambermaids.'

'They are women, Papa. And they work very very hard, I assure you. I think the laundry maids work the hardest. They have to heat all the water in a copper holding. And I do like clean clothes, Papa. Sometimes I feel guilty about that.'

It was moments like this when Jem really wished that Sally hadn't died. 'I suppose I didn't mean women. I meant ladies. Ladies often don't work terribly hard.'

'I haven't met very many,' Eugenia said thoughtfully. She accepted a toast finger with marmalade. And then: 'Papa, have I ever met a lady?'

'Yes,' he said. 'Your governess is a lady. And Mrs Patton is a lady. She visited last year, do you remember?'

The door opened and Cope entered. 'My daughter, Eugenia,' Jem said brusquely. 'Eugenia, this is Mr Cope.'

Jem rather liked the way that Cope eyed the quivering beef on his plate.

'I've already eaten twice that amount,' he told him unrepentantly. 'It'll do you good. With eggs to follow.' He gestured to a footman, who promptly placed two yellow eggs on Cope's plate.

The man wasn't a lily-liver. He clearly didn't like what was before him, but he took up a knife and fork and attacked it anyway.

Eugenia behaved very properly and waited

to be spoken to.

'I'm afraid I know little about the interests of small girls,' Cope said to her. 'What kind of things do you do with your day?'

That, of course, was all the invitation Eugenia needed. She reeled into a discussion of mathematical angles, her curiosity cabinet, her collection of tradesmen's cards. 'But what I like best of all is reading plays,' she finished. 'Papa owns the Hyde Park Theatre, and he causes the company to perform their dress rehearsal here, so I see everything before it goes to London.'

'I see you are a theatrical family,' Cope said politely enough.

The comment poked at Jem's conscience. He probably shouldn't have actors around Eugenia, not to mention the fact that he should be screening her reading material. When he had inherited the theatre from his father, inviting the actors to rehearse at Fonthill had been a careless decision when his attention was focused elsewhere, probably on the Game. It had turned into a tradition before he knew it.

'Beer for both of us,' he told the footman, who promptly poured a great foaming tankard for Cope.

Jem took a deep swallow. He wasn't a proponent of beer, in truth. After a good decade of hard drinking and hard living, he'd stopped drinking almost entirely when he realized that Eugenia was a person rather than a squalling nuisance off in the nursery.

Cope sipped his tankard. That was another thing he'd have to teach him, Jem thought, adding it to an ever-growing mental list. No sipping. Men don't sip.

'Papa won't let me quote plays any more,' Eugenia was telling Cope.

Cope raised an eyebrow. 'Is it the act of quotation that's banned, or the plays?'

'Her governess was concerned that she was forgetting normal speech. Everything she said was in blank verse and written by another person.'

'That's not correct, Papa,' Eugenia said with great dignity. 'It's merely that I love to memorize, and there are so many moments when a quotation comes to mind.'

'It wasn't only the fact that she spoke almost entirely in blank verse,' Jem told Cope. 'It was the selections she chose.'

'I like old plays the best,' Eugenia said.

'Old *bawdy* plays,' Jem said.

'They're funny!'

'I forbade her reading for a month after she asked me what it meant to have *sweet violet beds, pressed to death with maidenheads.*'

'Oh,' Cope said.

Jem saw with some satisfaction Cope's utter inability to answer that particular question reflected in his face. He pushed away from the table. 'We're going to have a

144

fencing lesson now, poppet. You'd better go back to the nursery.'

'Please let me come,' Eugenia said. 'I'm so lonely by myself.' She looked truly distraught, except that Jem had known her long enough to recognize instantly every dramatic scene she had in her repertoire.

'Ah–' Cope said.

'I'm all alone in the nursery,' Eugenia said, clasping her hands and getting into her stride. She tried fluttering her lashes at Cope, but he just looked bemused.

Jem snorted, but on the other hand, he didn't want to be alone with Cope. God forbid he should find himself in another discussion of hair colour. Not that it was Cope's fault exactly, but he just seemed to bring out a side of Jem that – that–

Didn't exist.

'All right,' he barked. 'You can watch us if you stay out of the way.'

He led the way to the portrait gallery in the east wing, listening with half an ear to the lively discussion behind them. Just as Villiers had described, it appeared that Cope had hardly even visited London, and so hadn't seen any current plays. But like Eugenia, he'd read quite a few. Eugenia was breaking the rules and quoting a line here or there, but Jem didn't feel like scolding her in front of a stranger.

Though Cope was quickly turning into

something other than a stranger.

A few years ago, Jem had had all the portraits in the gallery taken down and put in the attics somewhere. They weren't of his relatives, anyway, just mouldering old courtiers who came along with the house.

Instead the long corridor was lined with glass cases stuffed with curiosities. Some things still interested him, and others he'd ceased to care much about. But he liked the idea of collecting them all in one room – and the portrait gallery was the only space large enough for a stuffed ibis, not to mention the crown of an African prince, featuring orange-, blue-, and green-tipped plumage.

Eugenia pulled Cope over to the display cabinets. Jem leaned against a wall to watch. He hadn't let a male guest put a finger on Eugenia since she turned five, but there was something about Cope that told him clear as a bell that the man was no danger to a little girl. He might be unable to perform with one of the Graces when it came down to it, though Jem hoped for his sake that wasn't the case. He might even turn out to be a molly.

Jem had had plenty of men of that persuasion visit the house over the years, and he knew well enough that sin has nothing to do with the gender of a bed-partner.

Cope was nothing to worry about, not with those eyes. So he turned away as

Eugenia pulled Cope from case to case, pointing out the supposed unicorn's horn and the white swamp-hen from Australia.

Povy had the practice rapiers laid out. Jem pulled off his jacket and boots, tested the steel, and made some practice forays.

'Let's do this, shall we?' he finally called.

It turned out that Cope had trouble pulling his own boots off. Jem didn't curl his lip too much, merely noting the obvious: a man should be able to valet himself.

Cope didn't reply, just wrenched at his boots until one came off. Eugenia came to help, squealing with giggles as she tried to pull off the other boot, so finally Jem had to take over, to his disgust. He tossed the boot to the side of the room.

'Coat off,' he called. 'Waistcoat too.'

Cope took off his coat, but then got very obstinate about his waistcoat and claimed it was cold in the gallery.

'Are you cold, Eugenia?' Jem asked.

'Not at all, Papa,' she said promptly.

He turned to Cope.

'Her lips are blueish,' the man pointed out. 'Probably she would turn herself into a block of ice for the pleasure of your company, but I am not so taken with it myself.'

Jem looked closer at his daughter and cursed. He flung open the door and bellowed for a footman to bring Eugenia's pelisse, mittens, and hat. Of course, it was a trifle chilly in the gallery, but they were planning on exercise.

'Run around,' he barked at Eugenia. 'Keep warm or it's back to the nursery with you.'

Then he turned to Cope. 'The key to fighting with a rapier is to twist your wrist. As you parry a blow, a twist of your wrist will send the rapier sliding past the opponent's blade and into his body.'

He eyed Cope. 'Widen your legs. And hold your rapier in your right hand. You're going to have to rely on wit rather than strength.' He took him through the first three basic moves. Then:

'Let's have a match,' he said. 'Povy didn't provide rapier caps, so try not to injure me.' He laughed.

Cope looked startled, but Jem was already circling him. He could feel frustration surging through his veins – the frustration that had been building since the moment he caught himself looking at Cope.

It wasn't the man's fault, by God. But the blood was beating through Jem's body and he wanted to fight.

Eugenia clapped and cheered, and Cope started circling too. Jem could see the sudden wariness in his eyes. Suddenly he no longer looked like a child holding a rapier, but like an alert man, smelling danger.

Good.

It was all part of becoming a man, Jem told himself. Not that he planned to draw blood or anything.

'Now I'm going to parry,' he announced. 'See how my left arm has tensed? You need to watch every motion of your opponent's body because it will tell you what he's about to do before he does it.' Slowly Jem started a sweeping attack, a *demivolte*.

Rather surprisingly, Cope didn't fall back, but swung his rapier up and actually managed to deflect the blow before his rapier spun out of his hand and fell to the ground.

Jem barked with laughter. 'Not bad!'

Cope straightened from picking up his rapier. His colour was high and his eyes looked furious. 'You struck hard!' he accused.

'No point in babying you,' Jem said, grinning. He started to circle again. 'Some day you might grow up and meet someone on a duelling field at dawn. I'll do exactly the same approach again. Try parrying it on the horizontal, rather than the vertical.'

Cope backed up, his lips tightly pressed together. Already he looked less effeminate, Jem thought with satisfaction.

'All right,' he called. 'Watch my left shoulder. You can actually judge the type of blow once you get more experienced. The moment my left shoulder tenses, you should be assessing what and where I'm planning

149

to strike.' Again he launched into a swirling, driven *demivolte*.

This time Cope managed to get his rapier horizontal rather than vertical, and he didn't drop his blade, though the blow knocked his arm almost to the ground.

'Damn, but you're weak,' Jem said.

'That's not a very nice comment, Papa,' Eugenia said.

He blinked and turned around. 'Stay well away from the fight, poppet. I'm afraid that Mr Cope's blade might fly from his hand again.'

'She shouldn't be here,' Cope said, catching his breath.

Jem narrowed his eyes. 'I can watch out for my child.'

'You may be able to watch, but I can't guarantee that I can hold onto my rapier, given the forcefulness with which you are conducting this ... tutorial.'

Well, who would have thought? The little chicken was turning into a rooster. Jem turned to Eugenia, but she forestalled him.

'I'll go behind the cabinet, Papa. I can see through, but a rapier could never reach me.' She ran behind a tall glass cabinet.

Jem tossed his blade slightly until he had the right grip. 'Mr Cope?'

'One more time,' Cope said rather grimly. 'My shoulder won't take much more of this.'

'We'll play again tomorrow morning, and the next,' Jem said cheerfully. 'In a week or two you'll be on the attack yourself.' Then, seeing how low to the ground Cope held the blade, he added: 'Perhaps.'

Cope's jaw tightened and he raised the blade.

'Same again,' Jem said. 'Watch my shoulder.'

This time, as he came in a swirling attack from above, Cope's blade fell smoothly into the proper horizontal position, slid along his blade and damned if he didn't pink him.

'Bloody hell!' Jem said, dropping his rapier.

Cope put down his own blade in a very unhurried manner. 'How unfortunate,' he said, coming over and peering at the small trickle of blood coming from Jem's arm. 'Perhaps we should have waited for rapier caps.'

Jem growled.

Cope was grinning; he was definitely grinning. 'A mere twist of the wrist, I think you described it.' Then he turned to Eugenia. 'Shall we escort your father downstairs? He needs the attention of his valet.'

Eugenia was bending over Jem's arm. 'I think it's quite all right, Papa. Look, it's already stopped bleeding. You must be careful, though, Mr Cope. My father is not as young as you are.'

Wonderful. Now Jem felt ancient.

He strode to the door, Eugenia skipping before him. 'I'll go back upstairs now, Papa,' she said, trotting away.

'I'll visit before supper,' he called after her.

'Oh, Lord Strange,' Cope said from behind him. 'If you will allow me, I am the bearer of a letter for you.'

'What?'

Cope handed over a folded piece of foolscap. Jem opened it and then waved it in the air to dispense with the burst of perfume. 'My God, it's a poem. Anonymous too. Who gave it to you?'

'I couldn't say,' Cope replied.

He had laughing eyes. For a moment, Jem found himself grinning in response, before he pulled himself together and turned back to the letter.

He read it out loud:

'The dark is my delight,
So 'tis the nightingale's.'

He turned the page over. 'That's it? Two lines?'

He caught himself, about to ask Cope if he had written it. He? If Cope wrote such a thing he wanted nothing to do with it. Besides, obviously Cope didn't write it. The paper was drenched in perfume, and Cope actually had a clean smell, a bit like soap.

He was so angry at himself for knowing what Cope smelled like that he stalked out of the room without another word.

14

Friendship in an Unexpected Place

'So have you been regaled by dancing girls yet?' Villiers was reclining in bed, looking as haggard as it was possible for someone so beautiful to look.

Harriet sat down. 'It's been a grave disappointment, but no one performed at breakfast. How are you feeling?'

He grimaced. 'That pestilent Scottish physician of Jemma's, Dr Treglown, advised me not to travel and, though it pains me to admit it, he was right. More importantly, how is manhood treating you?'

'Being a man is exhausting,' Harriet said with some feeling. 'My rear hurts from riding, and my arm hurts from rapier play, and all my other muscles are sympathetically twanging as well.'

'I gather that Strange took my dictate to turn you into a man seriously. You'd better watch out; he's likely to introduce you to a demirep this evening. Part of the training.'

'It's all very well for you to laugh,' Harriet said. Then she put on a lofty air. 'As it happens, I already have a lady friend interested in my company.'

'No! How I wish I could get out of this damned bed. Promise me you won't dismiss her, at least until I see you being wooed.'

'I fully intend to avoid her.'

'That won't be easy,' Villiers said. 'Strange's house parties are surprisingly large and yet intimate. I didn't think you'd visit me.'

Harriet looked up. 'Why not?'

'You have every reason to hate me.' He said it without any particular inflection. But there was much unspoken: the evening when he had rejected her advances and dropped her out of his carriage in the middle of London, the fact that her husband had committed suicide after losing to him at chess.

'I did hate you.' It was strangely restful to admit it. 'I spent a great deal of time brooding over revenge. It was easier to hate you than to accept that Benjamin chose to leave.'

'Chose to leave is an odd way of talking about suicide.'

'How else would you describe it?'

He hesitated. He really had amazing eyes, black as pitch.

'You think suicide is cowardly,' she said when he didn't speak immediately.

'Am I wrong?'

154

'I thought that at first too. I raged at Benjamin the first year: for being such a coward, for not loving me enough, for caring so much about chess that he gave his life for it, for being such a fool. But then I started to think that cowardice is just a point of view.'

'The counterpoint to courage?' His eyes were sympathetic but unconvinced.

'Something like that. Benjamin cared most in the world for chess. I hated that fact while we were married, but it was true. Though he was always amiable, and was certainly fond of me in his own way.'

Villiers didn't say anything. Harriet made herself continue. 'But chess was his passion. And while he was very good at it, he wasn't the best. So let's imagine that he had been that wildly in love with me. Don't laugh!' she said fiercely.

He raised an eyebrow, surprised. 'I haven't the faintest impulse to laugh.'

'If he had been madly in love with me, or some other woman, and had killed himself because he failed to win her, would you call him a coward?'

'Merely a fool,' he said flatly.

'Perhaps.' Harriet couldn't think where this argument was taking her. 'But not a coward,' she persisted.

'It would have to be a grand passion, a love so great it was intolerable to live without the other person.'

'Yes, and everyone would have felt the grief along with him. Whereas if a person commits suicide for love of something other than a woman, no one shares their grief.'

'I count myself lucky to have escaped such a passion,' Villiers said. 'I can picture it, but I haven't been afflicted by it. Have you?'

'I–' Harriet stopped. 'I loved Benjamin. He was the first man to pay me any attention.'

'Then he's not quite the fool I thought,' Villiers said, more gently.

'You needn't.'

'Needn't what?'

'Give me that practised flummery you're so good at. We both know who I am, and exactly how attractive I am to men. Not to mention the fact that I am now wearing breeches.'

'Don't underestimate yourself,' he said. 'Nor your breeches. Your *derrière* is a pleasure even for me to behold and believe me, my wish to bed a woman is at a lifetime low.'

'You never wished to bed me,' she pointed out.

'I actually did,' Villiers said thoughtfully. 'When you kissed me, years ago, I was quite happy to reciprocate. But the fact that Benjamin was my friend leaped into my mind and I admit it took the pleasure out of it.'

'I can't believe I did that,' Harriet said

miserably. 'I would have loathed myself if I had been unfaithful. I really did love him.'

'Rage, I expect,' Villiers said. 'Did you try to seduce anyone else, or was I your only foray?'

She felt herself flushing. 'You were my only try at adultery, though the fact doesn't reduce my shame.'

'I am the more honoured,' he said.

'Don't be. I chose you because you were Benjamin's closest friend and I wanted so bitterly for him to notice me. To put me before a chess match, even just one time.'

Villiers nodded. But his silence said what she knew: even had she slept with Benjamin's friend, it wouldn't have meant she was loved above chess. Or even accounted above a good win at the game.

'Well,' she said brightly, 'this is a dismal topic. When do you think that you might be able to rise?'

'A day or two,' Villiers said. 'I wish I were better. I'm worried that you will be discovered long before you wish to be. Are you quite sure you wish to stay here?'

'I love being in these breeches,' Harriet said, looking at them affectionately. 'And not because my *derrière* shows to advantage, but because it makes me feel free. It is very nice not to be Benjamin's widow for a time.'

'Is it so terrible?' he asked.

'Everyone loved Benjamin. He was always

cheerful, always friendly, always ready with a kind word or a loan, if it came to that. That was easy, because he didn't care deeply for people or money. Only for chess.'

'It's an illness,' Villiers said.

She stood up and grinned, looking down at him. 'No chess for a month. I count it as my revenge.'

He groaned. 'I'm reading.'

'Not chess books, I hope.'

'The History of Tom Jones.'

'Who's Tom Jones? A politician?'

'It's a novel, not a real history. So far he's a naughty sort who has stolen a duck and seems doomed to be hanged. Given the length of the novel, I shall be surprised if he escapes the scaffold. Do go and amuse yourself. Strange's house parties exist for that sole purpose.'

'It is enormously entertaining to be male,' Harriet agreed. 'You can have no idea. Unless you tried to be female.'

His heavy-lidded eyes lowered a bit. 'I'd rather not.'

'From what I've seen, Strange's party is not so different from any other house party, beyond the fact that I can't name everyone's lineage. Should any dancing girls appear, I'll send you a message.'

'And will you pay me a visit and tell me how your manliness develops?'

Harriet smiled faintly. 'Saving you from

the high moral tone of that book?'

'At least tell me how it goes with the young lady who desires your further acquaintance. I am like to die of boredom here without–' He stopped.

'Without chess,' Harriet filled in. 'It's all right. I'm used to men who can't stop thinking about the white queen. At least you haven't acquired a wife, only to slight her for every chess match within three counties.'

'I have tried,' Villiers said.

'You were briefly engaged to Jemma's ward, weren't you?'

'She threw me over for Jemma's brother. Then I thought I was making inroads on a certain Miss Tatlock, but she threw me over for my heir.' The mockery in his heavy-lidded eyes almost made her laugh, despite herself. 'Do you suppose that there's something intrinsically wrong with me?'

'A chess malady. The irrevocable inability to make a woman believe that he will love her more than the chess game. No woman wants to be ranked below a set of toys, Villiers.'

'I suppose you're right. Well, Mr Cope, go forth and be wooed.'

15

The Tahitian Feast of Venus

'I don't know if I can make it downstairs,' Harriet moaned. 'Everything hurts! I can't lift my arm. My bottom is in excruciating pain.'

'I couldn't possibly go to the Feast of Venus by myself,' Isidore said, looking a little panicked.

'Why, Isidore,' Harriet said, laughing. 'You look a bit nervous.'

'If only Villiers would get up from his sickbed! I think he's malingering.'

'I doubt it. He looked played out, and he's not the sort to lie down if he didn't have to. What are you worried about?'

'Lucille said that there is to be a dance performed by six virgins this evening. Apparently there were supposed to be twelve, but they couldn't locate another six girls who would agree to the label.'

Harriet snorted. 'It sounds dissolute enough that Strange will enjoy it.'

'Why do you say that? Don't you like him?'

'He's a typical male: arrogant, irrational,

and rather snappish. He likes to make me feel like a fool. You should have seen how chagrined he was when I managed to prick him with the sword, though it was entirely his fault for insisting we didn't need rapier caps. At any rate, what's frightened you about the six virgins?'

'The obvious,' Isidore said. 'A French demirep put on some sort of impromptu performance here last month that involved a visiting sugar baron from the Americas. I am not ready to witness that.'

'Neither am I,' Harriet said, pulling out a cravat so that Villiers's man could tie it for her. 'If it looks as if the six virgins have found close friends, we'll leave.'

'Perhaps we should just eat in our rooms tonight.'

'Is this the brave Isidore, who wanted to create a scandal large enough to bring the Duke of Cosway back from deepest Africa?'

'It's one thing to create a scandal and another to see six virgins losing their status.'

Harriet couldn't help laughing. 'I thought you were so sophisticated. Frighteningly so.'

'I put on a good show,' Isidore said, with her lightning quick smile. 'But in fact, I'm a good daughter to my Catholic mother. She was very protective. I love to flirt but that's all.'

'I promise I'll drag you out of the room if it looks as if the entertainment is turning salacious. I'll probably need you to rescue me, anyway.'

'Why? Is there a man after you?' Isidore said. 'You know, I wouldn't have mentioned this, Harriet, but I have a funny feeling about Lord Strange.' She lowered her voice. 'He looks at you in such a way...'

'No, he doesn't,' Harriet said. 'He finds me incredibly irritating, but Villiers told him to look after me, so he has to do it.'

'I don't know,' Isidore said dubiously. 'Are you following what I'm saying, Harriet? He–'

'My problem is Kitty,' Harriet interrupted.

'Kitty?'

'One of the Graces. Have you met them?'

Isidore wrinkled her nose. 'I met Caliope. She has the biggest breasts I have ever seen, and she wears such a rigid corset that they swell up around her chin.'

Harriet laughed.

'Truly! She must have a very short neck. What's Kitty like?'

'Very pretty, rather sweet, and – and interested.'

Isidore started hooting with laughter. 'You have a suitor!'

Harriet stood up, wincing from all her sore muscles, and looked at herself in the glass. Tonight she was wearing black silk breeches with a scarlet waistcoat marked with a border of embroidered silver chains. 'Do you think I look too gaudy? Finchley says that I can't possibly dress all in one colour, though I think that the Duke of Fletcher looks wonderful when he does it.'

'No one wears a plain suit, except for Fletcher,' Isidore said. 'I like the embroidery on your waistcoat. It marks you as a protégé of Villiers, which is important. No one could think that Villiers would sneak a woman into Strange's house in disguise. What coat will you wear?'

'Velvet,' Harriet said, turning to the table where it was laid out. 'Scarlet. I'm a scarlet woman, in every sense of the word.'

'Lovely embroidery around the button-holes,' Isidore said. 'I do wonder how I'd look as a man. You look utterly delicious, Harriet. I'm not at all surprised that Kitty is chasing you.'

Harriet pulled on the scarlet coat and then glanced at herself. Even sore in every muscle, she looked – well – good.

Isidore appeared at her shoulder. 'Please don't be insulted, but I think you make a lovely boy.'

'I'm not insulted,' Harriet said. 'Just sad that I can't dress like this at all times. I've always disliked my hair, but I love it pulled back in a simple queue.'

'You could dress like this. It's merely a matter of eschewing ruffled and ribboned

163

gowns for a more masculine style. You could set a new fashion!'

Harriet shook her head but she couldn't stop herself from smiling. 'It's just so ironic. I feel beautiful, for the first time in my life. But no one of the right sex is interested in me!'

'Do you want me to scare off Kitty by telling her you are mine and only mine? We should probably go downstairs now, Harriet. That gong went off at least an hour ago.'

'I can manage Kitty,' Harriet said, loving the fact that she didn't have to pick up a knotting bag or a shawl, but could just stroll from the room.

Povy was outside the ballroom doors when they arrived. 'The entertainment is about to begin,' he whispered. 'If you would be so kind as to stand in the back, I'll seat you shortly.'

'Thank you,' Harriet said, remembering at the last minute to allow Isidore to walk through the door before her. As Duchess of Berrow, she was used to taking precedence over almost every woman below the level of nobility: it was hard to remember that a male always followed a female, with no regard for rank.

The company was assembled on rows of gilt chairs facing a raised platform stage, so Harriet and Isidore moved to stand behind the last row. One side of the ballroom was lined with tall narrow windows looking onto a formal garden. It was undoubtedly quite handsome in the summer, but at the moment it was a few degrees above arctic, due to a draught stealing under the windows.

On the stage a young woman glared furiously at the heavens. She flung out her arm and cried: *'Bright star of Venus, fallen down on the earth, how may I reverently worship thee enough?'*

'She must be freezing,' Isidore remarked, drawing her shawl closer around her shoulders.

The actress was wearing a gown made of twists of gauze, sewn all over with glittering bits of glass. Her hair was free and strung with glass beads.

'It's a lovely costume,' Harriet whispered back. 'Look how her hair glitters.'

'It shimmers with every shiver,' Isidore said.

Another woman appeared, wearing a crown and a scanty toga-like costume. *'Here be Venus of the sky. Ask me your request, fair maiden.'*

'I wanted to be at least a little bit shocked,' Isidore hissed. 'This is like a bad masque at Court.'

Harriet felt a pluck on her sleeve and turned to find Kitty beaming at her. 'Come join us,' she whispered. 'I saved you a seat.'

Lord Strange appeared from nowhere and

began speaking to Isidore. He didn't even greet Harriet, and when she glanced at them, he didn't raise his eyes.

Though obviously he knew she was standing there. Fine.

'Isidore,' she said, interrupting whatever Strange was saying. Isidore was laughing and there wasn't a trace of worry on her face any more.

Strange was one of those men who made everyone in his vicinity fade away. He was standing there looking a bit tired, but burning with fierce intensity and she felt like–

How ridiculous.

'Don't worry about Her Grace,' Strange said, not bothering to greet Harriet properly. 'She can join me in the front row. You trot off with the lovely Miss Kitty.'

Harriet ground her teeth. 'If the ballet of the six virgins grows too risqué, Isidore will not be comfortable in the front row.'

Strange gave Isidore a wicked little half-smile. 'I'll leave it entirely up to her,' he murmured in such an intimate way that Harriet felt her face grow a little hot. Not surprisingly, Isidore kissed Harriet goodbye with indecent haste.

'You go with your friend,' she said brightly.

Kitty had returned to her seat and was beckoning in an extremely unsubtle manner.

'What a lucky young man you are,' Strange murmured. He took Isidore's arm.

'I fancy Mr Cope will occupy himself this evening, Your Grace.'

Isidore smiled at him. 'I don't use the title. Please, *you* must call me Isidore.'

Harriet forced herself to walk away without looking back. Strange wasn't for her. By all appearances, he was interested in Isidore, which was good for Isidore's plan.

She felt a tinge of sympathy when she realized that her seat turned out to be next to Nell. Poor Nell, in love with Strange and soon to be disappointed, it seemed.

'Did you give him a letter from me?' Nell whispered eagerly.

On the stage, Venus seemed to be rather angry about something. *'I fear the sparkling majesty that issues from your most imperial eyes,'* the maiden said, falling to her knees.

'Yes, I did,' Harriet whispered back.

'What did he say? Is he coming to my bed tonight?'

Nell's eyes were shining the way Kitty's did when she looked at Harriet. Both Nell and Kitty had woefully misplaced affections. At the moment, for example, Kitty was almost leaning on Harriet's shoulder, although she was pretending to be interested in the histrionic acting on the stage.

'I tried to be more subtle,' Harriet said. 'I sent him the first two lines of a poem, and I'll give him two more tomorrow.'

Nell looked unconvinced. 'What did the

167

poem say?'

'The dark is my delight,' Harriet said.

When Nell smiled, her whole face transformed from an almost plain collection of features to something truly enchanting. 'Lovely!' she said. Then she leaned over and whispered in her ear. 'I told Kitty that you were the heir to a coal mine, so be sure to act like one.'

Harriet goggled at her. 'You what?'

'Not that you needed it,' Nell said, smothering a giggle. 'She's got a stupendous attraction to you.' She bent over and whispered in Harriet's ear. 'She says you're a gentleman of voluptuous beauty. Voluptuous! What a word to use for a man.'

Harriet's heart sank. She wasn't voluptuous even in female clothing. At that very moment Kitty's hand crept onto Harriet's knee. Harriet nearly jumped out of her seat and whipped her head around, only to meet Kitty's naughty little smile.

She picked up Kitty's hand and moved it off her knee; Kitty pouted but didn't say anything, so Harriet looked straight ahead and pretended to be following the performance.

Venus was gone, replaced by two more shivering, wailing virgins... Who knew that Lord Strange's disreputable house parties were so tedious?

Isidore and Lord Strange left after ten minutes, but Harriet didn't think it had anything to do with the six mournful virgins. More likely, Isidore was bored.

She was bored.

'You'll have to forgive me,' she whispered to Kitty, when the six virgins had been joined by six extremely scantily clad young men. Harriet fancied she could see their goosebumps from her seat.

'I think there might be a more interesting part coming,' Kitty whispered back. She hadn't taken her eyes off the stage since the male actors appeared.

'I'll see you tomorrow,' Harriet said firmly.

She escaped just as one of the virgins collapsed into her male counterpart's arms. Harriet could only be glad that at least they would be able to share a little warmth.

16

The Leaning Brothel of Fonthill

February 7, 1784

He walked into her room the next morning with hardly a knock on the door, but Harriet was ready this time. She was up and dressed, casually seated in an armchair reading, as though she hadn't flung herself there two seconds before.

'Oh!' Strange said, coming up short.

She rose, smiling, as if men strode into her bedchamber regularly. 'Are you ready to go, sir?' she asked, ignoring the fact that her bottom throbbed like a pincushion at the very thought of a saddle.

'Yes,' he barked.

He looked angry again. Obviously, something about her made him peevish. Harriet thought about ill manners all the way down the staircase. Benjamin used to feel free to be very ill-mannered as well.

But she had been trained that a lady should never exert her moods over other people. And she had adhered to that plan for years, never snapping at the people who obliquely blamed her for Benjamin's suicide, no matter how pestilently rude she felt they were being.

Strange leapt onto his horse with a sort of boyish enthusiasm that she found attractive, despite herself.

Or perhaps it was the way the muscles in his legs bulged when he settled on the horse.

That was one thing about attending a party notorious for its illicit liaisons: the atmosphere lent itself to frank assessments of bodily charms. There was a great deal about Lord Strange that Harriet found attractive.

When they reached the beginning of the

road, Strange rose slightly in his stirrups, bringing his horse to a trot. Harriet eyed him from behind, and revised her opinion. What she felt went beyond attraction.

She was almost helpless in the face of her desire. It was ... ravenous. As if she would do anything to caress him, to touch him.

And never mind the fact that he thought she was an effeminate male whose company he could hardly stand.

She gathered up her reins and urged her horse to a trot. Not to put too fine a point on it, the first blow of the saddle as the horse started trotting made her want to scream. But she wedged her boots into the stirrups and tried to hover above the saddle. It worked – to a degree. It was much better once her horse lengthened her stride and started galloping. She bounced along in opposite rhythm to the horse and it wasn't nearly as painful.

In fact, she actually found herself leaning over the horse's neck and beginning to enjoy herself, barring the icy wind whistling in her teeth and squealing in her ears.

Strange waited for her at the end of the road. Harriet pulled up her horse, her chest heaving.

'Better,' he said. He wheeled his horse and started back the way he had come.

'For pity's sake,' Harriet muttered, staring after him. Didn't he say yesterday that the horses needed to walk after a gallop? Finally she took out after him. If she paused even for a moment, the cold ate at her bones. The ground whirled by at her feet, frozen clods of brown earth flying from the horse's hooves, thin ice cracking.

It felt wonderful.

Her heart was pounding, blood thumping through her veins. She suddenly realized that she hadn't felt this alive in – oh – years.

Since Benjamin died, perhaps before Benjamin died. It was as if she had been living in cotton wool, and suddenly the woolly blanket lifted and the world flared out around her, brilliant, full of life, colour, and movement. A jay started out from a bush; she caught the tail of a rabbit bounding under a hedgerow.

At the entrance to Strange's drive, she hauled on the reins. Her mare had enjoyed the run, and slowed to a walk with a few graceless, stiff-legged movements that jolted every one of Harriet's bruises. But she was too interested in Strange's house to do more than wince.

It was the first time she'd really looked at it. It was a child's drawing of a country house, a castle and a house in one. Part of it gleamed in proper Portland stone, but the bit to the right looked like the left-over parts of a medieval castle without a turret.

Then there was a wing extending to the

left that sprawled low to the ground, with greenhouses sprouting from it like spokes on a wheel. And finally there was a tower-like affair that must be the famous re-production of the Leaning Tower of Pisa – except she didn't think the famous Italian tower leaned quite *this* much. It was made of brick, with a little brass peaked hat on top.

It looked dangerous.

A smoky voice said, 'You're frowning at my tower. Would you like to see it?'

'You really did design that?'

For the first time since she'd met him, Strange's eyes lit up with something more than lazy appreciation or sarcasm.

'Let's take a look.' And without waiting for an answer, he directed his horse through the archway.

Harriet shook her freezing fingers and picked up the reins.

Up close, the tower was made of bricks, with a wooden door. It leaned in an alarm-ing fashion. In fact, it didn't exactly lean: it toppled. It looked like a tree forced out over the edge of a cliff by repeated winter storms. It looked like a drunk man falling to the ground.

It looked, in short, like certain death.

Strange was already off his horse and unlocking the door when Harriet arrived.

'Come on,' he said over his shoulder, dis-appearing inside.

Harriet looked down. She had never dismounted without assistance. Ladies didn't. And Nick, her favourite groom, who had boosted her into place with plenty of whispered bits of advice that morning, was nowhere to be seen.

Grunting a little from her sore muscles, she pulled her right boot out of the stirrup and tried to slide to the ground.

She ended up falling with a wallop onto the frozen ground just as Strange came back into the doorway.

She quickly scrambled to her feet.

'You're the worst horseman I've ever seen,' he said, in a not unfriendly tone of voice. 'And yet you ride quite well in a neck-or-nothing sort of way. Didn't your mother let you on a horse?'

'My–' Harriet said, before remembering that Villiers had given her a sickly mother in the country. 'My mother is afraid of horse-flesh,' she said. 'What shall I do with the reins?'

'Just put them down. My horses are extremely well trained. You see how my horse is simply waiting for me? Yours will do the same.'

Harriet put the reins down and stepped back. Her horse, being no fool, instantly decided that she would rather be in the nice snug stables, and set off in that direction.

In a hurry.

Harriet didn't see any need to comment on it, so she walked past Strange, leaving him muttering some interesting curse words behind her.

She stopped short inside the tower. It was one round room, and rather than having floors, the ceiling simply receded and receded, so Harriet felt dizzy when she looked up and saw the roof veering off to the left.

The room was hung with great swaths of watered apricot silk. It had only two pieces of furniture: a large bed hung with matching gauze, and a solid oak desk piled with papers. It looked like an odd cross between a Turkish harem and the chambers of a solicitor.

Her mouth fell open.

'Isn't it interesting?' Strange said, appearing next to her. 'I pressured the vector to the most extreme that it could manage in terms of weight-bearing.'

'It's like looking up a crooked chimney pipe,' Harriet said, ignoring the bed and looking upward again.

'If you calculate the angles, Cope, you'll see that I achieve around a sixty-three per cent lean by fifty per cent of the extension. What do you think?'

'I think it's dangerous,' Harriet said bluntly.

'It's not dangerous. I calculated the weight of the bricks very carefully against the slant of the tower.'

'I'm sure you did. It's dangerous.'

'It's not dangerous,' he said in a controlled voice that told her other sensible souls had pointed out the same thing. 'The servants don't like to come near, and so I allow them their foibles. But any educated man has to recognize that the science of engineering dictates exactly what a building can and cannot do, in terms of angles.'

'No windows?' Harriet enquired.

'They altered the weight-bearing properties of the bricks.'

In other words, Harriet translated, the whole thing would have collapsed into a pile of dust.

'The tower in Pisa has been standing since the 1170s,' Strange said. He strode over and struck a flint to light a lantern hanging from a little hook. It cast a golden light over his shoulders that served to remind Harriet how cold she was.

When she didn't say anything to affirm his brilliance in tower-building, he added: 'In the summer, Eugenia and I often picnic here.'

She swung around from examining a couple of bricks she was sure were about to crumble into each other. 'You shouldn't do that.'

'Do what?'

'Your daughter should never be in this

tower. Ever. It's one thing if you want to put your own life at risk–' *and mine*, she added silently '–but your daughter should not come within a hundred feet of this building.'

He looked at her with a scowl. 'Villiers tells me that you spent your life so far under the wing of your mother. I don't mean to be rude, Cope, but if you want to be a goer, you'll have to stop parroting your mother.' He imitated her voice. *'It's too cold. It's too dangerous.'*

'Do you think it makes you more dashing to put a child in danger? How interesting that you don't force the servants to risk their lives in your creation. I really should make notes. To wit: manhood, achieved by risking nurslings but not underlings.'

'You are an ass,' he spat out.

Harriet felt a thrill. No man had ever called her an ass. No doubt Benjamin had thought she was an ass, but he would never have said such a thing to a lady.

'You too,' she said cordially. He seemed shocked at the broad smile she gave him. 'Don't ever allow your daughter in this tower, or near it, again. You love her too much. Why risk a broken heart?'

She caught his eye just long enough to make sure her words sank in and then stepped back out into the frosty air.

'One final point,' she said. 'That room is kitted up like a brothel. While it's enterprising of you to recreate that charming atmosphere on your own grounds, why on earth would you introduce your child to it?'

A look of pure rage crossed his face. 'It's not a brothel.'

'Did you pick those hangings yourself?'

'No, I–' He bit the words off.

'Let me guess,' she said, enjoying herself enormously. 'You asked for help from a London firm whose last employment was in a courtesan's boudoir.'

He didn't say anything.

'Well?'

'Miss Bessie LaMott arranged for the hangings,' he said through gritted teeth. 'I certainly didn't think of it as a brothel.'

'I expect Bessie just reproduced the environment she knew best,' Harriet said kindly.

He strode over to his horse and said, 'You'll have to ride behind me.'

Harriet took a look at his lean, muscled body and felt a qualm that had nothing to do with being a man, and everything to do with being a woman. 'I can walk. I feel much warmer, just from being out of the wind for a bit.'

'Nonsense. Eugenia will be waiting to watch our fencing lesson.' From his tone, he couldn't wait to face her with a sword in his hand. Strange swung into his saddle and then looked at her. 'I suppose you can't get up without assistance.'

He didn't seem to want to touch her, which was a little hurtful. But Harriet was starting to shiver all over, so she just shook her head.

He stuck out his hand. She went over to him, put her hand in his, and then looked up. 'What next?'

He was staring down at their hands. Her hand was engulfed in his, of course. 'What next?' she repeated. 'Should you take your foot out of the stirrup so I can get up?'

'For Christ's sake,' he said.

He gave a great heave. She flew through the air and landed just behind his saddle with a muffled shriek. The horse's rump sloped backwards, so she edged forward until she was actually sitting on the raised end of his saddle. It caused her to be plastered against his back, but at least there she had a chance of staying on the horse.

'Let go of my shoulders!' he said irritably.

'I clutched them in an effort to stop myself flying into the next county,' she managed.

'You scream like a woman,' he said, obviously disgusted.

She had the impulse to pinch him hard, but she controlled it. The horse didn't even seem to notice her weight. He was prancing, eager to return to the stables. 'You left your horse standing in the cold after a run,' she said pointedly.

'I was just thinking the same thing,' he said, his voice rueful. 'Horses, servants, children. I'm afraid that I get excited by this sort of thing.'

'Towers?'

'The engineering that goes into them. The calculations. The other day I figured out how we could put a false floor in the ball-room.'

Harriet let a moment go by before she asked the obvious. 'And the false floor would be good for?'

'For a banquet table,' he said. 'It would have been interesting, but I'm afraid that Eugenia has your hardheaded approach. I threw the calculations away.'

He was terrifyingly likeable when he was rueful and in love with his crazed engineering feats.

'Do you have to sit so close to me?' he asked, with an edge in his voice that made her forget that she ever liked him.

'How exactly do you think that I'm supposed to sit behind you, *on* the saddle, without being close?'

'Try moving backwards,' he said, very unfriendly. 'There's a nice space of the horse's rear to sit on.'

'I can't do it,' Harriet said, enjoying herself. So he didn't like her because she was too effeminate? Rank prejudice. Why, her mother's curate, Mr Periwinkle, was remarkably effeminate. He smelled like a flower and believed that life was always better with a cup of tea. Lord Strange probably wouldn't want to shake his hand.

She snuggled closer. It was good for him to feel uncomfortable. In fact, she would be grinning except her face was too frozen to move. It would be good for Lord Strange if he had to get to know someone – a man – who was a little different from himself.

The man was set in his ways. Obsessed with manliness. Mr Periwinkle enjoyed arranging dried flowers. And he gave lovely sermons about the lilies of the field. Everyone adored him.

The horse started climbing the hill towards the front of the house. 'You don't mind if I put my arms around you, do you?' she shouted against the wind.

'What?'

So she just put her arms around his waist. His body stiffened.

Her grin died a moment later. Strange's body was large and fierce and male, in a way that played fiddlesticks with her pleasure in Mr Periwinkle's company.

She could feel coiled muscle and steel, even through his greatcoat. It was dangerous to have her hands on him. It felt like nothing she'd experienced before. It felt heady, warm, crazed. It made her think about the bawdy songs in Kitty's book, the ones that talked about a woman folding a man in her arms and kissing him over and over.

It must be the influence of Strange's degenerate household, with Kitty and Nell and all the rest of them pursuing their desires without the slightest concern for consequences, or reputation, or society. If she weren't a duchess...

If she were just Mr Cope, young Harry who had no responsibilities and no history, she would throw away caution.

She would...

The horse stopped in the courtyard and Strange was off the horse so fast that she slid forward onto the saddle, into the space left by his warm body. He looked up at her, his eyebrow cocked disdainfully.

She looked back at him steadily until the scorn faded in his eyes.

'Do you still wish to fence?' she asked.

'Yes.' He turned away, and Nick came running towards her.

'I was that worried when your horse came home alone, miss,' he whispered.

'I'm all right. It was Strange's fault; he told me to drop the reins because his horses were so perfectly trained that they would stay in place.'

'Well, there's some that will do it,' the boy said fairly. 'But not many in this weather. So you didn't fall off, then?'

'No, and your tips helped. I think I know

how to manage a gallop, though trotting is a terrible thing to endure.'

'Perhaps we could get up really early one morning and I could show you how to manage a trot.'

'I'd hate to get you up so early,' she said.

'I'm already up. But night may be better. That way you wouldn't be riding with me, and then with Lord Strange. He might notice. But we should start with mounting a horse. It's a miracle he hasn't seen the way you climb your mount like a rocky hillside.'

'Perhaps even tonight?'

'I'll wait for you in the stables. There's generally no one around so it should be safe.'

She gave him a quick smile. 'Thank you!'

Strange was waiting for her at the door. 'You're very friendly with that stable boy.' His tone was unfriendly again.

'His name is Nick, and I like him,' she said, walking past Strange to get into the warmth.

'You *like* him?' Strange said.

She glanced back at him. 'He's nice.' But the only thing on her mind was to get warm without losing her manhood. 'If you'll forgive me, I'm going to take a piss.' She managed to walk half the way up the stairs, but then broke into a run. When she got to her chamber she dashed across the room and dived under the quilt, leaving only her boots sticking off the bed.

'Your Grace,' Lucille exclaimed, coming over. 'Are you all right? Are you ill?'

'Cold,' Harriet said with chattering teeth. 'So cold.'

'Tsk, tsk,' Lucille clucked. She ran over and got another quilt and piled it on top of Harriet. 'You'll be catching your death, riding around on a morning like this. Why, the Duchess of Cosway isn't even out of her bed yet. She's just breakfasting.'

'You can have my hot chocolate,' Isidore said, appearing in the doorway. 'Have you been pounding around on freezing roadways for hours?'

'Ye-ess,' Harriet said from under the covers. 'My horse went home alone and I had to ride behind Strange and it was *so* cold.'

'Sit up and drink this chocolate,' Isidore said. 'I know you English only drink it in the afternoon, but it is lovely in the morning.'

Harriet finally did, gratefully curling her fingers around the mug.

'What's next in the life of a gentleman?' Isidore asked.

'Fencing again,' Harriet said. 'Fighting with rapiers. He makes me take my jacket off and it's bloody cold up there in those galleries. The man must have cold blood, like a reptile.'

'Harriet!' Isidore said. 'I've never heard

you swear. I think all this masculinity is rubbing off on you.'

'I like riding,' Harriet said. 'You can't imagine, Isidore. It's all different with men. You know how we perch in the side-saddle and then pick our way down the road?'

Isidore nodded. 'I don't often bother, but I know how.'

'Men just fling themselves into the saddle and pound down the road – so fast the wind blows their hair directly back. They don't wear a wig because it wouldn't stay on. They just go. It's sweaty and tiring, but afterwards you feel so good.'

'Watch out,' Isidore said. 'You'll end up dressing like this for ever. You know, everyone always says that Lord Findleshanks is really a woman. Did you ever look at him closely? He does look like a woman.'

'He has a beard,' Harriet pointed out.

'So did my grandmother.'

Harriet swung out of bed. 'I have to meet Strange for fencing practice. Ouch!' She rubbed her bottom.

'I am going back to my bed,' Isidore said. 'Strange lent me a book of poetry.' She paused for a moment. 'Do you still dislike him?'

Harriet shrugged. 'He's acceptable. What do you think?'

'I think he's interesting,' Isidore said. 'Really interesting.'

Harriet looked at her. 'You are married, Isidore.'

'Not that anyone would notice,' Isidore said wryly.

'You know what I mean.'

'There's something about Strange,' Isidore said. Harriet noticed with a pulse of alarm that her eyes were almost dreamy – and Isidore *never* looked dreamy. 'He walks into the room and everyone notices. I like being with a man like that.'

'Well, he is the host,' Harriet said. 'Although I'm not sure he really knows who some of his guests are. Have you noticed?'

'Povy reads him a list of his new guests every night,' Isidore said. 'Lucille told me about it.'

Lucille popped her head in from the adjoining room. 'Do you need me?'

'Does Lord Strange know who his guests are?' Isidore asked. 'You said that Povy is in charge of informing him.'

'Well, Strange does and doesn't,' Lucille said. 'He may hear about them, but that doesn't mean he always knows who they are, if you see what I mean. This is a big house. That run of scientists in the east wing, for example. I'm sure he doesn't know all of them.'

There was a short knock on the door, a knock that Harriet was getting to know. Isidore gave a shriek as it opened. Harriet turned and looked at her through Strange's eyes.

Isidore was in dishabille, a sweep of curling black hair matching her eyelashes. Her nightgown was everything Harriet's wasn't. It could never be mistaken for a man's.

A smile of greeting appeared in Isidore's eyes for one second, before she gave another little shriek (entirely unnecessary, to Harriet's mind) and disappeared into the room next door, slamming the connecting door.

Harriet had never realized that a woman's legs could be seen straight through the thin lawn of a nightgown.

Strange didn't seem to be ravaged by desire, but what did she know? He had an eyebrow raised. 'An early morning visitor, Cole? You constantly surprise me,' he said. His voice was unfriendly again.

But this time he had a reason. It probably looked as though she were intruding on the woman he had selected for an *affaire*, given his flirtation with Isidore the previous night.

'We're friends,' she said quickly. 'Friends.'

'Ah, friends.'

There was a moment of silence while Harriet thought desperately. 'She's my – my mother's goddaughter. I've known her for years.'

'For years. How lucky.' There was something inscrutable in his face.

'Yes,' Harriet said. 'When my mother was ill, Isidore was often the only person who visited for months.'

'Are you ready for breakfast? I instructed the staff to put out a side of red beef for you and a good tankard of ale, of course. And Eugenia is eager to watch our lesson.'

Harriet groaned inwardly. The beef she could manage, barely, but she truly disliked the beer.

This time the fencing lesson went much better. Without saying a word, Strange put caps on the rapiers, which made Harriet feel more comfortable. She managed to keep a hand on her blade and even parried a *tierce*.

'I'll teach you the *prise de fer* next,' Strange said.

He walked behind her and reached around her body to hold her sword. 'Look,' he said, 'tilt your wrist like this, put your right foot at an angle.' He nudged her leg to get it into the right position.

Surely he didn't have to have his arms around her to demonstrate this move? His hand brushed Harriet's breast. Of course, her breasts were firmly wrapped in bandages, so there was nothing feminine for him to discover.

Still, she jumped away and turned, rapier at the ready. The truth was that every time he touched her, Harriet felt heat rushing up and down her body.

Eugenia sat behind a glass cabinet and called out instructions. Harriet couldn't help turning around and smiling at her, for all Strange insisted that she keep her attention on the rapier.

Eugenia was a strange little girl, with a huge mop of undisciplined hair and an old-fashioned quality about her. To all appearances, she had never played with a child her own age, and it showed. She spoke with all the quaint rhythm of the plays she loved to read.

Just when Harriet started to get tired, Strange said that they should try a match again. She leaned against the cabinet next to her and tried to catch her breath. 'Are you sure, sir?' she asked. 'You are injured from yesterday.'

'*Sir?*' he said. 'You drew blood yesterday; I think we might as well be on intimate terms. I like to be called Jem.'

'And your given name is?'

'Buried in the mists of time,' he said promptly. 'What's your given name?'

'Harry,' Harriet said. Suddenly this was all making her nervous. Strange – or Jem – kept coming up behind her, pulling her arms into the right angles. It made her knees weak. Having his lean, muscular body, clad only in thin breeches and a white shirt, touch hers made her skin flare. She kept beating back an all-over body blush.

This was so dangerous.

Strange – or Jem – strode into position in the middle of the room.

'Eugenia, you stay behind the case.'

'Yes, Papa,' Eugenia said. 'I hope you don't mind, but I'm going to cheer for Harry.'

'Not at all,' Strange said, shifting his rapier from hand to hand. Harriet couldn't help it. She looked at the muscles in his legs and nearly groaned – and it wasn't all her sore muscles this time. 'Come on, Harry. Feeling a touch of fear?'

She walked forward and fell into a defensive position. Strange began circling her, his eyes fixed on her face, a little smile curling the corner of his lips.

'Down with him, Harry!' Eugenia called excitedly. 'Down with him, down with him!'

'I only know one attack,' Harriet complained. 'This isn't really fair.'

Strange tensed his shoulder, and Harriet raised her rapier to blunt his attack. Unfortunately he spun in a circle and came in from the opposite direction. His blade stopped a hair's breadth from her shoulder.

'Not fair,' she grumbled, falling back a step. 'You've never described such a move.'

'You did watch my shoulder,' he said, starting to circle again. 'You're not a total loss.'

'I think you must have some sort of

hunter's obsession,' she said, turning to keep always in front of him. 'Are you one of those men who spend hours loping through the woods with dead creatures slung over your shoulder?'

'Why, Harry,' he said softly, 'you're surprising me again. I thought you were an avid hunter. I'm sure you told me so.'

'Humph,' Harriet said. Her arm was tired, and the rapier felt as if it weighed at least three stone. It was taking everything she had just to keep it to waist level. She had to try to attack. So without thinking about it very much she just stabbed forward.

His sword blocked hers instantly, moving so fast that she didn't even see it. The shock of the two swords coming together went right through her shoulder.

'To him again,' called Eugenia. 'Cut him in the leg, Harry!'

'Be quiet, you bloodthirsty child,' Strange said. He had turned his head to Eugenia, so Harriet took advantage and raised her rapier to his throat, stopping an inch from his skin.

'Ha!' she said.

He turned his head to look at her. 'Foul play, Harry?'

There was something in his eyes ... she let the rapier fall. Could Isidore be right? Could it be that Strange was interested in her – as a man? 'I'm finished for today,' she said, turning around to sheath her rapier.

When she straightened, she glanced back at Strange to find that he was staring at her bottom.

A little shiver ran through her. This was not good. It was one thing for Kitty to be leaning up against her, and another for a man like Strange to be thinking ... whatever he was thinking.

'I think you should just aim that sword a little lower and stab him in the leg,' Eugenia said, running up to her.

'You *are* bloodthirsty,' Harriet said. 'That's your father you're making into my pin-cushion.'

'Do you have another letter for me?' Strange asked. She handed it over and he ripped it open, waving it in the air.

'I don't suppose you could ask my secret correspondent to be a little less generous with her perfume?'

'No,' Harriet said. She'd used Isidore's best French perfume.

'*My music's in the night,*' Strange read aloud, '*So is the nightingale's.* Nice. Brief yet evocative. And it rhymes with yesterday's delight and night.'

Harriet shot Strange a look. 'Your letters are hardly suitable reading for a young girl.'

He ignored her entirely. 'So, Harry, do you have any sense what my mystery corre-spondent wants from me?'

Harriet frowned at him. 'I have no idea,'

she said, thinking his question as unsuitable for Eugenia's ears as was the poem.

'She wants your company, Papa,' Eugenia said.

Strange grinned at her. 'I agree.'

'It's a love poem,' she continued.

'Or something along those lines,' Strange agreed.

'I think she wants to meet you at night,' Eugenia persisted.

'Well,' Harriet said brightly, 'I suppose you'll have to wait until the poem is complete to find out precisely what the poetess requests.'

'Love,' Eugenia said flatly. 'My governess was in love with Papa for a long time, but she finally gave up. He's not easy to catch. Do you want to see the calculations I did last night, Harry? I stayed up till really late but I figured out all the angles on my doll's house roof.'

'How late?' Harriet said, before she thought.

'You're pitiful,' Strange said. 'I can hear your mother speaking every time you open your mouth. It may be impossible to turn you into a man, Harry, if you don't mind me pointing it out. Eugenia is perfectly capable of taking care of herself.'

'I'd like to see your calculations,' Harriet said to Eugenia, ignoring him. He was a fool to let his eight-year-old daughter stay up half the night parsing calculations but at least that explained the odd grey shadows under Eugenia's eyes. She almost looked ill.

Eugenia reached up and took her hand and even though Harriet was longing for a bath and a nap, she let herself be drawn past the barrier of the footman into the locked wing of the house.

'Who lives here besides you?' she asked.

'No one,' Eugenia said blithely. 'That is, there's always a maid with me, of course. Papa likes to keep me safe, so there's always a footman on guard.'

But when they got to the nursery, it was deserted. 'Where's your maid?' Harriet said, looking around. The fire was burning low.

'She must have gone downstairs for a bit,' Eugenia said. 'My governess will probably be here any moment. She's in love with one of the footmen, so I always know where she is.'

'And where is that?'

'Kissing the footman, of course,' Eugenia said. 'They kiss in the knife room on the second floor.'

'How on earth do you know that?'

'She told me.'

Harriet nodded. Then she squatted down, suppressing a groan over her cramped muscles, and allowed Eugenia to show her the angle of every wall and roof on her three-story doll's house.

'Did you demonstrate all the angles for your father?' she asked.

'Papa? No, Papa designed my house, so he knows the angles.'

'I mean, did you figure out the angles because it will make him happy?'

Eugenia looked at her with the clear, surprised eyes of childhood. 'Why would that make him happy? It makes *me* happy.'

Harriet, put in her place, began to sort out the tiny furniture that was toppled this way and that within the house.

'Do you have a cat?' Eugenia asked, sitting down next to her.

'I have a dog,' Harriet said. 'He is a silly old spaniel named Mrs Custard. Do you have a pet?'

Eugenia shook her head. 'I don't know very much about animals.'

'There's nothing much to know. You feed them; they love you.'

'But they need to run outside. And I'm in my room so often. It wouldn't be fair.'

'But you must go outside, don't you? A dog would be happy to be inside with you and then go outside for some exercise.'

Eugenia frowned down at her little house. 'I wouldn't want an animal locked in my room. He might start to hate me.'

'Of course he wouldn't! If my spaniel, Mrs Custard, were here, you'd see how much he would love it. He would curl up in front of the fire and be perfectly happy.'

'Actually, he might be cold. I'll add another log to the fire,' Eugenia said, getting up.

'Wait a minute,' Harriet said, hurrying after her. 'You're not going to do that yourself, are you?'

Eugenia cast her a pitying look. 'Of course I am, Harry. You *do* know how to feed a fire, don't you?'

'I leave it to the footmen,' she said firmly. 'And you shouldn't be doing it either. What if your skirts caught a spark?'

'They never do,' Eugenia said. 'I'm very careful.' And before Harriet could stop her she picked up a small log and tossed it on the fire. A huge burst of sparks sprang into the air and slid up the chimney. 'I like it when that happens,' she said. 'It's so pretty.'

'I'm going to speak to your father,' Harriet said, pulling on the bell cord. 'Where are your governess and the maid? What if there were a fire in this room, Eugenia?'

'You *do* sound like a mother!' Eugenia said, giggling. 'Papa never worries the way you do. I'd run out of the room, of course.'

'But the hallway is locked,' Harriet said. 'Is there another exit?'

'That's the only way out, but the footman is always there. Or do you mean a secret passage?' Eugenia's face lit up. 'I never thought of that.' She instantly started walking around the room and peering at the wainscoting. 'Anyway,' she added, pulling at a carved knob on the elaborate fireplace, 'I have a plan for escape in case I need it.'

'What is it?'

Eugenia nodded towards the window. 'I'll go out of that window. There's a huge oak tree there, and I'm sure I could scramble down without any problem.'

Harriet looked out of the window. The oak tree was a good two feet away and she wasn't sure that even she would be able to jump to it.

'You look so fidgety,' Eugenia said, giving up her search for a secret door. 'Tell me more about Mrs Custard, please. That's a strange name for a boy dog.'

So Harriet did.

17

In Which Harriet Finds Herself Shocked

Dinner that night was a formal affair. Rather to Harriet's surprise, she found that she was seated towards the head of the table, with Isidore between herself and Strange. Kitty was to Harriet's left.

'How are you?' Kitty whispered with an effusive smile. 'Did you have a good day? We practised for our next performance. We're going to sing madrigals for a bishop.'

'Madrigals for a bishop?' Harriet said, spreading her napkin in her lap.

Kitty started giggling madly, so much so that she couldn't speak.

There was something about being dressed in men's clothes that made Harriet far less patient, she was discovering.

'He wants us dressed as little angels,' Kitty finally managed to say.

'Angels singing before a bishop. I suppose it makes sense.'

'But wait until you see our costumes,' Kitty said. 'It must be very warm in Heaven, if you understand me.'

She gave Harriet her practised, naughty smile.

Harriet smiled back, rather more stiffly. 'Do you have wings?'

'Yes, really lovely ones, made of real feathers. Lord Strange has a French secretary who helped with the costumes. The wings are so soft and pretty. At one point we take them off and actually lie down on them.'

'Lie down?' Harriet said.

Kitty leaned closer. 'I could give you a private rehearsal if you wished, Harry. I couldn't sing a madrigal without three of us, but I could sing another love song.'

'Did you say rehearsal?' Strange said from the head of the table. 'Are you discussing the angel performance? I would love to see that.'

She instantly gave him the same dimpled smile that she had just bestowed on Harriet. 'I'd be happy to include you, my lord.'

'Isidore,' Strange said, turning to her with a touch on her arm, 'would you be interested in seeing a private concert given by an angel?'

'Of course,' Isidore said, but Harriet could tell from her voice that she didn't like the idea.

'I'm afraid I already have an appointment after supper,' Harriet said quickly.

'You do?' Strange said, looking at her from under his lids. 'Now who could that be with?' He looked down the long, glittering table, lined with people more beautiful than noble. 'Nell, perhaps?'

Harriet gave him a cool little smile. 'There are so many people in your house that it's difficult to enumerate one's acquaintances.'

'After your appointment, then,' he said softly. 'I stay up quite late and I'll warrant Kitty does as well. Shall we say eleven o'clock?'

All the stable boy had mentioned was learning how to trot. And mount. How long could that take?

'I'm not sure Kitty will want to stay up so late,' Harriet said. 'It sounds as if she had a strenuous day's exercise.'

'Oh, it's not so strenuous,' Kitty said with a giggle. 'I spent a great deal of it on my back.'

The little line between Isidore's brows deepened. 'I'm afraid that I couldn't possibly join you at that hour,' she said, politely enough. 'I'm quite exhausted.'

'What a pity,' Strange said. He stopped looking at Harriet and gave Isidore a lavish smile. 'It won't be nearly as enjoyable without you.'

Harriet had a sudden, shocking realization. If Strange ever gave her that kind of smile, she would lose her composure. She might even beg him to take her to bed.

'Eleven o'clock,' Kitty said. 'Would you like more angels than just myself? I'm sure–' she ogled Strange '–any number of Graces would love to perform tonight, Lord Strange. To sing madrigals, we need three.'

'I think all we need tonight is you,' Strange said smoothly.

Kitty erupted into giggles.

A thought occurred to Harriet. Something about what Kitty might be thinking. Her mouth fell open and at that same moment, Isidore's fingers dug into her arm.

'I need to speak to you. At once!' she hissed.

Strange was standing up, signalling a general move away from the table. He paused just for a moment. 'My guests await, and you, Mr Cope, have an appointment... Shall we say eleven o'clock in the library? Mr Povy can direct you.' Without waiting for a response, he walked away.

Isidore's grip strengthened. 'Harriet!'

Harriet turned to Kitty, wanting to say something. But there was a deep excitement and – yes – enjoyment in Kitty's eyes that stopped the words in her mouth. Kitty was perfectly happy with the idea of Mr Cope, Lord Strange, and one solitary angel. Harriet swallowed.

'Eleven o'clock!' Kitty said, trotting away.

Isidore dragged Harriet to the side of the room. 'Do you have any idea what Kitty is planning to do tonight, Harriet? Do you?'

'I just figured it out!' Harriet said, panic making her head reel. 'I had no idea!'

'You must stay in your room,' Isidore stated. 'Better: you can sleep with me in case Strange walks straight into your bed-chamber.' She looked around, but almost everyone had left the dining room. 'Harriet, this is a – a degenerate house! These people are – are – they are doing things–'

Harriet couldn't help laughing a little. 'Isidore, you *knew* that. Why do you think that Jemma said she wouldn't come here, even though she'd hosted all sorts of shocking parties in Paris? Her Paris events roused scandals because someone's costume was a bit risqué, or a married woman paraded around with someone else's husband. Strange's reputation – and his house parties – are on a totally different scale.'

'I didn't understand the reality of it. It makes me feel unclean even to be here! Where is Villiers? I thought he was supposed to protect us. Harriet, what are you going to *do?*' Isidore's eyes were bright and alarmed.

'Well, I'm not going to engage in any sort of hanky-panky with an angel,' Harriet said, practically. 'You needn't worry about that. I'll figure something out. Perhaps I'll claim to be ill and just leave Strange and Kitty together.'

'Ugh!' Isidore said. 'I don't like him at all now, Harriet. I don't like it here. Two men and one woman.' She shuddered. 'So far I've been bored to tears by half-clothed virgins and invited to hear madrigals sung by angels. I find the mixture of culture and nudity tedious. But you're having fun with Strange, aren't you?'

'It's nothing to do with Strange,' Harriet said, though she was lying. It *was* Strange. Half her pleasure, perhaps more, came from the time she spent with him, fencing with rapiers, fencing with words. Of course, it wasn't a real attraction. The pleasure had to be coming from the fact it was all so illicit to hunger for a man who didn't even think of her as a woman.

Not that she would ever consider going to that library to meet Strange – and Kitty.

Not even to see Strange unclothed.

'It's because of how much fun I'm having in male clothing,' she told Isidore. 'I've never been so free before.'

'I don't want to be this free,' Isidore said. 'I'm turning more and more staid by the moment.'

'I can lend you my breeches,' Harriet suggested. And then: 'I forgot my appointment!'

'What appointment?' Isidore exclaimed. 'Not another appointment with a woman, surely?'

'It's at the stables,' Harriet said. 'A very nice stable boy is going to teach me how to mount a horse properly. I keep almost falling off the other side.'

Isidore rolled her eyes. 'I am going to bed. I think I may announce a case of infectious red spots tomorrow. Anything to keep the Graces out of my bedchamber. And Strange. I certainly don't want him bursting in on me while I'm in my nightgown again. I hardly had my hair brushed.'

Harriet watched her climb the stairs, thinking about just how much she'd like Strange to visit her bedchamber, if he knew she was a woman.

She wouldn't care if her hair were brushed. She would just–

She wrenched her mind away. That was foolishness.

18

Harriet's shock, Part Two

Two minutes later she was walking into the warm stable. It smelled of clean horses, leather, and manure. The horses poked their heads over their stalls and whickered for a carrot.

'Good evening, Nick!' she said, as the boy appeared around the end of the stable. 'This is so very kind of you. You must be exhausted after a day's labour.'

'It's me good deed for the day, miss,' he said. 'My mother would never forgive me if I let you be discovered.' He hesitated.

Harriet smiled at him. 'You very likely want to give me a warning about Lord Strange's establishment.'

'Anyone can tell, miss,' he burst out, 'that you're not the usual sort of woman who stays at the house. It's not the place for you.'

'I'm a widow,' she said. 'I promise you that I'm not shocked, Nick.'

'Married is one thing,' he said stubbornly. 'But you're a lady, and ladies don't have a place here.'

She couldn't help smiling at that. She knew quite well that Isidore would agree with him. 'I promise you I won't stay even a moment if my disguise is uncovered,' she said. 'Would that make you feel better?'

Then she leaned to kiss his cheek because he was—

But whatever thought she had flew from her head as the door at the end opened, letting in a swirl of snow and wind. She leapt back.

Strange stood in the door for a second, and then walked forward, throwing the door shut behind him. He pulled off his gloves, one by one, with a silent precision that contained as much threat as a tiger's slavering yowl.

'Good evening,' Harriet said. 'I thought you were with your guests, my lord.'

'I had the suspicion that I should watch you,' he said. He turned his eyes onto young Nick. 'Off to your quarters, boy.'

Nick hesitated, throwing a worried glance at Harriet. She brought out the coin she had saved for him. 'I'm most grateful to you for your tutelage, Nick. Thank you. And I'll see you tomorrow.'

'But you'll—' he said, but stopped. Obviously, he needed the position, and she could see chivalry and terror warring in his face.

'Go,' Strange said. There was something flat in his tone that made the boy turn and flee.

Harriet turned to face Strange. He'd been irritable with her before, but now there was true rage burning in his eyes. He slapped his gloves into the palm of his hand with a noise like a gunshot.

'Is there some way that I can help you?' Harriet asked.

'Do you know, I thought the opposite?' he said. 'I thought that I should watch over *you*, to make sure that you weren't beguiled by one of the scum that sometimes float around the house. But I didn't realize that you would be a predator.'

Harriet blinked at him. 'Predator? I don't know what you're talking about. But I take umbrage at the insult, my lord.'

'You take umbrage,' he sneered. 'I catch you kissing my stable boy, a good boy, and giving him money, and you *take umbrage?*'

She frowned at him. 'He was helping me–'

'That sort of help isn't allowed in my house,' he said, and his voice was as chill as a frozen knife. 'Never. Under any circumstances. Do you understand?'

'I–'

'A simple yes or no is enough. Do you understand?'

Harriet stood there for a moment trying to figure out if she did understand. The only possibility that came to mind was–

Her mouth fell open and she could feel her eyes growing round. 'You couldn't – you didn't–' She spluttered. 'You degenerate *beast!*'

There was a moment of panting silence in the stable, and suddenly Strange threw back his head and started to laugh. The noise of it rang in the rafters and made the horses prick up their ears.

'You are a fiend,' Harriet said, moving to walk past him. 'Your mind is as black as a privy. I'll leave these premises tomorrow.'

He caught her arm, still laughing. 'I'm not a fiend, Harry. I'm not.'

She glared at him. 'No one but the most dissipated rascal could have such a thought in his head.' She jerked her arm away.

He was still grinning. 'It's your face,' he said, sounding utterly unrepentant.

'My face!' she said, feeling her cheeks go red. 'There is *nothing* in my face that would lead anyone to that conclusion. You, sir, are just as much a hellhound as they say of you, and I was a fool to come near your estate. I'll leave tonight!'

'Don't you see,' he said, grabbing her arm again, 'I was just trying to protect young Nick? You're damned beautiful for a man, Harry. It made me suspicious, and I shouldn't have been. You can't help the way you're born.'

'The very fact the thought came into your mind—'

'I'm an adult. I run a house party that makes no pretenses to follow the rules of decent society. Of course I thought of it. Among other things, I'm the father of a lovely little girl. I *have* to think about such things.'

Harriet shuddered. 'I pity you, then. Because my father and mother never worried about that.'

'Oh, they must have,' Strange said. 'Not worry about you? With that beauty you have? The way your eyes look, so innocent and that brown-violet colour?' His mouth curled up. 'They worried about you, young Harry. It's to your mother's credit that you never encountered this sort of ugliness.'

'If you have, it's because you live a licentious life,' Harriet said, feeling as if the moorings of her rage were slipping away from her. A moment ago she was about to leave the estate, and now he was looking at her, and there was a shadow of something on his face that made her feel odd. It was almost sadness, but how was that possible?

'Quite likely,' he said.

'You shouldn't have such people around you,' she snapped. 'Then you wouldn't have to have such invidious thoughts.'

'I would always have that kind of thought.'

'I pity you, then,' she said. 'I know the

friends who enter my home. I know their strengths and their weaknesses. I need not fear them.'

'No one knows what's in another man's heart. The greatest evil often lies under the prettiest face.'

Something went across his eyes that was pure pain, but he shook it away, and the laughter was there again. 'Now, you must forgive me, young Harry. Really you must. You see, I did think I knew you. And my rage was all the greater because I suddenly thought I'd made a mistake.'

Harriet smiled, a bit stiffly. 'It's quite all right.'

His charm was a potent weapon. He walked back to the house, talking of inconsequentials. But Harriet felt faintly nauseated. This was not the house for her, not a place where Strange clearly expected that sort of thing might happen to little Nick. She needed to leave. And what's more, she would take Nick with her. She could easily employ him on her estate. She had about sixty people there, and not a single lecher that Nick needed to fear.

When they entered the house she started towards the stairs, but Strange stopped her with a hand on her arm. 'Surely you haven't forgotten Kitty?'

'I'm sure the two of you can entertain each other,' Harriet said, not impolitely.

'Will you give her my excuses, please?'

'So you can go upstairs and instruct your man to pack your bags?'

She hesitated. It seemed so bald. And yet, why prevaricate? 'Yes,' she said. 'This is no place for me.'

He dropped her arm. 'Of course, I cannot stop you. Will you bid Villiers goodbye tonight or tomorrow morning? I was summoned to his room this evening.'

'Then I will join you and make my farewell,' she said. 'And I do thank you for your hospitality, my lord. It's not your fault that I am more naïve than I thought. I belong at home.'

'In the country? Do you live in the country, Harry?'

She nodded. 'I thought it was a boring existence, but now I am changing my mind.'

'I wish you would change your mind about Kitty. How often does one get to see an angel perform?'

Harriet didn't bother to answer that. He walked up the stairs beside her.

Villiers's chamber was hung with blue velvet and had the lush atmosphere that Harriet imagined one would find in a courtesan's drawing room. Villiers was lying on a settee next to the fire, wearing a dressing gown of rich black embroidered with pearl. Candlelight threw shadows on his face, on the exquisite drape of his gown, on the lavish velvet on the walls.

He put down his book when they walked in. 'Thank God you've taken pity on me,' he said. 'I'm thinking of hobbling to the window and throwing myself out into the snow from pure *ennui*.'

'Alas, I bring ill tidings,' Strange said, throwing himself into an armchair. 'I've insulted young Harry here, and he's determined to leave the house since my mind is *black as a privy*. I do have that phrase right, don't I, Harry?'

She scowled at him.

'Black as a privy!' Villiers said, his eyes showing some interest. 'I agree, I agree. What on earth inspired such a diatribe?'

'There is no need to go into particulars,' Harriet said stiffly.

'I have an uncommonly pretty stable boy,' Strange said, ignoring her. 'I'm afraid that I assassinated your protégé's character by jumping to the conclusion that Harry was interested in an intimate relationship with the boy. To do myself justice, he was kissing him. Such a neophyte as I am, I've never seen a man kiss a man, except in France, of course.'

'I kiss men often,' Villiers said. 'Just to make them flustered. Remind me to kiss you on our next meeting, Strange.'

'I shall look forward to it,' Strange said.

'You really should forgive him,' Villiers said

to Harriet. 'The man lives in the country. How does he know how civilized people behave to each other?'

'But he suggested–' Harriet said.

Villiers lifted his hand. 'Just so. One abhors to mention these things, dear Harry, but that does not make them disappear. Strange is right to look out for his people, stable boys and all.'

If put that way, Harriet had to agree.

'The proper thing to do in this circumstance,' Villiers continued, 'is to tell Strange that if he plays the fool with you again you'll pummel him so hard that he'll fart crackers.'

'Fart crackers,' Harriet said, laughing despite herself. 'You mean firecrackers? Right.'

'Like to see you try,' Strange said.

'Please don't leave tonight,' Villiers added. 'I was sadly brought down by the journey here, but this afternoon I felt the first glimmer of hope that I might actually be able to emerge from this damned velvet nest.'

'I thought you liked this suite,' Strange said.

'Inexorably vulgar,' Villiers said. 'Blue velvet. Paugh!'

'I am learning so much tonight,' Strange said. 'But here's another little problem for you to solve, Villiers. I don't think you've met the Graces. They're a lovely troupe of young women. If you'd like to paint them, they're agreeable. If you'd like them to sing or dance or otherwise inspire you, they're capable of doing that too.'

'Wonderful,' Villiers said. 'I'm not up to being inspired, but I grieve at my loss, truly I grieve.'

'At the moment they are rehearsing an inspiring performance of madrigals to be sung while dressed as angels,' Strange said.

'A performance designed for a bishop,' Harriet added.

'Dear me, how lucky the episcopate is sometimes,' Villiers said. 'Nothing half so thrilling ever comes my way.'

'That's just it,' Strange said. 'One of the Graces, a lovely young thing by the name of Kitty, has offered a private performance to myself and Cope. That is, I believe she meant to offer it just to Harry, but I elbowed my way into the party.'

'Ungracious,' Villiers said. 'You are growing more countrified by the moment, Strange. Don't ever do that if one of the young ladies offers me a private performance. I should be forced to run you through. Miss Kitty agreed to perform for both of you, did she? An enterprising young woman.'

'Exactly,' Strange said. 'Now, it occurs to me that perhaps young Harry here is not ready for some of the more exuberant aspects of Kitty's likely performance.'

'While in Rome, do as the Romans,' Villiers said cheerfully.

Harriet blinked at him. He couldn't possibly be suggesting that she...

'*Si fueris Romae, Romano vivito more,*' Strange said, in what Harriet presumed to be Latin. And then, disastrously, he turned to Harriet and asked her a question, again in Latin.

Harriet panicked. She didn't understand a word of it, and yet of course as a young gentleman she ought to. Every gentleman understood Latin.

Villiers smoothly cut into the conversation with a Latin remark of his own. Whatever he said, it seemed to shut up Strange. He nodded sharply. There was an odd, wild light in his eyes that made Harriet a bit nervous, but at least he didn't keep talking in Latin or expect her to say anything in reply.

Harriet shot Villiers a quick glance. She didn't dare look pleading in front of Strange, but obviously she had to avoid Kitty somehow. Because it was clear that what Kitty and Strange had in mind – whatever that was exactly – was nothing she wanted to join.

'I have just affirmed to my friend Strange that I certainly want you, young Harry, to come into your manhood,' Villiers said.

'You did,' Strange said. 'You did.'

'And yet...'

'Exactly,' Strange said. They smiled at each other.

Villiers's skin was so white it looked blue. Some might call him haggard due to his thinness, and yet somehow his loss of flesh just emphasized his masculinity. He looked like a fierce lion, temporarily caged, beaten and starved, but still deeply dangerous. Wild at the core.

Strange was entirely different: lean but muscled. He had the look of someone who walked through hell – or a lot of brandy – and came out the other side wiser, tougher, and with his sense of humour intact.

The sardonic lines by the sides of his mouth deepened every time he looked at her and she finally knew the name to put on that emotion: laughter. She was dying to know what they had said to each other in Latin, and yet she couldn't ask.

'Well, Harry,' Villiers said. 'Would you like to handle young Kitty alone?' He was daring her. She saw it in his eyes, the spark of delight there in the fact that he was putting her on the spot.

Villiers had told her that men were straightforward and use Anglo-Saxon words. Was fornicate an Anglo-Saxon word? It was the only one that came to mind, and it sounded too pedantic.

She raised her chin. 'I'm looking forward to meeting Kitty,' she said. 'Privately.' She turned to Strange with a show of deference. 'If you'll forgive me, my lord.'

'Not at all,' Strange said promptly, that strange laughing light in his eyes again. 'I think you and Miss Kitty will have a truly delightful time in private, and I would just be in the way.'

'Exactly,' Harriet said.

'Couldn't I watch?' he asked. 'I have a room with a hidden peephole.'

She blinked but there was laughter in his voice. She was beginning to tell when he was serious and when he was laughing.

'Stop mocking my ward,' Villiers said, his voice sounding more tired than it had a moment ago. 'The day you need to get pleasure by watching another couple perform is my last visit here, Strange.'

He laughed. 'You never know. I could whisper encouragement to Harry through the arras.'

'Some things are instinctive,' Villiers said, his words blurring together.

Harriet stood up. 'It would be most ungracious of me to keep Kitty waiting. Where did you fix our appointment, my lord?'

'I thought you were going to call me Jem.'

'Am I right in thinking you told Kitty your library? If you'll forgive me, I'll join her. I am naturally quite eager.'

'Naturally,' Strange drawled. 'What young man wouldn't be? Kitty is so nubile, so luscious, so charming in every way. I do wish you the best of evenings.'

19

In the Company of Angels

Kitty's angel costume was fashioned from a few twists of cloth and a pair of feathery wings. If angels looked like this, men were going to find Heaven a very interesting place.

Harriet's heart sank. Obviously, she was going to have to expose her own gender in order to get out of the room without disrobing. And she wasn't ready.

She loved being taken for a man, being given steak to eat for breakfast, being told to pummel someone until he farted crackers.

She didn't want to go home and have docile conversations with the vicar. She didn't want to get on a side-saddle and ride decorously over a field or two before her hip started aching from the unbalanced effect of the saddle.

She definitely didn't want to spend two hours staring glumly into a mirror while her maid dressed her hair into an arrangement that included a ship in full sail.

She closed the door behind her, but before she could say a word, Kitty flew across the room in a burst of giggles. Harriet recoiled for a moment, thinking she was about to be kissed, but it turned out that Kitty simply wished to loosen Harriet's cravat.

'I'm afraid that Lord Strange can't be here,' Harriet said, holding on to her cravat rather desperately.

Kitty bounded around Harriet, turning the key in the door, and giggling all the time.

'Oh dear,' Harriet said to herself, quietly.

Then Kitty came back and stood before her. 'Now, Harry,' she said. 'I know how you're feeling.'

Harriet felt pure, unadulterated panic. 'You *do?*'

She nodded. 'You're a little scared. Everyone has a first time. And of course it's a bit more difficult for a man, given as he has to perform. But I'm–'

It had to be said. 'I'm not–' Harriet began.

But Kitty was giggling again. 'Don't tell me this isn't your first time, Harry, because I'd hate to call you a fraud this early in our acquaintance!'

'A fraud?' Harriet repeated faintly.

Kitty had a look in her eye that made Harriet want to dash for the hills, so she took a deep breath and steeled herself. Goodbye breeches, goodbye wild morning rides, goodbye fencing...

'I'm not a man,' she said clearly.

'Well, not *yet,*' Kitty squealed. She reached

218

for Harriet's hand, but Harriet fell back a step.

'I truly mean what I say. I'm not a man.'

There was a moment of silence in the room. Harriet could hear the embarrassed thumping of her heart in approximate rhythm with the grandfather clock.

'You're not a man?' Kitty asked. 'Really?'

Harriet shook her head. 'No.'

'But how did that happen?' Kitty asked. 'Was it a childhood accident? Or something worse?'

Harriet blinked – and then she suddenly realized she had been offered the perfect escape. 'Childhood accident,' she said sadly. 'I couldn't bring myself to tell you, because I find you so beautiful.'

'Oh...' Kitty breathed. 'You poor thing.' Her eyes lost the luminous, excited tint they held, and began glowing with sympathy. 'It must be so embarrassing for you to tell me. Of course you don't want anyone to know.' Her eyes widened. 'No wonder you didn't want Lord Strange to join us!'

Harriet heaved a deep sigh. 'You can have no idea.'

'There's a eunuch in the Queen's Revels company,' Kitty offered. 'He sings all the high parts. I've never met him, but everyone says his voice is beautiful. You know, this all makes sense now. Your voice is very high.'

'It never changed,' Harriet admitted.

'I suppose it wouldn't. Is there anything I can do?' Kitty looked full of trepidation but willing.

'There's nothing anyone can do. It's all just too, too humiliating.' For a moment Harriet thought she'd gone too far, but of course Kitty was used to people dramatizing themselves, and she didn't even blink.

'We'll have a drink,' she said, patting Harriet on the shoulder. 'Brandy is a great help when it comes to humiliation. Why, there was the time when I was auditioning to be in the chorus at the Drury Lane theatre, and the manager asked me if I could play the part of an ape. He wanted a private audition.'

'What on earth did he mean?'

'Roll around on the floor, head over heels, in some sort of gymnastic feat.' She walked over to the sideboard and poured two hefty doses of brandy and brought them back. 'Here, Harry, this is for your health. You never know. Maybe you'll regain capacity when you're a bit bigger. Anyone can tell that you have a nice package there. It's just a dirty shame that it doesn't work.'

'Yes, isn't it?' Harriet said, silently blessing the wool stocking tucked down her breeches that formed her 'package'. They sat down on a settee, and Harriet said, 'So the manager wanted you to be a gymnast?'

'Private performance,' Kitty said. 'Unclothed.'

Harriet choked.

'Head over heels, around and around the stage. He offered me quite a lot of money for it. But I don't do that sort of thing.' She made a prim mouth. 'There's being naughty for the pleasure of it, if you see what I mean. And then there's just plain naughtiness, as my mother would say.'

Harriet drank some more. This was definitely the most interesting period of her life. There could be no comparison to the turgid conversations she'd generally had at balls. 'Is your mother still alive?' she ventured.

'Of course. She's one of the principal dancers with Prince George's troupe, down in Brighton. She always laid down the rules for me. I do a private performance now and then, but only for my own pleasure. If you do such things for money, you become hard and bitter.'

'Why?' Harriet asked curiously.

'You *are* a young one, aren't you? For one thing, you'll probably get an illness and then you'll look back and regret making yourself ill for twelve pence. Or whatever the sum happened to be.'

'But couldn't you get an illness anyway?' Harriet asked.

'It's not going to happen.'

'Why on earth not?'

'Because it's a different sort of thing,' Kitty said, rather obscurely. 'And if you start doing things only for money, well, then you're not enjoying yourself, are you?'

'I expect not,' Harriet said. She was starting to think that whatever she and Benjamin had done in their marital bedchamber had little to do with Kitty's idea of enjoyment.

'I shouldn't even talk of this to you,' Kitty said, looking stricken. 'You being unable to take pleasure, I mean. I do apologize.'

'That's quite all right,' Harriet said. 'I like to know, even though I can't partake.'

'That's even sadder,' Kitty said, her eyes growing a bit misty.

'So,' Harriet said hastily, 'will you take a husband someday?'

'I've had three proposals of marriage,' Kitty said. 'I suspect that I will take the next one. I've always liked the number four.'

There was something about Kitty's reasoning methods that made Harriet's head spin. 'But what if you don't care for the fourth man?'

'I like most people,' Kitty said cheerfully. 'Someone like you would be perfect. Except ...' she paused delicately.

'Yes,' Harriet said, finishing her glass of brandy. 'I see exactly what you mean.'

After a second glass of brandy, Harriet pulled off her peruke and loosened her cravat. Then Kitty took that cravat and illustrated an interesting way to tie someone to the bedpost (or any other handy pole, she explained earnestly), using just one wrist and the cravat.

Kitty didn't handle her third glass of brandy all that well, although she insisted on drinking it. She turned quite pink and it was hard to make out what she was saying between bursts of giggles.

'Come on,' Harriet said, hauling Kitty into a standing position. 'We need to find something to eat.'

'We can just ring for the butler. You can simply ring that bell and anything–' Kitty waved her arm wildly '–anything will be delivered right to you. You can't imagine what we all asked for during our first two days here. I demanded champagne for breakfast!'

'And they brought it to you?'

'Of course,' Kitty said, toppling to the side. 'Perhaps I should eat something. I was so excited about the evening that I didn't really eat supper.'

Harriet steered her towards the door. Once in the hallway, Kitty remembered that she was planning to marry the next man who asked her and started speculating about his age. And the size of his member.

Harriet cleared her throat. She was certainly learning a great deal that evening, never having seriously considered such a question before. But she was also feeling slightly dizzy.

Povy took one look at them and then

tucked Kitty under his arm.

He snapped his fingers at a footman. 'Fetch Lord Strange.'

'Oh, you needn't – you mustn't,' Harriet protested.

'His lordship likes to be informed of all events,' Mr Povy said, gliding across the corridor with Kitty in tow, as if a drunken young woman dressed as an angel was all in a day's work.

Which it probably was, Harriet had to realize.

'Come on, Harry,' Kitty called. 'Harry!'

Harriet reluctantly followed them into the sitting room.

'Strange is coming here, isn't he?' Kitty said, fixing her eye on Povy.

Povy said, 'I really couldn't say, miss. He might come if he's free.'

'I expect he'll ask me to marry him, and I think I'll accept. Unless you wish to ask me, Harry.' She appeared to have forgotten the manifest reason why Harry (or Harriet) couldn't engage in marriage.

The main thought that went through Harriet's mind was utterly surprising and fiercely violent. She pushed the thought away. It was none of her business whom Jem Strange asked to marry. Though he would never ask Kitty, any more than she herself would.

'If you'll forgive me, I won't ask you to

marry me at this time,' she told Kitty.

Povy deposited Kitty on a chair. 'Hot buttered eggs,' he told the footman. 'Hot tea, and I should think some salmon sandwiches as well.'

Harriet sat down.

Of course Jem appeared a moment later.

'Ah, it *is* Mr Cope,' he said genially. 'I wondered, when the footman reported that a young lady was the worse for drink.'

'I don't know why you'd think so,' Harriet said, looking up at him, finally, because there was nowhere else to look.

'Our Kitty does not usually drink to excess,' he said, bending over to peer at his guest. 'It must have been a great disappointment that sent her into such a pit of despair.'

'I really couldn't say,' Harriet said. 'I believe that she expects you to ask her to marry you, perhaps even tonight.'

'Yet another disappointment in play,' Jem murmured. 'Dear me, the poor girl seems to have gone to sleep.'

'I should go upstairs,' Harriet said, not moving. There was a strange excitement racing through her veins.

Jem looked at her. 'And waste buttered eggs? I love buttered eggs. When they are cooked correctly, they are silky, and my cook makes them excellently.'

He could make a salad of straw sound

delicious, Harriet thought. Two minutes later, a footman had picked up Kitty and carried her off.

'Tsk, tsk,' Jem said, sitting himself in Kitty's chair. 'Young women can't drink like men, you know. They're apt to topple off to sleep before they even think of taking their wings off. I suppose that's what happened to the two of you?'

'Exactly,' Harriet said. 'That describes it perfectly.'

'Never disappoint a woman, Harry,' Jem said. There was a glint of amusement in his eyes that said – said what?

'I've been thinking about the lines of verse you keep handing me,' he continued. 'I suppose you'll have another two lines for me tomorrow?'

'I expect so,' Harriet said, a bit cautiously. 'It depends on whether I am given another missive for you, of course.'

'*The dark is my delight,*' he said. 'And then that business about the nightingale singing at night. You know, it almost sounds like a theatrical song, the kind that appeared in old plays.'

Mr Povy opened the door and placed a silver tray in front of them. 'Buttered eggs,' he announced. 'Extra butter, as your lordship prefers. Hot tea with lemon.'

'The rest we can see to for ourselves,' Jem said amiably, but with an unmistakable tone of dismissal.

He wants to be alone with me, Harriet thought with a thrill. He wants to be – alone. With me or with Harry?

Obviously with Harry, since he didn't know Harriet existed.

'What were you working on today?' she asked, biting into a piece of toast.

'Letters,' he said. 'My Lord Chancellor tells me that the King is quite distraught over a debt to the King of Denmark. But since I advised two years ago that it was best to avoid giving any funds to the Guinny Company backed by Denmark, which they choose to ignore, I feel the Privy Coun-cillors will have to solve this debacle on their own.'

'I didn't know that you exchanged correspondence with the Lord Chancellor,' Harriet said.

'Money,' Jem said. 'If you have a great deal of it, it precipitates you into conversations in which you would prefer not to participate.'

'With the Lord Chancellor?'

'And the King. My guess is that the King will remove the first lord of the treasury by the end of the week. The only thing of interest I did today was unpack a box of curiosities sent to me by a man in London.'

'What was among them?' Harriet asked.

'A salamander,' Jem said. 'And a squirrel shaped like a fish. There's a piece of wood from the cross of Christ, which I utterly discount because it's the fortieth such piece I've been offered, and that number alone is enough wood to put a good wall on a privy.'

'Why did you buy it then?'

'It was part of the lot,' Jem said. 'Monsieur Bonnier de la Moson died last year, and his collection is being sold off.'

'I don't understand,' Harriet said. 'How exactly can you make use of a squirrel shaped like a fish?'

'I don't make use of it. Knowledge is my ultimate end.'

'That sounds very grand,' Harriet said. 'And yet knowledge generally has some use.'

'Not this kind,' Jem said cheerfully. 'I'm a feckless sort. I like to examine anything strange or unlikely very, very closely.' There was a light in his eye that suddenly made Harriet wonder exactly how he found her *strange*.

'Everything out of the common run of things is valuable in its own right,' Jem said. 'People, after all, are so similar. The majority of them bore me to tears.'

Harriet finished a bite of buttered egg. It sang to her mouth, if silky eggs had a voice. 'In that case,' she said, 'why on earth do you always have a houseful of guests? Either you find them boring, in which case you should send them all home, or you actually enjoy them.'

'Ah, but the people you find here are not in the common run.'

Harriet thought about that for a while. 'I don't agree,' she said finally. 'I have been enjoying myself enormously. But while it is true that Kitty is rather more forthcoming about her particular ambitions, she strikes me as similar to many young ladies.'

'Kitty is no lady,' Jem pointed out.

'And yet she is akin to most of them. There's a wistful look in her eyes, you know. I think she will marry the next man who asks her—'

'I must remind myself to hold my tongue,' Jem murmured.

'She will marry,' Harriet said firmly, 'and then she will have a great many children. And while she will likely have fond memories of being one of the Graces, and perhaps even keep a feather or two as a memento, she will have any number of delightful, noisy children and be very happy. In fact, I would guess that she'll never think about her past as a wild young angel.'

'You're remarkably cynical for such a young sprig,' Jem observed.

Harriet snorted. 'Cynicism is not the provenance of the elderly.'

'And what is it brewed from, then?'

'Oh, boredom,' she said lightly. 'When one is bored, one tends to spend an inordinate amount of time analyzing one's neighbours.

That's why I would suggest that there is no great difference between your salacious guests and the run of the *ton*.'

'They burn more brightly. Gentlewomen are tediously attached to concepts of marriage and fidelity, even as they carry on *affaires*.'

'Are they? There seems to be just as much anxiety here as I find in the *ton*,' Harriet said. 'Take Nell, for instance.'

'Nell appears to have something of a fascination for me,' Jem said. 'She caught me in the corridor the other day and I thought she was going to leap on me like a ravening lion.'

'There is no accounting for tastes,' Harriet said. 'My point is that Nell appears deliciously free of society's pressures. But secretly I believe she's rather desperate to marry you, rather than merely bed you.'

'I am afraid to ask about my true desires.'

She opened her mouth but he raised his hand. 'I truly mean it. I don't wish to know. Villiers?'

'He's different,' she said. 'He has a passion.'

'Chess.'

'Yes. When a person has a passion, his life is different.'

'And have you a passion?' He asked it quietly enough, but the question rang in Harriet's ears.

Had she a passion? Had she some reason

for living that would make a mockery of Benjamin's wish to kill himself? He had killed himself because he wasn't the very best at chess. *That* was a passion, if you wish.

'Not a true passion. And you?'

'I'm lucky,' Jem said, finishing the last of the toast. 'I have several. In fact, I am somewhat burdened with passions. I love creating things, like my rash tower. I love learning about odd things in nature, like squirrel fish. And I am very fond of watching how money moves through markets, which has been useful for my cash box.'

'You are lucky,' she said. 'If one of those things fails to please, you can turn to another.'

'You need to find something, obviously. Harry, you need a passion.'

20

More Buttered Eggs

When Harriet finally made it upstairs, she found Nell sitting on her bed. She suppressed a groan at the sight of her.

Nell leapt to her feet. 'It's working!' she cried.

'What is working?' Harriet said, dropping into a chair. The warm glow of cognac had faded away, leaving her bone-tired.

'Strange is beginning to notice me. I don't know how you're doing it, Harry, but it's working!'

'How can you tell?'

'We met in the corridor, and he grabbed me by the shoulders, looked into my face very seriously, and said, *Isn't your family name Gale?*'

She stopped.

'And then?' Harriet prompted.

'That was it. I leaned toward him a bit, in case he wanted to give me a kiss, but he set off down the corridor again. Still, his interest is definitely piqued. And now I have an idea.'

'What is it?' Harriet asked, smothering a yawn.

'I think I might marry him.'

Harriet couldn't stop a little laugh. 'Really?'

Nell was not the sort to be easily put off. 'Strange needs a wife. Obviously he is deeply attracted to me, and only waiting for the right moment to approach. If I play this correctly, he'll marry me.'

'How will you play it?' Harriet asked.

'I'll refuse to bed him,' Nell said. 'Only the first request, of course. And I need you to change the poem.'

'In what manner?'

'To signify matrimony, of course.'

'I can't see how to do that,' Harriet said dubiously. 'I've been talking about nights and delight. How can I turn that to marriage?'

'You can do it,' Nell said encouragingly. 'Unless you think I should just let him come up with the proposal himself.'

'I think that's a better plan,' Harriet said with some relief. 'The poem is already written. The last couplet will rhyme Nightingale and Nell Gale, obviously.'

'I can't say I think much of that rhyme.'

'I never said I was a poet,' Harriet retorted.

Nell bounded from her chair and bent to give Harriet a kiss. 'You are my knight in shining armour. I'm so grateful to you!' And she was gone.

Harriet stayed where she was, staring at her booted toes.

Benjamin had been such a passionate man that she had faded into his shadow during their years of marriage. It was only when she wore men's breeches that she was able to parry and fence with a person like Strange. Normally someone so beautiful would make her tongue-tied. He would look at her with indifference, and she would mumble and walk away.

It was only in breeches and stockings, with her legs exposed for the whole world to see, that she had courage.

A passion...

Beyond a passion for wearing breeches.

The word slid into her mind with the cool sound of steel. If I were allowed to have any passion I wished, Harriet thought, I would have one for the art of the rapier. Strange had started her lessons in order, he said, to give her a weapon, to make her a man.

It had worked. She felt powerful with that thin, dangerous blade in hand. She felt like the kind of person who should be listened to. Her blood sang with the beauty of matching her opponent's swirling movements with her own. It was a complex sort of mathematical thinking that she understood.

She got up and grabbed her rapier again, exhaustion forgotten. Pushing aside the chair so she had a good space, she began to practise the moves he had taught her. Attack, parry, feint, thrust. Jem's voice sounded in her head. *The straightest path between two points is with your tip, not the side of your blade.* She pretended she had an opponent opposite her, coming in with a swirling keen blade. She practised her move against him over and over and over again. Watching the silver gleam of his blade, seeing it cut the air, bringing her own up to meet it.

Blocking is a move of last resort. Evade the blade.

She practised that, over and over, imagining the angle of the blade, the position of the body, jumping to the side so that his invisible rapier slashed through space rather than her body.

By the time she bent over, clutching a stitch in her side, panting, sweat dripping from her brow, the house was deadly quiet. It had to be the middle of the night.

Yet somewhere she could hear—

Could it be a cat calling? It sounded like a cry. Harriet wiped her face and put down her rapier. Her shirt was a bit damp around the collar.

It was extraordinary how different it was to be a man rather than a woman. She never sweated in her woman's clothes. Now her heart was thumping, and her blood was racing. It made her want to laugh.

Without bothering to pull her boots back on, she opened the door so she could hear the noise more clearly. That was no cat. She started running.

Eugenia, the third floor, the locked door. Harriet flew up the stairs, came to the huge oak door that barred Eugenia's wing from the rest of the house.

She could hear her clearly now, little thumps from her fists beating on the door, and calls drowned by sobs.

'Eugenia!' she called. 'It's Harry. What's the matter?'

There was a rush of words, but she couldn't understand. So she raised her voice to a shriek. 'Is there a fire?'

A little voice said, close to the keyhole. 'There's a fire in my bedchamber.'

'Oh my God,' Harriet said, her head starting to swim. 'Where's the footman? Where is he?'

She heard sobs. 'I don't know where he is. I've been hammering for ages and no one came, and it's cold and dark, and my governess...' She couldn't hear the rest.

'Is there a lot of smoke?' Harriet asked in her sternest voice.

She only heard sobs and something she couldn't understand.

'Eugenia, I need you to listen to me. Put your ear to the keyhole. Is there smoke in the corridor?'

Silence. Then: 'No.'

'Excellent,' Harriet said, her mind racing. 'Now, did you pull the bell cord in your chamber?'

'I forgot,' Eugenia said, her voice catching in a sob. 'I was frightened and I ran out of there and I don't want to go back!'

'I don't want you to,' Harriet said. 'Can you see the fire?'

Eugenia sounded a little puzzled. 'Of course not.'

'Then stay right where you are,' Harriet said. 'Don't move. If the fire comes, stay low. I'll be back in one minute, Eugenia. Will you be all right until then?' She felt the door anxiously. It was chill, without the glow of a fire's warmth. Surely the blaze wouldn't swell into the hall immediately. 'Eugenia! Can you hear me?'

'Yes,' she said. 'But, Harry–'

'Just wait,' Harriet said sharply.

She turned around. She was on the third-floor corridor, and bedchamber doors stretched on either side of her. Without hesitating she pushed open the door closest to her, and felt for the bell cord. She couldn't find it so she ran to the windows and threw open the curtains.

She heard a confused murmur from the bed but didn't even glance that way, just ran back to the door. She could see the cord in the light cast by the moon. It was on the opposite side of the door from where she had thought. She rang it, rang again, rang a third time, as hard as she could.

'What's this all about?' came a male voice from the bed.

She looked over to find a man who looked like a walrus with a nightcap on. 'Fire in the west wing, sir,' she said, hauled on the rope again and ran out into the corridor and back to the door. 'All right, Eugenia?' she said, steadying her voice.

'I don't like it here,' Eugenia said, and the sob in her voice made Harriet's heart stop.

'It's dark and I'm all alone.'

'I'll kill your father,' Harriet said between her teeth.

'I want Papa,' Eugenia said, starting to cry again. 'I want Papa!'

There was no key. Of course, there wouldn't be a key since Jem wanted to make sure that degenerates didn't find their way into the west wing.

'Isn't your Papa's bedchamber in the west wing as well?' Harriet asked.

'He's not he-here,' Eugenia hiccuped. 'I went to his room and he's not here.'

Harriet ran to the top of the stairs and looked frantically down the long flight of steps.

'Don't go!' Eugenia called. 'Don't go anywhere, Harry. Please don't go.'

'I won't,' she said, putting her hand on the thick wood as if she could caress Eugenia's face through it. 'I promise I won't go anywhere.'

'Sing me a song,' said the voice.

Harriet thought madly.

'Do you know any songs? My papa doesn't know a single song. He says it's because he's a man.'

'Well, I know some,' Harriet said. But her mind was blank and all she could think of was the smell of smoke. She knew nothing about children's songs. Finally she thought of one song that her music instructor had drummed into her head, years ago when she was about to make her debut and was expected to perform.

'Drink to me only with thine eyes,' she sang, *'And I will pledge with mine.'*

'What does that mean?' came a sharp little voice. But it sounded less frightened.

'It means that the singer admires the eyes of his beloved, the person he loves.'

'Oh. Do you know any other songs?'

'No.'

'All right, then.'

'Yet leave a kiss but in the cup, and I'll not ask for wine.'

'How do you leave a kiss in a cup?'

'Good question,' Harriet said. But she didn't answer, just kept singing. *'The kiss that from the soul doth rise, requires a draught divine. Yet might I of Jove's nectar sup, I would not change for thine.'*

'Isn't nectar what bees eat?'

'I believe so.'

'I wouldn't trade any of that for a kiss either. What's a draught?'

But Harriet finally heard steps coming up the stairs and jumped to her feet. It was a footman, so tired that his face was white.

'Fire!' Harriet bellowed. 'There's a fire in the west wing and Miss Eugenia is alone in there.'

He stared at her for a second and then wheeled and tore down the stairs.

'Harry?' Eugenia said, through the door.

'Yes, sweetheart.'

'Did you say fire?'

'Don't worry,' Harriet said firmly. 'He's bringing the key and I shall have you out of there in exactly one minute. You're going to be fine, Eugenia. We'll put the fire out, and then we'll find your father and murder him.'

He must be in the wrong bed, she realized. Of course he was. A man like that had a mistress, though she hadn't realized it, with her monumental naïveté. He was snug in a bed, likely with one of the Graces.

'But Harry,' Eugenia was saying, 'the fire is in my room.'

'I know,' she said. 'Don't worry.'

'I'm not worrying about that,' Eugenia said. 'Do you know, Harry, you sound like a girl when you sing?'

Harriet cleared her throat. The whole subterfuge was ridiculous. She opened her mouth, but just then there was the sound of pounding footsteps and a crowd of footmen burst up the last flight of stairs, led by Povy, carrying a great brass key.

'Give it to me!' Harriet demanded.

Povy handed her the key.

She stuck the key in the lock, threw open the door, scooped up the small huddled figure in her arms and threw herself backwards, holding Eugenia.

'Thank God,' Povy was saying. 'Thank–'

His voice died. He was looking down the corridor. There it was, dim in the light of one lamp burning by the door. There wasn't a wisp of smoke. There wasn't even a–

'Eugenia,' Harriet said, putting the girl on her feet.

'Didn't you tell me that there was a fire?'

Eugenia sniffed. 'There was,' she said. 'There's always a fire in my room.'

Doors were opening down the corridor behind her. She could hear little squeaks of dismay.

'A fire,' the walrus gentleman suddenly roared at Harriet's shoulder. 'In the other wing.' He gave the impression of having too many teeth.

There was an answering little shriek from the assembled company in the corridor. Povy jerked his head and a footman ran into the west wing.

Harriet knelt down in front of Eugenia. 'You were crying. You were afraid.'

Eugenia sniffed again and tears welled up in her eyes.

'Was your bedchamber on fire?'

'No,' Eugenia said. 'But I – I woke up alone.'

Harriet looked up at Povy. She felt as if she were learning to breathe all over again. 'Where is the footman who is stationed here? And where is Miss Eugenia's governess or maid? Who sleeps with her?'

'I will certainly inquire in the morning,' Povy said. 'I will inquire as to–'

'You will inquire *now*,' Harriet snapped, standing up. Every inch of her had transmuted from being genial Harry Cope to being a duchess, a woman who had run the duchy estate, not to mention Judge Truder's court, for years. 'I suggest you discover the whereabouts of these people immediately, Povy. And you might–' her tone was withering '–you might wish to inform Lord Strange, if you can find where he bedded himself, what happened tonight.'

Povy pulled himself upright. 'I will do that, sir,' he said. 'Immediately.'

'I shall take Miss Eugenia to my chamber.' She looked down the corridor at the huddled folk. They looked a great deal less glamorous this late at night. 'There is no fire,' she stated. 'Go back to bed, if you please. We are sorry to have disturbed your rest.'

'Tea?' Povy asked rather desperately. 'Buttered eggs?'

'Enough buttered eggs,' Harriet said, at precisely the same moment that Eugenia said, 'Yes, *please*.'

'All right, buttered eggs,' Harriet said. She took Eugenia's hand. 'I'd like to know exactly what frightened you, but let's wait until we've washed your face.'

They went down the stairs in silence. Harriet's heart was still racing. She felt ill, an aftermath of shock and excitement.

They walked into Harriet's chamber and she looked with some disbelief at the chair still pushed to the side, at her boots and rapier.

'I'm sorry you thought there was a fire,' Eugenia said, perching on the edge of the bed. 'I didn't mean to give you that impression.'

'It's not your fault,' Harriet said. 'Did you have a bad dream?'

'Oh no,' Eugenia said. 'That wouldn't bother me. I'm not a baby, you know. I would go back to sleep. It was the rat.'

'*Rat!*'

'Yes,' Eugenia said, nodding. 'It ran across my bed and I woke up and there it was, looking at me. Right in the face. It was all black with a horrid pink tail.'

'It must have been a dream,' Harriet said. 'A rat would never do such a thing. They're afraid of people. You were dreaming.'

'I know the difference between a dream and a rat, Harry. The rat bit me. A dream would never do that.'

'The rat *bit* you? Where?'

'Right here.' She held out her right hand. Sure enough, just above her thumb there were four sharp puncture marks, the skin swelling around them.

'Oh, no,' Harriet breathed. She scooped Eugenia up and ran over to the water basin, poured some water from the pitcher and thrust Eugenia's hand into the water. 'Soap,' she said. 'Soap.' Her heart was thumping again.

'Right there,' Eugenia said, pointing to the ball of soap.

Harriet soaped and soaped.

'He wasn't a very dirty rat,' Eugenia said. 'I mean, he frightened me. And I didn't want to stay in the room with him. But he had a nice white spot on his stomach, as if he had a fancy waistcoat on. He was a clean rat, as rats go.'

Harriet groaned and scrubbed harder. 'How many rats have you seen?'

There was a knock on the door and Harriet swung around, ready to scream at Jem. But apparently they hadn't been able to root him out of whatever bed he was nesting in, because it was Povy with yet more buttered eggs. He set them down on the little table next to the armchair. A footman carried in another armchair.

'Yum!' Eugenia said, slipping her hand out from Harriet's and shaking water drops all over the floor. 'I'm so hungry.'

'I gather Lord Strange is nowhere to be found,' Harriet stated.

Povy bowed. 'I have not had success, Mr Cope.'

'Have you checked every bedchamber?' Her tone was only slightly acid.

He blinked. 'Naturally not. I cannot inconvenience our guests in that manner.'

'Do so,' she snapped.

'Lord Strange will be quite angry,' Povy said.

She fixed him with a look. 'Lord Strange will have other things to worry about. You might wish to inform him that his daughter has been bitten by a rat.'

He stood for a moment as she gave him her best duchess stare. Then he faded backwards, closing the door quietly behind him.

'I don't think Povy likes you, Harry,' Eugenia said, taking a huge bite of buttered eggs.

'I don't like him very much either,' Harriet said. 'If there is a rat in your room, it is Povy's fault.'

'I shouldn't think so,' Eugenia said after a moment. 'Papa told me that all old houses have mice.'

'Mice are one thing. Rats are another.'

'I expect the rat was hungry,' Eugenia said. 'I went to bed without my supper because I was naughty.' She ate another large bite of egg.

'What did you do?'

'I fell into a rage,' Eugenia said. 'I do that, and it is a great fault. My governess was so angry at me that she left.'

'And she didn't come back.'

'Yes, so I didn't get supper. But I knew I

245

wouldn't. I am never supposed to have supper if I am impertinent. And sometimes I just feel impertinent.'

'We all do,' Harriet said, feeling the rage bubbling inside of her. 'I think you should still be given supper.'

'I know the way I ought to behave,' Eugenia explained. 'But I just can't do it. My nanny wanted me to practise my French. But I very much wanted to do my calculations instead. And I couldn't pay attention; I just couldn't. And then I snapped at her.'

'Were you rude?' Harriet asked.

'Frightfully so,' Eugenia said cheerfully, starting on the toast. 'You know, Harry, your hair is standing straight up in parts.'

Harriet put a hand to her head and discovered that her hair had fallen out of the tie at her neck and was curling wildly around her head. 'It's that sort of hair.'

'It makes you look like a girl,' Eugenia observed. 'You would make a very pretty girl.'

Harriet was inordinately pleased by that compliment.

'Are you a girl?' Eugenia asked, with that remarkable straightforwardness employed by children.

Harriet nodded.

'I won't tell anyone,' Eugenia promised. 'I wish I was going to be as pretty as you are. But I'm not. I'm reconciled to it.'

'What on earth are you saying?' Harriet

said. 'You're beautiful!'

'My Papa says that the worst thing you can do is fib to someone just to protect his feelings,' Eugenia said, her grey eyes very earnest. 'My hair is peculiar and I have a big nose.'

'You do have very curly hair,' Harriet agreed. 'So do I. But your nose is not big, and you have lovely eyes.'

'I am used to it,' Eugenia said serenely. 'Papa is very rich, so I shall marry whomever I wish. I shall buy him.'

'Oh,' Harriet said, rather taken aback.

'Are you rich?' Eugenia asked. 'It makes things quite pleasant.'

'Yes,' Harriet said after a moment. 'I suppose I am. I haven't thought about it much.'

'Why not? You could buy yourself a husband, you know. I can tell you how to do it, as Papa told me all about it. You go to London and post how much money you have on a pillar in St Paul's Cathedral. That's a very big place and you can find everything from a horse trainer to a wife there.'

'Oh,' Harriet said. 'Is your father planning to buy himself a wife?'

'He loved my mama very much,' Eugenia said. She was starting to look a little sleepy. 'He didn't buy her, though. She bought him.'

'Why don't you sleep in my bed until your father comes to find you?'

Eugenia stumbled her way to the bed and fell asleep the moment her head touched the pillows.

Harriet stood for a moment and gently touched Eugenia's hair. It hadn't been brushed before bed. Which made sense given that the governess had stormed from the room before supper and hadn't come back, not even to wash Eugenia's face. But shouldn't Jem have visited his daughter to say goodnight?

She swallowed. If life had been kind enough to give her a child...

'I could have a passion for you,' she whispered. If Eugenia were hers, she could have felt as fiercely about her as Benjamin had for chess.

It was a bleak thought, and just made her feel more tired. So she stumbled back to the armchair and sat down. She finally fell asleep thinking of calculations and children.

When she woke again, from a dream in which a very clean, intelligent rat was doing calculations on a scrap of paper, it was dawn. Her neck was stiff from sleeping in a chair. She stumbled to a standing position and then fell into her bed next to Eugenia, fully clothed.

21

Of Rats and Their Ability to Change Their Spots

February 8, 1784

She opened her eyes to find him there, hanging over her, such painful anxiety in his eyes that she forgave him, although his sins were unforgivable.

'Is she badly frightened?' he whispered.

It was the first time that she'd seen the almost physical glow of intelligence and confidence that surrounded Jem Strange diminished. She felt an instant wish to bring it back.

And quelled the emotion by remembering what an ass he was, sleeping God knows where.

'It could have been a fire,' she said sharply, swinging her legs over the side of the bed.

He had no wig. Of course not: he and his mistress likely didn't close their eyes for a moment.

If he ever came to her bed, she wouldn't sleep all night.

'God,' he said, running his hands through

his hair. It sounded like a prayer. Harriet felt another wash of sympathy and choked it back down.

'She would have died,' she said, her voice steely hard, chilled, logical. 'No governess. She'd had no supper. No one washed her face. A rat woke her from sleep and bit her on the hand. I expect he thought she smelled like a buttered crumpet. Did you know that you had rats?'

He wheeled and stared at her, his eyes huge, the shadow of his lashes falling on his cheek. 'Did I know I had rats?' he said, sounding almost dazed. 'No. I suppose I should have known. I thought we had mice. Eugenia told me that she heard scurrying and little squeaks and I told her that old houses have mice.'

'Rat-bite fever,' she said, bringing her worst fear to the surface, but unable to say more than just the name of the disease.

'Which hand was bitten?' He moved to the side of the bed. Eugenia was sleeping in a tangle of dark hair. She was smiling a little, the tips of her lips turned up.

'The right,' Harriet said.

He picked it up. The four puncture wounds were a little swollen. 'God,' he said. Again it sounded like a prayer.

'When a man on my estate died of the fever, it came on a fortnight after the bite. You'll have to watch her.'

'I'm such a bumbling fool. I just thought I was keeping her safe!'

Harriet couldn't think of anything to say.

'You can't imagine what it's like to have a child,' he said, falling into the armchair where she'd slept part of the night. 'When her mother died, I thought I'd put her out to a wet nurse and then send her away to some female relative somewhere. That made sense, didn't it?'

Harriet nodded.

'But then I picked her up and she had this odd face, with all that corkscrew hair going on—' He stopped. 'You look a bit like her. I couldn't send her away. I had the wet nurse here. Later I should have sent her to Sally's aunt, where she'd be safe and with other women, but I couldn't. Idiot!' he cried, clutching his head.

'It's not that terrible,' Harriet said, speaking against every instinct she had. She simply couldn't bear the bleak look on his face.

'I know what I have to do. She must go to live somewhere else, away from this place and its dangers.'

Harriet cleared her throat. 'Couldn't you be less drastic? Why not simply invite people whom you trust to the house so that you can unlock the nursery wing? And get rid of the rats. It seems simple to me.'

'Simple! You don't know how easy death is. It's – it's like a door. A person simply walks through it, and she's lost to you for ever.'

'As it happens, I have lost someone very dear to me,' she said. 'But I did my best to keep him safe.'

'As I am doing!'

'By inviting her for picnics in that leaning tower?' she burst out. 'By filling your house with people whom you yourself don't trust not to be dangerous? By locking her in, and not even bothering to check on her before you go to bed?'

'I didn't go to bed,' he said. His voice grated. 'You're right about everything else.'

'The fact that you didn't go to bed is just part and parcel of the truth of it,' she said. 'Perhaps you *should* send her away. A father who spends the night gallivanting rather than bothering to check on his daughter obviously has no time for her.'

He put his head back in his hands. She felt that alarming sweep of vertigo again, as if she would do anything to make him stop looking so stricken.

'You're right. You're absolutely right.'

'I—'

'I'm a terrible father. My father was no father at all, but I thought I could improve on the model.' He straightened up again and his face shocked her, with such black shadows under his eyes that it looked as if he'd been punched. 'Hubris. I should have known. Men in my family can't be decent parents.'

'Why?' she said sharply. 'And I don't think you're a terrible father. You simply need to be less careless.'

'We're a disreputable bunch. Villiers did you no great service by bringing you here. I'll have to send her away.' His voice was as bleak as midwinter.

Harriet swallowed. 'She loves you,' she said, faintly. 'Don't send her away. Just change your life.'

'I let her be bitten by a rat,' he said, turning around again. 'This house is, metaphorically at least, full of rats. And I, like they, have no idea how to turn into a more civilized version of myself. I am no quiet country squire, Harry Cope.' Then: 'Is it rage that makes your eyes that colour?'

'Anger has no particular colour,' Harriet said. She was trying to work through what he had just said. Could it be that Jem allowed this house party to continue because he considered himself reprehensible? Flawed beyond the ability to change?

'Your eyes are the most peculiar colour,' he said. 'Sometimes they're brown, and sometimes they take on a violet tinge. When you disapprove of something they – what am I saying?'

Harriet was wondering the same thing. What sort of man stayed up all night making love to his mistress and then praised a *man's* eyes?

He turned away again and gently pulled the coverlet from Eugenia.

'Don't you wish to leave your daughter here until she wakes up? I can go to another bedchamber,' Harriet said. 'She's so exhausted.'

'So are you. I'll take her with me,' he said, and scooped Eugenia into his arms. She murmured something and turned her face against his chest. Her long thin legs fell from his arms like a crane's.

'We owe you huge thanks,' he said.

'You owe me nothing.'

'If nothing else, another lesson at the rapier.' His eyes swept around the room, seeing the rapier cast to the side, the rug thrown back.

'I find I love the sport,' Harriet admitted.

'In the afternoon. You have to sleep.'

22

Lay Me Down and Roll Me to a Whore. Or Not.

February 8, 1784

She woke without finding Jem standing over her, for a change. The room was utterly silent except for the song of a bird on the branch outside her window. Then there was a rustle of paper and she raised her head to see Isidore sitting by the fire, reading a book.

She sat up and stretched.

Isidore glanced over and said, 'You will likely shriek when you see your hair; I'm just warning you.'

'I've lived with this hair my whole life. My maid tames it by binding it back when it's wet.'

'It seems you had an exciting night,' Isidore said, putting her book aside. 'Will you please tell me what happened? I've heard of an invasion of rats and a fire and a missing host. It sounds like a bad play. Except for the rat part. That has a dismaying touch of reality to it.'

'There was a rat, in Strange's daughter's bedchamber.'

'Ugh,' Isidore said. 'I can't abide rats. I stayed in an inn that was infested with them. We were eating dinner and then realized that three or four of them were dancing under the table nearby. They weren't in the least afraid of us.'

'I thought there was a fire, but there wasn't. And Lord Strange couldn't be located. He wasn't in his bed.' The words made Harriet's chest feel tight, as if it were filled with small, hard stones.

'I wonder who he's bedding,' Isidore said. 'I suppose he has a mistress. There are a great many women here, you know. I keep encountering women in the ladies' salon whom I never saw before.'

Harriet didn't say anything. It was horrifying to discover that she still wanted Jem, even knowing that he had a lover.

'You are an odd female,' Isidore said rather obscurely, picking up her book again. 'What are you reading?'

'Machiavelli's little book called *The Prince*. It's all about how Italian princes keep their power. My mother says that a distant relative is mentioned in here somewhere, and so I thought I would read it.'

'Was your relative a prince?'

'No, as I understand it, he was an underling with a sideline in poisons,' Isidore said. 'My family is full of people with various talents.'

'My family is full of people of tedious virtue.'

Isidore turned a page in her book, but looked up. 'Tedious virtue?'

'Exactly.'

'Perhaps I am a long-lost relative. I find I am not enjoying this sojourn at Lord Strange's house. Last night Lord Roke said such an astounding thing to me about brandied apricots.'

'What was it?' Harriet asked.

'It was a suggestion of a physical nature,' Isidore said. 'I retreated into the ladies' salon and found myself in conversation with a lady wearing a great quantity of cosmetics. And a swath of gold hair that towered above her shoulders.'

'Everyone's hair towers,' Harriet said moodily. She was not looking forward to returning to the duchy and dressing her hair once more. 'Look at Jemma. She once told me that she had fifteen bows affixed to her hair.'

'Not like this. The lady in question could have had an entire rat's nest in there and no one would have known.'

'A distasteful thought.'

'Do you know what I find odd? Strange doesn't even like most of his own guests, let alone know their names.'

'How can you tell?'

'He and I were circling the room and some of his own guests were forced to introduce themselves. I thought that was appallingly rude.'

'On Strange's part?'

'If he bothers to invite people, shouldn't he take the time to greet them when they arrive?'

'I suppose so.'

'A juggling troupe arrived yesterday. I gather they are attached in some fashion to a theatre he owns in London. This troupe is a group of boisterous lads who have no place in a formal sitting room. They weren't even properly dressed. And yet he was trying to pretend they belonged there.'

'What did they think of the sitting room?'

'They were delighted by the ale,' Isidore said. 'And they complimented him on the bubble-and-squeak served at dinner. I was not offered that dish, to the best of my knowledge.'

'I think it's rather admirable,' Harriet said.

'Why?' Isidore said baldly.

'Because he doesn't decide who his guests should be simply on what kind of family they come from or what position they hold in society.'

'Then why not open a hotel? I myself have never stayed in a hotel, due to my mother-in-law's fixed conviction that ladies don't belong in paying establishments. But I was forcefully reminded of a hotel last night. Or perhaps a brothel, to call a spade a spade. I saw a great deal of glee resulting from Strange's free food, together with a certain thirsty appreciation of the Graces.'

'When would you like to leave?' Harriet asked, knowing precisely where this conversation was heading.

'Do you think tomorrow morning would show an unbecoming eagerness? Everyone at breakfast was cheerfully comparing rat bite stories they knew. I don't want to acquire such intimate knowledge of the animal kingdom.'

'Could we wait another day?' Harriet asked. 'I have engaged to deliver notes to Strange on the behalf of Nell, and I should do the last couplet tomorrow.'

'I am so staid compared to you. You're actually engaged in wooing Strange, albeit for another woman. It sounds Shakespearian.'

'Perhaps I should inform Nell that Strange has a mistress.'

'Do you think that she would care?' There was a snap in Isidore's voice.

'Perhaps not,' Harriet admitted.

'I do not care for the slipshod manner in which these people conduct their social affairs.'

'It's not so different from Jemma,' Harriet said defensively. 'At least, from what we heard of Jemma's *affaires* when she was living in Paris.'

'There's a world of difference. Yes, Jemma had a liaison or two. But she didn't have this careless, pleasure-for-the-sake-of-it attitude. You know, Harriet, I never think much about my husband, Cosway. Why would I? I don't know the man. But now I realize that if he is like Strange I simply won't be able to countenance it.'

'Like Strange?' Harriet's heart thumped. To have a husband like Strange ... with that wild beauty of his, with the way he smiled, with the lean muscles, the laughter in his eyes, the pure brilliance...

'Exactly. Never knowing whose bed he might be in. I suppose Strange will take up Nell on her offer. I gather it is for a night's pleasure and not marriage.' Her tone was scathing.

'Yes,' Harriet said. 'Though she has ambitions to marry him.'

'He'll never marry her. No man would marry a woman who allowed him to bed her.'

'You can't say that for certain,' Harriet protested. 'I know of many ladies whose first child came with suspicious haste.'

'*After* the marriage had been arranged.'

'Not in all cases,' Harriet said.

'Well,' Isidore said, 'as I said, I'm becoming hide-bound. I'm turning into one of those fierce old duchesses who thinks everyone is immoral.' She hunched her shoulders. 'I simply don't enjoy this kind of gathering. I was approached last night–'

'About the brandied apricots?'

'It was the jugglers. They became very drunk at some point. I was sitting at the side of the room with one of the Graces discussing French letters – in which I have no interest, Harriet, I assure you – and a couple of them came over, looked at us and said, *"I am very drunk, lay me down and roll me to a whore."* My companion thought this was remarkably funny. She giggled and giggled.'

'Oh, Isidore, I'm sorry.'

'Then they started comparing us. One of them said I looked like a virgin, and the Grace giggled at that. Then the other laughed and told me to lie down and he would *feeze* me. Do you know what that means, Harriet?'

'He said that he would lie with me tonight, and his friend could have me tomorrow. And do you know, I think the Grace was a little peeved? She wanted those drunken fools to desire her.'

'Oh, Isidore,' Harriet said. 'That's awful! How did you get away?'

'The drunker one grabbed my arm and pulled me to my feet. I was so stupid, I couldn't think of anything to say or do.'

Harriet wound an arm around Isidore's shoulders.

'Luckily he fell down. He just lay there.'

'Where was Strange?'

Isidore shrugged. 'Mr Povy appeared and they swore at him and said he was full of fleas. Povy didn't seem too bothered by this, and he got two footmen to drag them away.'

'All in a day's work,' Harriet said dismally.

'I want to go home,' Isidore stated.

Harriet gave her a hug. 'We'll go tomorrow morning. I'll give Strange the rest of the poem in one fell swoop. You ask Lucille to pack our things, and we'll be off.'

'I'm sorry. I know you're enjoying being a man.'

'It couldn't last for ever.'

It was like everything else in life. Nothing lasted for ever.

23

Of Ladies, Amazons, Whoremongers, and Prickles

Harriet copied out the last quatrain of Nell's poem for Strange and perfumed the stationery before taking her bath. She sat in hot water for a long while, thinking over the last week.

She was changed for ever – but that wasn't

necessarily bad. She couldn't stay a man. But she could change her life. Never again would she sit for two hours while her maid built her hair into a towering set of false curls. She would never wear ruffles again either. A mantua maker could fashion her comfortable clothing, fitted to the body, though made for a woman. She might even bribe Villiers's tailor into making her a gown or two.

And she would continue to learn how to fight with the rapier, even though women never did such a thing.

Finally, and this was crucial, she would like to have a child. A child meant a husband. It meant going to London and attending the balls she loathed.

Surely she could find a man who was interesting and intelligent. The picture in her mind was alarmingly familiar, clever and pale, but she threw that thought away. Strange was part of this bizarre, wonderful little interlude. And that was all.

She pulled on her breeches for the last time, helped Lucille wind strips of cloth around her breasts, pulled a white shirt over her head. Then she walked into the portrait gallery and looked for Eugenia.

'She's not here,' a deep voice said from the corner. Jem was leaning over a glass case. The top was up.

'What are you doing?' she asked, coming

to join him.

'Removing this chess set.'

He was taking them out, one by one, and placing them on top of the cabinet. They were carved little pieces of fantasia, each piece with its own expression.

'Look at the black queen,' Harriet said. 'She looks as angry as my cook when the fish is off.' The black queen had her hands on her hips. She had a fantastic headdress, made of a delicate ball carved with openings, inside of which was another ball, and inside that another.

Jem looked at her, over his shoulder, his dark eyes faintly smiling. 'I hardly know the look on my cook's face at the best of times. Now I think of it, there's a chef down in my kitchens.'

'Well, this is what my cook looks like at the worst of times,' Harriet said. The black queen's lip was curled, and she appeared to have just stamped her foot. 'Why are you removing them?'

'I'm sending them to London,' Jem said. 'I'll give them to the Duchess of Beaumont. She once expressed interest in them.'

'Really? They're so beautiful. My–' Harriet bit back the words. Benjamin would have loved the set, but Mr Cope had no husband, dead or otherwise.

'I'd give them to you, but they're cursed.'

Harriet laughed.

'I bought them from a Moroccan prince visiting London,' Jem said, as if he didn't hear her laugh. 'He told me that anyone who owns the set will never be happy in love. He called it an anger board.'

'That's absurd,' Harriet said.

'I thought so too, but I broke up the set by selling the white queen, just in case,' Jem said. 'And now I've decided to get rid of the whole set. I've seen a lot of queer things and I've learned not to trust my own sense of reality.'

'Given the way your tower stays upright,' Harriet said, 'I believe you.'

All the little pieces were out of the case now. The kings had their fists in the air and seemed to be screaming war cries. The bishops had odd masks pushed up over their heads. The look on their faces would make one shiver. She picked up a pawn, only to find that he was carrying a lance that poked her in the hand.

'I'll leave these for Povy to pack up,' Jem said.

'Don't send them to Jemma,' Harriet said. 'Sell them instead.'

He turned around. 'So you believe in the curse?'

When Jem smiled it did something to her stomach. Her much-vaunted common sense told her to run. Her heart told her to smile back. Maybe even lie back.

The company must be addling her brain. Before long she'd be sending men bits of erotic poetry. Which reminded her, so she pulled the perfumed sheet of paper out of her pocket.

'Just a minute,' Jem said. He was getting ready for their match, pulling off his jacket, rolling his sleeves up muscled arms. All this male beauty was all bound up in the sense of freedom she'd had this week – but that was a mirage, not real life.

She could find a gentleman to marry. Anyone who wanted children, and had a decent personality.

Jem raised an eyebrow when he read the full verse.

My body is but little,
So is the nightingale's
I love to sleep against prickle
So doth the nightingale.
And if you'd like to know my name,
You'll find me wearing a veil–
And nothing else!

'A veil sounds ominously like a proposal of marriage,' he said, tossing the sheet away.

'I believe the word offers a clue to your correspondent's name,' Harriet said.

'I can't imagine who that might be.'

He knew who it was. He knew Nell's last name was Gale. But he was pulling off his

266

boots, not looking up.

'Do you receive many letters of this sort?' she asked.

'No. I fancy the cleverness of it is to your credit. I do receive many propositions, generally more boldly phrased.'

'Why?'

He looked at her, eyebrow raised. 'You may not credit this, Harry, being as you're a prettier man than most of the women out there, but women do find me attractive.'

'I'm not pretty!' Harriet protested.

'Unfortunately, you are,' he said flatly. 'Just look at the effect you had on poor Kitty. And it's not as if she hasn't had many to choose from.'

'She didn't write me any letters.'

The way he looked at her made her feel like a fool and a king at the same time. And a woman, through and through.

You're a man, Harriet told herself. Remember you're a *man*.

'I'm not sure how good Kitty is with her letters,' Jem said. 'If you'd like, I could help her. The way you helped my little nightingale come up with rhyming words.'

Harriet opened her mouth to deny it and then sighed. 'Well, aren't you the least bit tempted? That's the first poetry I've written in years.'

'By the nightingale? No. But I'm shocked by you. Who would have thought you knew words like *prickle?* Or could employ them so ... usefully?'

Harriet felt herself growing a little pink. 'I know all sorts of words.'

'You'll have to give me a vocabulary lesson one of these days,' Jem said dryly. 'I'm sure I could use instruction.'

'Surely your mistress could do that service for you,' Harriet said, before she caught back the words.

His answer came a few heartbeats too late, after she'd had time to think about what a fool she was. 'I don't have one,' he said.

Harriet had her masculinity firmly in grip now. 'Every gentleman has a bit of muslin,' she said. 'You needn't lie to me, Strange.'

'Call me Jem,' he said with emphasis. 'My name is Jem. No mistress. I had one for a while a few years ago, but she wanted to meet Eugenia. That wasn't going to happen.'

'Has Eugenia recovered from last night?' Harriet asked.

'Yes. Her governess has been dismissed, and so has the footman who was supposed to be at her door. Povy discovered they were spending the night together in a knife room, of all places. Are you ready to fence, Mr Cope?'

It seemed to Harriet that Jem's eyes gleamed when he said *Mr Cope*, as if he relished the sound of it, but she said nothing.

Just went to the side of the room and hauled off her boots. For once, it was warm in the gallery when she stripped off her coat.

'Did you see that I had a brazier brought in?' he called to her.

Sure enough, a fat iron-wrought pot sat to the side, radiating heat.

'I'm trying to keep Eugenia warm. But then she decided not to join us.'

'Good,' Harriet said rather absently. She had just realized that she had a blister on her right palm from practising so long the previous night. It hurt to grasp the rapier.

'What's the matter?' Jem said instantly.

'Nothing,' she said, gripping her weapon. '*En garde*, sir.'

He fell into position, that long muscled body such an elegant pleasure to look at that Harriet made herself turn her head.

'*Never* turn your eyes from your opponent,' he said sharply.

Obediently, she looked again. 'I'll show you an *envelopment* today,' he murmured. 'Watch me.'

He held his rapier in his right hand, brought it up in a graceful looping arch, swung it around, slid it under, and lunged forward.

'Again,' she said, memorizing the way his arm came up, the way his other arm flew out in balance, keeping his body in perfect symmetry.

He did it again.

'Like this?' She tried it but knew something was wrong. Her arm went too high and then came down at a sharp angle.

'You're terrifyingly good at this,' he remarked. 'I didn't get that far for hours when I first learned.'

She didn't believe that, but her voice died in her throat. He was behind her again, reaching around her body to show her where to begin the motion, his long muscular arm lying against hers. She swallowed. His body touched hers, like a flash of fire, like a promise forgotten, and her whole body flamed in response.

'Now you try,' he said, coming in front of her again. He looked utterly unmoved. Well, of course he did: he thought he was teaching Harry Cope how to fence! The thought steadied Harriet. At least Jem could have no idea how his touch made her tremble. It was a humiliating secret – but it was a secret.

She tried the move. Tried it again while his eyes watched her. He stopped her, showed her again, demonstrating what she'd done wrong. After twenty minutes, she'd forgotten that his touch made her heart race. She was too possessed by the idea of reproducing the exact movements he was showing her. And twenty minutes after that – she had it.

'Perfect!' he said, his eyes smiling at her.

Just like that, her body turned liquid,

longing, female. Everything about her felt female: soft, curved, luxurious.

'What an odd expression you have on your face,' he murmured. 'You don't mind if I pull off my shirt, do you, Harry? I seem to have become quite heated with all this exercise.'

He had the kind of body that Harriet had only seen on labouring men. Not noblemen. Noblemen had slightly sagging physiques like Benjamin, the bodies of men who spent the evenings drinking copious amounts of brandy and playing chess.

Not Lord Strange.

Not Jem.

He looked as if he belonged in the golden light of a wheat field, swinging a scythe overhead. His chest looked powerful. Useful, as if a woman could throw herself there and–

Useful? Was she losing her mind?

'Harry?' Jem asked with a look of concern. 'Are you all right? Let me see that hand.'

He walked over and unfortunately the effect of his naked chest near hers sucked all the air out of her lungs and Harriet couldn't even protest as he uncurled her fingers. All right, she had a blister. But who would have thought she would be so affected by a muscled male body?

The very thought made her face burn. If she didn't watch out, she'd end up hanging over the rail and watching her own men scythe the fields. Like a hungry old maid.

Unless, a traitorous little voice in the back of her mind said, unless you...

'This is quite a blister you have forming,' Jem said. 'We need to wrap it up and keep it clean.'

'Yes, I'd better go and do that,' she said with relief, skipping back a step. If she was losing her mind and turning into a bawdy widow out of a ballad, she would prefer to do it in the privacy of her bedchamber.

'No need,' he said. He went out to the corridor and bawled, 'Povy, water! Soap!'

'He won't hear you,' Harriet said.

'Of course he will. You sit there and watch me while I show you the next move.'

Watch him? It was like some sort of torture, but not torture that Harriet ever dreamed of. Whatever this emotion was, it wasn't one that belonged to Harriet. Plain, country Harriet didn't feel surges of longing that practically brought her to her knees.

It was humiliating.

It was exhilarating.

Jem swung the rapier above his head like some sort of conquering warrior. She could see him in a Viking's leather breeches, scarred from many a fight on his longboat, his hair blowing in the ocean wind...

Her eyes were glazing over so she pulled herself back to the move he was showing her. It was an impossibly dizzying series of deft movements, darting forward and back.

'Are you watching, Harry?' he shouted at her. He raised those golden shoulders again, and Harriet slowly nodded her head. She was watching.

'Want to try it yourself?' he said, pausing.

'No,' she said, and her voice didn't even sound like her own voice. It sounded lethargic and sweet, like a trickle of honey.

His eyes narrowed and his mouth opened, but thankfully the door opened and Povy bustled in. 'A bowl of water, my lord, and dish of soap. May I enquire as to the injury?'

'Just a blister, Povy,' Strange said. 'I can take care of it myself.'

He was still standing in the middle of the gallery floor, looking as if he didn't even know that God had given him the kind of body that women dream of. Well, not that Harriet had ever dreamed of a man's body, because she hadn't.

She'd dreamed of *love*. Of affection and kisses. Once she'd married Benjamin, those dreams had clarified: she'd started imagining a man who would look interested when she spoke to him, who would show concern if she were ill, or sad, or just plain tired.

But she didn't think about the bed. Well, perhaps only a little bit. If Benjamin won an important game, he was always happy and smiling, and generally he would come to her bed. They would make love, and then he would tell her the entire game, playing the moves out on her breasts as if she were a chess board. Sometimes they wouldn't even finish consummating the act before he started recounting his triumphs.

'His development was slow,' Benjamin would say, rearing over her with a little grunt. 'He couldn't find a good square for his Queen's Bishop' – grunt – 'I made sure his bishop never got to King's Knight Two.' Grunt.

The memory made her feel a great deal cooler.

Jem was a much prettier package than her late husband. He even seemed to listen to her – but he thought she was a man. And if he knew she was a woman, would he be teaching her fencing?

Not likely. Or, as Harry Cope might say, 'Not damned likely.'

Povy left and Jem said, 'Now we'll clean your blister.'

'I can do it by myself,' Harriet said. She washed her hand carefully, with soap, and dried it on the fresh towel Povy had left.

'We can't play our match unless you bind up that hand,' Jem said.

'It hurts at the moment,' she said, shrugging. 'Tomorrow, perhaps.'

'You're not worried about a little blister, are you? All we have to do is bind it up.'

'We don't have any cloth,' she began but

he was circling her, rapier in hand.

'What are you doing?' she asked, not really alarmed. There was a dancing light in his eyes, a deep sense of laughter that made her treacherous heart thump.

'Looking for bandages.'

'I can't imagine–'

Flick! His rapier sang through the air and one of the buttons on her shirt skittered away across the floor.

Her mouth fell open.

Flick!

Harriet put her hands on her hips and gave him a ferocious scowl. 'Just what do you think you're doing? If you're planning on cutting up my shirt, I volunteer yours instead!'

'Can't do that,' he said promptly. 'My shirts are specially woven for me in the Caucasus mountains by three-legged goats.'

'It wouldn't surprise me. Nevertheless, my shirt is not bandage-making material, for all it's made of English linen.'

'Soft, white, easily cut,' he said. 'Why–'

And with one flicker of his rapier, he cut a slash down the front of her shirt.

Quick as she could, Harriet clutched together the two sides. 'How dare you!' she shouted furiously. 'No one unclothes me without my express permission. Are you mad?'

He had two responses to that. First he

threw back his head and laughed. And then, rather more ominously, he turned the key in the lock.

Harriet fell back a step, suddenly remembering that she was Mr Harry Cope, and that apparently Jem had decided to broaden his horizons by – by – she could hardly think. This couldn't be happening. Why, she was certain he was just joking.

Jem prowled towards her, silent in his stockings, a flicker in his eyes telling her that he was still laughing, inside. Apparently this situation made him feel happy.

Harriet waited one more step and then made a break for the door.

She didn't even feel the slash that separated her shirt in the back. She only felt the swish of cool air and then the billowing of her shirt. She shrieked, the enraged shriek of a female Viking and swung around into fighting position, wishing she had her rapier in hand.

'How dare you destroy my clothing!'

But he was laughing at her again. 'You're such a very odd man, Harry.'

'That's none of your business,' she retorted, stepping back one step so that she was almost within reach of the key. 'You, sir, are a wanton reprobate. I know what you're thinking and I assure you that I have no interest in – in being the object of your interest. *You* may wish to broaden your horizons, but I, sir, do not!'

'But Harry,' he said softly, his grey eyes gleaming with something like excitement, something like joy, something that – that she didn't know how to identify. 'I've decided that I truly love men. Shamefully, I never joined those they call mollys. Now I see the error of my ways.'

'You can do whatever you wish, but not with me,' Harriet managed. She had her hand on the key, but she kept her eyes on him, not knowing what would happen to her poor shirt if she turned around once more. As it was she could feel cool air all over her shoulders, though the bandages protected her breasts.

'But I only want you,' Jem said.

'Women are so boring,' he said softly, his thumb rubbing the line of her jaw. She jerked her head away. 'I had no idea how arousing it was to fence with someone ... with you. It made up my mind. I never thought I was that sort of man, but for you, with you, I'm going into new territory.'

'Not with me,' she said through clenched teeth. 'I'm not interested.'

'You won't be the Prince Charming who will lead me into a whole new world?'

'No!' she spat. She had her hand on the key, but there was something in his eyes that made her stop. He had a rapier in his hand and he was menacing her with God knows what kind of obscene behaviour and yet her heart was fluttering like a debutante's at her first compliment.

'Look, I'm dropping my weapon,' Jem said. 'The one that doesn't matter, anyway.'

It happened very fast. He reached out a hand and wrenched.

The English linen failed her, fell into two pieces and off her shoulders as if it were nothing more than a rag.

Heat flashed through her body like a gift.

'What have we here?' he asked, desire making his voice husky. Those long fingers curled around the top layer of her bandage. She let her hand uncurl and her rapier fell to the floor.

'Bandages,' he said quietly. His grey eyes drifted over her, claiming her, knowing her. Suddenly he fell back a step. 'Don't tell me! I'll never get to broaden my horizons now, will I?'

Her mouth fell open and then she saw the lines by his mouth deepen and realized with a giddy wave of pleasure that she, Harriet, knew what Lord Strange was feeling, even if no one else did.

He was laughing.

'When did you find out?' she demanded.

'Mmmmm,' he said. 'I always knew.'

'You didn't!' she said, shivering, trying to ignore the touch of those clever long fingers as he unrolled the cotton from her breasts, around and around. 'It's like the best present I never had,' he murmured.

'When did you find out?' she persisted, trying to stave off nervousness. What if he expected more than she had under those bandages? Someone more endowed?

'I guessed in the stables,' he said, grinning at her. 'And then Villiers confirmed it.'

'Villiers!' she cried. He unwound another circle and then she realized. 'The Latin!'

'Latin,' he agreed. But he didn't sound interested. His eyes were very dark, very intent, as he gently took away the very last winding of bandage.

When Benjamin first saw her breasts, on their wedding night, he said that they were small but that small was just as good as large, and he hoped she agreed. She had agreed, because she was just grateful to discover that he wasn't disappointed. Harriet looked down at herself, trying to see her breasts through Jem's eyes.

They were small. But they were perfectly shaped, like teardrops, Benjamin had said. It made her feel odd even to think of Benjamin, so she banished his name from her mind.

'It must be my birthday indeed,' Jem said softly. And then he reached out for her.

She thought he would take her breasts in his hands and rub them. That was what Benjamin would have done.

But Jem didn't touch her breasts. He pulled her against him and his tongue curled into her mouth at the same moment. Harriet went rigid with surprise. Benjamin had kissed her. Of course he had.

But he had never...

Sensations raced through her body as his tongue played a lazy game with hers. He was tasting her.

'What are you doing?' she managed.

He looked down at her. 'Kissing you.' He took her mouth again, cupping her face in his hands, and she was ready this time and melted toward him. But he licked her lips, as if she were a delicious sweet, savoured her, finally came to her like an old friend, like a cool drink.

That kiss...

The kiss changed Harriet. She could feel it, changing her sinews and her bones, changing the essence of who Harriet was: a sad, tidy little widow from the country. But with that kiss singing in her bones, she wanted to dance. It raced through her blood and made her want to scream.

She kissed him back.

And this time it was he who pulled back, breathing heavily. 'Damn, Harry,' he said, whispering it, his voice a silken rasp in her ears. 'Tell me – not that I'm fooling myself that it will make a damn bit of difference – tell me you're not a virgin.'

She cocked up a corner of her mouth.

He kissed her again, hard, and she could taste his gratitude. She felt it too. It hadn't been fun, being a virgin. In the first few months of marriage, she used to stay at balls and ridottos until she had black circles under her eyes, until Benjamin was tottering with drink. She challenged him to teach her chess and would listen for hours, prompting him to replay master moves with her, all to avoid the bedroom.

Because it hurt.

Even once it did get better, there had never been anything like the fierce desire that burned along her legs now, when Jem hadn't even touched her.

So she pulled his head down to her and threw herself into learning the new sport, the kind of kissing that's done with tongues and wet mouths and intimacy.

'It feels as if we're talking,' she murmured some time later.

'We are,' he said, kissing her sweetly. And then hard, fierce, so that she trembled, felt all female, every inch soft and desirous.

And still he didn't touch her.

'Let me put it this way,' he said. 'If you're not a virgin, Harry, you sure as hell haven't had much experience kissing.'

'I'm a fast learner.' She brushed her lips over his. How dare a man have that full lower lip? It tantalized her.

'So,' he said, 'I just want to understand the rules.'

This was pure Jem.

'Useful knowledge?' she said with a raised eyebrow.

'No back talk from you, young Harry,' he said. 'What is your name, by the way?'

'Harriet.'

She saw the name settle in his mind, grow into a smile. 'I like it,' he said.

'I like Harry better.'

'You're a virgin kisser,' he said, 'but not a virgin otherwise.'

'I kissed before! Many times. Just not – not that kind.'

'That kind?'

She had to show him what kind she meant, and they got distracted. Still he didn't touch her, though, so she brazenly pulled him close and put her body against his. He was speed and muscle and smooth skin. And she felt soft and curvy and delicious.

More so than ever in her life. More so than her wedding day, than her wedding night.

'Harriet,' he gasped.

'Harry to you.' She wiggled against him.

'I'm curious about the amount of experience you've had. That is,' he gasped a little as she managed to rub against something that was making a lump in his breeches. And it wasn't a rolled-up sock either. 'That is, are we talking about once or twice in a hay loft? I'm just wondering–'

He broke off, probably because she was tired of him not touching her and it occurred to her that no one said there was a law that she shouldn't touch *him*. So she cupped him there.

'I was married for years,' she told him, loving the hardness, even through his breeches, the strangled noise he made in his throat, the way his hips arched a little toward her. 'There's *nothing* I don't know about men.'

He froze. 'Still married? Because I am absurdly old-fashioned...'

'You? You, the owner of a house known for its *affaires?*'

'Ridiculous, isn't it?'

'Yes,' she said. 'Luckily, I'm a widow.' She ran her hand down the front of his breeches again.

'Good,' he managed. 'Excellent. I mean, I'm so sorry to hear about your loss.' And with that his hands came down from the door and slid down her back, leaving a trail of fire. 'You are a beautiful woman,' he said. 'I knew you were beautiful. I thought you were the prettiest boy I had ever met. But then when I realized you were a woman I knew you were the most beautiful woman I had ever met.'

It was so ridiculous that Harriet didn't even listen. Besides, he was stroking her,

283

dragging his fingers over her flesh in little circles and movements that made her shiver and gasp. Especially when he finally made his slow way to her breasts. He didn't grab them with endearing, if puppyish, enthusiasm, the kind of caress she was used to.

Instead he stroked them with his fingertips as if she were made out of glass, as if her skin were the most delicate silk in the world. His fingers sang across her skin.

Just like that, she lost the strength in her knees, but his arm was there to hold her up. 'I'm sorry,' he murmured, 'but I have to have a taste.'

'Ah...'

And then she was on the floor, being gently laid backwards on a little pile of discarded clothing: her ruined shirt, their jackets, his shirt. Her breeches were gone; he threw his to the side and came to her. When his mouth touched her breast, it was as sleek and fiery as his fingers.

She moaned, head back, her fingers burrowing into his thick hair and pulling it free from its ribbon.

He paid her no mind, kissing her over and over, lips brushing her bare skin until the caress was too much, until she started feeling as if she might start begging soon, crying.

'It's time,' she gasped, pulling him up.

He laughed down at her. 'Married, and

still so quick to draw?'

She arched backwards and said, 'Please. Jem.'

'How long were you married?' he asked, not touching her.

'Years,' she said impatiently.

'Years with no child?'

And she knew what he was saying. It was only a pulse of sadness: a second that passed. 'No need for a French letter,' she said, making her voice cheerful.

So he came to her, braced above her, hair falling forwards like silk around her face.

Harriet was used to making love: to the dry pull at the beginning that sometimes stung and hurt a little, giving way to a warming friction, to the delight of it. To the way a man's body felt in her arms, hot and slightly sweaty.

This was entirely different.

For one thing...

'I'm not sure about this,' she gasped. 'Wait a minute!'

'Anything for a lady,' he said, leaning down to capture her lips again.

But she raised her neck and peered down between their bodies instead. She was right.

'Um, Jem?'

He managed to capture her in a kiss so fierce and sweet that she almost didn't notice what he was doing with his hips, but her body did.

'Stop,' she ordered. 'Wait!' She was feeling – she wasn't even sure what she was feeling.

She peered down there again. 'What is that?'

'Last time I checked,' Jem said, 'it was my favourite body part. Happiest body part. Dare I say it – my *best* body part.'

'It's–' She shut her mouth. What she was thinking was disloyal. But still ... she peeked again. It had to be twice the size of Benjamin's. 'I'm not sure...'

'It will,' he said. He did a little hip dance that made her gasp. 'Please, can we try?'

'Yes,' she said.

There was no dryness, no pinch, no pain.

He came all the way inside her and then stopped.

'We fit,' she said, rather dazed. 'We fit like puzzle pieces.'

Jem looked a little agonized. 'You're small,' he said. His voice was hoarse.

'I know. My breasts are small too.' She smoothed her hands over his shoulder muscles.

'Believe me,' he gasped. 'It's not a problem.'

And he thrust deeply. This was Harriet's favourite part of making love: this part. It made her feel adored. Important. She wiggled a little, getting herself set to be a proper bed for him, a lifting platform for his work. The man's part seemed like work;

Benjamin's face had always turned a light purple colour. 'I'm ready,' she said.

Jem's face wasn't purple. He was looking down at her, eyebrow raised. 'I'm getting some very strange ideas about your marriage, Harriet.'

He really felt wonderful. She could feel her whole body relaxing, accepting, drawing him in. 'Hmmm,' she said. 'Maybe we could discuss it later?'

His chest was covered with muscles and just a dusting of hair. He was rubbing his lips against her forehead, which meant his chest kept brushing over her nipples.

Jem paused for a moment the way he used to when he was a young buck who couldn't always control himself. There was a problem here.

His lovely Harry may be a widow, but she didn't know how to make love. She looked about as engaged as a mattress, though she was giving him an adorable smile.

It would break his heart if she turned out to be one of the women who couldn't experience pleasure. Back in his wild days, before he had married Sally, he'd found himself in a few beds like that.

He used to do his best – and he knew quite well that his best was about the best there was – and if it didn't work, he gave up, took his own pleasure, thanked his partner warmly, and walked away.

But he didn't want to walk away this time. Harriet's round little body was female in every respect, all cream and silk. He wanted it. He wanted her to writhe in his arms. And damn it, he was going to make sure that happened.

It was painful, but he withdrew from the sweetest, tightest channel he'd had the pleasure to visit.

'What's the matter?' she said, blinking at him.

She wasn't nearly where she needed to be. Not nearly.

He gave her a sleepy smile, the kind an alligator gives its victim before he gobbles him up. 'I decided I'm hungry.'

Harriet looked totally confused. Her husband must have had a member the size of a peapod, and the technique to go along with it.

He reached down and licked her on her cheek, which was as smooth and delicate as the side of a peach. A man! How on earth was he ever so stupid as to think she was a man?

It was shaming. He ran his tongue along the side of her jaw. Harriet had a strong jaw. Maybe that was it. She didn't have a receding jaw like so many ladies did, the kind who sat around and clucked over their embroideries. She had the jaw of a woman who knew her mind, who fought with a sword and did a damn good job, who...

He forgot where that was going because he had reached her lips. They were lush and rose-coloured. He gave himself another two-second lecture about his own stupidity, and then let their kiss turn wild.

Just so she understood from the beginning, he took control of her mouth, and plunged into her, claiming her, naming her, making sure she knew she was a woman. No man. His woman.

The thought was dim in the back of his mind, but he knew it anyway. He hadn't waited eight years, ever since Sally had died, just to find himself another lover.

Whoever Harriet was, his own little widow, she was *his* now.

He pulled back, propped himself on one elbow, and moved to her breast. Claimed it. *Now* she was responding. Her hands started moving restlessly over his shoulder, clutching him, sliding over his chest and down his back. She even touched the curve of his arse but pulled back instantly, as if she'd been stung.

In a flash he knew what the problem was. Harry had done a pretty good job of being a man. But she'd been trained to act like a lady and talk like a lady – and make love like a lady.

Though she wasn't one.

She was an Amazon warrior at the heart, a

woman who would meet a man on her own terms and demand what she wanted.

'Touch me,' he commanded.

'Wh–what?'

Those wide pansy-brown eyes of hers were starting to look a little dazed, which was a good thing. His Harriet thought too much. What she needed was to be shocked.

And he was just the man to do it, Jem thought with a grin.

'Now, Harry,' he said, making his voice into a drawl, 'you know what sort of man I am, don't you?' Just so she had a vague idea, he started rubbing her nipple with his thumb. Like the sweet little angel that she was, her back arched a little.

But that annoying brain of hers was obviously still working, because she opened her eyes again, and said, 'I know what kind of man you want everyone to *think* you are, Jem. I'm not so sure about the real you.'

Obviously she wasn't quite at the mindless stage she needed to be at yet. 'I'm a libertine,' he told her, pulling back so that her body was before him like a delicious meal. Then he bent down and kissed her breast until he could hear soft pants. She liked little bites, so he moved to the other breast and gave it some special treatment. She was twisting under him now.

'Debauched. A whoremonger. A voluptuary,' he told her.

But he underestimated her, because those eyes of hers popped open and she said, 'Nonsense. You've never slept with a whore in your life.'

He opened his mouth and then he realized that given his extreme dislike of exchanges of coin for intimacy, he could hardly win that argument.

Instead he went for the kind of argument he knew best. The kind he knew he could win. 'We voluptuaries want *everything* when we make love,' he said, moving down her body. 'Open your legs, sweetheart.'

She was peering down at him, desire warring with alarm. 'Do you want to – to look at me?'

'Yup. You're so pink and soft down there' – he pushed her legs open – 'I wish you could see what I'm seeing. Sleek little leaves like rose petals. And the sweetest little door that a man ever saw.' In fact, it was getting hard to speak because his body wasn't used to all this wanton talk, and thought action would be a good idea.

Instead he pushed her legs wider and went for the kiss that turned every woman into an Amazon.

Naturally, Harriet was more resistant than some. Sally, for example, had just sighed and said, 'Thank God,' and laid back.

But Harriet had her legs out of his way and was scrambling to her knees before he

291

managed to catch her.

'Now, Harriet,' he said, 'you're simply going to have to go along with my depraved desires. I can't do this otherwise.'

'What?'

'I can't make love to you otherwise,' he said patiently, as his entire body signalled perfect willingness to do whatever was necessary. 'I have to taste you.'

'Nonsense!' she said. 'You were perfectly ready to bed me just a moment ago.'

'Not any more,' he said sadly, rolling over a little so she couldn't see the fact he'd an erection harder than he'd had since being fifteen. He kept up the gentle rub over her nipple, and he could tell she was a breast woman.

'I've never heard of such a thing,' she said suspiciously. But he could see her eyes going soft again.

'You can't expect that making love to me would be the same as to – to that country squire you married,' he said.

She opened her eyes and he knew he'd nailed her husband. Of course he was a country squire. It was the only thing that made sense. She hadn't been sheltered by some overprotective mama – it had been a hidebound country squire instead. Maybe he was one of those gentleman farmers.

'I suppose you have different demands,' she said, looking down her own body dubiously. 'I just don't think–'

'Don't think,' he said. Then he planted himself between her legs and started to give her little bites on her thighs.

Just like that, Harriet started making soft sounds. His erection was pulsing against the floor, begging him, but by then he'd reached her core, his tongue sliding over her sweetness, driving her to arch her hips again and again.

She wasn't being too coherent now, though words kept flying from her lips. 'No', and 'Yes', and 'Jem', and a few things he couldn't understand.

'I love the way you taste,' he told her, just in case she didn't know that by now. 'You taste like sugar and spice and lemon–'

'Lemon soap,' she gasped.

He took another few minutes on a particularly delicate spot, just to punish her for having been rational enough to mention lemon soap.

Then he stopped. 'What did you say?' he asked, keeping his tone innocent.

She raised her head, eyes wild. He knew those eyes and loved them: that was the look of a woman who was about to strike a man.

'Sorry,' he said innocently, 'did I lose track of what I was doing?'

She had her fingers in his hair, and she was panting.

All good.

A few minutes later, he raised his head

again. 'Lemon soap?'

She looked down at him, dazed. 'Please...'

'Please what?' He couldn't help grinning. He let his fingers play a bit, though he knew it wasn't the same. She writhed under him.

'Please,' she said.

'Say *kiss me,*' he commanded. His Amazon needed to put things into words, to own them.

'Please,' she sobbed, 'kiss me, please.' A lady to the end.

So he bent his head again and this time he let his fingers wander everywhere, because those 'No's' just kept being swallowed up by 'Yes's'.

And then he finally took her home.

It took all he had not to slip into her. But he coaxed her and commanded her and ignored her protests until she started curling her toes, and uttering little screams.

And he had her ... she cried again and again, and her sweet body curled towards him, convulsing with pleasure.

'That's it, sweetheart,' he said. 'Go ... go!'

Harriet stared at the ceiling of the picture gallery. It was far away, and seemed to be swinging slightly. It was as if the whole world had tilted a bit on its axis and dropped her off the side.

'Ah.'

Jem was above her again, arms braced. 'Would you mind if we made love now?'

She looked at him, unable to form words.

He nudged his hips towards her. A strangled sound came from her throat. Her knees slid up of their own volition.

'I'll take that as a yes,' he said. And then he stroked forward, hard.

It was unlike anything she'd ever felt before. The pleasure she'd just experienced was in her bones, but it turned instantly into a clinging kind of joyful fire. She lifted her hips towards him without even realizing what she was doing.

'That's it,' Jem said, his voice deep.

He was the most beautiful man in the world to her. She started running her fingers over his cheekbones, over those fierce, intelligent eyes, over his strong jaw. Down to his shoulders, hips, the muscles responsible for her little cascades of shivers.

He thrust again, and like magic, her hips rose to meet him.

And again. 'Do you see now?' he said. His teeth seemed to be clenched. His face didn't look purple, but there were little beads of sweat on his forehead. And his shoulders.

She tasted them – they tasted like salt, clean salt and Jem.

He kept stroking forwards, long and strong, and she couldn't keep her mind on her exploration of his body. She was starting to feel unmoored, as if her whole attention had narrowed to the fire caused by his movements. Long after Benjamin would have collapsed onto her, Jem just kept going, smooth, indomitable, as if he would never stop.

She couldn't breathe. All she could do was follow him into the storm, her fingers clenched on his shoulders, little cries coming from her throat.

'That's it,' he said hoarsely. 'That's it, Harriet.'

Her hands slid from his shoulders, clenched onto his arse. It was smooth under her fingers, muscled and strong. She could feel his body as if it were her own, throbbing, plunging, thrusting deep into her.

She didn't even hear Jem because her world shattered and flew, remade itself into a different place, a place in which a kind of deep pleasure was possible that she had never imagined.

Could never have imagined.

24

The Scandal! A Woman in Breeches

Dinner was an odd affair. Jem wasn't expected to join the company, but he suddenly appeared.

Harriet choked.

Povy flew into a flurry of activity, rushing to get a chair and put it at the head of the table.

'Don't worry so much, Povy,' Jem said. 'I'll slip in next to the Duchess of Cosway. If you don't mind, Mr Cope.'

Harriet hastily moved her chair to the left and allowed Povy to slip a chair between herself and Isidore.

'I'm upsetting our dinner symmetry, I know, and I do apologize for my late arrival,' Jem said, smiling around the table. 'I simply couldn't resist the chance to speak with the duchess.'

To her left, Nell was excitedly pinching Harriet's arm. 'Does he know?' she whispered shrilly into Harriet's ear.

Jem sat down and his leg instantly pressed against hers. Harriet snatched up her napkin. Jem accepted a plate of food and began talking to Isidore, on his right.

Nell pinched Harriet again. 'Did you give him the entire poem? That must be why he came down to supper. He almost never joins the company for supper!'

'I did give him the rest of the poem,' Harriet whispered back.

Nell took a deep breath and clasped her hands together. 'I am going to marry him, you know. I've quite made up my mind.'

Harriet discovered that she no longer felt this wish was as humorous as she had thought a few days ago. 'Really,' she said, a bit coldly.

'He must not be certain who wrote the note. Please, Harry, can you do something?'

'I am no bawd–' she cleared her throat '–that is, I am certainly not a brothel-keeper, Nell. I can't arrange your liaisons.'

'You already have,' Nell said, her eyes sparkling with deep excitement. 'And I won't charge Strange a thing. I never do that.'

Nell had a disconcerting lack of subtlety.

'Can you at least introduce me as the author of the poem?' Nell breathed in her ear.

Harriet turned towards Jem, at the same moment that his hand came down on her leg. She froze. Of course, Nell couldn't see. No one could. He had hooked the table-cloth over his arm.

His fingers ... those fingers ... her skin was instantly on fire. He was smiling at Isidore as he slid his fingers up, towards the crotch of her breeches.

'Harry!' Nell hissed.

Harriet cleared her throat. Jem finished his sentence and turned towards her. 'My dear Mr Cope,' he said. 'I truly apologize for not greeting you.'

Harriet inclined her head. 'It's a pleasure to have you join us, Lord Strange.'

'I always chase pleasure whenever I can,' he said carelessly. 'Now tell me, Mr Cope, what *is* your given name?'

Harriet narrowed her eyes.

'Your first name?' he prompted. 'Only the most hidebound of friends address each other in formalities.'

'I wanted to introduce you to the author of the poetry that has so intrigued and delighted you,' she said, ignoring his question.

'Ah, Miss Gale. What a surprise this is.'

'Nell,' she said, dimpling at him. 'I certainly hope it was not an unpleasant surprise.'

'Not in the least,' he said, giving her one of his most charming smiles. 'I don't suppose that *you* know Mr Cope's given name, do you? He's far too stuffy to share it with all of us.'

Nell had a little frown that indicated she wasn't very interested in his question. 'It's Harry,' she said.

'Harry! Oh no, no, no,' Jem said.

'Why not?' Harriet asked with an edge of unfriendliness. 'It's a perfectly good name.'

'It has no moral tone,' Jem announced. 'None at all. You couldn't be a judge with that name. Nor a bishop either. It would even be difficult for a parish priest. Now if you called yourself Harold, which likely is your true name, it would all be different.'

He paused, but Harriet wasn't going to encourage his silliness and kept silent. Nell leaned forward so that her bodice gaped open and said, 'How would it be different, Lord Strange?'

'Please,' he said, 'you must call me Jem.'

Harriet thought uncharitably that Nell appeared on the edge of a joyful apoplexy.

'Now if young Harry here would adopt his true name, Harold, he would quickly find a high moral tone was issuing from his mouth on all subjects. He could publish his remarks in *Gentleman's Magazine*, for example. They tell the most awful lies about women.'

'Such as?' Harriet asked.

'Apparently some dissolute women have begun shaking hands,' Jem said.

'Goodness,' Nell said. 'I've been guilty of that myself.'

'We don't approve, do we, Harold?' Jem asked.

'My name is Harry, not Harold!' Harriet snapped. 'And I think Miss Nell should shake hands with whomever she pleases.'

'One never knows where those hands might have been,' Jem said, inching his fingers higher.

She should stop him. She should, except the most delicious languor was creeping over her.

Earlier, after a bath, she had decided the whole episode that afternoon was like some sort of lovely dream, as unrepeatable as it was unacceptable.

But now her body was sending her signals that it would be happy to repeat every moment of it.

'I shan't ever shake hands again,' Nell said. 'What else do they say in that magazine, Jem?'

She breathed his name as if they were already in bed together. It rolled off her tongue with visions of bridal finery and wedding nights, Harriet thought sourly.

'The author is practically virulent on the subject of women,' Jem said. 'Imagine. He says that women are carrying pistols.'

'Mrs Grandison put one in her knotting bag and it went off and shot a great hole in her drawing-room carpet,' Nell said. 'So that is true as well.'

'This one must be an exaggeration. The author actually claims that some women have given up the sidesaddle for riding astride and – who could believe this? – are wearing breeches.'

'Breeches look dreadfully uncomfortable,' Nell said. 'I think that claim is rather un-likely, don't you, Harry?'

Harry – or Harriet – couldn't think all that well, as Jem's thumb had taken up a rhythm that was making her feel rather faint. 'I agree,' she managed.

'But breeches are so convenient,' Jem cooed. He was obviously enjoying himself hugely. 'A woman's costume is impossible, what with her panniers, her petticoats, her stays...'

Nell was giggling madly again. 'How well you know us!' she shrilled.

Jem leaned across Harry toward Nell, which allowed him to rub even harder. Harriet gasped and jumped in her seat.

'Don't allow me to bother you, Cope,' Jem said. 'I just want to make a point to Nell. Why do you suppose that women wear all that clothing?'

'To be attractive,' Nell said promptly. She cast a quick look down at her gown in a manner that suggested she felt that *she* looked very attractive indeed.

'But think how attractive they'd be if they merely wore breeches. Just think how a man's eyes would be able to feast on their limbs, on the curve of their – I'm not shocking you, am I, Nell?'

Hardly. Nell's eyes were fixed on him the way a baby chick looks at its mother. It was Harriet who could feel herself turning pinker and pinker.

'You'll have to forgive me,' she said, scrambling backwards and standing up. Jem's hand fell away. Her knees felt a bit weak.

'Have you finished eating?' Jem asked.

'Absolutely,' she said. 'Absolutely finished.' She was babbling, and tried to pull herself together. 'What I mean to say is since I shall accompany the Duchess of Cosway back to London tomorrow, I should probably supervise the packing of my clothing.'

Jem looked at her quickly, and she realized she'd forgotten to tell him.

Nell scrambled into the chair that she had vacated. 'Oh dear Harry,' she cooed, smiling at Harriet. 'I wish you a wonderful journey.'

'Yes, indeed,' Jem said, his eyes rather unfriendly.

'I'm sure we'll see you here again,' Nell said, taking on the role of the mistress of the manor.

'Indeed,' Jem said, and he turned back to Nell with a smile.

25

The Intoxicating Air of Fonthill

Harriet walked up the stairs thinking about three people to whom she had to say farewell: Eugenia, Villiers, and Jem. It was astonishing how differently she felt about Villiers than a mere month ago, when she had hated him with a vengeance. Last year she had talked Jemma into shaming him at chess; she'd spent hours wishing he would die of a loathsome disease. She had been intent on revenge.

And now...

Now he was the only person in the world other than herself who had apparently loved Benjamin. And she didn't hate him any more.

She walked into his room and was happy to find him clothed and sitting up rather than lying down. She walked over and threw herself into the armchair opposite him and stretched out her legs.

'Nicely done,' he said, eyeing her. 'There is a certain lanky freedom about your legs that certainly bespeaks the male. How is it with the young woman who woos you?'

'Unfortunately, I had to disclose a sad fact to her.'

'That you had no equipment to pleasure her with?'

'Precisely.'

'Did she tell everyone you're a woman?'

'In fact, she thinks I'm a eunuch.'

His smile was delighted. 'A eunuch! How in the hell did you supposedly come to that sorry state?'

'We left it vague,' Harriet said, grinning back at him. 'An accident or some such.'

'Some such! Most men spend a good part of their waking hours making sure that no such accident comes near their privates.'

'She wept for me.'

'Slayer of a young lady's heart,' Villiers

said with satisfaction. 'I've loosed a monster on Strange's household.'

'She didn't appear at supper at all,' Harriet reported.

'Pining in her room, unable to eat.'

'I doubt that,' Harriet said, picturing Kitty's abundant flesh. 'But she may have taken consolation elsewhere.'

'Any other exciting events?' he enquired.

'Do you remember that I was wooing Lord Strange on behalf of Nell?'

'With poetry?'

'Exactly. I introduced her as the author of the said poetry and left them together at the table.'

'It will come to nothing. Strange never dabbles,' Villiers said. 'Now I am a dabbler. It took me a few years to understand that though he surrounds himself with beautiful women who could certainly be labelled *loose*, he never takes advantage.'

'How odd,' Harriet said.

'He was wild to a fault after coming down from Oxford,' Villiers said. 'We were there together and I had some adventures of my own, but nothing like Jem. He was in a fair way to getting the title of the worst rakehell yet to grace London; he belonged to every one of the various clubs that delighted in women.'

'Were you also a member of those clubs?' Harriet asked curiously.

'I'm a chess man,' Villiers said, shrugging. 'I find an unadorned array of female breasts tiresome, if you'll forgive my bluntness.'

'I'm sure I would feel the same about the more interesting parts of males. Although,' she added, 'I might gawk for a few nights first.'

He snorted. 'You surprise me. Did you show this side of yourself to Benjamin?'

'Do you think it would've interested him?'

He was silent. 'No. He must have been a dreadful spouse, now I think it over. Do you suppose I shall be as bad?'

'I have no idea.'

'I do wish to marry someday,' Villiers said. 'And foolish though it may seem, I would like it to be a happy marriage. So please, give me some advice.'

'Don't ever recount a chess game to a woman when you're in bed together, no matter how splendidly you performed.'

'My goal in bed is always splendid performance,' Villiers murmured.

Harriet rolled her eyes. 'Pretend that chess is not your life's breath and blood, the reason for living–' She broke off. 'It won't work, you know. Perhaps you could find someone like Jemma, someone who likes chess too. Then the two of you could sit together and mumble, "Bishop to King's Four", when you're too old for other activities.'

'I tried to fascinate Jemma,' he said. 'But

then I found an odd qualm in me about Beaumont, since we were old friends. The end of my sorry tale is that I heroically refused Jemma's advances, then changed my mind and found myself wounded by her brother before I had a chance to impress her with my charms. I intend to make another foray when I am completely well.'

'She'll probably enjoy a recital of chess moves,' Harriet said. 'But if you wish to marry – and I believe that is what you said – you need someone else. Jemma is surprisingly married, more so all the time. But I came to tell you that we leave tomorrow morning. Isidore has discovered she is not nearly as prone to dissolute behaviour as she believed.'

'That is true of many ladies,' Villiers observed. 'Whereas you, on the other hand, look to have happily settled into life as a rake.'

'It's lovely,' Harriet admitted. 'I loathe panniers, powder, wigs, and all the rest of it. I haven't been so happy in years.'

Villiers narrowed his eyes. 'There's something different about you–' He sat up. 'I believe you have succumbed to the intoxicating air of the Strange household. Someone has discovered your true sex.'

She smiled faintly but said nothing, just stood up to leave. She gave him her best bow, the one that ended with a flourish of her right hand.

'Not bad,' Villiers said. And then: 'Are you certain you wish to leave with Isidore? You're quite welcome to stay as my ward, you know. I should be on my feet tomorrow, if all continues well.'

But Harriet was sure. There was nothing real about what had happened at Fonthill, with Jem. It had been deliriously wonderful. It had taught her things about men and women and her body. But her life was at home, not dressed up in breeches.

'This has been a wonderful few days,' she said, meaning it. 'I was able to finally bury Benjamin, if that makes sense.'

He inclined his head. 'And you're quite certain you wish to leave whomever it is?'

'Quite certain,' she said steadily. 'I must return to real life.' She smiled at him. 'I will never dress myself as Mother Goose again.'

There was an answering smile in his eyes.

She left.

Eugenia was building a castle out of pasteboard when Harriet made her way past the footman standing guard and into the nursery. She dropped to the floor next to the castle. It was remarkably good. The walls were cut with fair precision, and glued together. Eugenia had drawn little blocks to represent bricks. And there was a tower and battlements.

'That's wonderful,' Harriet said. 'What comes next? And how's your rat bite?'

Eugenia looked up. 'It's you! I was hoping you would visit. Look what I'm making.'

'A castle,' Harriet said.

'I made the castle before,' Eugenia said impatiently. 'But I'm going to have a battle, so I'm making the soldiers now.'

She was cutting out little men and placing them around the battlements. 'I was going to have the Saracens attack, but I changed my mind.'

'An army of dogs?' Harriet said, seeing what was arranged outside the castle.

'Rats!' Eugenia said proudly. 'See their tails? It's hard to cut out tails. I had to set up a hospital for all the wounded rats because my scissors kept slipping.' Sure enough, there was a careful little pile of mangled rats off to the side.

'How's the bite?' Harriet asked.

Eugenia held out her hand. 'Almost gone, see?'

Sure enough, the puncture wounds looked as if they were healing nicely.

'I have to go home tomorrow morning,' Harriet said. 'I came to say goodbye.'

'My governess went home too. And the footman. People are always going home.' She turned back to the rat she was cutting out and her hair swung before her face.

Harriet gently brushed it back. 'Would you

like to pay me a visit, if your father agrees?'

'I never leave Fonthill,' Eugenia said. 'Papa doesn't really let me out of these rooms, you know.'

'That's not true!' Harriet said. 'He just worries about you.'

'That's why he brings all the actors here, because he doesn't want me to go to London to the theatre,' Eugenia said, still not looking. 'He says someone might steal me, because we have too much money. He won't allow me to visit you.'

'I'll ask him,' Harriet said. 'But you don't really think that your father wants you in your rooms all the time, do you? He merely worries about your safety.'

Eugenia gave her a little crooked smile. 'It's all right. One of the maids said that our house is full of monsters. When I was little, I believed that, but now I don't.'

'Monsters!' Harriet exclaimed. 'Were you afraid?'

'Yes, but now I'm more afraid of rats,' Eugenia said. Her face brightened. 'But Papa is going to get me a puppy – the kind of puppy who can kill a rat! And it can live with me here, in the west wing.'

'I will speak to your father tomorrow morning. I promise you that, Eugenia. There are no monsters in this house. I will ask him to let you run free occasionally. *And* pay me a visit.'

Eugenia hopped to her feet and dropped into a curtsy. 'If you would do that, Harry, I would be tremendously grateful.'

Harriet bowed to her, but the simple kind, with no flourishes. And then she kissed her goodbye.

And finally she gave her a hug.

26

In Which Harriet Joins The Game. Finally.

He caught up with her as she was walking down the corridor, away from Eugenia's room.

'I've been looking everywhere for you,' he said without preface. 'Come on, it's time for the Game to begin.'

'Game? What game?'

'Primero. It's perfect for you.'

Harriet trotted a little to keep up. 'Perfect how? I need to pack.'

He just glanced over his shoulder and said, 'I've been holding the Game almost every night for the last seven years. You're the first woman ever invited.'

Harriet ran a little faster.

She walked into a study on the second

floor to find that there were two tables set up – and Villiers was seated at one of them.

'What a pleasure,' he murmured, as she sat down beside him. He looked at Strange and the corner of his mouth quirked into a smile. 'Sometimes you actually show signs of common sense, Strange.'

Harriet looked around. The room was hung with dark silk. Four or five men stood next to the fire. The room held no furniture other than two small square tables and a number of comfortable chairs.

'It's an honour to be invited to join Strange's Game,' Villiers said to her. 'We all refer to it with a capital G, in case you're wondering. And it's a point of honour to mention the Game to no one except a man who has participated, so I had to leave you in the dark.'

'And where does the honour come in?' Harriet saw that the most interesting of the Cambridge professors was there, and the man who played the lead at the Hyde Park Theatre. He had told her the other night that he hated *Hamlet*, and then explained all its stupidities so that Harriet felt she would never enjoy it again.

'It's famous. Some nights there are four people, and sometimes eight. No one dares complain if they are excluded for a night – or for ever. But I've known people to stay at Fonthill for weeks, longing for just one shot at the Game.'

Harriet looked around again. Povy was handing out small glasses of ruby-coloured liquor. There was a happy buzz in the room. 'Do we play for money?'

'High stakes,' Villiers said. 'Very. Does that bother you?'

'Benjamin always said it was paltry to play for money rather than for love of the game.'

'Cards,' Villiers observed, 'are different from chess.'

'What sort of game is primero?'

'Oh, a game of power. Of bluffing and lying.' He said nothing more. 'Look at this,' he murmured a moment later. 'It seems that your arrival has occasioned some interest.'

She looked up to find a wolfish man staring at her. 'Young Cope, is it?' he barked.

She rose and bowed. 'Indeed, sir, you have the advantage of me.'

'Lord Skipwith.'

'Lord Skipwith,' came Villiers's measured tone, 'is the senior man in Parliament on the question of the Irish Resolutions. You do well to meet him, lad.'

Harriet bowed again. Skipwith eyed her from head to foot, seeming to pause, narrow-eyed, when it came to her legs. Harriet held her breath.

But Skipwith turned away with a snort, and Harriet sat back down.

'He's decided you're a molly,' Villiers said.

313

'What does that mean? I keep hearing the term.'

'A man who prefers to sleep with other men, rather than women. They are sometimes effeminate in their presentation. Skipwith is quite conservative in his thinking.'

Harriet uncrossed her legs and stretched them out in front of her in a careless, manly fashion.

Villiers eyed her. 'You might wish to belch,' he suggested.

'You seem to be enjoying yourself,' Harriet retorted.

'That's the funny thing about coming near death,' Villiers said. 'I am finding life to be a great deal more tolerable.'

'You came to Fonthill to join the Game, didn't you?' Harriet said. It had puzzled her why Villiers had decided to come to Strange's house party. He seemed to have no interest in the various women being offered, nor had he showed any interest in scientific experiment or dramatic productions, the two forms of entertainment.

'One cannot live by chess alone. Ah, there you are, Strange. And Lord Castlemaine. How splendid that you join us. Do you know Mr Cope?'

Harriet stood up and made a leg to Castlemaine. He was a youngish man with a close-clipped beard and a pair of spectacles.

'Castlemaine is one of the top men at the

Exchange,' Villiers said, as Jem sat down.

'The Financial Exchange?' Harriet asked.

Castlemaine had a slow, toothy grin. 'Indeed.'

'I suppose you are up to your neck in this business between the king and the pursers,' Jem said, dropping into a seat.

Castlemaine pursed his lips. 'I'm afraid there will be certain charges made to the crown that His Majesty will not be happy with.'

'In that case, His Majesty must provide the victuals.'

Castlemaine glanced at Jem. 'Is that your word on the subject, Lord Strange?'

'Indeed,' Jem said, passing out cards. 'Now, Cope, in the game of primero each man has two cards. You may look at yours.'

Harriet looked. She had two queens, which struck her as a very nice hand.

'We shall go about the table. Your choice is to pass, in which case you must discard and draw. Stake, by putting some money down, or bid,' Villiers said. 'I, for instance, will bid one hundred pounds with a forty-seven.'

'Who has forty-seven?' Harriet asked, confused.

'No one,' Jem put in. 'Villiers wants you to think that he has it.'

It took a few minutes to catch the rhythm of the game, but quickly thereafter Harriet realized that the bets were much larger than she had understood. For example, Castlemaine staked, and unless she was mistaken, what he put down was the right to provision the pursers. For all England.

Villiers raised an eyebrow, but passed.

Jem bid a huge amount of money against the contract and it was Harriet's turn again. She looked at her hand … those points he was pretending to have. So she could win. But – but provisioning the pursers? She knew nothing of pursers. On the other hand, it was clearly a lucrative contract. And perhaps they would play again.

She won.

'You throw your heart into the game in a reckless fashion, Cope,' said Castlemaine, looking slightly displeased.

Villiers leaned forward. 'Cope is young but not foolhardy, Castlemaine, and there is play to go this evening. Perhaps more importantly, his estate could certainly manage the pursers, many times over. He *is* my relative.'

And so it continued, with laughter and the occasional bawdy insult. From what Harriet could hear of the other table, the play – and the bets – were the same. Large. Powerful.

They took a break between hands and she leaned towards Jem. 'This Game…'

'Centrally important to the governing of England,' he said. 'And so much more interesting than hanging about in Parliament and getting hoarse shouting at each other.'

'But what if someone wins who–'

'Don't worry,' he said. 'I'll take that provisions contract off you next round. Castlemaine knows I mean to have it.'

'Is that legal?' Harriet asked.

Jem looked surprised. 'Why in the bloody hell wouldn't it be? Of course it is.'

Another hand. Harriet was starting to enjoy herself. All the hours she'd spent in Judge Truder's court, reading the eyes of men who were accused of crimes – and the eyes of those doing the accusing – were coming in very handy. She knew when Jem was lying. Within two hands, she knew Castlemaine well enough to guess whether he had a good hand, and though Villiers was tricky, she managed to beat him as well.

But now Villiers was looking tired. 'I'm afraid I'll have to call it a night, gentlemen.'

The provisions contract was still in Harriet's hands, and she'd won four hundred pounds from Castlemaine as well. 'Does the money actually come from you?' she asked

'Discretionary funds from the Crown,' Castlemaine said. 'The king would love to attend the Game himself, but that wouldn't be effective. I'll post back immediately tomorrow morning and tell him the outcome. I admit that he'll likely be surprised to hear that such a young gentleman has taken over the provisions contract, but given what I've seen of your play, I have no doubt but that it's in good hands.'

Harriet thought with a little shudder about the king's reaction to hearing that the Duchess of Berrow now owned the contract. 'Pray do not write to him yet,' she said. 'Why doesn't the king stage his own Game?' she asked.

'Difficult to beat a king resoundingly,' Jem said. 'Especially an irascible one.'

'I never knew there was a Game like this,' Harriet said.

'There's always a Game, behind every government,' Jem said. 'Sometimes it happens in the king's own bedchamber, and sometimes in an anteroom. And sometimes at Fonthill.'

'Often at Fonthill, it seems,' Harriet said.

He bowed, and went to speak to his other guests.

So she left.

27

Leaving the Audience For Ever

Harriet couldn't sleep. Even though she didn't care to admit it to herself, she had thought Jem would come to her bed. She was leaving the next morning... Didn't he want to make love again?

And yet how could she call it making love?

She finally got herself to sleep by making a list of all the wonderful things she would do with Eugenia during her visit, from finding kittens (there were always kittens in the barn), to having tea with the Froibles's little girls, to playing dressing-up with all those Elizabethan gowns in the attic.

Harriet was having a wonderful dream, one of the best of her life. She was on her back, boneless, and Jem was kissing every inch of her. His mouth was open and his tongue was caressing her, soothing her until she craved more, until she was murmuring with...

Until she woke up.

'What are you doing here?' she gasped. Her nightgown was up to her armpits. He was sprawled out next to her, stark naked. 'How did you get into my room?'

He stopped kissing her ribs just long enough to say, 'I walked in.'

It was such a laconic, Jem-like thing to say that her heart thumped. His fingers were trailing up her ankle.

'And now,' Harriet said, with a little squeak–

'I'm going to make love to you.'

'We have to talk. I need to talk to you about Eugenia.'

'No. We need to make love.'

She pushed away his fingers and sat up. 'It's very kind of you, Jem, but I think I would feel more comfortable if you listened to what I said.'

He groaned and his fingers fell from her thighs.

'Eugenia needs the companionship of other little girls,' she told him.

He pulled a pillow over his head.

'I know you loathe the idea,' she said sympathetically. 'But you needn't send her away to school. If you would send her to me for visits now and then, I would invite children to my house. There are very nice girls just down the lane.'

He said something but it was muffled by the pillow. Years of marriage had taught Harriet a great deal about men, however, and she kept talking. If he really had something to say, he would remove the pillow.

'Eugenia thinks you have her locked in her rooms, as if she were some sort of prisoner. One of the maids told her the house was full of monsters.'

The pillow flew to the ground. His eyes were blank. But she couldn't shelter him; she couldn't.

'Apparently she was frightened by the monsters, but now she says she's more frightened by rats.'

'Damn it!' Jem growled, throwing himself off the bed. He walked across the room to the hearth, bent over, and picked up a log.

Harriet watched the lean powerful line of his body. 'She could visit me,' she said. 'There are often kittens in the barn. The family down the road has three little girls. I'll invite them over for tea. She can learn to ride a pony.'

'A tea party? I could...'

Harsh things needed to be said, Harriet felt. It was like lancing a wound. 'Proper little girls couldn't come to Fonthill,' she said flatly. 'Let her visit me, Jem.'

He slammed his palms down on the mantelpiece. 'I've bungled it all, haven't I? I should have sent her away.'

'I suppose you might have done that,' Harriet said cautiously.

'Sally died the night she was born. I couldn't believe it. I didn't believe it for months. Sally was so young – and I'd never even thought about death. It had never occurred to me, *fool* that I was!' His voice was savage.

'But if you had thought about it, what could you have done?'

He swung around, eyes burning. 'Don't you know? You're a widow.'

'No,' she said quietly. 'I've never found there was any way to prepare for death.'

'I could have said goodbye,' he said, his lips a thin line. 'I would have said goodbye. I would have told her that I loved her. I would have...' he broke off.

A tear rolled down Harriet's cheek. 'I'm sure she knew you loved her. She knew.'

'I doubt it. I never told her.'

'You don't need to be told those things,' Harriet said. 'People rarely talk of love.'

'My father arranged the marriage,' Jem said, his mouth twisting. 'I was too much of a hellion, he said. A danger to all of England.'

'Really?' Harriet asked, jumping at the chance to lighten his tone. '*All* of England?'

'The facts of the matter are rather ironic, under the present circumstances,' he said, smiling faintly. 'My father didn't mind when I was raising Cain at Oxford. He wouldn't have cared how many demireps I bedded. He had told me repeatedly, since I was five years old, that a bordello is man's version of paradise.'

'Oh.'

'My personal rebellion,' Jem said broodingly, 'is that I have never paid a woman for her attentions. And I never will.'

Harriet swallowed. 'I suppose that's good,' she ventured.

'As a youngster, I managed to find plenty of women who were happy to do the deed for free, thus following the family tradition while engaging in a little mutiny at the same time. It was only when my father thought I was pursuing men that he got the wind up.'

'Men!' Harriet exclaimed.

'Men.' He shrugged. 'It's not in me. But one of my closest friends from Oxford was of a different sort. He was a true friend. Not my lover, but my father couldn't be bothered to see the difference.'

'Isn't he alive any more?'

He shook his head. 'Killed. No goodbye there either. At any rate, my father thought I was learning to share his proclivities, so he married me off to Sally.'

'What was she like?'

'Funny,' Jem said. 'I resented her, of course. She was tall and slim, and I fancied my father had picked her because she looked like a boy. But she was a woman, all through. She could pull witticisms out of the air.'

Jealousy sometimes masqueraded as hatred. Sometimes it was just hatred, though. Harriet thought she probably hated tall, slim Sally.

'It's been eight years since she died,' he said. 'We had very little time together. But we had amusing times while she was alive.'

'Wonderful,' Harriet said flatly. And then she added: 'I can see why you wished you had said goodbye. I'm sorry that wasn't possible.'

'Did you say goodbye to your husband?'

'No.'

'Was it quite sudden?'

She nodded.

'They came and told me Sally was dead,' Jem said, dropping into a chair. 'And then they brought me Eugenia. She was ugly, of course. She had an odd head because Sally had laboured so long. I thought she looked like some sort of monkey. But she looked at me with her squinty little eyes, and I could see Sally there.'

'That's so sweet,' Harriet said, feeling a lump in her throat.

'Not really,' he said. 'I didn't see Eugenia herself. All I saw was that Sally had left a scrap of herself behind, and that I had to treasure it. So I bought this house and had the west wing secured to keep her safe.'

'But why on earth would you have to worry so much?' Harriet asked. 'I just don't understand...'

'I'm the richest man in England,' Jem said flatly. 'My father had a fair amount, as well. And my sister...'

'What happened to your sister?'

'A man kidnapped her and forced her into a false marriage. My father had him tracked down and killed, of course. Just like that, my sister became a widow.'

'She must have been so distressed by the whole event!' Harriet cried.

'She was distressed long before,' Jem said. But his tone didn't invite any more questions.

'There has to be some way that Eugenia can have more of a childhood,' Harriet said. 'If she visited me, no one would suspect who she was; she would be perfectly safe.'

'I'll think about it,' he said. 'All this talk of visiting ... you haven't left yet, Harriet. You're in my house...' She loved that look in his eye. 'In my bed...'

His hand slid under her and wrapped around her bare bottom; she started to say something but his mouth was on her breast. This was no whispery little caress. His mouth was warm and wet. A tremor went through her body. He sucked harder and whatever Harriet was going to say died on her lips.

He was shaping her buttocks in his hand, pulling her up and towards the pull of his mouth. He made his way down her body with tiny bites, and every touch of his mouth made her shake.

He reared up and she opened her eyes again. There was a wicked spark in his eyes, something that spoke of lust, pure lust.

'I want you. Now.' He ran his thumb over her nipple. 'Do you understand, Harriet?'

'Yes,' she whispered.

He rubbed a little harder. 'I think I'm going to want to make love to you in the morning as well.'

She opened her mouth to say something, but he ran his thumb down between her legs and she started gasping instead.

Eyes still on hers, he put a hand on her breast. 'You're part of this, Harriet. You're not just the audience.'

'I know,' she said, hearing the desire in her own voice. Then she woke up to what he was saying. 'What do you want me to do?' She looked rather wildly at his body. Would he like to be kissed?

He grinned, and the sparks were wild in his eyes. 'For now, lie back and tell me exactly what you feel.'

It took her a while. Harriet had not been raised to tell men what to do. Yet perhaps the fact that she'd practised that particular skill in a court of law lay behind her success: by twenty minutes later, she was very comfortable with the practice indeed. 'Yes,' she found herself saying. 'No, not there – *there!*' And finally she couldn't form words any more, but by then Jem had turned her body into a musical instrument. He knew her strings and chords and melodies...

He knew her song and he loved it.

They took a bath (Harriet made Jem go into the wardrobe and stay there until the footman came and went). The bath was ... interesting.

They sopped up the water with a sheet and crawled, exhausted, into the bed.

Harriet woke to find Jem's large warm body curled around hers. I'm not just the audience, Harriet told herself.

It wasn't a concept she'd ever imagined. She *was* the audience in most of her life: Benjamin's audience for chess, the court's audience for arguments.

Not an audience was a fascinating concept.

She ran her fingers over his muscled chest, through his chest hair, circled his nipple. Jem made a sound in his sleep and rolled onto his back.

A penis, Harriet decided, was an odd thing. Though she loved her breeches, she was just as glad not to have one of those. She slid her hand down his stomach and then touched him. It.

It was smooth and hard, like a piece of marble. It raised questions in her mind. What would it taste like? What would it feel like in her mouth? What would – what did it feel like to Jem?

He was sleeping so peacefully, long lashes resting on his cheek as his chest rose up and down. But the fact was that he kept kissing her in private places. An involuntary shudder ran through her body. Surely he would like it if she did so to him.

She had dared to touch him in the bath, a soapy hand running up and down his shaft. He had thrown his head back and groaned, as if he were in pain. But then he stopped her.

It had been stark desire in his face, the

same sort of tearing, itching lust that made her cry out when he was kissing her, arching her hips, begging him to come to her.

Yes, she had the idea that he might truly like it if she kissed him.

So she did.

He was warmer than marble, and he tasted like soap. Lemon soap, because it had been her bath.

She started experimenting, and forgot he was part of the picture until all of a sudden a male body erupted from the sheet and flipped her over.

For a moment Harriet relaxed, her body welcoming his touch, the fierce look in his eyes, the way his body...

But: 'No!'

Jem froze. Gulped, like a little boy caught with a stolen cake. Harriet started grinning and wiggled her body backwards. 'No.'

'Why not?' His voice sounded rusty. Not smooth and sensual, but desperate. She started laughing, slid out from under him.

'I'm not the audience,' she told him, leaning over, loving his chest and his arms, and the way his muscles defined his stomach. 'Right now, *you* are an audience.'

Then she pushed him down and began deliberately, slowly, powerfully taking over the game. Making it her own. His body ... hers. Owned by knowledge of its every crook and corner.

She turned his body into a musical instrument and finally held him helpless, groaning, begging, his hands clutched in her hair.

'I never lose control,' he said, warning her, reassuring himself, something like that. His teeth were obviously clenched. 'Harriet...'

She ignored him, slid over his body.

And took his control. Threw it away with her kisses, caresses, slow wet love...

No audience, she.

After, he lay there silent.

'Are you all right?' she whispered.

'I've never been so right,' he said, a moment later. He sounded awestruck. She let herself laugh, then tucked herself against his side.

When he rolled over this time, it was in a tangle of limbs that included a silent request, her affirmation, their utterly silent agreement...

Then he was pounding into her and it was as if she felt both him, almost too large, pulsing with life, and herself, soft velvet, wet. She felt his body as much as hers.

He lowered his head and they kissed. He never missed a beat; her body rose to meet his.

It's as if we're not two people any more, Harriet thought blearily. But those delicious heat waves were starting to spread, to grow from her toes, to rock through her body and everything slid away from her but the feeling of his strong body in her arms, the wildness of his tongue, the power of his body.

28

Marriage Proposals are So Romantic... Sometimes.

February 9, 1784

'I have to pack,' Harriet said the next morning, very early. 'And you have to leave this room. Any moment Lucille will enter to help me dress and she'll likely shriek the house down if she sees you.'

'I'm not leaving,' Jem stated.

Harriet had seen that look on a man's face before. It was the look Benjamin had when he had just started a game of chess and she wanted to leave a party and go home. It was the look her father used to get when her mother would demand that he wear jewelled heels.

'And,' Jem added, 'you're not going anywhere either. I'll send the Duchess of Cosway home with six outriders to protect her, if you wish. I'll send the entire household with her.' He rolled over and put a finger on her nose.

'You, Miss Harry, are staying with me.'

Harriet was conscious of a feeling of giddy joy. 'I can't stay here for ever,' she managed. 'There are things I have to do at home.'

'Your country squire is gone. My wife is gone. Neither one of us has any reason to be anywhere other than in this bed. You don't have children, do you?'

'No.'

'Harriet, do you really think that you're simply going to leave and go back to your little estate, wherever it is?'

She blinked at him. 'Of course I do.'

'You're not.'

She couldn't help smiling. 'I appreciate the moments in bed when you forcefully state your opinion, Jem, but this is different. I am not going to stay with you. I shall return to my own estate, and I would be very happy to bring Eugenia with me for a prolonged visit.'

'No.'

'Are you sure?' she said, biting her lip. 'It's not good for her being in that room by herself all the time. Did you see the game she's playing right now?'

'I thought some of the rats were very well fashioned,' he said. 'I do feel guilty because she wasn't adequately bathed before bed. We've had the rat-catcher into the house. He hasn't found any evidence of a rat infestation.'

'What would an infestation mean?'

'That this house held a whole village of them. He thinks the rat that bit Eugenia came in to escape the cold and was frightened. But she'll have one of the terrier puppies from the village to stay with her, just as soon as it's old enough to leave its mother. And no rat will ever enter her room with a terrier there.'

'I don't think my house has rats...'

'I didn't think mine did either!' he said, his voice raising.

'But I know there are little girls living next to me,' she said, pleading. 'Please let her pay a visit, Jem.'

'You don't understand. She's not paying a visit because you aren't leaving.'

Harriet was starting to feel a little exasperated. 'You need to listen to me, Jem. You have just as much trouble being an audience as I do, it seems.' She swung her legs out of bed. 'I wonder where Lucille is.'

'She'll be here within the half-hour, and your reputation will be ruined for ever.' There was a liquid note of satisfaction in his voice.

'Not mine,' Harriet said, 'Mr Cole's.'

'Well, then, my reputation will be ruined for ever,' Jem pointed out, 'since you are Mr Cole. All my father's worst nightmares come true.'

'You'd better leave then.'

'I'm not leaving.'

Harriet sighed and started looking about for her dressing gown.

'When Sally died,' Jem said chattily, 'I suspect that everyone thought that I would go back to my hell-raking ways. I didn't.'

'Because you loved her so much?' Harriet hoped her tone wasn't surly. She didn't feel surly ... much.

'No. I loved her, but loving a dead woman wouldn't necessarily stop a man from sleeping with a lively courtesan.'

This struck Harriet as male logic. 'If you're not leaving,' she said flatly, 'I am. Do not follow me; Isidore is certainly still unclothed.'

And she walked straight through the connecting door.

When he thumped on the door, she took the precaution of locking it.

Isidore stuck her head up from the covers. Her hair was tumbling around her shoulders. 'What's happening?' she asked fuzzily. Then her eyes widened. 'Is there a rat in your room?'

'Not exactly,' Harriet said.

'Harriet, open this door,' Jem bellowed.

Isidore fell backwards. 'Oh, Harriet.'

'You are going to marry me,' Jem bellowed. 'And you know it!'

Harriet choked. 'I am not going to marry you. But thank you for the proposal.'

'Lord Strange just asked you to marry

him,' Isidore said in a faintly awed tone. 'Harriet!'

'And I said no.' Harriet's heart was beating fast. It was the first time a man had asked her to marry him of his own volition. Benjamin's proposal had come about through an arrangement between their fathers.

'Why don't you?' Isidore hissed. 'I don't mean to be mercenary, but in case you've forgotten, he's terribly rich. And charming.'

The door shook as a fist pounded into it again. Jem bellowed: 'Harriet, open this door or I'll break it down.'

Isidore gave a little shriek. 'Open it!'

'Let's see if he can really break it down,' Harriet responded.

The entire door frame shook and there was the groan of splitting wood.

'He can,' Isidore said happily. She was sitting up in bed now. 'This is so exciting. And romantic! I wish my husband would break down the door to fetch me.'

The door shuddered under the next blow. 'I listened to everything you said!' Jem shouted. 'You have little girls next door, and kittens in the barn, and what you're really saying is that you love Eugenia.'

Harriet unlocked the door and swung it open.

He was standing there, hair on end, eyes fierce. 'You'll marry me.'

'No, I won't.'

He narrowed his eyes. 'We'll discuss that later. If you stay, I'll let you take Eugenia for a visit.'

'I can't stay here for ever, in breeches. This won't work for me, Jem. I'm not who you think I am.'

'I know exactly who you are,' he said promptly. 'You're the wife of a country squire, who died in some sort of accident.'

Isidore made a sharp little movement but said nothing.

'My husband didn't die in an accident!' But she didn't want to tell him the truth, either. Benjamin's death was still her secret.

'Call it what you wish,' Jem said. 'He died in his own bed, then.'

It was more or less true, so she nodded.

'You came here on a lark, and now you want to fly back to your tidy little nest. But I'm not going to let you. I've never asked a woman to marry me, ever. Do you realize that?'

'You didn't ask me,' she pointed out. 'You issued an ultimatum. And while I am gratified to think you are having new experiences, I don't mean to marry you.'

Jem, being Jem, instantly switched tactics. 'The real point at issue now is whether you want Eugenia to pay you a visit, or whether you can reconcile it with your conscience to leave her here, locked up in the west wing like a cracked, ageing relative, vulnerable to rats and Lord knows what else.'

'You shouldn't use Eugenia as blackmail,' Harriet said, frowning at him. 'She's your daughter.'

'She's my wild card,' he said. 'You're in a fair way to loving her, Harriet, which is a good thing because when we marry, you'll be her mother.'

'I haven't said I'd marry you!' Harriet said with some exasperation. 'You just won't—'

He grabbed her. You'd think his kiss would have been as aggressive as his talk, not to mention the way he practically beat down the door.

But it wasn't. It was so sweet it melted her heart. His lips were hot on hers, silent, delicate. But she was no fool. It was a diplomatic parley, his kiss. It was a shot over her bow from a pirate ship, a notice that she wasn't going to leave his territory without a fight.

And God help her, her arms went around his neck. He rewarded her by tightening his arms around her. She opened her lips to him like a starving woman, and what he brought her – what he brought her made her heart bloom, made the current in her blood turn to sparks, hot and burning.

'Will you stay?' he asked her a bit later, his voice quiet and steady. 'Please stay, Harriet. I know I'm not very good at listening, but I'm learning to be your audience. I remember everything you've said to me. Please.'

Harriet heard Isidore sigh, behind her. 'I'll stay with you, Harriet,' she said softly.

'All right,' Harriet managed.

His long fingers cupped her cheek. 'I can't let you go.'

'Will you keep me locked in the west wing?' She didn't know where that came from, but it made sense.

He froze for a moment, that long graceful body still. 'I suppose you are giving me a lesson, Harriet mine.'

'Good morning, Lucille!' came a sprightly voice from the bed behind them. 'Just ignore these two.'

Harriet turned, but Jem pulled her back against him. 'You see, Lucille,' he said, bending to kiss Harriet's neck, 'I have discovered your mistress's secret and I must say, it makes me very happy.'

'I'm going to stay a few more days, Lucille,' she said.

'I'll stay as well,' Isidore said promptly.

Lucille looked bewildered. She was carrying a stack of perfectly folded stockings, ready to be packed in Harriet's trunk.

'I can send you home with outriders, Isidore,' Jem said. 'You'll be perfectly safe. I could find a good woman from the village to accompany you.'

But Isidore was giggling. 'No. It's like watching one of my favourite plays.'

'But Your G–' Lucille began and then

337

stopped, catching Harriet's eye.

'I plan to stay in my male clothing, of course,' Harriet said calmly, as if Lucille had said nothing. 'We shall continue our visit for a brief period of time.'

Jem laughed. 'There goes my reputation.'

'All you have to do is act in a normal fashion,' Harriet said, twisting around to look at him.

'How much you have to learn, love.'

'I shall enjoy watching it,' Isidore said, with a honey-like satisfaction in her voice. 'I have a feeling that Lord Strange's reputation is about to dive to a new level of disreputableness, and I shall be here to see it!'

'Nonsense,' Harriet said briskly. 'I shall stay away from Jem when in public, and all he has to do is keep to his normal impolite habit of ignoring his guests. I see nothing in that situation that should threaten his reputation.'

Lucille obviously didn't approve. Harriet saw all sorts of questions trembling on her lips, some stopped by Jem's presence, others by the barriers between maids and duchesses.

'Be off,' she said to Jem, giving him a little push towards the door.

'Look at Harriet's lashes,' Jem said, draping himself in the doorway.

Isidore and Lucille looked in the general

direction of her face.

'Lushly feminine,' he said, his voice deepening. 'I knew she was a woman the moment I saw her.'

'You certainly did not!' Harriet exclaimed.

'No man's lip has such an erotic curve.'

'When did you discover Harriet's sex?' Isidore asked curiously. 'Did you really know from the beginning?'

'Villiers told me,' Jem said. 'Though I guessed before he confirmed it.'

'I'll thank you to take yourself out through the door before you ruin Isidore's reputation,' Harriet said. 'You might find yourself in a duel. Remember, Isidore has a husband to protect her.'

'In a manner of speaking,' Isidore murmured. 'I feel as if I'm learning so much about men and women just from watching the two of you. I may shock my husband if he ever arrives.'

'His arrival is a given,' Harriet pointed out. 'Still, I would prefer that the household doesn't find Lord Strange standing in your doorway, and you in bed. Your husband will arrive only to divorce you.'

Isidore's eyes widened. 'Out!' she said, pointing to the door.

And this time, Jem obeyed, only sticking his head back in to say, 'Fencing at eleven.'

29

Sources of Inspiration

February 10, 1784

'It's very frustrating,' Isidore said, the next morning. 'I would have thought to receive at least an answer from my husband's solicitor by now. I first wrote to everyone with my plans months ago. My mother-in-law should have been able to work her magic by now.'

'Your husband is a dunce,' Harriet said. 'Are you coming to breakfast?'

Isidore was lying on her bed, deliciously gowned in a French negligée, reading a book. 'Absolutely not. I've just started Tacitus's war manuals.'

'Who is Tacitus?'

'Was,' Isidore corrected her. 'A Roman tactician. If I ever need to lead an army into battle, I am entirely prepared.'

'I will keep that in mind,' Harriet promised, and left Isidore happily sipping hot chocolate and wiggling her toes.

Nell was waiting for her outside the breakfast room. Harriet slowed when she saw her, but Nell took her arm and pulled her to the side. 'I just want you to know,' she said, 'that I don't blame you for it.'

'For what?' Harriet asked, confused.

'For taking him away from me,' she said. 'It was as if my eyes opened up the night before last, because after you left the table, he went all drab and silent. And I knew that he had been witty for you, but he couldn't be bothered for me.' Harriet felt a terrible pang of guilt.

'I–'

'I just want to know one thing,' Nell said.

Harriet blinked at her.

'Did you laugh at me? Were the two of you making up that poetry and laughing at me all the time?'

'No!' Harriet cried. 'Absolutely not. I wrote the poetry for you because I thought...' Her voice trailed off.

'You thought he was interested in women,' Nell said. 'I did too, obviously. You know, in a way that makes it easier. I really thought he had a fancy for me. I just want to say that if it had to be someone else, I'm just as glad it's you. Because it's not another woman.' Her eyes flashed. 'I'd have to *kill* you if you were a woman, Harry!'

'Goodness,' Harriet said faintly.

'I've been thinking about it ... this is why no one ever hears of Strange actually being with a woman.'

Harriet gulped.

'I should have known. I mean, I work in the theatre. But I was just blinded by the way he is.'

'I know,' Harriet said, feeling a surge of sympathy.

'We're giving our final performance tonight, and we'll be off to London,' Nell said. 'And do you know, I was talking to Miss Linnet last night. She was the lead at Drury Lane last year, and she had a very nice understanding with a prince. I think a prince would suit me just fine. Don't you think so, Harry?'

'Absolutely,' Harriet said, nodding. 'A prince would love you, Nell.'

After breakfast, Jem crooked a finger, and they ended up in the gallery, fencing. Except the fencing turned into something else. They went to visit Eugenia, and on the way back, Jem suddenly whirled her into a spare bedchamber.

That night at the Game she had won the patent to a curious calculating machine that cast sums. It was very pretty, but not useful, to Harriet's mind. So later she allowed Jem, who thought he could make improvements to it, to win it from her at another kind of game they played at night.

'I want to know exactly when you guessed I was a woman,' she said, sometime near midnight.

'Are you sure you don't want it to be a

secret? I could tell you on your fiftieth birthday. As a surprise.'

She snorted.

'I'll take that as a no,' Jem said. 'This is a bit embarrassing. I didn't know from the very beginning.'

'Obviously.'

'In fact, it was utterly demoralizing, the way I kept looking at you and – well – desiring you, and there you were, a man.'

She laughed.

'You're going to think I'm a fool.'

She just turned her head and looked at him.

'All right, I *am* a fool,' he said with a groan.

'Let's take that as a given and move on,' she suggested, smiling at him.

He started kissing her and they both forgot the subject of conversation.

'I was idiotically slow in discovering your secret,' he said, some time later.

'Let's take that as a given as well,' Harriet said. 'Just when did it first occur to you?'

'The moment I accused you of kissing the stableboy. You were so horrified – and yet you *had* kissed him.'

Harriet snorted. 'Degenerate beast that you are. I remember you suddenly got very cheerful.'

'I was. Do you know, I was actually starting to contemplate the unthinkable?'

She laughed. 'For me?'

'There's something about you that's just ... mine,' he said. 'Male, female ... I'm not so sure it would really have mattered.'

'I'm glad I'm a female. So what exactly did you and Villiers say to each other in Latin?'

He frowned. 'I can hardly remember. I thought up the test. Obviously, if you didn't know Latin, you were a woman. And you didn't. But then Villiers took the opportunity to tell me that if I allowed Kitty anywhere near you in a state of undress he'd take off my head.'

'I love Villiers,' Harriet said with satisfaction.

'Now love me,' Jem said, rolling over.

Days passed like strings on a pearl necklace: luscious, erotic, sweetly spaced, beautiful.

Harriet understood the Strange household now. Its secret revolved around the Game. No wonder Jem rarely came downstairs to meet new guests. It was the Game that mattered, and half the new guests were merely there to provide entertainment for the players.

And now Harriet knew why the Graces stayed so long at Jem's house, though Jem himself showed no interest in their talents. And how sundry other young ladies came by their jewels and the smiles in their eyes.

Sometimes the Game continued until two

or three in the morning. One night Lord Sandwich started a conversation about how to raise three hundred thousand pounds for the use of the Home Secretary. Villiers suggested a poll tax. Jem shook his head. Harriet suggested a wine tax.

'And why is that, young man?' Sandwich said.

'Wine is a luxury,' Harriet said. 'Alcohol is the primary cause of most criminal incidents adjudicated in the family courts.'

'I don't know who you are,' Sandwich grumbled.

'You must study your Collin's more closely,' Villiers said, with a cutting edge to his voice. 'I have very few relatives, Sandwich. I can't afford to have any ignored.'

'It's scurvy few relatives you have on the right side of the blanket,' Sandwich said.

'Young Cope is one of them,' Villiers said, unruffled. 'A wine tax is a fine idea.'

'I don't like it,' a man said, who turned out to be the Lord of the Privy Seal.

But conversation evolved around Sandwich's love of fine claret, and in the end the idea of the wine tax carried. It was a heady sensation. She, Harriet, had influenced the policy of England.

Jem began coming to dinner every night. And luncheon, many days. Some nights he sat beside her, and others he sat at the head of the table and flirted with Isidore.

The heady pleasures of being male – of being able to ride freely, fence, and argue – grew more and more dear to Harriet. She found every conversation interesting. One night she got into an argument with one of the scientists about the recent discovery of a new planet called Uranus. Mr Peddle argued that the head of the Royal Society shouldn't have given Herschel, the man who discovered the planet, a Copley medal.

'What did he really do? The man spends his time stargazing, that's all. And now he's elected a fellow of the Royal Society! For nothing. You know, Sir Giles, down there–' he nodded down the table at a bespectacled professor '–Sir Giles identified the genus of the Purple Swamphen. Now *that's* a good reason to become a Fellow. This man just looks at the sky and notices a star. Bah!'

'But we need to map the night sky,' Harriet said. 'We have to understand our world. And stars are no different than wings on a butterfly, to me.'

'I disagree,' Peddle said. 'When you're older, you'll understand how very different it is to spend a lifetime doing exacting scientific analysis, versus sitting outside of an evening with a glass of wine and waiting for a star to catch your attention!'

Jem elbowed her. 'Turned down as a Fellow of the Society,' he murmured into her ear. 'Migratory habits of the grasshopper not considered an adequate topic. The study took him seven years.'

'Strange was admitted to the Royal Society by right of his experiments on frog's legs,' Peddle said. 'No one can dispute that.'

Harriet raised an eyebrow at Strange. 'Indeed.'

'Changing all sorts of things to do with electricity,' Peddle said, rather vaguely. 'Frogs' legs and metals; you must have read about it.'

'It was five years ago,' Jem said. 'Frogs are well in the past.' He had that secret smile in his eyes. He was proud, but he was pretending it didn't matter.

Harriet turned to Mr Peddle and asked him about how grasshoppers make music.

Later that night Harriet enquired about frogs' legs, but Jem wasn't interested in them any longer. 'They twitch,' he said. 'It was all rather fascinating, but then I wrote up everything I knew. It pointed toward mathematics, so I followed my nose and I never ended up back with frogs.'

Harriet shook her head. 'Aren't you proud of being made a member of the Royal Society?'

He shrugged. 'Proud ... I'm proud of *this*.' And he got out of bed, completely naked. It turned out that what he was proudest of was a bridge. 'Five arch ribs,' Jem said. 'Over one hundred feet across the river.'

'It's beautiful!' Harriet said, tracing the drawing with her finger.

'I couldn't have done it without Darby's cast iron. See, each one is cast in two halves?'

She nodded. She was beginning to understand how the combination of Jem's wildly powerful mind and his inventiveness was changing the world. Literally changing the world.

'What are you most proud of?' he asked her later.

There were no bridges to mention, so she said, 'In the town where we live, the judge is a drunkard. So sometimes, if he was incapable, my husband would sit in the court.'

'Is that legal?'

'It's always been done that way.'

'Aristocrats,' Jem said, amused. 'So the country squire would stride in and save the day, would he?'

Should she tell him? She should ... she should... *I am a duchess.* How hard was that to say aloud? Very hard. The words made her afraid. She couldn't help thinking of Jemma's words – that no one makes love to a duchess without thinking of the rank. The title changed everything.

'I can see Villiers doing that,' Jem said, idly tracing a pattern on her shoulder with one fingertip. 'What happened after your husband died? Did the next squire take over?'

'I did.'

He sat up and his mouth fell open in a very satisfactory manner. But then he snapped it shut and said, 'Of course you did. Of course you did!'

They ended up talking about Loveday Billing and women like her, women whose lives could be changed, perhaps, by a sympathetic voice and two pounds. 'It's amazing what a very small amount of money can do,' Harriet found herself saying. She told him things she'd never told anyone, about her view of the world and its injustices.

But he liked stories of Sibble best, Berrow's most creative criminal. 'He plagues the town,' Harriet said heart-feltedly. 'No one is safe. It's all a game to him.'

Jem laughed and laughed.

One night Jem rose from dinner and announced that the men would retire to take port together. The ladies left for the sitting room with looks of discontent. The men sat around the flickering candlelight for hours, arguing about slavery, tax relief, advances in taxidermy, whatever came to mind. There was no Game that night.

Harriet put her elbows on the table. She refused a cheroot, but drank more port than was good for her. Jem sat at the end of the table, his eyes laughing, not looking at her much.

But then he said something about the

artwork at the ancient Roman site, Pompeii. Apparently every single drawing featured a phallus.

Even more interesting, it became clear that most of the men in the room had given those drawings plenty of study while touring Europe.

'My favourite object from Pompeii is the birdbath,' Jem said lazily. 'Cope, you saw the birdbath, didn't you? When you took the grand tour, I mean?'

He was playing with fire. 'Of course,' Harriet said firmly, dropping her voice a notch. 'It was inspiring.'

Lord Pensickle hooted, and shot her an edgy look. 'Found it inspiring, did you? That's rather revealing.'

'One must assume that *you* found your own inspiration elsewhere,' Villiers said. Harriet loved the fact that she had two champions: her supposed relative, Villiers, and her host.

'The brothel,' Pensickle said promptly. 'Nice-looking frescoes. Nice-looking women. I see nothing particularly interesting about a birdbath that pees water. And no one has equipment of that size.' He gave them a squinty look, and Villiers smiled into his sleeve.

Jem left his seat at the head of the table and sat down next to Harriet. 'After all,' he said, *sotto voce*, 'there are only men here.'

Harriet was so happy she didn't worry about it. Jem poured her port, and laughed at her jokes. When all the men launched into a rousing version of *The Westminster Whore*, he elbowed her until she joined in the chorus. When Lord Oke staggered away from the table and pissed in the corner, Harriet squealed and Jem elbowed her silent.

'I thought there was a chamber pot there,' wailed Oke.

Jem rang for Povy and ushered everyone out of the room so cleaning could commence.

They lay in bed that night and Jem played with drops of forty-year-old burgundy, trailing them across her breasts and licking them clean.

'You haven't said anything about my offer of marriage,' he said, once they had bathed and fallen back into bed.

'What?'

'I asked you to marry me last week,' he said, hair falling over his eyes so she couldn't see them. 'Remember?'

'I – that was a joke. Wasn't it?'

She held her breath, but he said: 'What was your husband like?'

'He liked porridge in the morning.'

'That's not what I meant.'

'He didn't make love the way you do.'

'I know that. Tell me what I don't know.'

'He loved chess. More than anything, he loved chess.'

Jem was silent, but she knew him now, knew that his mind flew directly to the implication that Benjamin didn't love her as much as the game. 'Did he like playing judge?'

'No.' She hesitated. 'I actually started sitting in the shire court before he died. He was so busy.' That was a lie, but it was a wifely lie.

They spent the rest of the night talking about the bonfire on Guy Fawkes' day last that burned down Peter Nicoll's dairy, and how hard it was to apportion blame to a crowd of drunk men. She told him about the theft of six oranges and then they talked again about Loveday Billing and her five husbands.

'Five!' Jem said. 'Loveday was an energetic woman!'

'They kept leaving her,' Harriet said. 'I think she just wanted one, but she couldn't keep one in the house.'

'I wouldn't be able to stop thinking about my other wives,' Jem said. 'It would never work for me.'

'For Loveday, once a husband was in jail, or in Italy, he was gone.'

Jem's hair was over his eyes again. 'It wasn't like that for me, when Sally died. She was *there* still for so long. At the breakfast table, or down in the garden. I kept thinking I would turn a corner and she'd be there.'

'It sounds heartbreaking.' She brushed back his hair.

'Wasn't it like that for you as well?'

'No.'

'So when your husband was gone, you never thought you saw him through a door, forgot he was gone, remembered something you had to tell him?'

How could she tell him what it was like when someone committed suicide? It was the one fact that she lived with, day in, day out, for months, for a year. She never forgot the cause of death long enough to think she saw Benjamin in the garden. The pain was in her bones, in her feet.

'He killed himself.'

She made herself say it, the deepest most self-hating thing she could do, because she couldn't keep it quiet any longer. 'You might want to reconsider your proposal. Quite a few people think that Benjamin was so deeply unhappy because – because of me.'

He gathered her roughly into his arms and held her against his chest and said one word. It was an ancient, Anglo-Saxon word, the kind of violent swear word that never came from his mouth.

The wall she'd built up to keep him out cracked a little. And perhaps there was even a small crack in the wall under that one, the wall she'd put between the world and herself after Benjamin had shot himself.

'Sweetheart,' Jem said huskily. He was kissing her hair, and squeezing her so tightly that her chest hurt.

She stifled a sob because she didn't want to cry, not now. She wanted to hear what he was saying.

He wasn't making a good deal of sense. He kept saying how sweet she was, and then what a total idiot her husband had been. And as for the people who could possibly imply that his suicide had anything to do with her, well, they were idiots too. And worse.

'It wasn't that,' she said, 'that didn't matter so much. It was that he didn't love me enough to stay here.'

'He was a fool,' Jem said roughly. 'You know that, don't you? I can't not speak ill of the dead in this case.'

She nodded. But then: 'Benjamin wasn't a fool. He was just so unhappy that he forgot about me. There wasn't room in his mind for me.'

'There's nothing in my mind but you,' Jem said.

And then he set out to prove it to her, in an entirely satisfactory manner.

30

An Unexpected Marriage

February 19, 1784

Harriet walked into the drawing room un-
prepared to find Isidore glittering like a bird
of paradise. Or a princess. Harriet actually
blinked for a moment, watching her. Isidore
was clinging to Jem as if he were the tree she
was determined to nest in – which was also
strange and unexpected.

She was wearing a gown that fitted her like
a second skin. It was made of a silver material that shimmered every time she moved.
At her waist it revealed soft billowing folds,
transparent, pulled back to show watered
silk of a deep blue colour. It was a dress for
Marie Antoinette. It was a dress for a
princess...

Even more so when Harriet got close
enough to realize that the bodice and skirts
were sewn all over with tiny glittering stones.
Diamonds. And there were diamonds in
Isidore's hair too.

It took her a few minutes actually to reach
Isidore's side; gentlemen were clustered

around her as thickly as salmon swimming upstream, with Jem like a rock in the middle. He met her eyes over Isidore's head and mouthed something, but she couldn't understand.

'My darling Mr Cope,' Isidore cried lavishly. Her eyes were sparkling and yet, to Harriet's eyes, they were wild.

She bowed. 'Your Grace.'

'Do look at this amusing missive I received today,' Isidore said, dropping something into Harriet's hand as she turned away to greet Lord Castlemaine.

Harriet unfurled a wrinkled bit of parchment.

I discover I have some missing property, read the note. Harriet frowned. The words were written in a strong hand, dashed off as if the writer cared little for penmanship. She almost missed the one remaining word. *Tonight.* And then: C, scrawled in the lower right corner.

Harriet gasped. The duke. Isidore's Cosway. Isidore's scheme had worked. He was here, not just here in England but *here.*

She started back towards Isidore, elbowing one of the jugglers sharply in the ribs.

'Mr Cope,' Isidore said again. She was utterly exquisite – and as white as a water lily.

Harriet took her arm and pulled her away from Jem, who looked rather relieved.

Naturally all the men turned to follow, as if Isidore were some sort of rabbit and they the foxes.

Isidore smiled, that lavish erotic smile she had, the one that promised men everything and delivered nothing. Harriet could actually see the man closest to her shiver a little. 'My dear Mr Cope will escort me to – to...'

'We will return, gentlemen,' Harriet said, towing her away.

'I'm not ready,' Isidore cried, the moment they were free of the crowd. 'I've changed my mind, Harriet! I don't want–'

'You've brought the man all the way from the Nile,' Harriet said. 'Of course you want him.'

'I'm not ready,' Isidore said fiercely. 'In my *bed*, Harriet. I'm not ready for that. With a stranger. *Tonight!*'

In truth, it was a daunting prospect, put so bluntly. Isidore came to a halt. 'It's worse because of watching you and–'

Harriet pinched her. 'Hush!'

'You know what I mean...'

And Harriet did. When she was married, if she'd had any idea how much pleasure, joy, a man and woman could have together ... the comparison to her own life would have broken her heart, probably.

'Isidore,' she said, as they went through the door into the entrance hall. 'You must–' But the words died in her throat.

When she had walked into the drawing room a mere two minutes earlier, the great foyer to Fonthill had been populated only by a group of lackadaisical footmen. But now the front door was open, bringing with it a little swirl of snow and darkness.

She heard Povy's measured tones. 'Indeed, Your Grace, it is an unseasonably cold winter.'

And then a deep laugh. 'I'm not used to it, and I'm shivering like a shorn lamb, I assure you.'

Isidore went utterly rigid, and made a little sound of distress. The man was inside now, but his back was to them. He was huge, wrapped in a greatcoat and an enormous fur hat.

'I have to go upstairs,' Isidore breathed.

'Too late,' Harriet said, stopping her. 'He'll see you on the stairs.'

'I can't...'

Harriet gave her the frown she gave repeat visitors to her courtroom. 'Yes, you can.'

It was as if everything was happening in slow motion. The greatcoat was gone, and the hat was gone. Harriet had hardly time to see a great tumble of inky black hair, un-powdered and not even tied back, before he turned.

Her first thought was that he couldn't be English. She'd never seen an Englishman that colour – a sort of gorgeous mahogany.

He wore a jacket that Villiers would envy, made of pale blue but he didn't have it buttoned in the front, as was proper. She could see brown skin, right down below his throat. Where was his cravat? He wore no waistcoat. Long white cuffs tumbled over his hands, but rather than have them caught at the wrist by a pearl button, he wore them open. He was half dressed.

There was a moment of utter silence in the anteroom. The duke was looking only at Isidore.

Just as Harriet was about to say something – some sort of introduction! – he swept into an extraordinarily deep bow. Her eyes fixed on his face, Isidore sank into a deep curtsy. Still without saying a word, she held out her hand.

'My duchess, I presume,' he said, carrying the hand up to his lips. His voice was dark and foreign, like that of a man used to speaking foreign languages.

Harriet felt as if she were watching a play. How did Cosway know that he was facing his wife? And didn't he wish to retire to his chamber before he greeted Isidore? His face wasn't clean-shaven. Gentlemen – dukes! – never had stubble on their faces, to the best of her knowledge. That's what valets were for: to make sure that dukes pinned their cuffs, wore waistcoats, buttoned their coats...

No valet could tame the wildness of Cosway's face.

'I'd like to introduce a dear friend of mine, Mr Cope,' Isidore said.

Harriet bowed, and the moment she straightened she saw that he knew precisely what she was. Instantly.

His eyes were dancing with amusement.

'Mr Cope,' he said, softly. 'Had I known that my wife's friends were of this ... calibre, I would not have rushed across all England to rescue her.'

'I need no rescuing,' Isidore said coolly, just as if she hadn't planned precisely that.

'I had no doubt,' he said. 'Alack and alas, my mother is of a nervous disposition. I do believe she would have swum the Nile and bearded the crocodiles herself in order to bring me home.'

'Would Your Grace like to refresh yourself before joining the company?' Povy asked. Harriet had forgotten he was there.

The duke shook his head. 'The duchess and I leave in the morning, and I positively long to see the decadent pleasures offered by Fonthill. I've just come from a rather extraordinary wedding given for the Princess Ayabdar and yet from my mother's descriptions of Fonthill I expect to find myself shocked to the bone by Lord Strange's bacchanalian scene. I confess myself all anticipation.'

'I fear Your Grace will be sorely disappointed,' Isidore said. 'As shall I, if you are forced to leave in the morning. I myself do not plan to leave for several days.'

He took her hand in his again and raised it to his lips, smiling. Harriet almost fell back a step.

'Ah, but sweetheart,' he said, his voice too low to be heard by Povy and the footman, 'I am all eagerness for our wedding.'

'We are *wed*,' Isidore said sharply. 'You may have ignored that fact for years, but I assure you it is true.'

He shook his head. 'We signed some papers, or at least I did. I'm not sure you were old enough to know your letters. As I said, I've come from a proper wedding. It lasted four days, or perhaps longer; it was hard to keep track of the days or the pleasures.'

'Indeed,' Isidore said. 'How fortunate for you.'

'I spent the time thinking of you. And planning our wedding.'

She frowned.

'We are going to be married,' he told her. 'As befits a princess – or in this case, a duchess who waited far too long for her duke to kiss her into life. Surely you feel as if you have been sleeping one hundred years?'

Isidore was silent. Harriet hardly took a breath, so fascinated was she by the charged sexuality that flared between them.

'I have never considered myself in need of a prince,' Isidore said, finally.

'I shall have to ... persuade you of your need,' the duke said. And he smiled. He was by no means classically handsome, in an English sort of way. He had a big nose, and all that tumbling black hair, and that golden-dark skin. But Harriet realized her mouth had fallen open anyway.

'A wedding,' the duke said. 'The kind of wedding celebrated in Gondar, from which I just returned. My mother is preparing the estate and invitations will be delivered all over England. We may have to send a special invitation to Mr Cope, of course. For some reason I think my mother may not know his name.' His eyes slid to Harriet, and she realized with a start that she was simply standing there like a dunce.

'I would be honoured,' she said weakly.

'You'll forgive me for not taking your arm? Under the circumstances?' There was a devil laughing in those eyes.

Harriet fell back and bowed, and Cosway swept Isidore through the door into the drawing room. There was a moment of dead silence and then a clatter of tongues that she heard even out in the antechamber.

31

In Which Lord Strange's Reputation Takes a Strange Turn

February 20, 1784

The next night it started all over again – a table of half-drunk Oxford professors together with some odd and highly intelligent actors, Lord Pensickle and Mr Nashe. Villiers came to dinner and stayed for port. Everyone talked of little other than the Duke of Cosway's return, and the way he had swept his duchess away to London after one evening at Fonthill.

'I suddenly realized something,' Harriet said to Jem. He was sprawled next to her in a chair. Now they had a routine. Once the ladies left he moved down the table and sat beside her without a word. It allowed him to do naughty things with his hands.

They felt happy sitting together. They never said it, but silence didn't make it any the less true.

'What?' he asked lazily. He was watching Mr Nashe play chess with Lord Pensickle. Pensickle was a little the worse for port, and kept picking up the wrong pieces and galloping them across the board.

'The only dissolute persons in your house are women.'

'Oh, I wouldn't say that,' Jem said. 'Look at Villiers, for instance.'

'No, I mean it,' Harriet said. She looked around the room. There were perhaps twenty men around the table. Down to the left, two of the Oxford professors were chattering about a recent visit to the Duchess of Portland's collection at Bulstrode Park. Sir Joseph Banks, the President of the Royal Society, was talking about something called a Florilegium, and the need to raise funds for the project. His audience looked unconvinced. Nashe and Pensickle were playing chess.

Sullenly congregating in the drawing room (the ladies had made it clear that they did not approve of the new custom of separate evenings), were Nell, and the Graces, Sophia Grafton and the rest.

'Your house gains its reputation from the women you invite.'

'That is true of any house,' Jem said, with a flash of anger in his eyes. 'It's one of life's great unfairnesses. Mr Avery, for example, maintains Mrs Mahon in royal style. She's doubtless out in the drawing room right now boasting about the little silver boxes he's bought her. But is his reputation any the worse for it? No.'

'It's grotesquely unfair.'

'The world is unfair,' Jem said. 'Reputation is ephemeral and unfair. Why should the Duchess of Beaumont be famed for her *liaisons* and yet Mrs Mahon be an outcast?'

'Jemma married before she had an *affaire*,' Harriet said, jumping to the defense of her childhood friend. 'And then she didn't stray until she found her husband on the desk with his mistress.'

'A bitter moment, I expect,' Jem said.

'Very!' Harriet said. 'Did you maintain a mistress while married to Sally?'

'No. Sally was enough to keep me busy.'

Harriet spared a moment for a pulse of dislike for tall, slim, busy Sally.

'What are you two talking about?' Lord Pensickle said, raising his head from the chess board.

'Checkmate,' his opponent said.

Pensickle gave a little snort of disapproval and pushed away the board. 'Every time I look across the table, you have your heads together.'

Harriet gave him a cool look. 'We were actually discussing mistresses.'

'Don't tell me you have one!' Pensickle said, with a guffaw. 'I wouldn't have thought your instrument was old enough to function.'

Harriet stiffened.

But before she could answer, Villiers cut in. 'Now that is surely a matter of the pot calling the kettle black, Pensickle. Now according to the laments so widely distributed by your former mistress, you have some difficulty there yourself. All due to age, no doubt!'

'I must admit,' Jem said, 'I found the poem published in *Gentleman's Magazine* rather amusing myself. Though undoubtedly it had nothing to do with you, Pensickle. You have to admit, all those jokes about the pen that would cast no ink were very diverting.'

Pensickle's eyes narrowed. 'My pen has more than enough ink,' he flashed. 'And at least I'm dippin' in the right kind of inkwell, if you don't mind the presumption, Strange.'

For a moment Harriet thought that Jem would leap across the table. There was a sudden calmness around his large body, but he just grinned.

'Villiers and I are educating Harry about the responsibilities of manhood, including lessons in proper treatment of the fair sex. Perhaps we'll take you on next, though I doubt things would go as well. Harry, after all, has found himself in the favour of one of the Graces.'

That was true enough. Kitty was so saddened by the terrible accident that had befallen her darling Mr Cope that she sought

Harriet out at every possibility, hanging on her elbow and smiling sadly at her.

'It ain't Harry's inclinations that I'd question,' Pensickle said, pushing back from the table. 'I think I'll be going in the morning, Strange. I don't mind the house being a little *strange*, but we all have our limits.'

'By all means,' Jem said, smiling at him. 'Why don't I ask my butler to help you now? No need to wait until morning. Just think. You might get lured into another game of chess and lose, or worse – one of the young ladies in the other room might request the use of your pen.'

Pensickle knocked over a chair on his way out of the door.

Harriet felt a little sick. The table had gone stone silent, naturally, but now eased back into talk as if nothing had happened. She felt the nearness of Jem's leg, even though he had turned away and was chatting with the man on his right.

She turned to her left. Frederick Sanders gave her a queasy little smile and his eyes skittered away from hers. He was a middle-aged man with a cheerful red face and a parcel of coal mines, here to ask Jem to invest in coal.

As a matter of fact, Harriet had talked Jem out of the investment, based on the fact that the mines were dangerous for workers, but Sanders didn't know that. He'd been perfectly friendly to her up to this moment.

Then Villiers, across the table, leaned forward. 'Want to go for a walk, Harry?' he said, rising.

She gratefully rose as well. And left without saying goodbye to Jem, though what good that would do from a gossip point of view, she didn't know.

'I need to start walking, or so my valet tells me,' Villiers said with a little sigh.

'You look much better than you did a few weeks ago,' Harriet said. All the footmen were standing around the corridor. How much could they have heard of Pensickle's fury? Would he say something to his valet?

'I mend,' Villiers said. Povy bundled the duke into an enormous greatcoat, and Harriet shrugged into her own.

They walked out into the night. There was just a thin fall of powdery snow in the air. It came onto their hats, not seeming to fall as much as to appear suddenly with its chill greeting on lips and noses.

The windows of Fonthill spilled dusky orange-red light onto the snow. They walked silently to the opening of the great gates, and then Villiers paused, leaning against one of the pillars. 'Damn, but I'm a husk of a man,' he said, a trace of an apology in his voice.

'So am I,' Harriet said. 'Have I ruined his reputation for ever, Villiers?'

'It would take an idiot not to know you were bedding each other.'

'I don't see why!' Harriet cried, frustrated. 'He rarely whispers anything to me, or touches me.'

'It's in your eyes when you look at each other,' Villiers said. 'But they're a strange crew at Fonthill. Most of the women are here for the free bed and board, and they'll not let a little thing like choice of bedfellow stand in their way of free champagne.'

'That's – do you really think so?'

'They are hardly acquaintances of Strange's,' Villiers said. 'Sometimes he doesn't even know the women's names. I have no idea why he opens his house to every light-skirt who makes her way here, but he does.'

'Never to actual night-walkers,' Harriet objected.

'I suppose he has some standards,' Villier said wryly. 'The majority of them are fen ing for themselves – either as actresses c sole practitioners, if I might emplo term.'

'That makes them more interesti many ladies,' Harriet said.

'Exactly. If we're discussing n said, 'then yes, some of them There's the Game, of course think men chiefly like this ligent conversation, in c

cheerfully loose women.'

'Is that why you're here?'

'I'm not yet in a position to avail myself of female company,' he said, still leaning against the pillar.

Harriet threw back her head to look at the stars. Somewhere up there was the new planet, except it wasn't truly new. It was just new to them. The stars looked cold and very far away.

'Should I leave?' she asked. And she held her breath, because she didn't want to leave. She wanted – oh, so greedily – more days like these, full of vigorous exercise, vigorous argument, vigorous love-making.

'They'll discover your true gender soon,' Villiers said. 'And if they discover that you're a duchess, Harriet, then the fat is truly in the fire. It would be disastrous – not for Strange. For you.'

'But it's just a joke,' Harriet said feebly.

'I saw it that way. If it had been nothing more than a short masquerade, we could have carried it off. But I thought we were talking about a few days. Now it's a matter of time. The way Strange looks at you...'

'Damn,' Harriet said, heartfelt.

'You haven't told him who you really are, are you?'

Harriet shook her head.

'He won't take it well. And, Harriet, the longer you conceal your rank, the more he

370

will see your revelation as a betrayal.'

'I tried to tell him,' Harriet said, near tears. 'I couldn't... I'll leave.'

'After telling him the truth, I hope. He deserves that.' Villiers had a touch of a smile on his mouth. 'How lucky you are.'

'To be so close to complete loss of reputation?' she asked, startled.

'I would pay for such intoxication. I might give up the final shards of my reputation for it. Give yourself one final day to savour. Leave the following day.'

And he began to walk back to the house, favouring his right side, moving slowly.

But Harriet stayed behind, staring at Villiers's back through the thin, icy veil of snow. She couldn't squash the hope in her breast.

Surely, surely, Jem would not be able to see her go. They separated during the days, of course. She read in her bedchamber or played with Eugenia.

But when they came together it was with such joy, such intellectual curiosity, such – physical pleasure. Surely he would not just watch her go.

The idea of waving goodbye was as bitter as the faraway stars.

He would tell her that it didn't matter who she was. He would follow her. Eugenia and he would follow. He would say goodbye to his guests, and come to her estate.

Surely he would.

32

Double the Pleasure

February 21, 1784

The next day was clear and cold.

'Riding?' Jem asked, glancing at her when she entered the breakfast room.

She gave him a slight nod, and then turned to greet Kitty. Kitty dragged her over to the side of the room. 'I heard all about it!' she said in a thrilled whisper. 'I know you must be feeling terrible, but don't. I told *everyone* that you weren't a molly.'

'Oh. Good,' Harriet said.

'You know what a molly is, don't you?' Kitty asked.

'Yes, of course.'

'It's what that foolish Pensickle thought you were. As if he's one to talk! We *all* know about him. Anyway, I told them–' she leaned over and whispered in Harriet's ear.

'Really?' Harriet exclaimed. 'You–'

'Not only that but that you made myself *and* Roslyn happy. Roslyn thinks you are perfectly adorable, and she's so sad about what happened to you. She's telling everyone about last night. Roslyn is the muse of lyric poetry, you know, and she can really tell a lively story.' Kitty giggled.

'On the same night?'

'Together! You had been only mine, but last night you were so mortified by those horrid untruths that you surpassed yourself!'

'Goodness,' Harriet said, rather faintly.

Kitty kissed her cheek. 'I'm your friend, Harry, for ever. Don't forget that.' She went back to her seat.

Jem rose to leave, but paused for a second. The memory of what had happened in the middle of the night flashed between them, and Harriet felt herself turning pink. In the dark they had pleasured each other until they were breathless, begging, taking turns with sweet torment...

'From what I hear, I should be taking lessons from you in manhood,' Jem said, his voice just loud enough so that it could be heard by the room.

There was a stifled burst of giggles from Kitty's direction.

Harriet grinned at him. 'There are times when youth is an advantage,' she said. 'Perhaps I could give you a few pointers.'

'Ouch!' Jem said, and everyone started laughing.

It would be all right, Harriet thought, sitting down with weak knees. All the men were grinning at her. No one's eyes danced away; no one looked uneasy. Frankly, they all looked envious. She squared her shoulders and accepted a slab of roast beef, hardly cooked, from the footman.

Breakfast passed in a flash. Kitty giggled every time she looked at Harriet and so did Roslyn, who kept giving Harriet slow winks.

Sanders came in, and sat down at Harriet's side. 'Heard about last night,' he said, under cover of the conversation. 'We all should have known that Pensickle was uttering rot. Everyone knows about the man's capabilities in that direction. Jealous, no doubt.'

Harriet murmured something.

'Had a brother with a friend of that persuasion,' Sanders confided.

Harriet really wished he wouldn't.

But Sanders was done with that topic and onto another. 'When I was a youngster, I would have loved to get up to the sort of high jinks you engaged in last night.' He eyed Kitty in a toothy sort of way. 'Married too young, that's what happened to me.'

He thumped Harriet on the back so suddenly that she choked on a mouthful of beef. 'You're doing it the right way, Cope. Spread your wild oats, and spread 'em wide, I say.'

'Thank you, sir,' Harriet said.

It was a relief to escape. By the time she'd

negotiated all the winks and thumps from men, and all the giggles and veiled invitations from women, she was so tired that she felt like going back to bed.

Instead she pulled on her riding breeches and trailed outdoors to the stable. The day had started clear but was beginning to look grey again, with a hint of snow.

'We're actually working today,' Jem said, when she walked in. Nick was waiting for her, holding her horse. 'We're going out to check the north stables and make sure all's snug and tight. My stable master thinks we may need to buy some grain to make it through the winter.'

Harriet swung up on the saddle with a little puff. She was a much better rider now, and she didn't think that the tender ache in her thighs could be put down to riding astride.

At least, not riding a horse.

The thought made her smile and she looked up to find Jem's eyes on her. He abruptly wheeled his horse and left the stable. She followed, wincing as the bitter air hit her face.

He was waiting and leaned over, took her mouth in a hard kiss. 'Don't ever smile like that if there is anyone else in the room.'

Harriet's heart sang. He would never let her go.

'Jem–' she said, but he was gone, and with a little shout she let her mare leap after him.

She was a good rider now, able to go around turns at a gallop, although native common sense led her to slow her horse. Jem simply clung to the side of his mount and went faster.

Snow was in the air, the smell of it and the taste of it on the wind.

Harriet was just starting to get tired when a large barn loomed into view to the right. Jem immediately slowed his horse and picked his way across the frozen field. Then he jumped off and led his horse over to a small door in the side, not the huge door that accommodated the hay wagons.

'Come on, Harry,' he shouted over his shoulder.

Harriet clambered down rather painfully. That extra bit of gymnastics in the middle of the night – though it was wondrously fun – had taken its toll.

She led her horse into the warmth, out of the wind. Stacks of golden hay towered over their heads, winding towards the wooden loft far above.

'This is the largest barn I've ever seen,' Harriet said, awestruck.

'Your husband's storage barn isn't so large?' Jem asked. There was just a touch of satisfaction in his voice that made her smile. If she didn't like Sally, Jem didn't seem to like Benjamin either. Though she hadn't told Jem anything much about Benjamin.

Not that it mattered, not with the true, clear emotion that strung between them. She'd tell him when the moment felt right. Jem tied up the horses, then took her hand and they wound their way through a narrow pathway in the straw

'I just have to check the grain stocks,' he said.

'Where is it?'

'Back here, in the lofts. We have a terrible mouse problem.'

'Perhaps rats. You were so lucky with Eugenia's bite,' Harriet said with a shudder. 'By yesterday afternoon I could hardly see the punctures at all.'

'The shepherd brings his ratters to the barn once a week,' Jem said. 'Ironic, isn't it? I take excellent care of my barn, but I let my own child be bitten.'

Harriet's fingers tightened, warm, around his. 'It was an accident.'

'She seems fine. Did she show you what happened to the castle?'

Harriet laughed. 'Trust Eugenia to turn a disaster into a triumph.' A ham-handed footman had dropped a log on one side of her paper castle, crushing it. So Eugenia promptly declared the castle a ruin, and said the rats had won. 'Last night she was busily cutting out baby rats.'

'I saw them,' Jem said. 'They looked like little puddings with tails, but I didn't tell her that. Here's the grain.' He wrenched open the wooden top and they stared down into a huge bin. 'I'll tell him to buy a bushel or two,' Jem decided.

Harriet reached out a hand and let the smooth kernels sort through her fingers. 'It smells so good.'

'Not as good as you do.'

He was looking at her again with longing in his eyes. 'Do you suppose this will ever go away?' she asked, hearing hunger in her own voice.

'I doubt it. But why worry? We're having so much pleasure at this moment.'

He pulled off her greatcoat and ran a hand under her shirt, only to be frustrated by her, bandaged chest. So his hand started to roam downwards instead.

At first they just stood there, leaning against the rail, kissing until they were both panting a little, until Jem's heart was pounding under Harriet's hand.

'If only they could see us now,' he said, amusement in his voice. 'I'm afraid no amount of fibs from Kitty would help.'

But Harriet wasn't interested in imagining what they looked like together. She wound her fingers through his and tugged. 'Let's lie down,' she said.

'A tussle in the straw like shepherds ... I can't.'

'Why not?'

'Straw gives me hives. I itch for days,' he said, his eyes on hers. 'But I think we could manage standing up, don't you, Harriet?'

His hand was doing a slow caress of her hip. 'Yes,' she whispered. 'I think so.'

Two seconds later he was kneeling in front of her, she was holding onto the railing for dear life, and he was – he was–

He pulled back his head. 'You know, Harriet,' he said thoughtfully, 'I sometimes get the feeling that you would like to scream. May I remind you that there's no one for miles around this barn?'

Harriet gulped, but then he pulled her towards him again and that wicked tongue of his turned her knees to water.

In the end, she didn't really scream. It was more like–

'That was a scream,' she heard Jem say. 'I knew you had it in you.' But it was her turn, so she slid to her knees before him, and satisfactorily proved that Lord Strange had no control at all when it came to Harriet.

None.

Then he was turning her around, belly to the railing, his large hands shaping her bottom. 'God, you're beautiful, Harriet.'

She wanted to say that no, she wasn't beautiful. Her hips were too round and her bottom was too round and her breasts were too small, but there was something in his voice that made the comment die in her throat.

His voice made her beautiful. His hands caressed her and she felt as if they were her own hands: from him, she learned the beauty of a woman's sweet curve, of a generous hip, of the delicate, mysterious space between a woman's legs.

They were so together that her body knew what he wanted before her mind did. She arched back, welcomed him, sobbed when hard velvet stroked into her. His hands encircled her, protecting her from the railing.

He took it slow, each stroke a promise, to Harriet's mind. The days strung forward, days and nights with Jem...

Exclamations aren't enough. There are times when screaming is called for, especially when Jem slipped a hand in front of her body and began a wicked dance with his fingers. He rode her until she shattered; turned her about so he could kiss her again. Lifted her onto the railing so that her legs wrapped around his hips, saying that he didn't want to come without seeing her face.

She cried. What's a scream, after all, but a prelude to tears?

He was so deep within her that they didn't feel like two people.

Just one.

33

Fear

They came home slowly, walking the horses most of the way because Harriet admitted that her thigh muscles hurt.

'I'd take you in my lap,' he said, 'but we'd be seen.'

Harriet laughed. 'I can't put Kitty's story-telling abilities to waste.'

So they walked the horses home through the gathering snow. She gratefully gave her mare back to Nick, and walked back to the house.

They were met by Povy.

'A fever, my lord,' he said, without pre-amble. 'Miss Eugenia has a fever and it's quite high. I've sent for the doctor.'

Jem's whole body froze. 'When?'

'An hour ago. I sent to the stables, but they said you had to be on the way back home already.'

Jem pounded up the stairs, gone in an instant.

Harriet turned to Povy. 'What have you done for it?'

'I've ordered the maids to make a snow

bath. We'll use it if we have to. At the moment I have her snug in bed. I'm sure you will be a comfort.' In that instant she realized that Povy knew precisely what she was (a woman), and quite likely, *who* she was (a duchess) as well. Povy was simply that sort of man.

'I'll go,' Harriet said, moving towards the stairs. She was thinking desperately about the labourer on her estate, the man who had died of rat-bite fever. It had been a few weeks before the fever came on; yes, just the same as for Eugenia. But he had had some sort of rash...

'Is there a rash?' she asked.

She saw the same awareness in Povy's eyes. He probably knew symptoms of every disease. 'Not yet.'

That *yet* was no comfort.

34

Hell

February 23, 1784

The first two days Harriet tried to stay out of Jem's way. How long had she known Jem and Eugenia? A matter of weeks, even if it felt like years. She stopped in the morning and the evening to see Eugenia. She asked Povy for news every time she saw him. She wondered if she should leave, and couldn't bear to go out even for a brief walk.

In case ... in case Jem needed her. In case Eugenia needed her. In case something so awful happened that she couldn't put it into words.

Most of Jem's guests didn't appear to notice that their host was never to be seen. They heard his daughter had a fever, and having ascertained that it wasn't contagious, continued with their pursuits. The Graces left to travel to the house of the bishop for a week-long 'performance'. Presumably the Game continued, though Harriet neither knew nor cared.

On the third day, Harriet peeked into

Eugenia's room in the evening to find Jem slumped in a chair by her bedside, asleep. He woke with a start.

The feverish patches on Eugenia's cheeks told their own story. She wasn't in a deep sleep: every once in a while she would shake her head, back and forth, as if she were in an argument.

'What's she doing?' Harriet whispered.

'Fighting,' Jem said. His voice was leaden with exhaustion. 'She's fighting as hard as she can.'

Eugenia shook her head again and said something indistinct. There was a *no* somewhere in the mumble.

'She's a good fighter,' Harriet said. 'Where's her nurse?'

'Eugenia doesn't like her. I'll have to find another one tomorrow.'

'Is there any way I can help?' Harriet said. She'd asked before, but he had said no.

Now he looked at her, gaunt and exhausted. 'I have no right to ask you this.'

'Please,' she said. 'Please allow me to help.'

'She doesn't like the nurse the doctor sent. But she likes seeing you. She asked for you once.'

Harriet came forward in a rush. 'I was trying not to be in the way. You should have called me when she asked for me.'

'It was the middle of the night.' He stood up, rubbing his hands over his eyes. 'Could you sit with her, just for an hour or two? I need some sleep.'

Harriet pushed him towards the door. 'Go. Come back in the morning.' She curled up in a chair next to Eugenia's bed. At some point the little girl woke up and asked for water. She smiled blearily at Harriet. By morning she was fretful.

'I don't want water,' she cried. 'My side hurts. Where's my papa? Papa!'

A maid entered the room and Eugenia's voice escalated. 'Don't want her here! Make her go away!'

Harriet cast an apologetic look at the maid, who scuttled away.

The only thing that settled Eugenia was singing. So Harriet sang.

She was singing 'Drink to Me Only' when Eugenia woke again. Harriet put a cool cloth on Eugenia's forehead.

'Are you ever going to marry someone, Harry?' she asked sleepily.

'I don't know.'

'If you had a baby, I could hold her. When I grow up I'm going to have fourteen children.'

'Really? Fourteen?'

'Mrs Billows in the village has fifteen, and Papa says that's far too many.'

'So is–'

But Eugenia was asleep, a little smile on her face. Perhaps she dreamed of fourteen children. At least she didn't shake her head. But an hour later she woke again, feverish.

'I want a different song,' she said fretfully. 'A song about Papa. Sing me about Papa.'

Harriet panicked. She was singing the refrain of 'Papa's Tower is Falling Down' for the fourteenth time when Jem entered the room. 'I've sent for another doctor from London,' he said by way of greeting. 'How are you feeling, poppet?'

'I'm hot,' Eugenia said, her lower lip trembling. 'I hate it in bed. I hate it here. I want to go outside. I want to sit in the snow.'

Harriet stumbled up from her chair and Jem sat down. And that's how it went. For years, it felt like.

The fever and the chills chased each other in an endless circle. Harriet sang song after song.

Nights were so much worse than days. Sometimes the fever waned slightly in the daytime, though it raged at night.

Sometimes in the daytime when Harriet said, 'Hello, sweetheart,' to Eugenia, she would open her eyes. Every once in a while she woke up and seemed completely rational. Even when she cried and said it hurt, they took it as a sign of strength.

But at night she never slept for more than an hour. When she wasn't sleeping, she went back to fighting, as Jem described it. She thrashed her head, back and forth, and shouted until her voice cracked. When she did sleep, it wasn't a natural sleep, but the kind from which people don't always wake.

One day Harriet realized that Eugenia had been ill, really ill, for two weeks. She was sitting by the bed, wringing out a cold cloth to put on Eugenia's forehead when she heard Jem outside the door. 'Can't you do anything?' he asked the new doctor fiercely.

And the man's voice, low. 'God, and I wish that I could. We just don't know enough. There's people studying fevers, but they've little to say about rat-bite fever.'

And then she heard Jem walk away, down the hall, break into a near run. He never cried in front of her. But every day his face was more strained, the lines by his mouth more cruel.

When he returned, later that day, Harriet went to take a bath. The house was quiet, just a huge house and somewhere in it the rat that had given Eugenia a fever.

Just a house, and a father and his dying daughter.

She stopped and rested her forehead against the corridor wall.

Days stretched into another week.

Eugenia was shrinking every day. Her little face grew more peaked and tired, her eyes larger.

One day Harriet went out for a walk, and when she came back, she saw with fresh eyes what she had known inside for days. Eugenia was dying. It literally felt as if her heart stopped, and not silently, but with some great screeching pain.

Eugenia was shaking her head again, back and forth, back and forth. Her cheeks were red and she was moaning, a little slipstream mumble of words, but Harriet knew what they were: a litany of pain.

She stumbled forward and fell on her knees by the bed.

Jem was perfectly stark white, his eyes surrounded by black circles. 'It's not going anywhere,' he said hoarsely. 'It's taken hold for good.'

'You can't know that,' Harriet whispered. 'No one can know.'

'She can't bear this much longer.'

Harriet swallowed, buried her head in the covers, as if not to hear.

'The doctor says perhaps today.' Jem's voice didn't even sound like his own. It sounded like a voice echoing from far away.

Harriet's tears burned her hands, burned the inside of her nose, burned her heart. 'Would you like to be alone with her?' she said, raising her head. Tears dripped from her cheeks.

He shook his head. 'Stay with me. With us.'

So they sat together.

The day wore on. Towards evening, Harriet found herself thinking the oddest

388

thoughts: that twilight is not really dark. It's grey. The sun gone, the world turns grey, without emotion, without colour. It seemed a fitting time for a little girl to slip free of all this pain, to let go.

But Eugenia never did. She would fall into silence, and panic would grip Harriet's heart, and then she would start shaking her head again.

'She's fighting it,' Jem said suddenly, after hours of silence. His voice cracked mid-sentence. 'She won't let go.'

Harriet managed to smile at Eugenia. 'Good girl,' she said.

'No.'

'No?'

'She has to know it's all right to go. It's all right, darling, it's all right.' His voice broke, and tears were rolling down his face. 'Your mama's waiting for you. There's just too much pain here, poppet. It's all right. You can let go, Eugenia.'

'She can't hear you,' Harriet said.

'Yes, she can.' He bent over the bed, cradled his daughter's little face, told her again. And again.

Harriet buried her head in the covers and wept. Then she suddenly heard him say in a different voice: 'Hello, poppet.'

She reared up her head. Eugenia was looking blearily, irritably, at her father. ''Lo, Papa.'

They were the most beautiful two words that Harriet had ever heard.

Eugenia frowned. 'Stop telling me to go, Papa. I'm too tired to go anywhere.'

'Of course you are,' he said. 'Of course you are. I know that.'

'Where's Harry?'

Harriet leapt up and tangled on her own feet and half fell on top of Eugenia. 'I'm here.'

'Sing me that song,' Eugenia said, closing her eyes again. 'I want that song, Harry. My favourite song.'

So Harriet sat down on the bed and started to sing. Her voice wavered and cracked. *'Drink to me only, with thine eyes...'* she sang. *'And I will pledge with mine.'*

'Put your hand on my cheek,' Eugenia ordered. 'Like you did before, Harry.'

So she did. *'Yet leave a kiss but in the cup–'* She couldn't manage the high note and slid low instead. *'And I'll not ask for wine.'*

As they watched, Eugenia fell into sleep. It was a deep sleep this time. She was so far away that her chest hardly moved.

'I can't take it,' Jem said suddenly, stumbling to his feet. A great cracked sob came from his chest. 'I can't – Harriet–'

'Go for a walk,' she said, looking up at him. 'She won't die, not this hour. Not this moment.'

He stood, frozen in the doorway. 'I can't

390

watch. I – can't – watch.'

'Go,' she said, loving him, loving Eugenia. 'I promise I'll watch and she won't die. Not yet.'

He stumbled from the room. She lied, she had lied. It seemed obvious to her, as it undoubtedly was to Jem, that Eugenia was leaving them now. If not this minute, in five minutes, in an hour.

35

Yet Leave a Kiss But in the Cup

March 15, 1784

Harriet picked up Eugenia and carried her over by the fire to the rocking chair. Her little body was all bones.

She stayed by the fire, rocking back and forth, tears sometimes falling on Eugenia's face. The odd, funny little girl with a logical mind and a passionate wish for babies had crept into her heart.

When Benjamin was alive and they were first married, she had thought they would surely have children. Those unborn children tumbled through her dreams, teething on chess pieces, strutting the way Benjamin did, smiling at her with his eyes.

But then the children never came and somehow those dreams became faded and tired, rather like their marriage.

More tears fell on Eugenia's hair. She had found a child, only to lose her.

Once Eugenia stirred, but Harriet shushed her, kissing her forehead, and singing a few bars. She slipped back into that deep sleep.

Harriet was still rocking when Jem came back.

He walked through the door and she saw the question in his eyes and shook her head quickly. 'She's here, still here.'

He looked down and despair was written in every inch of his body. 'I'll take a bath and then I'll hold her,' he said. His voice was toneless.

Shock, she thought. He can't let himself face it yet.

Harriet kept rocking, her arms aching with exhaustion.

A slanted hint of pearly light came in through a crack in the curtains. Dawn had arrived.

The light wasn't grey any more. Rose, dusted with pearl, played over Eugenia's closed eyes. She didn't stir. Harriet freed one arm and put a hand on Eugenia's forehead.

Jem entered the room, deep in the cotton wool in which he had somehow wrapped himself. He felt like a snowman come to life, cold, emotionless, walking by some miracle.

Harriet was still by the fire, but she'd stopped rocking. He registered that was a bad sign, walked towards them. Harriet had patches under her eyes like bruises. Her hair was tied back with a simple ribbon, and strands of curled silk were falling about her cheeks. Eugenia was curled in her arms like a baby hedgehog.

There was something in Harriet's eyes... He looked at his daughter again. Put his hand on Eugenia's forehead.

Harriet's smile was so beautiful that he felt it in the fibre of his bones. The cotton wool peeled away, left him reeling.

Morning light came towards him like a blow of colour.

'The fever,' he whispered. 'It – is it?' From the earliest days, the fever had waned, but it had never really left. But Eugenia's forehead was cool. Cool.

Harriet tried to say something but she was crying.

Eugenia opened her eyes. 'Papa,' she whispered.

He scooped her up. 'How do you feel?' He heard his voice crack with no embarrassment.

'Hungry,' Eugenia sighed, putting her head on his shoulder.

Harriet's wonderful, husky chuckle was a shadow of its former self – but she hadn't laughed in weeks. Eugenia hadn't asked for food in weeks either. She'd protested every spoonful of soup they gave her. Jem laughed, felt something wet on his cheek and realized he was crying.

'You're going to be all right,' he whispered, tightening his arms around his little girl. 'Harriet, she's going to be all right!'

Harriet laughed again.

He looked down at her. The joy was almost painful. 'I love you,' he said suddenly. 'Do you know that?'

Harriet turned a little pink. 'Oh.'

'Eugenia and I both love you. Our Harry.'

Eugenia was asleep again, so he tucked her back in bed and then picked up Harriet and put her in his lap instead.

She put her head against his shoulder and they just stayed like that, staring into the smouldering fire. It took an hour, perhaps. But finally he heard her voice, like a kiss. 'I love you, Jem.'

He tightened his arms.

36

Games

March 16
The following evening

Jem walked out of Eugenia's room and his
feet turned of their own accord towards
Harriet's bedchamber. Eugenia was well.

She would live. The doctor agreed. She
would live.

Mr Avery was strolling down the corridor.
'We've missed you at the Game,' he said.
'How's your daughter?'

'Better. Perhaps I can join you tonight.'

'Children are pesky creatures. I'm quite
proud of myself for not spawning any. Will
Cope join us?'

'Of course.'

Avery accepted that without a blink of an
eye. Jem's heart sang. Everything could go
back to normal now. Except of course it
wouldn't be the same, it would never be the
same. He had Harriet now.

He pushed open the door of her chamber
without knocking, hoping to find her un-
dressed. Bathing.

She was writing a letter. He knew there was a smile in his eyes, saw it echoed in hers. He came around behind her and pulled Harriet's hair out of its ribbon.

'I need you,' he said fiercely.

She stood in his arms and turned, silent and sleek.

He pulled her to the edge of the bed, standing before her, so that he could make love to her, and still see her, all her sweet curves and delicious roundness. Harriet had no shyness, no modesty. She lay before him like a gorgeous feast, her legs wrapped around his hips.

Being Harriet, she never really stopped talking. 'Deeper,' she said. Her lips, crimson and plump, caught his attention and he bent forward, taking her lips without missing a stroke.

Making love to Harriet was like nothing he could describe.

So he didn't try, just tugged her out of a nap a few hours later. 'Come on, Harry, on your feet.'

She rolled away into the pillow. Her lips were bruised and swollen from his kisses. His body flared and did one of those instant calculations men can do in their sleep. Do it again now, or wait? Wait.

'Put on your breeches,' he said. 'The boys are waiting.'

'What boys?'

'The Game,' he said, giving her a kiss just because he could. 'They've missed us. I promised we'd go tonight.'

She blinked at him. 'The Game has kept going? Without you?'

'Of course.'

'And they think we're going to join them tonight?'

'They think their host and Mr Cope are going. I told Povy that we'd take the seventh and eighth seats.' Her thighs were irresistible. He ran a hand up her right leg, stopping right where her sweet plumpness began.

She frowned at him and turned away. But that just meant that the curve of her bottom caught his eye.

He ran a hand slowly over her hip. 'Have you ever played master and slave girl?' he asked, not expecting a yes. Whoever that gentleman farmer was Harriet had married, he didn't sound like a master.

She gave him a look and sat up. 'Are you really telling me that the whole cohort of wastrel game-playing men are still here and you agreed to meet them tonight?'

He thought she had phrased that quite succinctly. 'Exactly. Let's go.'

'Jem, don't you think...' she started. And then lapsed into silence.

'If you'd rather stay here,' Jem said, having a change of heart, 'I'm perfectly willing. I can teach you a lovely game called Master and Slave.'

'Oh, really,' she said. 'I suppose you're the master and I'm the slave.'

'Other way around,' he said, pulling her legs to the edge of the bed and then falling to his knees. 'Command me, O master.'

He loved her chuckle. It made his heart dance; it made him harder than a rock.

But she was persistent too. 'Get up, Jem. You don't really think that we're going back to – to the Game this very night?'

'Are you tired of primero?' He got to his feet. 'I can go by myself, though they'll miss you. Povy can easily find someone for the eighth seat.' He wandered over to the fire. 'Eugenia had two eggs for supper tonight.'

'That's wonderful,' she said.

But something was sinking into his mind. He knew that tone. Every man in the world knew that tone.

'Harriet?' he said warily.

She was standing with her arms folded. 'You don't think everything is going to go back to exactly as it was, do you?'

He cleared his throat. 'Um.'

After a moment or two, she prompted. 'Jem.'

'Of course, it won't be the same,' he said. 'I love you, Harriet. I mean, I loved you before but now I know I love you. That's different.'

'So you think that Mr Cope will be coming out to play primero tonight?'

It was starting to feel like a stupid decision to wake her up. Harriet's eyes had darkened. Even though she was so angry, she was standing there naked.

He couldn't help noticing.

And she saw that he noticed. Her eyes slid down his body and then narrowed. 'I suppose there's an alternative to a night of primero.'

'Yes,' he said, warily, feeling he was walking into a trap. 'We could play a different game,' he added hastily. 'Chess, for example.'

'Or Master and Slave.'

'That too.'

'Life is not all about games, Jem.'

He couldn't help what his body thought, so he grabbed a dressing gown and wrapped it around himself.

'You said you loved me,' she stated.

'I did. I mean, I *do* love you.'

'Don't you see that things have to change?'

'How?' He could feel tension building in his chest.

'I can't be Mr Cope for ever,' she said.

Relief flooded his chest. He grabbed a dressing gown and gave it to her, because he still couldn't concentrate. 'Of course, I don't want you to be Mr Cope. I want you to be Harriet. I have an idea about that. We're going to kill off Cope, in an unfortunate carriage accident. I'll go away for a few days and meet you. Then you can come home with me, and just be Harriet.'

'I can't be just Harriet.'

'Why not?' He could feel himself almost gabbling, but there was a look in her eyes he didn't like.

'I can't live like this.'

'But–'

'Like *this*, Jem,' she said sharply. 'With the Game, and the Graces gallivanting around the house when they're not out entertaining bishops. I'm not–'

The truth slammed into him like a brick wall. Of course she wanted to get married. And he meant to do that, of course he did. He'd only asked her once, through the door, and she hadn't answered.

He walked across to her, cupped her face in his hands. 'I know what you mean, darling,' he said. 'You don't have to ask me.'

'I don't?' She sounded rather stunned. He had meant to ask her to marry him again, because he'd known from the very first time they made love that she was his. That he would never let her out of his sight.

'You know, when I married the first time, I thought of marriage as some sort of jail. Like a little cage. A prison sentence.'

'Charming,' she said and he loved her dry wit so much that he almost smiled, but the moment was too important.

'Marrying you will be completely different.'

'Not a jail sentence?'

She still looked a bit peeved.

'I love you. I mean, I did love Sally, but not when we first married.'

'Yet Sally was so amusing to be with.'

'Yes, but–'

'I'm guessing she enjoyed the Game, if she was allowed to play.'

'Well, actually she was very–'

'Good at primero, was she?' He didn't like the way her eyebrow shot up. And how on earth had he got onto the topic of Sally? The love he felt for Harriet was far deeper than what he had felt for Sally. She seemed like a long-ago playmate.

'I can't remember whether she played primero well or not,' he said, going for a safe bet. 'We were like two puppies together, Harriet. Not like you and me.'

'Oh? And what are we like?'

'Grown up,' he said firmly.

'Grown up.' She said it slowly, as if she were tasting the words. 'And how do such aged people as ourselves behave?'

She was obviously furious. Jem's self-preservation instincts finally took over and he said, 'I think we should discuss this later.'

'You might miss the Game if we actually discussed the future,' she said.

'I'm happy to discuss the future!'

'So ... the future. Harry Cope dies. Harriet, who happens to have an unusual resemblance to Harry Cope, appears at your estate and after a brief flirtation, we marry. A nine-days' wonder.'

'It could work.' But he could feel anger building in him too. What had he done to deserve her scorn? Ask her to marry him? Only that. Ask her to marry him.

'We'll spend our days learning a little fencing, riding, trading quips with the Graces or their ilk, greeting any new people who happen to appear uninvited–'

'I invite everyone who comes here!' he said, stung.

'Wander down to greet our guests around twilight, have a bite to eat, start the Game – oh wait, I won't be part of that any more, will I? I suppose I'll teach the Graces how to embroider or something ladylike.'

Tenderness seized his heart. He would hate to be shown a glimpse of the freedoms allotted to men – and then forced to give them up. It would break his heart.

Obviously, it was doing the same to Harriet.

'We'll change the rules,' he said, putting a hand on her cheek. 'All men ... and Harriet.'

She struck his hand away from her face and spun away. Surprised, he stumbled back.

'You don't understand at all!'

He caught his balance on a chair. 'I would have to agree,' he said finally. 'I asked you to marry me. I offered to change the rules of my household so that you could continue to join the Game because I know you enjoy it.'

'You don't understand anything!'

He felt a swell of rage but he caught it back. 'Why don't you try to explain it to me?'

'It's all games with you. Life is not a game!'

'Are you suggesting that I don't work hard enough?' he said. His lips seemed to be numb. 'I assure you that I manage my holdings.'

'I'm certain you do,' she said scathingly.

He waited a moment to see if she wanted to explain herself. Then he said, 'It takes a great deal of work to keep a vast estate and income the size of mine afloat, Harriet. You wouldn't understand that, but I don't see why your ignorance should result in scorn.'

'I manage an estate as well,' she flashed.

Of course, the farmer had probably left an estate. It must not have been entailed, which suggested that Harriet's husband was a commoner. Not that it mattered to him.

'It's the way you approach life,' she said. 'As if it were one long *game.*' Her face had a stony look to it.

'I don't understand your criticism. I assure you that I take no unnecessary risks with my estate.'

'Just with your child,' she flashed.

He felt himself growing paler. She dared –

dared – to say that he took risks with Eugenia? Still, he forced himself to respond calmly. It was almost like a miracle, the way he heard his own voice enquire mildly, 'And how exactly should I have protected Eugenia from the rat, Harriet?'

'I'm not talking about that! Anyone could have that happen – but she was alone when it happened.'

'I gather you're criticizing my ability to hire nursemaids.'

'That governess was as feckless and beautiful as the rest of the women in this house,' she said flatly. 'She had no real care for Eugenia: none.'

'She was in love. That could happen to anyone.' Though he was starting to wonder if it had really happened to Harriet.

'She was part and parcel with the women who pay you visits,' Harriet snapped. 'My mother would have called her a wag-tail. She was nothing more than a ladybird, looking for her next meal!'

Jem could feel himself growing rigid. Ice poured down his back. 'I regret that you think I willingly hired a ladybird to care for my daughter.'

'You didn't hire her willingly,' Harriet cried. 'I suspect you simply don't know what a decent woman looks like.'

'I am not a hermit,' he pointed out, counting to one hundred in the back of his mind.

'I frequently visit London, which is stiflingly full of boring women who must, therefore, be virtuous.'

'Oh, of course virtue is boring!'

'Exactly. And it makes such claims for itself. The very smell of virtue makes a woman utterly tedious, and at the same time, utterly conceited.'

'I am a virtuous woman,' Harriet said through clenched teeth.

'We'll have to agree that you are an exception,' Jem said. He was vibrating with rage over her criticism of his childrearing. 'I shall do my best to engage a truly virtuous nanny for Eugenia. Or else I'll just try to find one like yourself.'

'What do you mean by that?'

'You came to my house under a false name, dressed in breeches,' he pointed out. 'When it became clear to both of us that we were of compatible genders, you fell into bed with me without showing an undue amount of virtue. Thank God.'

'In short: you think I'm a strumpet.'

'Only in the best meaning of the term.'

'A ladybird.'

His back stiffened again and his jaw tightened. 'There would be nothing so terrible about being a ladybird, Harriet.'

'So is that the future you have in mind for Eugenia? Is that why she is locked in the west wing, hardly able to enjoy fresh air –

while all the ladybirds trot around your estate?'

'I have never kept Eugenia from the fresh air. Neither have I unreasonably immured her from our guests. She has come to know a few of the young women very well.'

Too late, he realized this was a mistake. Harriet's eyes flashed and she made a sound that could have been a growl, on a man. 'I gather it *is* your ambition to turn her into a ladybird, then, since you give her such excellent companionship.'

'Can you please find some other term for this conversation?'

'Doxy?' Her tone was delicate but sharp as knives. 'Drab or strumpet? There are so many appropriate words.'

'And as a virtuous woman, you know them all,' he said, pushed beyond endurance. 'Good women delight in throwing terms at those less fortunate – even while they gaily engage in precisely the same behaviour.'

She paled and he knew that went home.

'I suppose you're right,' she said, a second later.

'You virtuous women shun and scorn those whom you believe to be weaker, less righteous. And yet–'

'You're saying I've played the doxy in your house, and now I have no right to condemn you for your taste in companionship. After all, I transformed myself into precisely what you always desired.'

He was never very good at sorting out a whole swirl of emotions, and he felt buffeted by them. 'I'm not sure–'

'Luckily, I am quite certain. You are right.'

She waited until he said, cautiously, 'Oh.'

'I had no right to ask you to change, or to think that you were even capable of it. I thought–' and something flashed across her eyes '–I thought you saw my heart. I thought you *knew* me. What a fool I was.'

She almost whispered the last.

'Don't look grieved,' Jem said, catching her arm. 'I do know you, Harriet. I *love* you.'

She didn't even hear him. 'I wove it all in my head, of course, fool that I am. I was playing the doxy and you saw me as a doxy, and that–'

'I never saw you as that! Never!'

'That is that,' she finished.

'What are you talking about?'

Finally, she looked at him again. 'I am extraordinarily slow in my understanding, Jem.'

'So am I,' he said. 'Because I have no idea what is going on here.'

'This will make you laugh.' There was something empty in her eyes that made him want to scream at her. 'I actually thought you would – you would change.'

'I *will* change! I told you I would change. I want to marry you.'

'Not that.'

'I've never asked anyone to marry me, by my own impulse and reckoning. I didn't think it would be thrown away so lightly.'

'I thought you knew what kind of woman I am. I thought you would – I thought you would become that sort of man.'

'Jesus,' he said. 'I am the sort of man for you, Harriet. Don't you understand that?'

She shook her head. 'You are a wonderful companion. I thought you could be something you're not at all. I thought you could be the sort of man who marries a woman like me – the real me, not Mr Cope. Not me under a secret name and having a wild *affaire*. The me who runs an estate, Jem. The me who sits in judgment in the shire court. I did behave like a ladybird.' She must have seen him flinch. 'But I thought you knew that it wasn't the real me... I thought you would come home with me.'

He laughed, heard his own laugh, like a bark. 'To the little farm your husband left you?'

'It's not little.'

'Whatever size it is, darling,' he said, reining in his impatience, 'Fonthill is hundreds of acres. It's not practical to leave my estate and move to yours.'

'I meant – I meant not just physically come with me. Come with me in other ways.'

'Do you mean become some sort of country squire, like your husband?'

'My husband wasn't a country squire.'

'Whatever he was,' Jem said impatiently. 'A gentleman farmer, living off in the country with his hogs. I don't care if he wasn't a gentleman, Harriet. I've never cared for rank. You should know that about me.'

'I see that,' Harriet said. 'But Jem, I haven't been honest with you. I played the doxy, and I'm not one. I – I frolicked with the Graces, and I led you to believe that I could live in such a way for my whole life.'

There was something in her face, something almost resigned, that made him feel slightly crazed.

'I don't care–'

'I lied to you by omission,' Harriet said flatly. 'My husband was a duke. And I am a duchess.'

The moment she said it, he knew the truth in his bones. Of course, she was a duchess. She had the spine of a duchess, and the natural tone of command.

She didn't expect people to love her: she expected them to fear her. To bow and scrape before her. That was why she loved being Cope so much. It set her free, in the same way that not being a woman set her free.

'A duchess,' he said, fury burning its welcome into his heart.

She inclined her head. It was a duchess's nod. But there was a tear sliding down her cheek.

'You pretended to be other than you are – why?' But he knew, he knew. 'I'm not good enough for a duchess. You deceived me, day after day – because of *rank?*'

'It wasn't rank. You are – yourself,' she said. 'And I am a bird of a different feather, for all I pretended to be someone I'm not.'

'You're saying I fell in love with an illusion.'

'Something like that.'

'And you? Did you fall in love with an illusion too, Harriet?'

'No. You never lied to me. I don't think you're capable of lying, Jem.'

He folded his arms because it was ungraceful to clench one's fists in polite conversation. Especially with a duchess, one had to presume. 'Ironic as this may seem, I would have thought it below myself to pretend to a lower rank than my own. I gave you myself, such as I am.'

'I know you did,' she cried. 'You have been utterly honest with me. This is your life, and – and that's wonderful. You love your life. And – and that's wonderful. Truly. I – I'm a fool, that's all.'

'Would you mind explicating the nature of your foolishness?'

She looked at him for a moment, as if she

were memorizing his face. His heart turned over. She was really going to do it. She was going to leave him.

'You're – you're the only gentleman I've ever met who truly doesn't care about rank.'

'So?'

'I honour that. But I can't live like this.'

Jem felt his tone hardening before he even said it. He knew why she couldn't live in a house without rank: she was a duchess, for God's sake. That would be like giving away her most precious possession. 'Like what?'

'In a house in which people just come and go, like some sort of changing play. You don't even know all of them, Jem.'

'They're not good enough for a duchess. I completely understand.'

'It's not a question of good. Well, perhaps it is.' He could see her make some sort of decision. She looked up at him. 'I'm a staid person, at the heart, Jem. All I ever wanted, really, was to have some children and a husband who loved me. That was it. I never–'

She turned away but he saw the gleam of tears again and it tore his heart.

'I never dreamed I would be as wild as I've been here. Playing primero for huge stakes, having an *affaire*... It's not me. But I also – I can't live with people like the Graces, not for the long term. I don't want to be in a house that is an inn for itinerant players and drunk jugglers, not to mention the scientists

411

and politicians. Yet I loved every moment of it. It's changed me, changed my life. I don't blame my husband for dying any more.'

Ice and anger slammed into his heart. 'I am happy that Eugenia and I could be of use to you.'

'Don't– Don't–' she cried, holding out her hand. 'Don't leave in anger.'

'You lied to me. I thought you were the widow of a *farmer*–' He spat the word '–and all along you were merely playing with hoi polloi. Amusing yourself with me.'

'It wasn't like that!'

Bitterness seized his throat. 'Do you know what I think about people, Harriet? I think the worst lie was not when you pretended to be a dumpy widow. I have that phrase right, don't I?'

Her face was stark white. 'I am–'

'Stop it,' he said through clenched teeth. 'It was when you pretended to be a squire's wife. Villiers was having his little duke's game, bringing along two duchesses. I don't know why I didn't see that; it's just the kind of twisted humour people of your rank appreciate.'

'It wasn't a joke!'

'It was the kind of joke that only a duke would appreciate,' he said tonelessly. 'I know Eugenia won't.'

'Oh, you mustn't say that to her. It's not true!'

He just looked at her, and the silence grew bitter and thick between them. 'I'll try to keep the uglier parts of the truth from Eugenia. You go, back to the duchy. I'll stay here. And God, I hope that we never meet again.'

Her face was tear-stained, but she kept her chin high. 'I don't see what I did that was so terrible, that deserves this level of rage.'

'I loved you. I thought I knew you. My anger should be at myself, not at you. I will endeavour to make it so.' And then he said, 'If you'll forgive me, I have an appointment.'

'Wait!'

He waited while she tried to say something that got caught on a sob, raised her head again. 'Are you sure you – couldn't you come with me, Jem? I love you. I love you so much.'

It was maddening to feel sorry for her. To still feel love for her, even. She was a liar who had entered his house and amused herself with him.

'I'm not a toy that can be bought,' he told her, finally. 'I'm a man with a large estate and a child.'

'And a house party,' she said with a touch of bitterness. 'Don't forget all your guests.'

'I have a life. It's not a perfect life, and it's not a duke's life, but it's my own. I am Lord Strange. I earned my reputation and–'

She interrupted him. 'You didn't! And you know you didn't! I don't believe you slept with any woman since Sally died. Did you?'

'My lovers are irrelevant.'

'Did you?' she shrieked at him.

'Only once.'

'So why – why couldn't you just love me, instead of all these other people?' Her voice choked again. 'Why do you need the Game so much?'

'I loved the person you presented yourself as – a funny, wise, intelligent person who loved learning to fence and ride and play poker. But that person's not real.' He felt merciless, and yet it had to be said. 'You're a duchess. You're not Harry.'

'You knew I wasn't Harry!'

'I thought you were someone I could love,' he said flatly. 'And someone who loved being here, with me. But you're right. A duchess can't have anything to do with Lord Strange. No duchess should ever darken the door of this house. You shouldn't have come.'

He left her small white face behind him, and walked away. Her voice stopped him at the door.

'I love you.' Her voice didn't even tremble. 'I may have misrepresented myself, and I suppose you can't forgive me. Or don't want to forgive me. But I saw you for what you are and could be, Jem, and I love you. I want you to know that.'

His eyes burned suddenly so he didn't turn around. 'You saw me for a loose screw who welcomes riffraff into his house. That's not what you want.'

'I saw you for a man with a heart too generous to turn anyone away based on something as frivolous as reputation or rank. A man who loves his daughter so much that he pulled her back from death. A man who honoured his wife's memory by not having careless *affaires*, though doubtless many were offered him.' Her voice wavered and she steadied it. 'A man who loved me.'

He turned around. 'Your husband didn't love you, did he?'

'Oh yes, he did.'

'But not enough.'

'Not as much as he loved chess. He was always honest about that. And you – you are honest too. It seems I have a genius for finding men who care more for a game than for myself.'

'I'm certain that you will find someone of your rank,' he heard himself say. The flash in her eyes could have been agony – or dislike, so he opened the door.

He wasn't walking away, because she had left him, really.

He wasn't good enough for her. And she didn't even know the whole of it. His mouth twisted. His valet took one look at him and practically threw his clothing towards him.

Then he was away: pounding down the road, down the slick road, hating her, hating himself, his heart bleeding for Eugenia. How would he explain to her? Harriet didn't love us enough? What do you tell a little girl who thinks–

Actually, what did Eugenia think?

She knew that Harriet was a woman. But she'd never said much other than that. He hadn't told her that he meant to marry Harriet.

Although he had always meant to marry her, he realized with another sickening lurch of his stomach. Almost unconsciously, he had decided long ago that he was going to do Harriet a favour by marrying her and rescuing her from her boring little backwater of a farm. Bring her to a life of luxury. He kicked his horse and they went faster, until the wind screamed in his ears.

A life of luxury, he was offering. In a tawdry house full of strangers and primero games. While she probably lived in a castle.

If he cried, which he never did, his tears would have turned to icicles on his cheeks.

37

To Be Better Than a Game

March 18, 1784
Berrow House
Country Seat of the Duke of Berrow

Harriet got home, all the way home, two days later. Villiers's man, Finchley, gathered up her clothes, and Harriet gathered up the shards of her self-esteem and her love, and took it all home in the carriage with her.

She didn't even cry until her spaniel, Mrs Custard, ran to meet her. And then she dropped right down on her knee in the dirt and hugged him. His tail wagged furiously.

'He checked the front door for you every day, Your Grace,' her butler, Wilson, said from somewhere above her right shoulder.

Harriet bit her lip hard. She couldn't cry in front of the servants. She had never cried in front of the servants, not when Benjamin died, not when...

When had anything worse than that happened?

Besides having her heart ripped out and rejected, thrown back in the dirt at her feet.

You'd think she'd be used to it. Benjamin hadn't really loved her; neither did Jem. They both loved their games better – the game of chess, with all its intricacies and power struggles, the game of being Lord Strange. With all its odd generosity, male camaraderie, celebration, and the game of primero, with all its intricacies, power struggles, and bets.

A tear dropped into Mrs Custard's greying fur.

Once, for once, she wished that someone would love her more than a game. The way she loved him.

'The servants await you, Your Grace,' her butler said. He meant they would be all lined up inside the front door, waiting to curtsy.

'My goodness, Wilson,' she said, striving for a light tone. 'It isn't as if I've been gone for months. Disperse them, please.'

'But–'

'Disperse them.' She didn't use that tone often.

'You have a visitor,' her butler continued. His training did not allow him to betray a wounded tone, but she could tell he would have liked to.

'A visitor? How odd. No one knew I was coming home today.'

'She arrived two days ago and has been awaiting your arrival,' Wilson said.

'And?' Harriet said, rising and brushing

fur off her hands. 'She is?'

The butler pulled himself to a standing position. 'The Duchess of Beaumont.'

'Oh, goodness,' Harriet said, walking towards the great stone arch that led to the inner courtyard. 'Where is she now?'

'In the conservatory, I believe, Your Grace.'

Harriet walked into the courtyard, and through the west door that led to the conservatory, avoiding the front entry and the waiting servants. She was conscious of resentment. She didn't want to see Jemma, fond though she was of her. She wanted to fall into the nearest bed and cry. She wanted to cry until she had hiccups and couldn't stop. She wanted to cry as many tears as she had for Benjamin.

Which was ridiculous.

Jem was not dead. He just didn't love her enough. A tragedy for her, for no one else. And yet she could feel her blood beating to the rhythm of the tears she wanted to shed.

Because she had thought – she had really thought – that he would come home with her. That he loved her truly, saw her truly. But he didn't.

She found Jemma sitting in the section of the conservatory that Harriet called the orange arbour. She had tried to grow oranges, but they flowered and never grew fruit. She couldn't bear to discard the trees, so they stayed in a corner, all scented shiny leaves.

By the time she saw Jemma, tears were hanging on her eyelashes.

Jemma was seated on a bench under an orange tree, playing chess, apparently by herself. Harriet walked up quietly. It felt odd to be in a dress. Slippers were much quieter than boots. As she watched, Jemma moved a white piece, and then one of the blacks.

She glanced up and sprang to her feet. 'Darling Harriet, you've come home!'

Then Jemma had her arms around her, and a white handkerchief out, and Harriet collapsed against her. 'It's just– It's just–'

'I know, I know,' Jemma murmured. 'Isidore told me.'

'She told you that he doesn't love me? She *knew?* Why am I the only dunce? Why am I the only one who never knows?'

'Isidore didn't say that,' Jemma said. 'She said that you were having a lovely time together but that–'

'He didn't love me,' Harriet said.

'I can only identify a man in lust,' Jemma said. 'I have no idea how reliable Isidore is in these matters.'

'He was in lust,' Harriet said, hiccuping. 'But I thought he loved me.' The words wrenched out of the bottom of her heart. 'His daughter fell ill, and he asked me to be there with her. And I thought – I thought it was because – I'm such a fool!'

'What?' Jemma said, rocking her a little.

'I thought he was thinking of me as being Eugenia's mother.'

'I'm sure he was thinking that,' Jemma said.

'I was good enough,' Harriet said, 'at least while I had my trousers on. He said we could kill off Harry Cope, and then he'd marry Harriet, and I could go right back to playing primero with the men every night.'

'A fool,' Jemma diagnosed.

'And then when I said I was leaving, and I even – I even begged him to come with me, but he wouldn't. He was so angry with me. He said I was a typical duchess, that I thought he was a toy that could be bought. It wasn't like that, it really wasn't like that.'

She was crying so hard now that she was bent over at her waist, arms wrapped around herself, crying in big ugly gulps and odd noises.

'I loved him and he didn't love me enough,' she said, her voice wavering. 'And I'm sick – I'm so *sick* of always being second rate, of never being enough. The moment he found out I was a duchess it all just changed.'

'Oh,' Jemma said, softly. Her hand paused for a moment, stroking Harriet's hair. 'People always treat duchesses differently,' Jemma said. 'A duchess is the highest in the land. There are many men who would never even flirt with a duchess.'

'He didn't have to flirt with me,' Harriet said, sitting upright again and wiping her nose. 'He just had to marry me! And then I wouldn't be a duchess any more. I'd be plain Lady Strange.'

'Maybe he wanted to but he couldn't imagine it,' Jemma suggested.

'He didn't love me enough. And you know? I'm tired of people who don't love me *enough*,' Harriet said, her voice rising. 'I'm not so terribly second rate. I'm really not like Mother Goose. I'll never be as beautiful as you, Jemma, but I am beautiful. I am. I look best in boy's clothing, but – but he saw me in boy's clothing. And I look really good with no clothes at all!'

Jemma chuckled. 'I believe you.'

'I'm clever. Maybe not as clever as you–' Her voice stopped. 'Oh God, listen to me. I said it myself. You are beautiful and intelligent, and I'm just good enough, and clever enough.'

'I really don't have much intelligence,' Jemma said matter-of-factly. 'I can't figure out much except chess, for example. And how far has that got me? I have won a lot of chess matches. And where am I because of it?' The bitterness in Jemma's voice silenced Harriet for a moment.

'Chess didn't stop my husband from

having a mistress. Chess didn't stop me from ruining the prospect of our possible happiness by retaliating and bedding a man. Chess didn't make Elijah love me, or care what I was doing in France. Chess won't do anything.' Her tone was fierce. 'There's nothing special about a head for chess.'

Harriet blew her nose.

'Strange is a fool,' Jemma said. 'You are wonderfully intelligent, and gorgeous clothed and unclothed, and you don't even play chess – what more could a man want? You would have been loyal to him–'

'I would kill him if he took a mistress,' Harriet said fiercely. 'I started to think about him taking a lover on the way home and I almost turned the carriage around.'

'See what he gave up?' Jemma said. 'The potential of being married to someone who loved him enough to become homicidal. You have a broken heart but broken hearts do mend. You are free to find a man who knows exactly what an intelligent, beautiful person you are.'

Harriet sniffed.

There didn't seem to be much more to say on the subject, so after a time they both retired to their rooms.

Harriet fell onto her bed and waited for a tide of misery to wash over her – but it didn't.

Instead she kept thinking that she deserved better. Anger made it too hard to lie still, so she leapt to her feet and walked the room. She deserved someone to love her.

She *wasn't* second rate, she really wasn't. Perhaps she was clumsy in panniers, but Jem didn't know that. What he knew was that she was nimble at fencing.

And perhaps she looked like a partridge in women's clothing – but again, he didn't know that. He'd seen her at her best. And she felt beautiful, those times when they made love. Even thinking about their afternoon in the barn made her feel a little teary – and very angry. What was he doing, throwing away something as precious as what they had?

She almost dissolved into tears, remembering the way he had cupped her face, and said that he'd make love to her in the stable on her eightieth birthday.

The crucial thing was that she had said – she had actually managed to say that she loved him. She'd begged him not to leave her.

And he had still let her go.

That was the only thing that mattered, not how he felt about her being a duchess, or whether he thought she was a liar, or those other things he had said.

It was like a cold knife, but it was also good. If she'd had the time to beg Benjamin not to leave her, he would have done so anyway. She knew that. But she would have liked the chance to tell him one last time that she loved him.

It was the same thing all over again, except that Jem was alive, presumably sitting around at the Game, flirting with the Graces...

It was the same thing, all over again.

He was dead to her.

38

The Definition of Manhood, Under Discussion Again

March 21, 1784

It was time for the Game, so Jem made his way to the study. Lord Brouncker arrived with news of a great quarrel between the East India Company and a man named Stally-brass, which was inflaming both Houses of Parliament. Jem didn't care.

He bet wildly and without interest. He ended up betting that Fox would not prevent passage of the Mutiny Bill, even though he hated engaging in that sort of random expenditure of money.

The Game dissolved into nothing more

than a series of drunken reminiscences, all of which had to do with a certain opera singer named Noelle Gray who seemed to have a generous temperament, to say the least.

Jem could hardly control his irritation.

Villiers was smiling his secret little smile across the table. It provoked him, so he said belligerently, 'What?'

'I was maintaining a dignified silence,' Villiers observed.

'Distasteful,' Jem snapped. 'Gentlemen, shall we have another hand?'

'Noo,' Brouncker said, shaking his head. 'Can't manage it. My stomach's upset. Might shoot the cat.'

Jem decided never to invite that idiot again. He looked around the room. He didn't want to see any of these men again, with their belching and pettiness. Lord Oke was peeing against the wall again, though he knew perfectly well that there were chamber pots in the hall. Now he would pretend that he saw—

'Damn me if I didn't see a chamber pot there but a moment ago!' Oke roared.

'Missing something?' Villiers asked.

The tone of his voice was nicely calibrated to sting. Jem turned and snapped at him. 'If you wish to say something, just do so. Be a man, for once.'

'Isn't that really the subject at hand? What *is* a man, after all?' Villiers asked softly. He was magnificently dressed in a flared coat of raspberry, edged with an elaborate braided twill. He had his hair tied back and unpowdered, of course. Only fools like Oke bothered to powder their hair for the Game.

'A man,' Jem said, 'is not a woman.'

'Concise.'

'Men are not fools who...'

'Who?'

'Who turn out to be what they are not.'

'Ah, the beauty of your logic,' Villiers said amiably. 'Really. I marvel at it.' He leaned closer. 'I miss Harriet. She showed remarkable spirit for someone of her sex.'

'And rank.'

'Ah,' Villiers said, sitting back. 'And therein we have the serpent in the Garden of Eden, do we?'

'You must admit there is some discrepancy in how she was presented to me.'

'I have never been one to overlook rank,' Villiers said, waving his hand. He wore a ruby on one finger.

'No, you wouldn't.'

'And yet if I judge Harriet correctly, one could not say that *she* takes rank as seriously as do I – and oddly enough, as you appear to do.'

'I thought she was the widow of a country squire,' Jem said, scrubbing his face with his hands. He might as well tell Villiers. 'I thought I'd be doing her a favour, by taking her out of a dreary country existence.'

Villiers laughed.

'Exactly,' Jem said. 'More the fool I.'

'The duchy of Berrow is no small hamlet,' Villiers said.

'Berrow?' Jem's head shot up. *'Berrow?'*

'What duchy did you think we were discussing?'

'I never asked.'

'There aren't very many of us,' Villiers observed. His ruby ring seemed to wink at Jem.

'Her husband...'

'Benjamin.'

'He came to the Game once,' Jem said.

'You never invited him again,' Villiers guessed.

'No. He wasn't really interested.'

'Benjamin was one of my dearest friends, though I didn't understand that until after his death. One can make terrible mistakes when it comes to love, you know.'

Jem ground his teeth. The last thing he needed was a lecture from someone famous for spawning illegitimate children. 'You are an unlikely font of such wisdom,' he said.

'I couldn't agree more. I have never been in love with a woman, for example.'

Jem looked at him startled.

'No, nor yet a man,' Villiers said, shaking his head. 'But I have *loved*. Here and there, here and there. I know the worth of the emotion.'

'I loved Sally,' Jem said.

But Villiers had known him for years, since those long-ago days, and he said nothing.

'All right, I didn't love her in the same way. But Harriet is a duchess.'

'We established that.' Villiers pushed his small glass of claret towards Jem with one finger. 'Here. I haven't touched it.'

Jem looked at his own empty glass and picked up Villiers's, cradling it in his hand. 'She is a good woman. A decent woman. She said the Game would have to stop, and I'd have to follow her. But she has no idea. She knows nothing of my family.'

'Pesky things, families.'

'My reputation would ruin her. She'd come to hate me.'

'I suppose you are saying that I must give up the chance of falling in love as well?'

'Why would you?' Jem tossed back the claret.

'Oh, I do have some children out of wedlock, you know. Do you?'

'No.'

'What, only the daughter that you've tended so carefully? It shows a shockingly conservative turn of mind, Strange.'

Jem snorted.

'I suppose you are saying that due to my notorious lack of interest in my illegitimate offspring, and my accompanying reputation, that I must never fall in love?' Villiers's question was delicately barbed.

'You don't follow. I can't – the Game...'

'Ah, the Game.' Villiers glanced around the room. It smelled of urine, thanks to Oke, and the air was redolent of cheroot smoke. 'A charming tradition.'

'I've fixed the majority of my contracts here. I–'

'Of course, one can always use more substance,' Villiers said. 'I wonder how my estates keep multiplying when I give them so little attention.'

Jem shot him a look of extreme dislike.

'I would guess that Harriet does not care for the Graces, and the other ladies of their ilk.' He raised a finger at a footman, who bounded forwards and brought him another glass of claret.

'It's not that she disdains them,' Jem said, taking another deep swallow of wine.

'She doesn't want to breakfast with them? I must admit that Chloe's laughter was making me tetchy earlier this evening. That story she told at dinner, about the bishop and the champagne bath. Hardly in good taste, don't you think? Especially with those details – it was his mitre she was talking about, wasn't she?'

Jem took another swallow.

'No good woman has ever loved me,' Villiers said, putting down his glass with a little ring. 'I was engaged, you know. Last year.'

'I heard.'

'Beautiful girl. She fell in love with the Earl of Gryffyn and dropped me. Do you know how I found out? Because she looked at him that way. There was a sort of look in her eyes.'

'What sort of look?'

He shrugged. 'I see it now and then.'

Jem knew where Villiers had seen it. In Harriet's eyes, when she looked at him. 'I know Harriet loves me,' he said roughly. 'But it would ruin her life, don't you understand that?'

'And they always say that women are the more sacrificial sex,' Villiers said. 'How touching all this recrimination is. I wish that Roberta had seen her way to such a sacrifice, but she went off and married Gryffyn anyway. I do believe they are most happy together.'

Jem grunted.

'I thought perhaps Miss Charlotte Tatlock might fall in love with me,' Villiers said. 'She paid me visits while I was ill.'

'For God's sake, you sound like a pitiful case.'

'One thing about nearly dying is that you quite lose the wish to disguise your own weaknesses,' Villiers observed.

Jem silently thanked God he was feeling healthy.

'Miss Tatlock fell in love with my heir,'

Villiers said.

'You're cursed in love,' Jem said. 'Next thing you're going to tell me that you have your eye on Harriet.'

Villiers said nothing.

Jem felt a punishing heat rising in his chest. 'You're joking, right?' he said in a stifled voice.

'No one could not have their eye on Harriet,' Villiers said, looking back to Jem. 'She's utterly delicious, as you well know, especially in breeches. Do you know that she and I almost had an *affaire* once?'

Jem thought he might vomit. He shook his head. 'I approached her but she slapped me. She was married then, of course.'

'I thought you just said that Benjamin was one of your closest friends.'

'Annoying, isn't it? I just seem to have the kind of constitution that simply *can't* pay attention to the claims of friends. If you had a claim on Harriet, for instance, I would do my best. But of course,' he added gently, 'you haven't.'

Jem gave him a leaden-eyed look. 'Stop it.'

'Stop what?'

'Your ham-handed attempts to manipulate me.'

'Dear me,' Villiers said, sipping his wine. 'I must be losing my touch.'

'If − *if I* go after Harriet it won't be because I'm afraid that you'll snatch her up.

She wouldn't have you, anyway.'

'A terrible blow,' Villiers murmured. 'It takes a friend to dash one to the ground.'

'She...' He stopped.

'I suppose it could be that she loves you, and therefore she would reject me,' Villiers concluded. 'How unfortunate, under the circumstances. Luckily, I am used to the circumstance. Well, I must to bed. This has been an utterly charming conversation, Strange.' He rose and bowed, magnificently.

'Jem,' Strange said, looking up at him.

'Dear me. First names are so very intimate. In that case, my name is Leopold, but I'll thank you not to use it.'

'Leopold,' Jem said, trying the name out. 'It suits you, in an imperial type of way.'

'I dislike it,' Villiers said.

'You must call me Jem. So much advice and delivered with such poisonous precision ... we must be the best of friends.'

Villiers paused for a moment, and a smile warmed his wintry eyes. 'Indeed,' he said. 'That is my impression.'

He turned with a swirl of his magnificent coat, and was gone.

Brouncker was sick in the corner.

39

The Origins of Paradise

March 21, 1784

'Harriet said I could visit her,' Eugenia reported. 'I can, can't I, Papa? I know she has kittens in the barn, because she told me so.'

'Of course.'

Eugenia climbed up onto his lap, and Jem's heart thumped when he felt how light she was still. 'Did you have a big lunch?' he demanded.

'Stew,' Eugenia said. 'And a special egg that Cook made me.'

'What was special about it?'

'It has a very fancy cheese called *fromage bleu* mixed into it,' Eugenia reported.

'You eat like a lady of eighty,' Jem said, tightening his arm around her.

'I like *fromage*,' Eugenia said, obviously relishing the sound of the French syllables on her tongue. 'I like Harry too. Or Harriet. I miss her.'

'I miss her too.' In fact, the pain of missing her was almost like a physical pain in his chest. He couldn't imagine how to get through yet another day.

'I thought she might stay with us,' Eugenia said.

He cleared his throat. 'I hoped she would too, poppet. But she's a duchess, and she had important things to do.'

'I asked her what they were.'

'What did she say?'

'She kind of laughed, and said that people on her estate needed taking care of, the same as your people do. And that she had a very old dog, who would miss her. His name is Mrs Custard.'

Jem opened his mouth – and shut it again.

Harriet had a very old dog waiting for her. She was going back to an empty house. It hit him like a brick in the head.

Eugenia was looking at him with concern. 'Don't worry, Papa,' she said sweetly. 'I'll never let you be all alone. When I grow up, I'll have a house and you can stay with me.'

He was an idiot. He was beyond an idiot. He *loved* Harriet. And love meant that you didn't let someone go home to an empty house and an ageing dog, even if she did turn out to be a duchess. And even if she was infuriating, and holier-than-thou.

And even if...

He looked down at Eugenia and suddenly realized something so obvious that he couldn't believe he hadn't understood it before.

That pain in his heart, the one that was so deep it made his bones ache, that was his fault. He had accused Harriet of lying. But in reality, *he* was the one who had concealed who he was.

He was a fool, an idiot, a child who was unable to stop looking for his father's approval – even when he knew his father was dead, and immoral into the bargain.

Why else did he turn his house into his father's version of Paradise? Why wasn't he the sort of father he truly admired – a father who created a house that was safe?

Because he wanted his father's approval ... a man who was dead and gone, and before that, drunk and dissolute.

Eugenia was pulling at his sleeve. 'Papa, don't look so sad. I *promise* you can always live with me.'

He buried his face in her hair. 'I know that, poppet. I'm sorry.'

'Sorry for what?' Eugenia asked, snuggling close but, as always, logical.

'Sorry for not being a better father. For allowing a rat to bite you, and keeping you in the west wing so you wouldn't meet my guests.'

'It's not your fault the rat came in from the cold, Papa. Goodness!'

How could he have been so stupid as not to see the pattern of his life? Fonthill was designed and driven by his boyhood wishes.

He wasn't ashamed of that deep, driving wish he had always had that his sister's life hadn't been ruined by circumstances outside her control, that she hadn't been able to marry and have babies, as she deserved. But he *was* ashamed that he had taken his guilt and love for her and allowed it to blind him to the kind of household in which he was raising his own child.

But he was even more ashamed of the way he had allowed a boy's wish for his father's approval to linger and shape his life, even when as a man he understood his father's corrupt nature. The way his father's shallow, careless attitude towards women had led to his only daughter's violation.

He couldn't give every woman in peril a safe harbour ... and his father would never come back to life and recognize that Fonthill was his version of Paradise.

If Harriet would just take him back, he would never sit down at the Game again. And every brick in Fonthill could crumble to the ground, that blasted bordello of a tower included.

'Eugenia,' he said, 'do you think that perhaps if we went to Harriet's house, she might see us?'

'Of course she would, Papa.'

Despair plunged through him. She wanted a Jem who didn't even exist. 'We can't just go and fetch her,' he said, thinking it through.

437

'We have to move to her house.'

'Harriet has kittens,' Eugenia said, reasonably. What if she wouldn't take *him?* How could she possibly take *him* – and she, a duchess? With his house and his reputation and his habits and...

'That will make Harriet very happy,' Eugenia said. 'I could tell she didn't want to leave me, Papa. She doesn't have a little girl of her own, you know.'

'I know.'

Harriet had said that she loved him, there at the end. She'd begged him, and he had thrown it back at her. She had given him the most precious gift in the world and he had flung it at her feet.

Jem felt as if he had been hit on the head and suddenly started thinking rationally. He *loved* Harriet. And yet he'd hurt her so much. If there was even a chance that she would take him back...

He would do anything for her. Sell the house, disperse the Game, say goodbye to the Graces...

All those things were easy compared to the possibility of living a lifetime without her.

40

Duchess by Day

March 30, 1784

The Berrow estate was easily as grand as
Fonthill. Probably the grounds weren't as
large ... but he couldn't fool himself. The
old stone house was settled into the ground,
surrounded by ancient orchards. It made
Fonthill look like a presumptive younger
neighbour.

'I don't want you to feel terrible if Harriet
decides not to keep us,' he said to Eugenia.

She looked at him with her serious,
straightforward gaze. 'Don't be silly, Papa.
Harriet loves me.'

The footmen opened the carriage and he
handed Eugenia out. They were announced.
They waited.

After fifteen minutes, Eugenia got restless
and started dancing around the drawing
room. Jem was feeling sick. This was absurd.
Likely Harriet had come back to her
beautiful estate and realized what an idiot
she had been ever to entertain the idea of
marrying a loose fish like himself.

All of a sudden the door opened. The Duchess of Beaumont. And ... the Duchess of Berrow. Two gorgeous women of the very highest rank, bedecked and bejewelled, dressed in silk and satin.

Jem called Eugenia to him and bowed.

Harriet was exquisite as a woman. Her hair was piled on her head, all the curls tamed. In a gown she was even more sensual than in breeches. Now she didn't have a cravat under her chin, but a gown that plunged in front to show creamy skin, her small waist ... her gown's billowing skirts made him long to tip her over, uncover her secrets.

Her eyes met his with all the curious welcome one might give a mere acquaintance. 'Lord Strange,' she said, holding out a hand to be kissed. 'You do me too much honour. I had not expected a visit at such short notice.' Then she turned to Eugenia and gave her a true smile. And a true kiss.

Eugenia leaned in and said something in Harriet's ear.

'Of course!' Harriet said, and without a glance in his direction, she took Eugenia's hand and led her away. 'The kittens are in the barn,' she said, as she left.

The Duchess of Beaumont lingered. Jem stood in the centre of the room.

'Why are you here?' she asked.

Jem just looked at her. 'You know, don't you?'

'You've come for Harriet. You won't let her go.'

'Never.'

'I thought you weren't such a fool. I'll make her come back to the room.'

He sat down and waited. And waited.

Presumably Harriet was exacting some sort of revenge. Or screwing up her courage. It didn't even make him angry. He felt a strange sense of peace. His whole life had been defined by degrees of dissipation. He had thwarted his father by never entering brothels – but he certainly lived in his father's footsteps in other respects. Since the moment he turned fourteen he had flaunted himself and his life as debauched.

Harriet was the only person he'd ever met who thought that he was worthy of a better place than a brothel. She was worth the demise of Fonthill.

So he waited.

Finally, after two hours, she walked into the drawing room and quietly closed the door, leaning back against it. 'Eugenia is having a bath. She slipped into the horse's trough.'

He came to his feet. She was fifty times more sensual, more delicious in a dress than in breeches. 'I love you.'

'I know you do,' she replied, rather un-expectedly. But she didn't leap into his arms, the way she had in the stables. Instead she just stood there.

He thought desperately about what to say. 'I like your dress,' he said. Her face looked duchesslike. Polite. 'I thought you didn't like having your hair up in the air like that.'

'I met with Judge Truder this morning and we heard outstanding cases.'

His mouth snapped shut.

'The duchy's administrative powers are exceeded by those of the government, of course,' she said, standing ramrod straight, every inch a duchess. And a judge. 'As you know.'

He fumbled, trying to think how to start. 'I didn't mean the things I said.'

'It's quite all right,' she said, with a cool incline of her head. 'I entirely understand. In the heat of the moment one often makes rash comments. I shan't give them a second thought.'

'But you don't know what I'm apologizing for,' he said, watching her closely.

Her eyelids fluttered and he knew she wasn't as calm as she was pretending.

'I assume that you were referring to the rather wounding things you said after I disclosed my rank,' she said. 'Believe me, I do not remember them.'

'I remember every word.'

'I'm ignoring the horrid things you said because you are an ignorant fool.' She said it with great precision.

'I am. I am, Harriet, I really am.'

She looked away.

He had to tell her everything. And then she would still have a hundred reasons to throw him out, but he would have tried. So he dropped to his knees, because when a man really wants to beg...

That's how he does it.

'Don't!' she said, frowning at him.

'I must.'

Her mouth trembled and then straightened into a firm line. 'Very well.' She folded her hands.

The floor was very hard under his knees, and her face was even harder. He knew, he knew in his heart that it wouldn't work. She didn't love him any longer.

'I didn't know I loved you, not really. Men just don't think that way.'

'I know that,' Harriet said.

'Because your husband didn't really love you?'

'You already established that,' she said. 'Right at the same few moments when you pointed out how unattractive I was as a woman, and how stupid I was to think I could get away with calling myself Mr Cole.'

Jem's heart twisted with the pain of it. 'I didn't mean those things.' Then he couldn't stay on his knees any longer, even though that's where a man was supposed to be. He leapt to his feet and brought her hands to his lips. 'I was furious that you were a duchess.

You suddenly moved out of my reach – out of anyone's reach. I couldn't bear it. All the time I was thinking – do you know?'

She shook her head.

'That I would never have you. I knew how much every man at that party would have lusted after you, if they knew you were female. And they were able to go off to London and court you, without my reputation.'

'You thought I would fall into marriage with the next man I saw?' She looked at him more with curiosity than anything else.

'I can't help it,' he said jerkily, not letting her draw her hands away. 'I had one image of you in bed with someone else, and I lashed out at you. But God, Harriet, you're so beautiful. In a dress, in breeches, in just your skin. Any man under God's sky would wish to make love to you.'

She managed to pull her hands away. 'That's good to know.'

He looked down at her and he loved her so much that the words piled up in his chest and couldn't come out. Not in the right order.

'You don't believe that I love you.'

'Actually, I do,' she said. 'But I don't believe that you really want to be with me. With me, Harriet. I'm just a boring widow, you know. I wore black for a whole year. I never met a courtesan before I entered your house, and while I found it interesting, I'm not enamoured of the experience. I'm boring, Jem, and you're not.'

'I sent everyone away. The Graces, the guests, everyone.'

She looked at him.

'They're tearing down the tower this week.'

He had her hands again, was kissing them and trying to tell her all the things he couldn't put into words. 'I told them to tear down the tower, and Eugenia will tell you, I found a governess. Eugenia hates her.'

For the first time, Harriet felt a gleam of hope. 'What's she like?' she asked cautiously

'She has a remarkable figure. I can hardly describe it other than saying that it goes out in the front as much as it goes out in the back. She wears black in honour of her husband. He's been gone a few years.'

'How many?'

'Twenty-six. I can't think about anything but you, Harriet. You left, and there was no point to the Game any more. I had no interest in riding. I found myself walking up and down that damn picture gallery four times a day I dreamed only of you.' He pulled her close again and caught her lips in the most passionate kiss she'd ever experienced.

'I can't be feeling this alone,' he said, voice low. 'Don't tell me that, Harriet. I never felt like this before. Sally and I – we laughed. We were like children together. She never scolded me, or noticed what my faults were. She never made love to me the way you did.'

Harriet smiled.

'I couldn't have made love to her the way I make love to you,' he said, cupping her face in his hands. 'Something happened since we made love in the barn. I can't stop thinking about you. I meant to leave you alone. You're a duchess, for God's sake. My family and my reputation are equally black. You do realize that, don't you?'

'I don't care.'

The truth of it must have been in her voice because he said, 'You don't know the worst of it yet,' but something eased in his eyes.

She was tempted to kiss him, but she made herself pull away and sit on the sofa.

He stayed there, a bewildered-looking man, with his dear lean face and a dark glower that made him look like a gypsy king.

'What if you miss all your friends?' she asked. 'The problem is that you shouldn't have to give up all your friends just to be with me. And someday–' she wrapped her hands in her skirts so they wouldn't tremble '–someday you'll be tired of me and you'll miss the Game.'

He looked at her, his eyes dark grey and clear. 'Do you think that I will ever get tired of Eugenia?'

A little snort escaped her.

'Then why would you think I'd get tired of

you?' He didn't sound challenging, just interested, the way he always was when there was a question of logic involved. 'I love you, Harriet. Love is not something that comes easily to me.'

Her smile was wobbling.

'I didn't want to love you. Especially when I thought you were a man. And even more when I knew you were a duchess.' He shrugged. 'But there we are. I tried to cut you out of my heart, but I love you. How can I let you go? It's the same question I had with Eugenia, so be warned. I never could send her to school.'

'Are you going to keep me locked in the west wing?'

He walked a step closer and looked down at her. The look in his eyes...

'I think the west wing is too large for you. I'm thinking more about just one chamber.'

'Oh,' she whispered. It was almost too much to take in. He did love her, plain widowed Harriet. He loved her.

And she knew Jem. He *would* never let her go.

He reached down to her at the precise same moment she flew to him. They kissed for... Harriet didn't know how long. They were talking to each other silently. Once she broke it off, only to whisper, 'You'll never leave me, will you?'

He knew what she was saying, and kissed

her again before murmuring, 'I gave up the Game and it was never that important to me. What happened to Benjamin will never happen to me. Never. I'm staying with you, wherever you are, Harriet.'

'When my nephew is old enough, he'll take back this estate.'

'By that point, we'll have Fonthill shaped into a perfect habitation for a duchess,' he said promptly.

'Not a duchess,' she whispered. 'Lady Strange.'

He started kissing her again, and only stopped to say foolish things about how they'd be together until they were both eighty-five years old, and her hair was white as snow, and she was a toothless crone...

She had to kiss him to make him stop.

41

A Chapter of Revelations ... of Fathers and Brothels

They had tucked Eugenia into bed together, only to discover a dismal meowing noise coming from under her covers. The kitten was rescued and taken back to his mother. Then Harriet thought to lift up the cover again and discovered an unfortunate accident involving that kitten.

After the maids had come and gone, Jem whirled her against the wall in the corridor.

'I can't do it without you,' he said, his voice husky.

'Yes, you could, and you have,' she said, not bothering to pretend she didn't know what he was referring to. It felt as if she might be answering his unspoken thoughts for the rest of her life. 'You're a wonderful father.'

But he shook his head. 'I need you. I don't think about rats and cat piss and falling towers. I didn't – I didn't have much of a father, and I think that's why I don't know what I'm doing.'

He wouldn't tell her anything more, and it wasn't until the middle of the night, when he was lying on the bed, his chest still heaving, that Harriet propped herself up on one elbow and said, 'I want to know why you were so angry when you found me in the stables with Nick.'

He closed his eyes, shutting her away, but she had one great fear and wanted to say it. 'Did someone harm you when you were a boy?' she asked quietly.

His eyes snapped open. 'Thank God, no.'

She waited.

'But it could have happened. Anyone with a story and a joke was welcome to our

449

house. Sometimes they would stay for weeks, and my father thought it was all great fun. We were the lucky ones, he would say.'

'Did you live at Fonthill?'

'No, we lived in Lincolnshire. One of those men was a hell-hound by the name of Sattaway. My sister was thirteen. Perhaps twelve. I can't remember.'

'Oh no!' Harriet cried.

'He left after a few weeks but it was too late. She bore a child.'

'And then?'

'The child died because he had given her syphilis. A disease.'

Harriet swallowed. Jem didn't say anything else. 'And after that she was kidnapped by a different man?'

'Yes.'

'Did she die soon after?' Harriet finally ventured.

'Oh, no. She's not dead.'

She put her head on his chest, but he just kept stroking her hair. 'You really may not wish to marry me,' he said finally. 'And–'

She reared up her head. 'You'd let me walk away?'

There was a smile in his eyes. 'I'm a reprobate to do this to you.'

She rolled over on top of him, as if he were a mattress. 'You are everything to me, Jem Strange. Don't you dare try to send me away again. Ever.'

'My sister owns a small, quite select brothel in Belfast, County Antrim, Ireland. She's quite happy, or so she says in letters. It's called the *Ladybird*,'he added.

'The Ladybird!'

'I'm sorry I reacted so badly when you labelled my guests ladybirds. They are, of course.'

Harriet stayed quite still for a moment as the truth of Jem's life became clear to her. 'How could you not include them?' she said fiercely. 'I didn't understand. You are a wonderful man, do you know that? I'm proud of you.'

His mouth twisted. 'What's there to be proud of?'

'You have never turned away a woman who reminded you of your sister, have you?'

He swallowed. 'No.'

'Is your father alive?'

'Wouldn't it be nice to say that he died of parental guilt?' The twist to his mouth made Harriet's throat burn. 'He died four years ago, after drinking too much and deciding to prove that he could walk along the top of the stone fence that surrounded his kitchen garden in Bath. He couldn't.'

She kissed him again.

'But I realized after you left that I had created Fonthill for him... It was he who told me, my whole childhood, that a house full of loose women, a brothel, is a man's paradise.'

'You created the house, but you never took advantage of that aspect of it,' Harriet said slowly.

'I don't feel comfortable taking advantage of women who must trade their favours for their next meal.'

Harriet put her head back down on his chest and listened to the steady beat of his heart. 'We can still help women in distress,' she said. 'In every way possible. Just perhaps not in our own house.'

'After you left, I realized that Fonthill had virtually become a brothel. *I* have a brothel. *I* who never willingly entered a brothel, not since my father forced me into my first one at the age of thirteen.'

'Fonthill is *not* a brothel,' Harriet said.

'Close enough.' His voice was bleak.

'Not,' she said firmly, sitting up so she could look in his eyes. 'Your sister runs a brothel. You do not. You had a wonderful, exuberant house party to which you invited all sorts of people, from scientists to women. And if some of them found friendships under your roof, you never profited from that. They did.'

He was silent.

'The Game was not dependent on female entertainment,' she said gently.

'I'm a damned poor bargain, Harriet,' he said. 'Are you sure you want to do this?'

She couldn't even speak: her heart was too

full. 'You are–' she swallowed '–mine. At the heart I'm a tedious country widow.'

He rolled over so fast that her words disappeared into his lips. 'You are my Harriet, the most intelligent, funny, wise soul I have ever met. And, though it hardly matters, the one person who has ever driven me utterly mad with lust with your beauty.'

She couldn't help smiling up at him. 'Do you want a similar catalogue?'

He shook his head. 'I don't care about any of that, if you think...' But he couldn't put it into words.

'You are everything to me,' she whispered, tears in her eyes. 'I love every bit of you, from the wrinkles by your eyes, to your crazed architectural plans, to your generosity and your sweetness. You are a wonderful father, who never dishonoured your own father by disowning his idea of paradise – and yet you kept Eugenia warm and safe and loved. You welcome every woman with your sister's background, and yet you never take advantage of them. How could I not love you, Jem?'

She was crying now, and he was kissing her. But he had something to say too, so he made her stop crying and listen to him.

'Benjamin was a fool, Harriet. A fool. I've never met another woman with your joy, your beauty, and your sensuality. But what I love most is your deep-down sense of fairness, the clear judgement that allows you to see people as they are, whether they are criminals or fools like myself, Villiers or Nell...'

There didn't really seem to be much else to be said.

So they talked with their hands. And their lips.

And finally, with the greatest gift of all. With their bodies.

EPILOGUE

Eugenia Strange's arm was starting to tire. Her little brother was much heavier than he looked. He was lolling back in her arm now, looking as if he were about to fall into his nap and yet he never seemed actually to do it. It was awfully frustrating.

Sure enough, the moment she stopped walking he opened his eyes and smiled gummily at her. Colin had his mother's velvety brown eyes. Since he was wearing a little blue shirt, they had a tinge of violet.

'All the ladies are going to be in love with you,' she told him.

He sighed and closed his eyes. 'You're right,' Eugenia said. 'It *is* a bit tiresome, all this adoration.' For example, she happened to know that right now there were eight gentlemen in the drawing room. Povy kept popping his head into the nursery and holding up his fingers silently to give her the new count.

But she hadn't met a single man in London who could entice her away from Colin. 'Why won't you nap?' she sang to him. 'Oh, why won't you nap?'

The door opened and she turned, thinking that it would be Povy, perhaps holding up all his fingers. But it was her papa.

He looked tired but happy, bone happy. Eugenia had the feeling that her darling, adored stepmother must have made the most of the hour since they had disappeared after luncheon. Not that she noticed where they were going, of course.

'You never napped either,' her papa remarked, strolling into the room. 'You were an awful infant.'

Eugenia snorted. 'And how would you know, Lord Strange? Since you spent my childhood racketing around with a house full of gorgeous courtesans and mongrelly men?'

'Mongrelly men?' he said. 'Here, let me have that baby.' Colin had stuck his head up and was making cooing, gurgling noises at the sound of his father's voice.

'I was just getting him to sleep,' Eugenia complained, handing him over.

'You look very fine to be in the nursery,'

her father said, looking her up and down. 'New gown? And not to be indelicate, my daughter, but you *are* wearing something under it, aren't you?'

Eugenia turned up her nose. 'This is Madame Carême's very finest new creation, Papa, and I'll thank you not to insult it. *Or* ask questions that don't concern you.' But she smiled down at her gorgeous morning gown. It was made of the finest silk taffeta. It fell straight from her breasts and then frothed into an enchanting little ruffle at the bottom.

'Well, go on then,' her papa said. 'All those gentlemen downstairs aren't here to see me, you know.'

'They might be,' Eugenia said, checking her reflection in the nursery mirror.

Her father snorted.

'They would love to snuggle up to the newest marquis in London,' she said.

But her father wasn't listening to her. He was humming to Colin, and rocking his arms in a way that Eugenia almost felt she could remember in her bones. She went over to him and put her head on his shoulder. 'I love you, Papa.'

'You too, sweetheart,' he said. 'You too.'

And then she went out of the door, knowing exactly why she didn't care about all those gentlemen down in the drawing room. Because not one of them was a scrap on her papa, that's why.

She met Harriet coming down the corridor. Her beloved, sweet-faced stepmother didn't look nearly as tired as her papa. In fact, she had a sort of glow about her that made Eugenia secretly grin.

'I think Papa is finally getting Colin to sleep,' Eugenia whispered. 'I couldn't quite manage it. I was about to give up and call for his nurse.'

Harriet fluttered her hand towards the drawing room. 'There's twelve of them in there now,' she whispered back.

Eugenia groaned, but turned and sauntered down the stairs.

Harriet smiled, watching her go. Her awkward, big-nosed child had turned into the most ravishing girl to debut on the *ton* in years. She had all the eligible gentlemen – and most of the ineligible ones – at her knees, if not her feet. Not that Eugenia gave a damn.

Jem looked up from the cradle where he was just putting down Colin.

'You're a miracle,' Harriet said softly. Colin gave a little snore and turned over. She looked down at him. 'He's so beautiful, isn't he?'

Jem caught her in his arms. 'Not as beautiful as you. He takes after his father. I can already see the wrinkles starting by his eyes.'

Lovingly Harriet pushed back the hair

from his laughing eyes. Her body still tingled from the pleasure they'd shared and she knew that he still felt it too. 'Remember when I first met you? I thought you were the most beautiful man I'd ever seen, and since I arrived at your house with Villiers, that was really saying something.'

'My first thought was that if Villiers had any idea of switching sides and seducing you, I'd kill him first. I should have known from that moment. I've never given a damn where men find their pleasure, and suddenly I was like a dog with a bone.'

'A very strange bone,' Harriet laughed.

He nuzzled her. 'I must say, I am glad that you've given up your breeches.'

'It wasn't hard once I realized that everything I learned in breeches I could simply employ in my gowns.'

'Still, you never sit quietly as ladies are wont to do, during dinner conversation.'

'No,' she said, grinning.

'And you're the most bruising rider in five counties, although no one knows that the duchess goes forth at twilight scandalously clad in breeches.'

'Let's not forget the fact that I took you in our last two rapier matches.'

'No more,' he whispered, his hand rounded on her belly. 'No more riding and no more rapiers, Harriet.'

'Not for a while.' She couldn't help smiling.

'Where do you suppose this baby came from?' he said wonderingly.

'The usual places.' He loved her laugh.

'But we were married for years without children. And then Colin, and now...'

'I didn't think I could.'

Under his hand was just the smallest flutter of life. 'I never used to cry, not a single damp eye, before I met you,' he said accusingly.

She kissed him until he didn't feel sentimental any more, just hungry. But he didn't want to wear Harriet out, so he didn't follow that kiss to its natural conclusion.

'Povy told me that a letter arrived from your sister,' Harriet told him. 'I think she is happy in London, don't you?'

He nodded. 'She loves being a matron at Magdalen House ... the way she talks about the head of the Metropolitan Police. Do you think, Harriet? Perhaps?'

Harriet grinned. 'She'll be lucky if he doesn't arrest her. The letter I had last week described two young women whom she stole out of a brothel, as best I could understand.'

'She's not always prudent about her own safety.'

'She told me she carries a knife in each boot,' Harriet said, running her hand along his cheek. 'I expect Eugenia to start carrying weapons at any moment. She adores your sister, you know.'

He was silent for a moment. 'I couldn't have imagined our life when I first met you in those breeches.'

Harriet stretched. Her body was ripe with happiness. Pregnancy didn't make her cantankerous or nauseated. Instead she was singing with happiness. 'I ruined you. There you were, happy as a house in the queen's mattress, surrounded by concubines and courtesans and actresses...'

'And having nothing to do with any of them.'

'You were waiting for me,' she said. 'You know, someone to wear the breeches in the family.' She looked up at him, but he was laughing.

Silently, of course.

A Note About Card Games, Fashionable Vices, and Family Courts

This novel opens with a scene from Judge Truder's court. Judge Truder does not exist, but the 'criminals' prosecuted in his court do. Poor Loveday Billing married only two men (though there are cases that reference as many as seven wives or husbands), but she was acquitted, precisely as described here. The arrangement by which nobility presided in court was unusual but not unheard of (though for a woman to be the 'judge' would be highly unlikely). The English countryside was patched with little jurisdictions and shire courts whose procedures did not follow the dictates laid out by the English government, but were moulded by local tradition cobbled together with necessity.

At one point, Jem says that every king's court has a Game such as the one he runs – whether it's conducted in court itself, or at a country house, or in a tavern. I thought up the Game after reading Samuel Pepys's wonderful diary. Pepys, who lived from 1633–1703, kept a diary that detailed everything from his fights with his wife over her penchant for 'laced' gowns, to his *affaires* with various women (details written in code), to his various positions in and about the English government. I was fascinated by the casual way by which crucial business was conducted, often over a chance meeting or a game of cards. At one point Pepys describes the king summoning a gentleman to play with him, where the said gentleman lost fifty shillings, but said he was pleased, since the benefit of playing in a high-level card game was worth the loss of fifty shillings. Thus was born Jem's 'Game'.

Pepys lived before the Georgian period – but the *mores* of his diary, in which gentlemen routinely have mistresses, and ladies take lovers, are true of the Georgian period as well. We might turn to another diary for a glimpse of a Georgian gentleman's life. James Boswell lived from 1740–1795; by age twenty-nine, he had already detailed the seduction of three wives, four actresses, Rousseau's lover, three middle-class women, and over sixty street girls.

To be a high-born Englishman in the Georgian period was to live at a time when adultery was a fashionable vice, rather than a crime. And yet ... if indelicacy was a fashion, love was another one. It was Lord Byron, a mad, bad, Georgian Englishman, who wrote that 'our sweetest memorial [is] the first kiss of love.'

This Large Print Book, for people
who cannot read normal print,
is published under the auspices of

THE ULVERSCROFT FOUNDATION